KRONOS' RETURN

MICHAEL WEST

Hydra
Publications

ISBN: 978-1-948374-54-5

Second Edition

Hydra Publications

Goshen, Kentucky, 40026

www.hydrapublications.com

*For Chris, David, Dione, Ericka, Maurice, Natalie, Niki, Robin,
Rodney, Sheri, Stephanie, and most of all, for Sara.*

*Some began this long trek with me, others joined in along the way,
but I wish that all could have been here to witness the journey's end.*

For Stephen King and Clive Barker, who set me on the path.

*For Peter Jackson, Hayao Miyazaki, and Guillermo del Toro, who
inspired me to imagine.*

*And in loving memory of John Barry, Jerry Goldsmith, James
Horner, Michael Kamen, and Basil Poledouris, who made my
imagination soar.*

"And there shall be destruction and darkness come upon creation, and the beasts shall reign over the earth."
~*Them! (1954)*

"The place you made your stand never mattered. Only that you were there & still on your feet."
~Stephen King

"It is better to die on your feet than to live on your knees."
~Emiliano Zapata Salazar

"The world is a fine place and worth fighting for."
~Ernest Hemingway

"Whoever fights monsters should see to it that in the process he does not become a monster..."
~Friedrich Nietzsche

"To the righteous we bring hope. To the tainted we bring fire. I am the Hammer. I am the Sword. I am the Gauntlet. I am the Bane of foes and the woe of the treacherous. I am the End."
~Grey Knight prayer, *Warhammer*

PART ONE

Twilight World

CHAPTER ONE

New York, New York.

So nice, they named it twice.

Mitch chuckled bitterly.

This city might be many things to many people, but it sure as fuck wasn't nice. In fact, it had a long and bloody history of being harsh and unforgiving. People died here every day, turning the news into a dark version of *Mad Libs*, just insert a name, a place, and a manner of execution. Crime and death had become as much a part of the urban DNA as the brick, the steel, and the asphalt, and after reading the same stories day in and day out, people had become numb, detached.

Nobody cared.

City of the dead. Hell on Earth.

Mitch took another long drag from his cigarette. He stared up at the faint slice of night sky that hung between the buildings above him. A billion stars up there, maybe a billion times a billion, and in his life, he thought he must have wished on damn near all of them.

But they were no different from the people of this city. They didn't give a shit. And just like people, they were born, they burned bright for a time, and then God just went and snuffed them out whenever He felt like it.

The real kicker?

Assholes here on Earth didn't even know the stars were gone. Their light just kept right on shining up there, growing fainter and fainter. It could be years, hell, maybe even centuries before anybody down here even knew that they were dead.

That would be just my luck, he thought, glancing at the crumbling, brick facades on either side of him, *die in one of these rundown shitholes, in some stinking alley, tossed aside with all the other garbage. Nobody'd look for me, nobody'd* find me *until I was nothing but rot.*

Snakebit. That's the term his mother had always used. Bad luck clung to him like dog shit to fur.

And as if Mitch needed yet another reminder of just how fucked-up his life and his luck truly were, now the spider-man was back. It was there in the darkened alley, standing right behind him. Mitch sensed the thing even before it opened its mouth and spoke with that now-familiar British baritone. He felt a trickle of ice water down his spine, felt the hairs on the back of his neck stretch and rise to attention, and he had that heavy sinking feeling in his gut, as if he'd just swallowed a stone.

Spider-man.

That's what Mitch had called the thing in a delusional fog brought on by blood loss and pain. An accurate title, sure, as the centaur was, in fact, half spider and half man, but the name called to mind the comic book hero instead of the insane nightmare that this thing truly was.

"I'm chuffed," the limey prick said. "Here I was, thinking you were all mouth and no trousers, but no. You're a real corker, mate."

When Mitch spun around, he saw the monster crawl out from behind a graffiti-covered dumpster. It moved on those elongated spears it called legs, the serrated points of its claws clacking and scraping against the asphalt, the same spears and serrated points it had used to lance the other members of Mitch's crew, to stab *him*.

Mitch found that his hand was shaking, the beat of his heart booming like thunder in his ears. He dropped his smoldering cigarette onto the concrete, then ground the butt to ash beneath his shoe. "What the fuck are you talkin' about? Did you find that goddamn crystal skull you wanted or not?"

"We found it," the creature, Benedict, replied, razored mandibles twitching. "It was right where you said it would be."

"Great." Mitch curled his trembling fingers, making tight fists at his side. "So, now that you've got what you want, you can get the hell away from me and leave me the fuck alone."

Benedict shook his insectoid head, the dark nodes of his many eyes all focused in on Mitch. "I'm afraid there's been a bit of a wrinkle."

Of course! With my luck, I shoulda seen that comin', right? Snakebit.

"Oh, yeah?" Mitch tried to keep the tremble in his hands from reaching his voice. "What's that?"

"You see, when we reached the warehouse, we ran into some resistance."

"Resistance?"

"Afraid so. Some friends of yours, I do believe, Preston and the others. They tried to queer our efforts."

"Look," Mitch narrowed his eyes, "I don't know nothin' about no queers, okay, and I don't know anybody named Preston."

"Come now, Mitch. You told them about the skull, didn't you — where to find it? Why else would they have been there? How else would they have even known?"

That stone in Mitch's gut grew heavier still, as if it were being dragged all the way to China. "How the fuck should I know? I found out from a guy, who musta found out from some other guy, but *I* didn't say shit to anyone else but you. You think there's a leak somewhere, it ain't me, okay? So you can just crawl back up the waterspout and go fuck yourself. You're welcome!"

"You said nothing to Preston?"

"What did I just say? I don't even know anybody named Preston."

"No?" Benedict was obviously unconvinced. "Well, then, I've brought along someone I believe you *do* know."

A second figure emerged from the shadows, stepping out into the glow of the lamplight. No monster this time, at least, not at first glance. It was a man dressed in a dark suit with a blood red tie. He was an imposing figure; tall, muscular, with close-cropped hair and a scar that seemed to completely encircle his throat, as if his head had come off and been reattached somehow.

It took Mitch a moment, but recognition finally took hold.

No...You gotta be shitting me...

The man strutting toward him shouldn't be here. This guy...he was supposed to be locked up in some New England hellhole, stuck in a maximum-security cell, serving more life sentences than Mitch had fingers and toes. No possibility of parole, no chance of escape, and yet, somehow, here he was.

Mitch's face fell, chasing after that hot stone in his belly. "Horror Show?"

The hitman nodded.

"Wow, man, jeez..." Mitch gave his own neck a nervous scratch. "When did you get out?"

How *did you get out?*

Horror Show smiled. He had become something of an urban legend, this guy — the gangster's boogeyman. For as long as Mitch could remember, there had been stories uttered in hushed, terrified whispers, that he'd filed his teeth down to points, like fangs. In the flesh, however, coming ever closer to Mitch, his pearly whites formed a wide Hollywood grin, gleaming in the dimness like the stars overhead. "Our new friends here just sprung me," he said.

"Oh...that's cool." Mitch glanced back at Benedict, then his eyes shot to the door of the run-down brick building behind him. Inside, there were half a dozen guys, Mitch's new crew. They were packaging drugs for transport and sale, and they were armed, all of them. If Mitch screamed now, cried out for help, they would all come running to his aid, guns blazing, and they would...

They'd be just as dead as my last crew. Just as dead as me. *But I ain't goin' out alone.*

Mitch swallowed, and his quivering hand crept slowly over to the butt of his own gun. Bullets had proven useless against Benedict, but boogeyman or not, he knew they would have better luck with Horror Show. "Good. Good for you."

"Yeah," the hitman agreed, "good for me." He took another menacing step forward, his smile widening even more, reminding Mitch of the cover to Alan Moore's *The Killing Joke*. "Not so good for *you*."

Horror Show towered over him, close enough now for Mitch to get a good whiff of the man's cologne. Not rancid in the slightest. On the contrary, the hitman smelled of musk from a high-priced, designer bottle. The wells of Horror Show's eye sockets were dark, swallowed by shadow, almost as if he had no eyes at all. This, coupled with that wide sinister grin, granted his face a skull-like appearance.

Now, Mitch understood how Horror Show had garnered such a fearsome reputation. He'd been wrong before. This wasn't a man at all. No. This was the Grim Reaper, this was *Death,* and it had now come for him.

Before he could draw his weapon, Mitch felt a sudden punch to his chest. He knew instantly what had happened, recognized the internal pressure, the horrid sensation of a foreign object being thrust deep into his flesh. And when he looked down, his worst fears were confirmed.

He'd been stabbed.

No shoulder wound this time. Nope. This one went straight for all the good stuff.

Mitch watched in stunned silence as Horror Show withdrew his blade. It was the length of a small sword or bayonet, and he saw thick, heavy droplets of his own blood fall from its sleek serrated edge. The blade's golden hilt appeared scaly, reptilian. It didn't look like a knife at all, at least, not like any Mitch had ever seen. If it resembled anything, it was a single, disembodied claw, a talon ripped straight off a monster.

A familiar copper tang hung thick in the air, drowning out the foul stench of the alley, the masculine scent of Horror Show's musk, everything. Mitch instinctively moved his hand to cover the wound between his ribs, feeling heat pulse against his palm. The warmth oozed between his fingers while everywhere else he felt suddenly cold.

"Thanks for your help," Horror Show said, still smiling, "but I'll take it from here."

The hitman's hand blurred out and Mitch felt a sting across his throat, a burning sensation that went from ear to ear. His head lolled. He hissed through clenched teeth, then heard the horrible sound of his own gargled gagging. Mitch slumped back against the crumbling brick, reaching up with his free hand to feel the sticky, wet heat of an open wound where his neck had been.

Snakebit, Mom, just like you always said. One last time...

The shadows crept in, dimming all the stars and the lamplight overhead, consuming everything. Mitch had spent most of his adult life in the gloom of alleyways, of warehouses and old buildings, all of his work done under the cover of night. Now, the darkness had come to claim him forever.

As he died, Mitch wondered who would find him, wondered what if anything would be said about his life and his death. After all, people died in New York every night. He would be just another statistic, another crook come to a bitter end.

Nobody'll even know I'm gone, he lamented, numbly. *No one will even remember my name.*

His blood and his spirit abandoned him, and he slid down the brick a corpse.

———

Horror Show released a long, stuttering breath; he stared down at the corpse at his feet, admiring his handiwork in the same way a sculptor might study his latest piece of art. It had been a while since he'd slit a man's throat, since he'd watched the light dim in someone's eyes. And until this very moment, he hadn't realized just how much he'd missed it.

He held up Vivian's bloodied claw. It didn't have the same feel as his trusty pearl-handled straight razor, the same elegance. The cold, reptilian hilt was too bulky in his grip, but the blade had done its job.

Mitch was dead.

The spider-centaur crawled alongside him, its talons gripping him by the shoulder. "Well done, mate," it said.

"Thanks, Benny."

"Looked to me like you were having a bit of fun with it."

"What can I say? I love my work."

"I'm sure, and I'm sure Vivian will be pleased with it, as well."

"That's my goal in life," Horror Show said, his tone unapologetically sarcastic, "to make Vivian Song happy."

"Mine, too."

Benedict's grip tightened, putting Horror Show's beefy shoulder in a vice. Could this thing sense the hitman's true intentions? Did it know that Horror Show was going to slay the dragon lady, that he was going to watch her pilot light go out, watch the life drain out of her the way he'd seen it drain from Mitch just now, that he would relish her death more than any of his other kills?

Horror Show smiled. He took a handkerchief from his breast pocket and wiped the blood from Vivian's claw.

It was good to be back.

CHAPTER TWO

Carol Miyagi had come back from the dead. At least, that's what she had been told. Now, she didn't know what to believe.

She remembered opening her eyes, but it felt as if she had yet to fully awaken, as if this moment were nothing more than a dream within a dream, a *nightmare*. She stared blankly down at the ornate table before her, shaking her head, denying it was real. Was this the alien Ark's twisted replica of an Aztec altar, or had it in fact been the original, what the Mesoamerican people had attempted to emulate with their own primitive constructs?

Is it live or is it Memorex?

She honestly couldn't tell. The Ark held many wonders, many secrets, some of which Carol now understood completely, though she had no idea how she had come by her knowledge, and others she felt as if she might never fully comprehend.

Whatever this object was, for example, be it *Chabudai* table or ceremonial altar, it was not forged of gold, nor was it carved from wood or stone. Instead, it had somehow been crafted from an uneasy marriage of organic and inorganic materials, a nightmare fusion of bolts and bones, of tissue and tubing.

On the side of the raised structure was a design resembling a cross, but with a loop in place of the top arm. The glyph was not Atlantean, not Aztec, but Egyptian: an ankh, the symbol for eternal life.

The woman atop the altar was dead, however. Her body lay splayed across its textured surface in the supine position, raven hair spilling out from a parka stained in blood. The girl's chest had been slashed open as if in sacrifice, an offering to the gods.

Carol gaped down at her, this corpse that had bled out onto her own coat, uncertain at first of what she was seeing.

That face...

Staring at this woman was like gazing at her own reflection, every hair, every pore, a perfect duplication. Carol repeatedly wagged her head, denying it all.

Soreha dekimasen, she thought numbly in Japanese, then heard herself mumble aloud in English, "It cannot be."

"What the fuck are you?" Alan Everson blurted again, nearly screaming it at her this time.

Carol winced at the words and her eyes shot up to lock with his.

He knelt down on the opposite side of her doppelgänger, clutching the dead woman's limp fingers tightly within his trembling grasp. All the while, he glared up at Carol through tears of anguish, spittle flying from his lips, *"Answer me!"*

Carol shrugged, helplessly. She felt as if this was one of the Ark's mysteries she should *know*, that she should have the answer perched and ready on her lips, but she didn't understand any of this. She took a step back, retreating from the hurt in Alan's eyes, from the rage in his voice, wanting to put distance between herself and this imposter who had somehow stolen her face and now wore it as a death mask.

Or maybe Alan's right, Carol's reeling mind began to wonder. *Maybe* I'm *the thief...the* imposter...

No.

Is it live or is it Memorex?

No! *It's not possible.*

She glanced back down at the body, remembering stories from people whose hearts had stopped beating while on the operating table, how they said they felt as if they were floating, how they looked down and saw themselves lying lifeless below them. Carol felt that way now. As she pulled her gaze away from the body and looked around the Ark's vast storage chamber, it was as if she were suddenly seeing everything from outside of herself, everything strange yet somehow familiar.

Stasis tubes surrounded her, not made of cold fiberglass and steel, but somehow warm and alive. They grew from the rippled floor like odd tree trunks, roots of corrugated tubing snaking out from their curved bases, crisscrossing in every direction; the transplanted forest of some far-off alien world. Hideous, inhuman faces stared back at Carol through their veiny, translucent walls — misshapen creatures, genetic mishaps, every failed attempt at creation; a carrion zoo, perfectly preserved and entombed in all its rictus agony.

Carol had been sealed in one of these fluid-filled containers herself. She'd awoken there, naked and confused, but she'd been *alive*, possessing awareness... memories of a life she'd lived, of goals yet unrealized. Everything had been nebulous at first, remote, but quickly crystallized with her dawning consciousness; her parents, her grandparents, her education, the loves of her life, Kari and Alan, her obsessions with Atlantis and later the Ark, Poseidon's children, the sword-wielding weretiger, Gagan and the Yeti, her mission...*her*.

She *was* Carol Miyagi.

She had to be.

Carol's grandmother had been Buddhist. In Buddhism, death was just a natural part of life, but it was not the end; it simply led to rebirth, reincarnation. After the body died, a person's spirit remained close by, seeking out a *new* body, a *different* body, and new life.

Was that what had happened to her?

Could it be possible — could she, somehow—?

"What's going on?" The female voice came from behind, and Carol felt a gentle hand on her shoulder. Her knees buckled, she crumpled, fell backward, and Kari Hannigan was there to embrace her. "Jesus," she said. "Carol, are you all right?"

Alan spat more venom from across the room, "That *thing* isn't Carol!"

"What are you talking about?" When Kari turned, her eyes went wide with dawning horror; they darted back and forth between the two Carols, one quick and one dead. "Oh, my God."

Carol watched Kari's face fill with unspeakable sadness; it tore at her.

Gagan, the goat-man, stood by them, his cloven hooves motionless, his horizontal pupils fixed on the body, the gaping wound, the *face*. He lowered his hand-carved bow, the bowstring going slack in his clawed grasp. "Two Miyagis?" he asked in disbelief. "What magic is this?"

Kari swallowed hard. She stared down at the corpse on the table before them, studying it for what seemed like an eternity. Finally, something ignited within her eyes, some great epiphany to which Carol remained ignorant.

"It's not magic, Gagan," Kari told him. "It's *science*."

Is it live, Carol's mind began again, *or is it—?*

Stop.

Would the real Carol Miyagi please stand up?

STOP IT!

"*Onegaishimasu*," she said aloud, straightening in Kari's embrace, steeling herself. Her eyes travelled over each of their faces in turn. "Please...don't be afraid. I don't know what has happened, what is going on, but I know who I am, and I *am* me. I can prove it to you. Test me. Ask me anything, something only I would know."

"Carol," Kari began, "you don't have to—"

"No," she glanced over at Alan, at the disgust in his eyes, at Gagan, whose bearded maw hung open in stunned silence, then back to Kari once more, "clearly I do. Please, just...just ask."

"Okay." Kari took a deep breath. She looked up at the ribbed ceiling of the chamber. After a beat, she tucked her fiery red hair behind her ear and moved closer. When she spoke again, her voice had an odd timbre to it, thick with emotion, "The day we first met."

Carol blinked. "In college?"

"Yeah, if you really want to do this; year one, day one, minute one. Tell me everything you remember about it."

"All right." Carol thought for a moment, trying to recall the details. "I walked into our dorm room. It was small, cramped. I had a box in my arms, clothes, I think, but you were already there, all moved in, and you...you came over to give me a hug."

Kari nodded, confirming it. "And what did *you* do?"

"I backed away, looked down at the floor."

"Why? Do you remember what you told me?"

"I said that I was Japanese, and that we do not hug. And then you said—"

"I said that I was Scottish, that I was descended from a long line of huggers, and that, if we were going to be friends, you were just going to have to get used to it. And then I—"

"And then you hugged me so tight that I couldn't breathe."

Kari smiled, and a single tear ran down from her eye to her chin. She pulled Carol to her, this new embrace even tighter than the first. "You don't have to prove anything to me," she whispered, "never to me."

———

Alan watched in disbelief as Kari Hannigan embraced an obvious imposter. The woman held a monster in her arms. That wasn't Carol; it was some alien *thing* this place had created to try and fool them, like a pod person from an old *Body Snatchers* movie. Meanwhile, the real Carol Miyagi lay right here in front of him, stretched out across this weird replica of an Aztec altar — still dressed in her mountaineering gear, still covered in blood.

He shook his head grimly, fighting to stem the intolerable tide of grief and rage that rose up within him.

It's not fair, his mind cried again and again; desolate, child-like. *It's not fair!*

He lifted the real Carol Miyagi off the altar's textured surface and held her up to his chest, cradling her. She was just as limp and lifeless as she'd been when they first entered the Ark, when the alien mantis had pried her from his arms and carried her off, disappearing into the living walls of this damned place. Now, however, she trailed a tangle of odd-looking wires and segmented cables. Like leeches, the tendrils burrowed into her *everywhere*, draining away her life's blood, her tissue, her identity, everything that had made her the woman she was, the woman he *loved*.

Alan stared down into the fog of her clouded eyes, into the gory depths of that great chasm between her breasts — the empty gulf once filled by her strong and loving heart, by her incredible soul. Alan clenched her fingers in his hand; he brought them up to his mouth, felt their icy touch against his lips.

Carol was dead.

Alan knew that now. There could be no denying it. Not anymore.

He'd just celebrated her return, her rebirth. He'd been over the moon with joy. But it had all been a cruel joke; a disgusting *lie*.

I'm so sorry, Carol. I should have known it was too good to be true. I should have known it wasn't really you. I should have known!

Numb, trembling, he reached up and brushed a stray lock of raven hair from Carol's face. Even in death, she was still the most beautiful, the most remarkable woman he'd ever laid eyes upon. In fact, he thought she was perhaps the most amazing creature to ever have graced this Earth.

It's not fair!

Alan's eyes filled to the brim with acid. He blinked, sent a few scalding tears sliding down the length of his cheeks. They fell onto Carol's body like drops of hot rain.

Not fair!

She'd been a gorgeous woman, yes, but it had been her mind, her *spirit*, that had truly captivated him all these years. Her intelligence, her drive, her integrity; they were all traits that he'd admired in her, qualities that had first inspired him to be a better archeologist, then a better friend, and ultimately, a better *man*. Her inner fire, her *passion*, had been an endless source of strength.

And now?

Now, that fire had been forever extinguished. Her light, her spirit, her love; they'd all taken their leave. She was left hollow and cold, a shell, a husk, and Alan felt just as empty.

The giant mantids had desecrated her remains and left her here all alone. They'd just tossed her aside like a worthless piece of meat. That's all she was to them. But to Alan, she was still so much more.

"Watashi wa," he muttered aloud in Japanese, even though he knew Carol was now beyond hearing, *"anata o aishiteimasu."*

His lip began to quiver. He kissed her lightly on the forehead and rocked her in his arms.

I loved you, Carol Miyagi, and I know that you loved me. I think I knew it even before you did. You were a good woman, a strong woman. I did my best to make you happy. I hope I succeeded. I think I did.

Oh, but Carol, you deserved so much more than I could ever give you. You deserved so much better than this. You were so young, so brilliant. You had so much life left to live, so much left to discover. We had so much yet to do together.

It's just not fair.

Alan looked once more at the lengths of black and silver cable that trailed from her, the semi-transparent corrugated tubing that had defiled her body. Why had he let them do this to her? What had been the point? Wounds this grave...they didn't heal. Not overnight. Not *ever*.

He *knew* that, he'd always known that, but he'd let his heart override his head.

Alan felt so stupid for listening to Kari, for believing that the Ark held some arcane sway over life and death. He felt cheated. He felt angry and betrayed.

Slowly, he lifted his head once more, shifted his focus to the charlatan that now stood across the room from him, the creature who had stolen his lover's face, pinched her memories. That thing over there was no different from the goat-man who stood beside it, no different from the tiger-man who'd tried to kill Carol back in Japan, and no different from the Yeti who'd managed to finish the job.

He swiped at his cheeks, his sorrow suddenly overshadowed, overtaken. In that moment, he was owned solely by rage.

Carefully, with the utmost love and respect, Alan laid Carol's body back down on the altar. Then, he reached for his ice axe. He gripped its handle so tightly that his knuckles flared white.

This is for you, my love.

———

Kari Hannigan held tightly onto the woman she loved, savoring the moment. She knew now how the Ark had brought Carol back, the process by which the mantids had given new life to the dead, but that awareness had not lessened her affections. If anything, hearing Carol's recollection of their first meeting had only served to intensify them.

Of course, Kari had her own memories of that day. She would never forget that very first glimpse of her future lover; how the sight of this striking, exotic young woman had literally stolen her breath away. Fit, yet curvy in all the right places. Toned, gorgeous legs. Long, raven hair. And those *eyes...*

But Carol Miyagi was more than a body. She was so much more than a body. She'd spoken softly, but even in her youth, Carol's beautiful voice had held this firm, dogged undertone that proclaimed all of her various theories and ambitions with such infectious confidence. As they'd grown to know each other better, as Carol had shared every inner working of her amazing mind, there had been no denying her brilliance, and it wasn't long before Kari's initial attraction had developed into a full-fledged crush.

Kari hadn't been out yet, and she'd been unaware of Carol's sexual orientation, which made having those burgeoning feelings all the more difficult to deal with day after day. Carol had shown little interest in either sex, far more focused on her marks, on her books and her research, than on any form of campus social life. But from their conversations, Kari had just assumed that the girl was completely straight.

Still, there had been no denying their connection. Kari had felt it whenever they were alone together, whenever their eyes met. Carol's were a deep brown, but they held a light within them, a brightness that paled the moon, the stars, even the sun. And whenever Kari gazed into those eyes, she saw herself. Not a reflection, not like a mirror. Kari saw herself the way Carol saw her; everything she was, all the glorious possibilities of what could be.

Kari had never experienced anything like it before or since, which explained why all her other relationships had failed. After graduation, after Carol went away, she'd actively searched for it, Lord knows she had, but she'd never been able to find it again.

Not until today.

This body Kari now held in her arms...it might be newborn flesh, but the spirit within was much older. Carol Miyagi was in there. There wasn't a shred of doubt in Kari's mind.

"What is going on?" Carol asked. Her voice was just as soft and beautiful as ever, but Kari heard fear punctuate every word.

"Oh, sweetie." Kari took a step back. She wiped the joyous tears from her cheeks then she reached up and lovingly combed a few errant strands of sable hair from Carol's face. "As clever as you are, you really haven't figured it all out yet?"

Carol shook her head.

"Think about it." Kari nodded at the lifeless body on the altar across the room, not really wanting to look at it again, not when the living breathing woman was standing right here in front of her. "Yes, that *is* you over there. You died out there on the slope. *But* this place, it did exactly what you said it would. It brought you back in the only way it knew how, the only way it *could*."

"I don't under-"

"They *cloned you*," Kari blurted.

"Cloned?" Carol slumped in her grasp, almost as if she'd been kicked in the gut.

Kari pulled her upright again, refusing to let her fall. "Your body was too damaged," she told her, "but there was nothing wrong with your mind. So they just...they grew it a new home."

Carol stared back at her, clearly dumbfounded.

"Dēvatāharu dvārā," Gagan gasped over her shoulder; the satyr's tone was one of wonder and reverence. "They moved Miyagi's brain? Is such a thing even possible?"

Kari nodded, her eyes still fixed on Carol. "You remember what you told me back in the tent — how these aliens, these creators, had mastered genetics and genetic manipulation? You said their skills created all of us, created this ship we're in right now. It's the basis of their whole technology."

"Yes," she agreed, "I remember. I said the possibilities were limitless, that maybe they might even have the cure for death itself."

"And they do...sort of. They hooked you up over there, took some genetic samples—"

"And they grew new, living cells," Carol interrupted. Kari watched the light in her eyes burn just a little bit brighter as she finally grasped it. "They re-created me. I was reincarnated, reborn in a new body."

"Hello, Carol 2.0."

The women shared a smile.

Still in awe, Gagan took another step toward them, his cloven hooves clicking against the uneven chitinous flooring. "But Hannigan, to grow a new Miyagi...would it not still be a *baby?*"

"I don't know what progress they've made in research laboratories, but yes, Gagan, if *we* tried it, I think the clone would still be a fetus; maybe not even that — just a collection of multiplying cells. But take a look around." Kari indicated the forest of cylinders that surrounded them, all the various specimens contained within. "The Ark is light years ahead of us when it comes to this stuff."

"Sugoi ne..." Carol began in Japanese, then she switched over to English before Kari could chide her for it. "They must have controlled the growth rate of my cells, made this body mature until it was no different from...from that one over there."

"More or less," Kari agreed with a shrug. She thought of Carol's missing belly button, of the organic ports that now ran up and down the length of her spine; those bits were all unique to Carol 2.0. "Then, your memories, your personality, everything that was *you*, they just transferred it all over to your beautiful new brain. They did it just as easily as we would download files from one computer and upload them onto another."

"It's everything you said they could do and more, and it's the only thing that makes any sense."

And now I get a second chance, a chance to tell you how much you still mean to me, how much I still—

No. Kari couldn't give those feelings voice. Why do that to Carol? What would be the point? She was now in love with—

Alan?

Out of the corner of her eye, Kari saw him rise up off his knees. She did a double take, and that's when she noticed the ice axe clutched in his hand.

Alan suddenly bared his teeth, his eyes wide as he stalked toward them, ready to strike.

———

Carol saw the threat, too, although at first, she couldn't believe her eyes. She continued to feel like a voyeur, as if she were seeing everything from a distance; her dead body on an altar, that terrible crazed look on Alan's face, the ice axe he clutched in his hands — they were all so impossible, so unreal to her. She felt as if she were floating, as if she were still submerged in one of these stasis tubes, unconscious, in the throes of some terrible dream.

But no, she knew it was real.

All of it.

Alan let out an awful howl and swung at Carol with malignant rage.

Acting on pure instinct, she broke free of Kari's grip and quickly pushed the woman back out of harm's way. Then, her arm flew up to shield her face from the coming blow.

Her wrist muscles flexed and tightened, the rapid motion triggering something within the cuff of her bio-mechanical armor. A hidden blade shot out from just above her wrist with a loud SCHLIKT; it extended over her fisted hand, stabbing through the air, instantly doubling the length of her forearm.

A sword!

Yes. That's what it had to be. But this was nothing like her grandfather's katana; it wasn't even metal. No, this sword appeared to have been carved out of bone. Where the shank met Carol's wrist, it was jagged and segmented like a fused spinal column. The sharpened blade, on the other hand, had a smooth polished face and a toothy serrated edge — the jawbone of some deadly predator fashioned into an equally formidable weapon.

Carol's new sword blocked Alan's ice axe.

For a moment, their eyes met across bone and steel, his shocked expression clearly echoing hers.

Carol recovered quickly; she managed to bat his axe away with a strong, controlled swipe.

Alan stumbled back. Then, his eyes narrowed, and he made another fevered lunge.

The move was sloppy, and Carol easily avoided it. *"Nantekotta i,* Alan!" she yelled, keeping to his left, just out of reach. "What's the matter with you?"

Alan didn't answer; he turned away from her, his eyes searching for Kari. "How could you?"

His voice was horribly rusty, as if he'd suddenly grown ancient.

"How could I *what?*" Kari stood with her back pressed against one of the stasis tubes; she held Carol's katana limply in one trembling hand.

"How could you stand there and hug this *thing?"*

"Alan...it's *Carol."*

"Bullshit!" he spat, pointing back at the altar, at the body, with his axe. *"That's* Carol. She's fucking *dead!"*

"Mr. Alan," Gagan ventured. He rushed to Kari's side, ornate bow in his clawed hands, but his arrow was still aimed harmlessly at the floor, "Did you not hear? She has been reborn!"

"You," Alan said with disgust, "you're both the same. You weren't *born.* You were grown in one of these goddamn tubes!"

He suddenly whirled around and drove the curved point of his pick into a nearby cylinder, rupturing its veiny translucent membrane.

His irrational outburst gave everyone a start.

Carol's arm and skeletal sword snapped on guard. On her other hand, she felt a tingle — the glowing alien weapon, "the wrath of the gods." She'd almost forgotten she was even wearing it.

The golden orb was nearly a foot in diameter, held in the sculpted clutches of a bizarre, six-fingered hand. Like the Ark itself, this unearthly claw appeared to be a bizarre marriage of organic and inorganic materials; exposed muscle and corrugated tubing intertwined, ending in jagged bony talons. Blazing like a dwarf star on the end of her wrist, the weapon fed off her growing fear; its blue-white fire intensifying, its power building, begging to be discharged.

"Alan," she pleaded. "Stop. Please."

He craned his neck to glare at her. "Or what?"

It was a valid question. Could she really use her armaments against him, even in defense? She hoped to never know the answer.

"Watashi wa, anata o aishiteimasu," she told him. "I love you."

"You can't *love*," Alan raged on; he withdrew his axe from the stasis tube, liters of amniotic fluid flowing from the open wound, bleeding out onto the rippled flooring at his feet. "You're *manufactured!* You're *programmed!"*

Alan whirled around and lashed out at another nearby cylinder; he buried his axe deep into its side then yanked the blade free again.

Carol suddenly saw insectoid movement behind him. A gigantic mantis. It had been there this whole time, completely motionless, blended right into the textured wall.

Antibodies. This ship is a living thing, these tubes one of its many organs, and Alan has just made himself a threat to the system.

She watched as the creature unfolded itself, emerging from the confines of its resting pocket. It scuttled across the rippled flooring, moving rapidly over, around, and between the remaining stasis tubes with unyielding purpose.

"Alan!"

His ice axe still dripping fluid, he turned to face her. He didn't even see the creature coming up from behind. Instead, he raised his weapon, took a menacing step toward Carol and—

In a single graceful move, the enormous mantis reached down and plucked him up off the floor.

Carol's eyes followed Alan into the air. She watched as he kicked and writhed, a fly in the insect's grasp. He swung his axe wildly back and forth, but the giant mantis held him far enough away to render the weapon harmless.

"Let him go," she yelled at the creature. "Put him down!"

The mantis ignored her completely, ignored everyone but Alan. A living machine, it had one task and one task only, neutralize the threat. Carol focused in on the huge hooked daggers that extended in place of its forefingers; they were curved and serrated, just like the point of Alan's axe, and it did not take much imagination at all to picture what the thing might do with them if given a chance.

Carol yelled at the mantis again, this time in Japanese, *"Yameru! Kare o tebanasu!"*

The overgrown bug turned away from her and continued toward the wall as if it hadn't heard a word she said.

Then, something in Carol's panicked brain urged her to try again, to speak in Atlantean. She barked her orders once more in that dead language, hoping her pronunciation was correct.

This time, to her amazement, the mantis responded. It suddenly paused and its antennae perked up. Its head swiveled all the way around on its neck and its huge eyes, dark and bulbous, focused in on Carol, on the ball of spectral fire that engulfed her right hand.

Its body spun and it advanced on her, its skittering sounds echoing through the vast chamber.

"Over here!" Kari suddenly shouted, waving the katana, trying to draw the massive insect away from Carol. "Over here!"

The alien creature paid her no mind. It was intent on Carol. There was no one else in the room.

I'm the only one wearing this armor, the myrmidon. I'm the only one with the "Wrath of the Gods."

Carol stood her ground, feet braced. As the mantis towered over her, she glared up at the creature, stuck out her chest, and tightened her jaw. When she spoke again, it was with great authority; in Atlantean, she made her orders clear, release the man and hand his weapon over to her.

The mantis was quick to comply. With great dexterity, its elongated fingers pried the ice axe from Alan's grip, then let the man drop. Alan tumbled to the floor, landing on his back between them, and the creature bent low over him, holding the axe out for Carol's inspection.

She hesitated, but eventually reached out and took possession of the tool. "Thank you."

Carol turned in slow motion, as if still in a dream. She smiled awkwardly at Kari and Gagan, unsure of what to do next.

Kari looked as if she wanted to say something, but simply shook her head in disbelief.

The goat-man did speak, however.

"Miyagi commands the angels!" Gagan fell to his hairy knees, still clutching his bow and arrow. "Servants of the gods obey *her* words!"

Alan looked stupidly up at her from the floor at the mantis's feet; his pain and fury had abandoned him, and in their place, Carol now saw only fear.

CHAPTER THREE

The Yeti had feared the gods since time began, but for countless generations, they'd been far more frightened of Zeus. There were legends, thousands of years old, that told of a terrible night of violence, of bloodshed and death. It was said that Zeus, using some dark magic the Yeti had yet to fathom, tricked the creatures into turning against one another; Yeti killed Yeti until few remained.

That bloody night of chaos had brought their race to the brink of extinction, but they had survived. They endured centuries of exile, cowering in caves, huddled in the bowels of the earth. They persisted. And despite their many adversities, or perhaps because of them, they somehow managed to thrive.

Within the last era, Yeti had grown enough in courage to venture back out into this harsh, unforgiving wasteland. Their hunting parties walked single file through Himalayan snows, leaving large footprints for all to see, but concealing their numbers. At first, the creatures clutched their jade axes, their swords, and their spears in anxious hands. Deep-set eyes, still fighting the sensitivity they'd developed in the dimness of those mountain hollows, now scanned rocky crags and icy barren slopes, forever on guard against any manifestation of their long-feared bugaboo.

And then, one day, out of a white void of wind-blown flurries, the devil appeared to them.

That initial encounter proved shocking. For all of their lives, and the lives of their forefathers before them, they'd been so afraid, so utterly paralyzed by fright, that the very mention of Zeus could quicken their pulse and turn their innards to cold slush. But these men, these *humans*, they were nothing like the legends had warned.

Small, frail, clearly not native to Himalayan peaks, Zeus possessed no fur of their own. Instead, the humans covered their bodies in slaughtered animal skins for warmth. They couldn't even breathe on their own, strapping metal cans of air to their backs in order to survive the great heights.

Peering at these fragile, pathetic creatures, the Yeti's long-held terror deserted them quickly, and in its place burned a sudden hatred that was every bit as intense — a consummate *rage*. Zeus didn't belong here in the mountains. They were invaders, transgressors, murderers still guilty of the genocide that had been perpetrated by their ancestors.

And they could not be allowed to continue on these slopes.

In the years that followed, the furious, vengeful Yeti made it their mission in life to execute Zeus with ruthless proficiency. Once their eyes fixed upon a target, its fate was sealed, and the fatal blow was always dealt with great speed and savagery.

Again and again, blood gushed over Yeti claws, but never enough to wash away the sins of Zeus' past, never enough to erase the countless, empty, wasted years the Yeti had spent in hiding, consigned to a life of darkness and dread. And so, the slaughter went on and on.

Nothing dodged the Yeti's blades. Nothing escaped their wrath. No Zeus left alive. No climber reached the mountaintop.

No exceptions.

Until now.

————

Now, Shekhar lifted his great head, his hot breath turning the thin frigid air into vapor, his white frosted fur twisting in the squall. He gazed up at the sky. Days were quite short here, no matter the season, and the sun had already dropped below Makalu's horizon, taking with it any whisper of warmth. But as night gripped the summit, clear as it was cold, it ushered in its own brand of illumination.

He lowered his eyes once more.

The frozen drifts beneath his huge hairy feet normally glowed and sparkled like crushed diamonds in the moonlight. Not tonight. Tonight, they were dark, painted red with the blood of fallen warriors. Shekhar frowned. He was a chief, the leader of a great clan, yet he felt utterly powerless.

Too many good Yeti had been struck down in their prime, their bodies now fused to the mountain by scarlet icicles. The deep wells of their eye sockets, their nostrils, and their open mouths had all filled in with fresh snow, but Shekhar could still make out their faces. In life, they had been his friends, his family, now they were just...*gone.*

He turned away from the icy funeral mound, looking instead to the slanted monolith they had died to defend.

Failed to defend.

Shekhar's lips, thick and cracked, quivered at the thought.

We failed to protect the God Stone, failed the gods themselves.

Gigantic, the black rock protruded from Makalu's peak like an outstretched finger of some long-buried titan. It pointed up to the heavens, towering over the creatures that now gathered in its shadow.

All around Shekhar, a congress of Yeti knelt down in the drifting snow — hundreds, perhaps thousands strong. They swayed back and forth; some waved their furry arms about in the sub-zero air. Shekhar could hear their low, guttural voices, the sporadic wails of their communal mourning. The sounds rode frigid winds, flowing down the mountainside in invisible streams.

The Yeti prayed. They prayed for the fallen, yes. But most of all, they prayed for the creators' mercy and forgiveness.

It had long been said that, one day, the gods would return to this world. That they would reveal themselves to the Yeti. That they would enlist them to restore the natural order of things.

It was foretold that the gods would help the Yeti punish Zeus for their sins.

Shekhar believed it. And all of his life, he'd dreamt of a time when the Yeti would gather here on the black pyramid of Makalu, when they would watch the creators descend from the heavens on mountains that flew like eagles on the sky. It was a dream shared by all Yeti, no matter their age or their clan. And when the ice melted, when the snow fell away, when the Yeti saw the God Stone appear on the mountaintop for the first time, many thought that the dream had finally come to fruition.

But the rock did not open to the Yeti. It did not speak to them. It remained petrified and mute. Until tonight.

Until the arrival of Zeus.

A handful of humans had managed to escape the Yeti blades and spears. They had been allowed to reach the summit, to look upon the God Stone. Not just to see it, but to lay their filthy hands upon it, and the holy rock responded to their touch.

The God Stone had suddenly come to life. Its back and its belly were smooth and hard as the peak that entombed it, but its flank was more animal than mineral, reminding Shekhar of a half-eaten carcass — a twisted mass of bone and gristle that seemed to move beneath the Yeti's collective stare, to pulsate, to *breathe*. Once black and foreboding, the living rock now glowed brightly from within as if it had swallowed a swath of stars.

The stone opened for Zeus, allowed the invaders entrance, and they had stepped into the realm where the gods had walked alone.

Now, if Shekhar listened very carefully, beneath the chanting and wailing of his kin, beneath the roar of frigid winds, he could hear music. The God Stone hummed. It sang. Or, more precisely, something *within* the holy rock caroled to him.

Zeus and the gods had been reunited, and the God Stone seemed to be rejoicing.

The Yeti might have been frightened by Zeus for generations, but they had feared the gods since time began. And now...now they had no idea what the creators would do next.

A single tear formed in the corner of Shekhar's eye, freezing to his fur. He fell to his knees, his chest heaving, and he joined his brothers and sisters in prayer. Shekhar hoped he was wrong. He hoped the gods were not angry or disappointed, hoped they had not chosen Zeus over Yeti. But no matter how much he hoped and prayed, Shekhar knew only one thing for certain: their world had suddenly changed, and it would never be the same again.

CHAPTER FOUR

The world was a scary place, and with each passing day, it grew even more frightening.

There was an old saying Patrick Tate had learned in school; history is written by the victors. He'd never been overly concerned about that before. He just did what he knew was right and gave little thought to how his actions might be viewed by future generations.

Tonight, however, as he drove down this back-country road, for the first time he found himself fretting about his legacy, nearly consumed by it. If his efforts were even recounted at all, he worried this chapter in history had the potential to be a very dark one indeed. And worst of all, Tate couldn't even be sure that those who might read it would even be human.

He'd dealt with impending threats most of his adult life, and he'd always found a way to combat them, always found a way to *win*. Of course, in the past, he had been able to rely on intelligence reports, on empirical data, statistics and probabilities, all manner of prognostication at his disposal. Now, however, he could trust none of it. This new threat was unlike anything he'd ever confronted, and recent events had caught him with his pants around his ankles.

Things were escalating quickly, spinning out of control, and he didn't have the first clue on how to stop them, on how to make them *right*.

Tate tried to concentrate on the road in front of him. A drive in the country often helped to clear his head, to soothe him, but not tonight. Tonight, his mind continued to race. He had a churning in his gut, as if some living thing had taken up residence, and that unsettling thought had only served to deepen his anxiety.

As a special director for Homeland Security Investigations, his superiors, the president, congress, and most of all, the American people all looked to him for reassurance. They wanted to know that this great country was safe, that everything was secure, and that all Hell was not about to break loose. Normally, Tate could provide them with such an assurance, but on this weird new supernatural battlefront, he could offer little comfort. Shapeshifters, armies of heavily armed monsters, ancient gods...He couldn't even share what he knew without sounding like a raving lunatic.

That was the enemy's biggest advantage, the fact that no one believed in them. Tate recalled a line from one of his favorite films, *The Usual Suspects*: "The greatest trick the Devil ever pulled was convincing the world he didn't exist." It was the absolute truth. Over the centuries, these creatures had been relegated to myths and legends, fairy stories. And that gave them the ability to be anywhere, be any*one*, and to act with absolute impunity.

But they're crawling out of the shadows now, these monsters. They're emboldened, unafraid, showing themselves more and more.

There had been witnesses. Too many witnesses to ever be

quelled with some lame cover story. The creatures hadn't picked some desolate battlefield this time, an isolated coastal town in the middle of nowhere, or even an old warehouse in some run-down section of the city in which to stage their assaults. No. These latest attacks had been out in the open, in full view of the public, every action taken in front of countless cellphones and security cameras.

Either these beasts were insane, or their plans were far enough along that they felt nothing could stop them. Tate hoped it was the former. Insanity, in *people* at any rate, bred mistakes, and mistakes resulted in captures, mistakes led to *victories*. But the thought that it might be the latter...that's what spawned this churning in his gut.

Something horrible was about to happen.

He could feel it in the air, like the hot desert wind before a sandstorm.

Sure, horrible things had happened already, but whatever was coming down the pike, Tate knew it would be a thousand times worse. The word "apocalyptic" got thrown around casually these days, but he could think of no other word to adequately describe his fears. And next time, whenever that next time might be, he knew they could not afford to be taken by surprise.

This world's not going to end on my watch. I know that much. No way. Not gonna happen. We're going to write our own history, not going to have it dictated to us by these things.

Tate's dark sedan left the main road and made its way up a long gravel driveway, his headlights illuminating the surrounding trees. The safe house lay nestled in the woods of upstate New York. It was little more than a glorified cabin, really, and completely off the books. Few knew of its existence, even fewer knew that it was currently occupied, and only Tate knew by whom.

The clock in his dash read twenty-two hundred hours when he

finally parked. He shut off the engine, grabbed his briefcase, and made his way inside.

On the opposite end of a dimly lit room, a hospital bed had been positioned to face the door. In it, Agent Andrews now sat upright, his left leg in traction, a pillow comfortably propped behind his head, and his right arm cradled in a canvas sling. In his left hand, he held a Glock Model 22 pistol, its barrel aimed squarely at Tate's chest.

"Director," Andrews said calmly. His face did not betray even the slightest flicker of concern or alarm, no emotion whatsoever. After everything this man had been through, everything he'd seen, Tate thought that must have been quite a feat.

"Agent Andrews," the director replied. "You're looking much better this evening."

"Thank you, sir."

Andrews lowered his weapon. He placed it on the bedside table that crossed his lap, right next to a glass of water, some reading material, and of course, his laptop. The computer sat open, bathing him in light, the contents of its screen reflected in the man's eyeglasses.

To say that Andrews had been at death's door was no exaggeration. The man was shot, his arm and leg were broken, and he'd lost a great deal of blood. He'd been rushed to a hospital, patched up, stabilized, but if not for the efforts of his partner, Agent Earl L. Preston Jr., Andrews might have been murdered in his sleep.

His own goddamn doctor...a snake-woman in disguise.

Hades' disciples. That's what Preston had called these creatures. And his warning, delivered with grim sincerity, still echoed in Tate's ears, *"Just...be careful who you put your trust in."*

Tate had seen the snake-doctor's bullet-ridden corpse, her reptilian body sprawled out across the floor of that hospital elevator.

An ID badge had still been clipped to the thing's scrub jacket — a much different portrait. The idea that the smiling person standing next to you could suddenly morph into something so horrifying, something so *lethal*...

With each new incident, each new photograph and video, each new addition to the body count, it grew easier and easier to accept, even for so-called "rational" human beings. And with this mounting proof came an overwhelming sense of personal relief, validation for Tate's own nightmarish experiences during the Gulf War — a battle with literal monsters that had ended in another Preston, Earl Senior—

Link. My friend.

—sacrificing himself to save the director's life.

Valor, it seemed, ran strong in that family.

You'd be proud of your boy, Link. He's like you in so many ways; smart, strong, sure of himself, and loyal to a fault. No soldier left behind.

Tate took another step toward Andrews. The agent continued to study his laptop screen; though haggard, his eyes were as sharp as ever. "I've been reviewing the traffic camera photos and enhancements you sent me," he said.

The director nodded. He'd been contacted by the NYPD. Someone had shot up a busy New York highway, the FDR — a truck and two motorcycles exchanging gunfire during a late night, high-speed chase. Traffic cameras captured all the action, yielding photographs of the perpetrators. The images were startling, and local authorities simply didn't know what to make of them, or how they should proceed.

Hanging off the back of that speeding truck was the Big Bad Wolf, leapt straight from the pages of the Brothers Grimm. And that wasn't all. One of the pursuing motorcycle riders appeared to be a great white shark with arms and legs, similar to the remains of creatures they discovered a few years back, when the sea-side town of Colonial Bay was bombed off the map by Roger Hays and his henchmen. Best of all, facial recognition software had identified the other rider as a dead man, a former Coast Guard officer turned federal agent — none other than Earl L. Preston Jr.

"So much for keeping a low profile." Tate stepped up to the left side of the hospital bed, frustrated and unsure of what to do with his rogue agent, uncertain if he should do anything at all.

"Agent Preston's methods have always been... unconventional," Andrews pointed out, "but take it from me, sir, his instincts are never wrong."

"Yes, well, as much as I would like this to be solely a referendum on Agent Preston's performance, there are obviously much larger concerns at work here." Tate rubbed his temple. "I have all the resources of the United States government at my disposal, but I have no idea where to deploy them or how to direct them.

"We don't know what that truck is carrying. No radiation sensors have been tripped in the New York area, but it could still be a cache of conventional weapons, or even something biological — a viral agent to which these creatures are immune, but one that could wipe normal human beings off the face of the Earth."

At that, Andrews glanced up from his laptop. "You imagine some pretty cheery scenarios, Director."

"It's in my job description. I have to imagine *every* scenario, and I have to make damn sure that they don't succeed. We need to get it right every time, but our enemies...they only need to get it right *once*."

Tate opened his briefcase and reached inside. He produced a black USB flash drive and held it out to Andrews.

"What's this?"

"Our enemies getting it right," Tate told him. "There's been a prison break."

"Where?"

"New Hampshire."

Andrews paused for a beat, and Tate actually saw a flicker of concern in those normally clinical, emotionless eyes. He took the flash drive from the director's fingers and quickly plugged it into the side of his laptop.

"We were able to obtain security camera footage—"

"I'm opening the file now."

A new window popped up on Andrews' screen, and he immediately clicked to enlarge the video, black and white footage of a prison hallway. The corridor sat empty at first, then something moved into frame, something as absurd as it was horrible: a scaly head driven forward by a sinuous neck. Curved horns and sharp teeth glinted in the light. The creature walked on two muscular legs, its clawed arms outstretched, and huge leathery wings folded against its spiny back.

"A dragon," Andrews said aloud, and from his lips it actually sounded plausible.

"You don't seem surprised."

The agent shrugged as best he could with one arm in a sling. "I've seen a giant's hand burst from an Indiana farmhouse and reach for the moon, been attacked by a werewolf brandishing an automatic rifle. Such things tend to open your mind to...various possibilities."

Andrews turned his eyes back to the laptop screen, but not Tate. He'd seen the footage once already, seen the immolation of a dozen or more guards as they were engulfed by the dragon's fire, and he couldn't bring himself to watch it again. It brought back too many memories.

Tate had never undergone counseling for post-traumatic stress. Perhaps he should have. But more than the memories and the nightmares, Tate feared that, if he told his story to anyone, uttered aloud what really happened in that Iraqi desert, it would only serve to lose him both his credibility and his job.

If he closed his eyes even now, he could still see them there — members of Hussein's Republican Guard, transforming into a pack of blood-thirsty hyenas right in front of him. He remembered the strings of saliva that hung down from their toothy grins as they gunned down his platoon. He remembered the pain of being shot. But most of all, he remembered their laughter. They had been laughing at him, laughing at *them all*.

Tate couldn't shake the feeling that, somewhere, they were still laughing.

"Jesus," Andrews said aloud. The action on his laptop screen finally at an end, he leaned back heavily in his hospital bed. "That was Roger Hays' man with the creatures, wasn't it — the one Preston helped to put away?"

"One Dante Vianello, a.k.a. 'The Horror Show,' sociopath and hired killer. Yes, that was him."

"And the werewolf they took with them, who was that?"

Werewolf. Jesus. At least Andrews wasn't fighting back laughter as he said it.

"We don't know," the director admitted. "It could be anyone, a guard or an inmate. At the prison, they're still sifting through the ashes, literally, trying to account for both. More than the 'who,' I want to know the *'why?'* Why bust them out — why risk such a public display to do it, and why now?"

"Without more information, it's impossible to say," Andrews told him, "but, obviously, they think there's nothing we can do to stop them."

Tate's frown deepened. "That's what scares me."

The director's mind returned once more to thoughts of future children reading through their history books, reading about the end of civilization as he knew it, about his failure to stop it. They were hyena children, and they were laughing.

CHAPTER FIVE

onsters!

They were hairy, rabid, bat-shit crazy things, and they were coming for Earl L. Preston Jr. No, not just for him. They were here to take everyone he cared about. Everyone he *loved*.

Earl snapped awake and managed to cover his mouth with his hand just in time. A sound had been climbing up the back of his throat, groan or scream, he didn't know which; but whatever it was, he stifled it before it could escape his lips. He hadn't called out in his sleep since he was a child—

Pavor Nocturnus, the doctors called it. Night terrors.

—when he'd lost someone close to him.

Monsters...monsters killed my Daddy!

Hades' disciples, the same clan who'd stolen his father from him as a boy...they'd nearly claimed—

Zuri.

She slept naked beside him on the narrow cot, a warrior in

repose; candles surrounded them, their flickering light playing across the elegant curves and hard muscular lines of her body. And though she now looked at peace, Earl had no doubt that some preternatural sense would spur her awake if any real danger threatened — her bright eyes suddenly alert, her lupine claws and fangs ready for a fight.

The perfect soldier, he thought with a mix of admiration and envy. *Dad would approve.*

All his life, Earl had lived in the shadow of his fallen father; the decorated warrior, the *hero* — a figure far larger and more mythic than any of the shape-shifting creatures they now fought. And everything Earl had done up to this moment, every choice he'd made in his life and in his career, had been in the hope of making that dead man proud, of meeting expectations that had never been voiced, and yet rang in Earl's ears every waking moment.

But falling for Zuri, making love to her last night...those decisions had been Earl's and Earl's alone. They'd stemmed from his heart for once, not from his head. There was no second guessing them now, and best of all, no regrets.

Earl heaved a sigh of relief that Zuri was alive and safe in his embrace, that the bad dreams he'd experienced had been just that and nothing more. He thought of waking her, decided against it, then touched his lips to her forehead, his kiss as soft and as gentle as a moth landing in the night.

In sleep, she looked no different from any other woman, but Earl knew better. He'd been fully prepared to find the wolf lying there in his arms when he opened his eyes, yet somehow, Zuri managed to hold onto her humanity, even in the depths of slumber, when Earl had been so certain the guise would slip through her fingers. Not that it really mattered to him one way or the other. Wolf or not, whenever Earl looked at her, he saw only Zuri.

He saw the woman he loved.

Her face appeared more relaxed than he'd ever noticed it, softer, yet still so serious. His chest had become her pillow, and she rode the crest of his every breath, nuzzling him with the nub of her nose and the fullness of her cheek, her own breath warming his bare skin. As she pressed close against him, Earl felt her supple breasts and taut abdomen; he felt the strong, steadfast beat of her heart, and the tight curls of her afro tickled him pleasantly whenever she moved her head.

She really was perfection, pure and simple.

After the freeway chase, when the spider-centaur had sent her flying from the back of that speeding truck into oncoming traffic, when Earl had picked her battered body up off the crumpled yellow hood of that Ford, when he'd watched over her as she lay here unconscious on this cot for what seemed like a hellish eternity, unable to change, unable to heal, Earl had prayed more feverishly than he'd ever prayed in his life. No, it was more than that. He'd made a bargain with God. He pledged again and again that, if Zuri lived, if she came back to him, he would love her completely. On his mother's life, he swore that he would love her true. And he meant it, every word.

Zuri suddenly roused. Her eyes fluttered open, and when she saw Earl lying there beside her, the corners of her mouth rose like the sun. After all the horrors this woman had lived through, the thought that it was *he* who could bring a smile to her face filled him with warm satisfaction.

"Mornin', sleepy-head," he told her.

"Good morning," she replied, her voice thick, her accent cracked and broken by sleep. "I see that you are smiling."

"You're smiling, too."

"Yes, well, for once in my life, Earl Preston, I find that I have much to smile about."

"Same here." He leaned in and her lips met his in a kiss; it was slow, passionate, but all too brief.

"Did I hurt you last night?" she asked, pulling away from him, her tone serious, almost apologetic.

What the hell did she have to apologize for? Not a goddamn thing. If anything, it was Earl who felt the need to try and atone for the past sins of his sex, for the monsters who'd taken her innocence by force and left her with wounds that had never fully healed, wounds that he hoped he hadn't re-opened. "I'm fine," he told her. "It's *you* I'm worried about. Did I—?"

Her hand shot up and she pressed her fingers to his lips. "No, beloved, you were wonderful, gentler and understanding than I could ever have hoped for. Being with you, I felt things I never thought I would be able to experience. I felt passion. I felt *free*."

"Good." He flashed a grin. "I'm glad."

"Now, please," she went on, still obviously concerned, "I must know this, so do not feed me any of your macho bullshit."

"Macho bullshit's part of my charm."

"Yes. It is the part that I find most annoying, but I see through it. You are a good man, Earl, with a strong heart, and so I have grown to love you, anyway."

"Thanks...I think."

"Last night," she pressed, "when I changed, showed my true nature, did I *hurt* you?"

Earl shook his head. "Not a scratch, Zuri. Honest. I'm fine. Hell," his grin widened, "I'm better than fine. After last night, I'm fan-fuckin'-tastic."

She didn't look convinced. "Have you tried to transform yet this morning?"

"Funny you should ask. I was just practicin' my new snarl right before you woke up. Whatcha think?" He contorted his face and bared his teeth at her. *"Grr... Argh!"*

Zuri gave his chest a rough slap.

"Ow! *Now*, you hurt me."

"I am serious, Earl."

"I get that..." He rubbed the sting from his chest. "But I'm tellin' you, I don't feel any different. And even if I did, I don't know how this *American Werewolf* shit works."

"Hold out your hand," Zuri commanded.

He held up his left arm, showing her his palm, his fingers splayed. "Now what?"

"Now, you must breathe," she told him. "Relax."

Earl rolled his eyes. "This is some yoga bullshit right here."

"It is not bullshit. You must trust me."

"Zuri, I trust you, you know I do, but this here is—"

"Zeus, Hades, Poseidon...All different, yes?"

"Sure."

"No. No different. We all come from the same wellspring, the same ancestors, and no matter what the clan, the struggle is always the same, in *here*." She placed her hand over her breasts, covering the pair of paw print tattoos which marked them. "Instinct over reason, savagery against civilization—"

"Good vs. evil."

"You paint with such broad strokes, Earl. Do you really think that our enemies are waking right now and saying to themselves, 'Today I will go out and do great evil in the world?' No. No one sees themselves or their own methods as wicked, but they are quick to find wickedness in others. Those we fight are only doing what they think is best for the clans, for the planet, just as we must do."

"Yeah, but Zuri, their *best* includes the mass murder of civilians, rape, torture, and slavery. I think most people would consider that shit to be pretty fuckin' evil, don't you?"

She stared at him for a moment. Then, her eyes swung back to his outstretched hand. "Now, relax," she told him. "Do not struggle against those baser instincts. We all have them. Surrender to yours. Give in to your primal nature."

Earl took a deep breath and did as she asked, trying to let go. He focused on his fingers, willing them into doing something unnatural.

Go go werewolf hand, he thought and then tried not to laugh.

"Do you feel anything?" Zuri asked.

"You mean other than ridiculous?"

She reached up and pressed her hand against his. Earl watched as her lethal claws unexpectedly lengthened to dwarf his fingers. A black wave of hair crested over her knuckles and flowed down her arm, covering her skin in a sleek coat of ebony fur. She made it look so damn easy, but no matter how hard Earl tried to force his muscles and bones to follow her lead, they simply refused him.

"Nothin'," he told her. "Guess you're stuck with me the way I am."

"I like you the way you are," she told him, her claws dulling as she let the wolf melt away. She reached out to stroke his cheek with delicate human fingers, and he saw the relief in her eyes. "It makes me very happy that I have not changed you."

But that was just it; she *had* changed him.

Earl had never been one for making long-range plans. He'd always been goal oriented, focused on the mission at hand, on insuring his own survival. But when it came to Zuri, as corny as it might sound, he now saw something more than just himself. He knew he wanted to be with her, to stay with her, to grow old and grey with her, and whatever trials might come their way, he knew without a shred of doubt that he wanted to face them together.

He thought of Larry Neuhaus. The shark-man had taken a bullet down in the Gulf of Mexico, but he'd still managed to swim thousands of miles back here to New York, desperate to find and protect his wife, Peggy. Gazing into Zuri's eyes, Earl thought he knew just how the man felt. There was nothing he wouldn't do for her.

Nothing.

Zuri kissed him then, as if she'd somehow peered into his brain and knew his thoughts. Or maybe no special powers were needed; maybe his feelings were just out there, scrawled plainly across his face for all to see. Her lips moved slowly to his earlobes, whispering, "Do you want me now, my love?"

"Hell, yeah, I want you now." *Now and forever.* "Do you still want me?"

"I do." Zuri's kisses moved down the length of his neck. When she reached the hard ridge of his collarbone, she smiled up at him. Her eyes shone bright in the dimness, as if lit from within. "Please, tell me you have another condom?"

Earl's hand blurred out for the bedside table. He felt around the base of a makeshift candelabrum, his eager fingers finding one discarded Trojan wrapper after another, some ripped neatly in two, others left shredded, depending on the urgency of their need. All were now empty and useless.

Jesus, how many times were we together last night?

Earl remembered the first time quite clearly. He'd been so nervous, so tense, searching Zuri for signs of PTSD, watching without letting her know he was watching, afraid that his touch, his kiss, his every move might prove to be some sort of trigger for her. The last thing he'd wanted was to add to her trauma, to spark some panic attack, or worse, send her spiraling into nightmare flashbacks, forcing her to relive the pain of past torments.

There had been some initial trepidation, but after she climbed on top of him, Zuri seemed fine. Better than fine, actually. To Earl, it appeared as if the experience had empowered her, invigorated her, and when she climaxed, he'd had the distinct impression that she'd achieved some personal victory.

It wasn't long before she asked Earl for a second go around, and he'd been more than happy to oblige. There was really no down time between their second and third couplings, and by then, Earl was confident that Zuri was no longer fearful, that she could be comfortable in his embrace. Then, and only then, did he allow himself to lower his guard, to become lost in the moment and rejoice in their subsequent unions.

At last, Earl managed to find a single still-sealed Trojan packet. He held it up for her inspection. "Last one," he lamented.

"Then, we must make it count." She snatched the condom from his hand and brought it to her mouth. Her teeth were already sharpened to canine fangs and she tore the wrapper open with ease.

"Careful," he warned, rising up on his elbows, "you'll poke a damn hole in it."

"Be still, my beloved," Zuri whispered, her voice deepening, "and I promise that I will be very careful, indeed."

She placed her hand firmly on his chest, still human, but supernaturally strong; it pushed him back against the cot. Earl found that he didn't mind surrendering to her. After all, Zuri's strength was what had drawn him to her in the first place. Then, he felt her other hand slide gracefully down to his groin.

Zuri gripped him, stroked him slowly up and down, her fingers massaging every inch of his length. Her hold tightened as he stiffened. He felt her palm thicken, her flesh bubbling and pulsating around him. The sensation was incredible, the friction of her movements slow and deliberate. Now, the bones of her fingers began to bulge and shift, each digit lengthening just as Earl was lengthening within her grasp.

"Lord, Zuri, *fuck*..."

He neared climax several times, but she wouldn't allow it. Not yet. Just when he thought he would explode, her grip loosened and she slowed her stroke. Finally, she halted altogether and sheathed his hardness in rubber. The thin barrier was meant to protect him, but it could not shield him from Zuri's heat. When she straddled him, when he felt himself plunge deep inside of her, her warmth enveloped him, stoked him like a raging inferno, and Earl wanted nothing more in that moment than to let it burn.

Zuri's hips began to writhe. She ground against him, her motions hard and furious, almost feral. Earl did his best to hold onto her, his hands firmly in the curves of her waist. He'd witnessed her transformation at least a dozen times by now, but the bright wonder of it all had yet to fade from his eyes. He studied the ebb and flow of her skin, saw her ears grow large and sharpen to points; watched her full, beautiful lips stretch thin as her jaw changed shape to form a snout.

Earl felt the coarse black hairs of the wolf sprout from Zuri's every pore, growing lush between his fingers. And between her legs, inner muscles worked against him; they quivered, fluxed, and convulsed, bringing him ever closer to release.

Zuri leaned forward. She pressed herself against him, pinning him to the cot, her snout nuzzling his neck. She let out a whimper, then a low guttural growl built up in her throat. Finally, she managed words, a husky whisper, "Do you really love me, Earl Preston?"

"Yes," he replied. "You know I do."

"The real me, as I am now?"

"Yes." He wrapped his arms around her, buried his nose in her furry neck, becoming lost in her scent. She smelled of heat, of musk, and it drove him wild.

"Then, please," she begged, "tell me again...speak the words."

Earl lifted his lips in her oversized ear. "I love you."

"Yes."

"I've never loved anyone in my life the way I love you."

"Make me to come, Earl," she growled. "Please, make me to come."

In reply, he began to thrust deeper, harder, *faster*.

After a few moments, Zuri broke his grip. She reared up and threw her head back with a loud, deafening howl.

Earl's eyelids slammed shut and he spilled himself into the condom, answering Zuri's cry with one of his own. When he opened his eyes once more, he found her hovering over him, still fully transformed. She was panting, propped up on quivering arms, gazing down at him without saying a word, her ears relaxed and her tail wagging pleasantly behind her.

She was never more beautiful.

He reached up and pulled her to him, kissing the coarse fur of her forehead, holding her tight. "Girl," he said, still more than a little out of breath, "*that* was amazing."

"It is you who are amazing, my love."

"Jesus, when you had me in your hand...where the fuck did you learn that shit?"

"Did you enjoy it?"

"Hell, yeah, I enjoyed it."

She shrugged in his embrace. "It is something I learned many years ago. It is how I brought my jailor to arousal before I tore his manhood from his body."

"What the—?" Earl felt his stomach do a barrel roll. "You serious? Why would you even tell me somethin' like that?"

"Because you asked and because it is the truth."

"I'm not even tryin' to hear that right now." His hand moved unconsciously to cover himself. He'd gone completely limp, the rubber, still slick from Zuri, growing cold against his skin. "You know, you don't have to be completely truthful all the time."

"You want me to tell you lies?"

"Well...maybe not lies, but, you know, pillow talk... it's supposed to be sexy. And you tellin' me how you learned to give hand jobs so you could rip guys' junk off? Don't get me wrong, that shit makes you bad-ass, but it sure as hell's not sexy."

"Before I met you, I did not know that I could *be* sexy," she told him. "I thought I knew who I was. I made myself strong, *bulletproof*, but there was always this place deep within me, this small refuge of weakness and fear, and the light could never touch it. No matter what I did, I still felt like a victim, still lived in shame. No more. I have found my complete strength, reclaimed it for myself. Those men...they wanted to destroy my spirit, my will. They did not succeed. They *did not* win."

"No," he agreed. "They didn't."

"And our enemies, they will not win, either."

"No." His thoughts went back to his father, to justice that desperately needed to be served. "They won't."

"Last night," Zuri went on, her bright eyes fixed on his face, "for the first time in my life, I truly felt like a survivor. That young girl the soldiers kidnapped all those years ago... I thought that she was gone forever, like my family, like my village. I thought those men had killed her. But you have shown me that she is still here. When I clawed my way out from that Hell, I carried her with me.

She was badly wounded, and she is still healing, but she is very much alive, and she is capable of love as well as hate.

"With you, Earl Preston, I have new purpose. No longer will I only be fighting *against* something. I now have something...some*one* who I will be fighting *for*."

Earl shook his head. "Unbelievable."

"What?"

"English isn't even your first fucking language," he told her, "but there you go, putting into words everything I've been thinking, everything I'm feeling for you right now, and you go and do it better than I ever could."

Zuri exhaled. "You flatter me," she said. Then, she ran her clawed fingers through his fro. "For a human, Earl Preston, you are very wise."

They both laughed at that, and for Earl, the night terrors were all but forgotten.

"Well," he told her, "as much as I'd love to lay here on this cot with you all day, we need to get our asses up and get dressed.

"We got work to do."

CHAPTER SIX

T he worksite was cluttered, frenzied, but that didn't bother Graeme King, not in the slightest. He was in his element. This was science, after all, the very thing that had driven him all his life, a physics experiment on the grandest possible scale, the physics experiment to end all physics experiments. And if experience had taught him anything, it's that unproven science was always raw, and usually quite messy.

Graeme knew that he was a captive, a prisoner, but it didn't *feel* that way. On the contrary, here on the floor of this cavernous old aircraft hangar, he felt as if he were the one in charge of these proceedings. And why wouldn't he? When these creatures needed direction, they all looked to him for guidance.

They need my help. These creatures, and the ancient, technologically advanced beings behind them, need me, a theoretical physicist from a small Indiana university, to complete their work.

Graeme still couldn't get over it. Each night when he laid down on his cot and his head hit the pillow, he kept expecting to awaken back in his own bed, to find that this had all been nothing but a dream.

He stood by watching as heavy machinery was positioned, then repositioned around triangular metal scaffolding. The massive structure pointed upward, aimed at the curved corrugated ceiling, toward the heavens that lay beyond it, and ultimately, into the icy heart of space itself. Arc welders worked to fuse this framework together, creating intense bursts of light, flares of ultraviolet and infrared radiation, like tiny supernovas; they appeared, burned brightly for a time, then were snuffed out completely.

Nothing is forever, not even the stars.

The stars were a subject to which Graeme's mind made frequent voyages. He'd stared into the night sky for so long he was surprised his neck hadn't strained beyond repair. Each constellation, every pinpoint of light, all scrutinized as he formulated his hypotheses and formulae, trying to bridge the gaps in Man's understanding of the universe.

Bridge the gaps.

As Graeme looked at this massive gateway they had cobbled together from the materials at hand, he had to laugh. That was his mission in a nutshell, wasn't it?

"What's so funny?"

Graeme turned toward the voice's owner and found one of his ever-present bodyguards, the man-bat. This same creature had kidnapped him from the hallowed halls of far-off Stanley University, had literally flown him here on its huge leathery wings, and in the process, it had made him both a hostage and a willing accomplice to one Vivian Song.

Its pointed ears perked up. Its dark eyes narrowed. "You see something wrong, professor?"

Still laughing, Graeme offered the thing a dismissive wave, his head wagging. How could he explain to this creature that the feathery concepts of quantum mechanics, complex theorems which had puzzled the likes of Newton, Einstein, Schrödinger, and Hawking, were finally being offered sturdy skeleton by a menagerie of whimsical beasts?

Mathematics was the only truly universal language. Whatever country you found yourself in, whatever planet you might hail from, one plus one would always equal two. Pi would always be equivalent to approximately 3.14. And equivalent energy (E) would always be calculated as mass (m) multiplied by the speed of light (c $= \sim 3 \times 108$ m/s) squared.

Numbers. Unlike men and monsters, numbers don't lie. Numbers don't have an agenda. Numbers are neither good nor evil. Numbers solve every mystery. Numbers explain everything.

Mathematical descriptions of cosmic motion, of the interaction of subatomic particles...it was all being made tangible in this looming edifice of wire and steel that now stood before them; an Einstein–Rosen bridge, a mechanism that would connect two vastly separate points in the universe, two completely alien worlds.

After a lifetime of conjecture and theory, Graeme found himself staring at possible proof, at *validation*, and he could scarcely believe it. He glanced down at his clipboard, at the schematics he held in his hands; a child who'd always wanted to know how the magic worked and had suddenly been handed an instruction manual by the magicians themselves.

Magic and science...both require sacrifice.

Graeme nodded.

The pages of history were filled with cautionary tales of researchers who had surrendered comfort, personal fortunes, families and relationships, even their own health and sanity, their *very lives*, all in the pursuit of scientific progression. These men and women claimed to have done it for the betterment of mankind, to make the future brighter and safer for us all. In reality, Graeme knew their motivations had been far more selfish in nature.

Scientists gave up everything because, deep down inside, they all possessed the same voracious hunger for understanding, the same unquenchable thirst for answers. Over the centuries, they did what they did, not for any church, not for king and country, but because they had to *know*.

And of course, there was no denying a certain amount of vanity existed in all scientific endeavors. Discovery equaled immortality; your name forever engraved alongside your findings for all to see, an epitaph that could never be erased, no matter what advancements might follow you. In this respect, Graeme was no better, no worse, and no different; he wanted to learn that which had yet to be learned, certainly, but he also wanted to learn it *first*.

"You have the chance to make scientific history, doctor," Vivian Song kept assuring him. *"Right here. Right now."*

He could only hope she was right. To hell with her motives, her *cause*; she had provided him with the opportunity of a lifetime, and he had no choice but to see it through.

Graeme thought of Wernher von Braun and other aerospace engineers who made deadly rockets for the Nazis during World War II, only to become essential players for America in the space race of the 1960s. All their sins were forgiven and forgotten. Their discoveries, their advances and their scientific triumphs, *that's* what history cared about.

He only hoped that, when this business was finished, no matter what the outcome, the same could be said of him.

Graeme took a deep breath to calm himself. His nostrils filled with welding fumes, a complex mixture of metallic oxides, silicates, and fluorides, and his analytical eyes resumed their slow climb up the tall scaffolding. He studied the project both as a whole and in minutiae, inspecting each seam, counting every last rivet, judging the overall placement of various cables and connectors, seeking out imperfections, no matter how slight. All the while, he compared their steady progress to Vivian Song's master plan.

No, not Vivian's, he corrected himself, his grip on the clipboard tightening. *If she's to be believed, then these instructions are extraterrestrial in origin, beamed to Earth from the farthest reaches of the cosmos, from a planet called Kronos, the product of vast and ancient intellects far different from our own...*

By design, small alcoves had been placed in the unfinished superstructure, thirteen to be exact. They were spaced at regular intervals. Six went up one leg of the isosceles triangle as it reached to the rafters, each one mirrored on the opposite slope. The thirteenth and final one had been placed high above all the others, in the dead center of the vertex point.

Graeme now knew that these cubbyholes were reserved for mysterious crystals, energized chunks of quartz that Vivian claimed were powerful enough to punch a hole through space and time. These crystals would charge the gateway, regulate the Casimir effect, and provide for a stable event horizon. He only wished he could examine them himself, could somehow test their properties. Then, perhaps, he would feel a bit more confident.

As a scientist, Graeme was accustomed to failed experiments, to self-judgement and course correction, but never had the stakes been so high. If this gigantic contraption failed to work, what then? He shook his head, trying to keep his mind from wandering too deeply down that dark path, trying to stay positive.

It will work, he told himself. *It has to.*

Behind him, large metal doors came to sudden grinding life. Graeme thought nothing of the sound; he'd heard it countless times throughout the day, doors sliding open to allow for the movement of equipment and the changing of personnel. But now, for the first time since construction began, the roar of those doors brought the creatures' work to a complete stop.

It took Graeme a moment to comprehend what was happening. Around him, the beasts began to freeze in their tracks. They stood wide-eyed, staring in Graeme's direction, but none of them looking at *him*. No. The awe in their collective gaze was reserved for something else. A murmur of recognition passed between them, then the entire crew suddenly dropped to their knees; they knelt upon the metal scaffolding and the concrete floor of the hangar, their heads down in a show of reverence and respect, as if to honor some powerful god or Earthly king.

Graeme looked to either side and saw that his own beastly bodyguards had prostrated themselves. They'd fallen on all fours. The man-bat's wings folded tightly against its back, and the long horns that extended from the minotaur's bowed head now scratched the cement.

In the entire hangar, only Graeme was left standing, aware that the object of his crew's shared awe and veneration now stood directly behind him.

"Isn't it beautiful?" The voice over Graeme's shoulder was just as cold, dark, and deep as the gulf of space he sought to bridge. And he didn't just hear the words; he *felt* them, every syllable reverberating through his ribcage.

Graeme clutched his clipboard to his chest. Against his better judgement, he forced himself to turn around.

A reptilian form loomed over him, its size every bit as shocking as it was intimidating. The thing stepped forward on two oddly jointed legs, an illustration from a children's fairy tale come to stunning life. Its golden wings spread wide, rivaling those of the man-bat, and a long, spiked tail sliced through the air in its wake.

A dragon, Graeme thought. Despite being confronted by something so far removed from the boundaries of any science known to him, his mind readily accepted it and was unafraid. He stared up at the creature as if he were studying an advanced equation, confused not so much by what it was, but rather *who* it was.

He'd been told about Vivian Song's inhuman form and even witnessed red-hot sparks fly from her lips whenever she grew agitated, yet a part of him still refused to believe. Now, here she was, standing right in front of him in all her glory. There was no denying the creature was real.

Vivian's eyes seemed to burn from within, stained glass windows to Armageddon, but she wasn't looking at Graeme. Her gaze was exclusive to the gateway. Dark, leathery lips peeled back in a toothy, delighted smile; her incisors were thin and needle-sharp, but her canines were thick as dwarf tusks.

"The Incas called it *Amaru Maru,*" she said to no one in particular.

Graeme saw a forked tongue flitting about in her mouth as she spoke. He also noticed the long catfish whiskers that trailed from either side of her snout; they seemed to float on the air, defying gravity. As if aware of his focus, Vivian reached up to stroke one of the protrusions, running it slowly through her clawed fingers. The mannerism reminded Graeme of a clichéd villain twirling their handlebar mustache, like some old Snidely Whiplash cartoon from his youth.

"The Doorway of the Serpent," she went on, and Graeme noted that her voice, now deeper, more authoritative, had lost none of its seductive femininity. "Our means of returning the gods to their rightful place here on Earth."

Vivian hadn't entered the hangar alone. The insectoid Benedict stood by her side, truly her right-hand man. Riding high on eight spindly legs, he studied the construction with a multitude of eyes, his mandibles wriggling as he spoke. "It's a real cracker, all right. I'm proper impressed."

"So, when do Kurt Russell and James Spader get here?"

It was the big man in the dark suit to Vivian's left who had spoken — human, at least for now. He reached up to straighten his crimson tie and Graeme could see a scar there on his neck.

"More jokes, my friend?" This final voice sounded much older, wiser. "Your tendency to trivialize is a façade, a mask to cover true feelings. You would live better without it."

Graeme's eyes shot to the source, a large grey wolf. It was bipedal, standing tall on two elongated hind legs, while its clawed hands were folded as if in prayer. Graeme had been so fixated on Vivian; he hadn't seen it standing there until now.

"Wrong, Preacher," the man in the suit snapped back, his attention shifting from the gateway to the werewolf. "Sometimes, hiding your true feelings is the only thing that keeps you breathin' — alive to fight another day."

The man glanced over at Vivian for a moment and smiled. It was an unstable, unpleasant smile that gave Graeme chills, but the dragon appeared not to notice it. She was far too intent on the wolf right in front of her, this "preacher."

The wolf stepped forward, edging nearer the gateway, but Vivian hung back, keeping a respectful distance, one clawed hand stroking her whisker, the other pressed against her scaly breast.

"Does it please you?" she asked him.

"Oh, yes, child, it pleases me beyond words. You've done well here, exceeded even my wildest expectations."

Vivian's lips peeled back even farther. She shut her eyes and her long neck dipped, bringing her head low. "Thank you."

Preacher unfolded his furry hands, then raised both his claws and his voice to the crowded hangar, "You all have done very well. Now, please, you mustn't kowtow to *me*. Get up off your knees, save your adoration for the gods."

Graeme had assumed it was Vivian — appearing before them au naturel; such a powerful, menacing creature — who had inspired the demonstrative show of respect from his construction crew. Now, he knew better. Graeme watched as the workers honored Preacher's wishes and slowly rose to their feet, many of them smiling. Some of them were even weeping.

A large, heavy hand fell on Graeme's shoulder and squeezed him like a vice. He jerked, startled. His eyes shot up to find gleaming teeth, and above them, a pair of bright, pale eyes.

"You," Preacher told him. His tone was devoid of any threat; it was actually quite warm. "You are Zeus, a man of science. It is *you* who have helped us to open this door."

"Dr. King has been instrumental to our cause," Vivian assured him. "He has quite the gifted mind."

Preacher released his grip on Graeme's shoulder. He pointed to the physicist's forehead with one clawed finger. "Yes, another gift from the gods, all a part of their grand design." He glanced back at the big man, the one in the dark suit and red tie. "Just as you have been, Dante. Zeus and Hades, working together after all these centuries, just as the creators always intended."

The big man, Dante, looked unconvinced.

"All that is missing," Preacher went on, "is Poseidon."

Benedict spoke up, "Actually, your grace, we've got one of them as well. A bright little bird in a cage."

CHAPTER SEVEN

Peggy Neuhaus lay curled up in the dark, cold concrete against her bare skin. She felt the chill intensely. She felt everything intensely, especially the pain.

How long had she been there, held prisoner in this cell? She had no idea. For what seemed like days, her world had been nothing but hot agony; it erupted steadily from the burnt-out crater of her right eye socket then flowed across her entire face, every nerve catching fire, consuming her.

Finally, the pain had cooled, subsided, or maybe she'd simply grown numb to it. She dared to open her remaining eye. The move failed to trigger fresh shockwaves. It still hurt like hell, but at least the ache had grown manageable — a dull throb that rang through her sinuses like a warning bell, cautioning her to take things slow.

I don't have time *to take things slow.*

She blinked away tears then glanced around. Bioluminescence from her translucent body provided the room's only light. Normally, her sight was impeccable, even in the endless night of ocean depths, but a dense black cloud had settled at the edge of her vision, thick as octopus ink, obscuring much of her surroundings.

Peggy let out a frustrated, mournful sob. She tilted her head, craning her neck to see the right side of the chamber.

The light her body generated was more of a bug light than a Maglite. There was no focus to it; just a soft, blue-white glow that illuminated a few feet in every direction. And because Peggy was trapped on dry land, and not swimming freely through the ocean depths, it pooled brightly on the floor around her.

As she tried to orient herself, she felt an odd pang of déjà vu, suddenly reminded of her very first day as one of Poseidon's children. She'd survived an assault, been baptized without her knowledge or consent, then she was ripped away from Larry, left stranded on a cold stone slab; abandoned in the dark, naked and afraid.

On that day, the stone had belonged to Colonial Bay's hidden temple, buried deep in the earth beneath a more traditional church façade. Peggy recalled how it felt to be stuck down there, how she had spent the lonely hours pining for her lover. She'd hoped and prayed that he would find her, save her, kiss away all of her ills and return her to *normal*. And once all that had come to pass, Peggy dreamt that she and Larry might finally get to live their happily ever after, like some glorious Disney fable.

Peggy sat up. She gave her cheek a violent swipe, clearing away the remaining tears.

A lot had changed since then.

She had changed.

Every moment with Larry since Colonial Bay, both in and out of the water, had been a blessing, not a curse. She embraced her transfiguration, cherished it, burning to shed the confines of her human guise each day the way most women longed to be free of their bras and their high-heeled shoes.

Would she have welcomed that initial bite, Peggy often wondered, given everything she knew now? Honestly, she couldn't say. But what was done was done. The old woman, the priestess of Varuna, Barbara DeParle, she'd been right: this truly had been a gift, and that younger, weaker version of herself had been naïve, *foolish*, to ever have wished it all away.

She rolled up onto her knees; her tail lifted, paddling the air.

Peggy made her living selling romantic fantasies to the highest bidder, but she no longer believed in girlish fairy tales. No champion was going to ride to her rescue. No prince, not even Larry, had the power to make things better with a simple kiss. She was a grown, powerful woman. She'd survived that first assault in Colonial Bay; she would survive this one as well.

She had to.

Peggy unclenched her clawed fist. She saw divots there in the glowing skin of her palm, dug by her talons during the worst of her pain, all now healed. She also found a small wadded slip of paper.

Baby's first picture.

She laid the sonogram down on the cement floor beside her, gently smoothing out all the wrinkles. It showed a tiny bright blotch suspended in a black, kidney-shaped void. The fetus had no discernable features, not yet, anyway. There were no eyes, no visible arms or legs, no obvious claws or fins of any kind, no way to even tell if Peggy were carrying a boy or a girl. But this baby was hers, hers and Larry's, and she loved it with all of her heart.

My little Sea-Monkey...

Dr. Brahm had printed the image off for Peggy right before he...

Before these assholes murdered *him!*

Another mournful sob stuttered in Peggy's throat, like tail rattling from the dread coiled up in her belly. She took a deep breath to try and quiet it.

Again, Peggy had no illusions, not anymore. She was all too aware of just how bleak their situation was, how *dire*. Even if Larry did exactly what these creatures wanted, she knew that there was no guarantee they would ever let either of them go free.

No. These monsters planned to kill her, to extinguish the dawning spark of life within her, just as they'd slaughtered Brahm back at the Medical Center, without thought, conscience, or regret.

No!

Peggy drew herself up off the floor and stood tall on her own clawed feet. She began to move around the darkened room, searching for a way out.

Her jailors had not shackled or chained her up in any way. Why bother? After all, it would be difficult, if not downright impossible, to adequately bind a shapeshifter. Secure Peggy in one form and she'd simply change into another, slipping cleanly from her bonds or breaking through them altogether.

She thought her captors had to be well aware of this. How could they not be? They were just like her.

No, her mind spat. Not *like me. Not like me* at all.

Peggy supposed they could have put a leash around her neck, chained her to one of these walls, or tied her to a spike in the floor like some junkyard dog. That might have worked for some creatures, but Peggy and Larry's throats expanded rapidly when they changed; their flesh rippled and bulged, tearing into ribbons in their innate desire to form undulating gills. Such a violent shift might rip through any collar, or instead, it could become a noose and strangle the life right out of them.

She wasn't sure what would've happened, and since these creatures seemed to have little experience with Poseidon's children, she doubted any of them had a better idea.

Can't have me accidently hanging myself, now, can we?

Peggy's frown deepened.

No. They can't.

That realization re-awoke the dread nestled down deep in her gut. She felt it slither once more, tightening its heavy coils, making her limbs and tail go numb in its grip.

While these creatures were eventually going to kill her, Peggy still had no doubt about that, for the moment, they were content to keep her breathing. Her welfare served as an incentive for Larry, of course, a threat that compelled him to dive to the bottom of the sea, to retrieve some sunken relic as ransom, but Peggy sensed another, much darker motivation at work here. These creatures needed her for something else, something special, but what?

Peggy shook her head, tried to calm that sick feeling in her stomach. She was alive. That's all that mattered. No need to waste valuable time fretting over the reasoning. If she didn't want this cell to become her eventual tomb, she had to think clearly, she had to focus on finding a means of escape, and she had to be quick about it.

Light from her body played across the nearby walls. So far as she could tell, there was no bunk here, no cot, no sink, and no toilet. A metal bed pan sat in the corner, filled with her own reeking piss. Peggy recalled peeing on those home pregnancy test sticks back in the privacy and security of her bathroom, safe at home, remembered the mix of emotions she'd felt as she waited and watched for confirmation. She held fast to the sonogram, quickly moved on, and the island of light moved with her.

Her next step resulted in a very loud CRUNCH.

She jumped, startled; her heart skipped a beat and her remaining eye shot down to the floor. An empty plastic water bottle lay flattened beneath her clawed foot, one of several littering the concrete in her path. She remembered hurling each of them blindly across the room, hoping to strike her jailors squarely in the face. Whether or not that actually happened, Peggy had no idea, but she hoped her aim had been true at least once.

She reached out, inspecting the cinderblock walls; they were thick, too thick to claw through, and damp to the touch. The whole room stank of mildew and rust, of dereliction and neglect, yet Peggy could sense rivers of electricity flowing all around her, current pulsing through the floor and the ceiling as well as the walls. And there were other heartbeats here in this place, so many that it was impossible for Peggy to get an accurate census.

Yes, one thing was for certain, wherever they were holding her, it might be off the beaten path, but it was in no way abandoned, at least, not anymore.

Peggy thought back to when she first arrived, to when she was pulled from her kidnappers' van. A stiff breeze had buffeted her, a wind that carried with it the unmistakable salty tang of the sea. Her head had been covered in a canvas coffee sack, a feeble attempt to block her heightened senses, but there was no disguising that wonderful, glorious scent.

It was the smell of home.

There'd been no way for her to get her bearings, but she knew that they had to be somewhere near open water. They *had to be*. If she could somehow reach it, there would be no stopping her, no catching her.

She'd be free.

That's a pretty big "if," don'tcha think?

I've got to at least try!

Peggy whirled in the dimness, searching once more for an exit, any exit at all. There were no windows she could find, boarded or otherwise. Above her, in the faint upper edge of her glow, she saw vents and ductwork suspended from the ceiling, all too small to accommodate her in either form.

She had seen movies and television shows as a kid, watched wizards and shapeshifters who could transform themselves into tiny mice or honeybees in order to escape from their captivity, crawling under doors or flying through the cracks. Even as a child, she'd seen the impossibility of it all. Magic or no magic, there was no way in hell a human being could instantly shed so much of their bulk.

Says the shapeshifter.

Yes, but she didn't lose any mass when she went through her changes, not really. She simply...stirred it all around. When she turned aquatic, her existing muscles lengthened, her bones grew; she became taller, sleeker — a rubber band stretched by unseen hands. Then, when it was necessary, she simply snapped back to her original human self, but she never actually *shrank.*

Right about now, however, it would certainly be nice if she could.

Come on, Peggy, you're a smart girl. Think! If you were writing this scenario for one of your books, how would you get your heroine out of here?

Before Colonial Bay, before her work had turned so autobiographical, she used to spend countless hours doing research. Truth be told, it often felt as if Peggy had spent more time with her nose in other people's books than she'd spent writing her own. She would look at various romantic times and exotic locales, studying every historical detail. She'd learned what people who lived in a given period or place wore, how they might think and speak, memorized all the proper names and colloquialisms, anything and everything to give her fiction a much-needed dose of reality.

It never got you published, though, did it — reading about all the things that other people did? You didn't taste any real success until you'd actually gotten out there and lived.

True enough. And, now, all those years of research were proving to be more of a hindrance than a help. She'd educated herself about everything, you see, including various methods of torture and death, and it was all still there, filed away at the back of her mind, ready to be recalled at a moment's notice.

She kept thinking of all the ways those assholes might hurt her and her baby if she didn't get away. They had already proven that they could make her suffer. They'd used a dragon's claw, not a hot poker, but the result had been the same; they had taken one of her eyes. How long before they wheeled in a Judas cradle, or a rack, or an iron chair?

She had no intention of finding out.

Peggy felt along the wall, made her way to the opposite end of the room. Like the possibility of those medieval tortures, in her mind, she'd built up an image of some heavy black dungeon gate blocking the entrance. It would be solid, she thought, with a huge lock forged of iron, something that would feel right at home in the halls of Azkaban or the Tower of London. Instead, what came into her circle of light was a normal, unassuming door — metal, yes, but not unlike the one that led from her kitchen to her garage. This one appeared blighted with patches of rust and flaking paint, as if it had been completely forgotten, not used in ages.

Peggy knew that was a lie, of course. They'd brought her in here, hadn't they? Her eye found a single tarnished doorknob, a knob that begged to be turned, and she took a step toward it.

Just then, as if sensing her approach, the door swung open, flooding the room with light.

Peggy held up a claw to shield her surviving eye. Through splayed talons and back-lit webbing, she saw a shadow.

The specter loomed across the threshold, a dark figure with feathery wings, as if the Angel of Death himself had come to pay her a visit.

"Frau Neuhaus..."

The griffin...Hans.

At the sound of his Germanic lilt, Peggy felt a cold shudder race across her skin like a rush of morning tide. She lowered her hand. His face was backlit, and she couldn't yet make out the details, but she had no problem picturing his horrible grin.

"So good to see you up and on your feet once more! I will admit that, for a moment, we were all a bit concerned."

"I bet," Peggy snapped back, making no attempt to hide her disdain. She retreated a few steps, shied away from the light, away from *him*.

Hans followed her into the room, closing the door behind him. Peggy heard pin tumblers and realized there had to be someone else out there, someone unseen, who'd just locked them in.

A guard, standing watch in the hallway...

Peggy concentrated, listening for the beat of that hidden heart. She found it; steady, relaxed, as if its owner didn't have a care in the world.

The jackal...Mark?

Yes. He was the other half of this deadly duo, wasn't he? They were the team tasked with stealing her away from Black Harbor Medical Center, the pair who'd whisked Larry off to ports unknown while Peggy had still been writhing in pain on the floor.

Wait. If they're both here, then...

"Where's my husband?" she asked, surprised by just how strong her voice sounded, how forceful, seemingly unburdened by the weight of that nesting dread in her stomach.

Hans said nothing at first. He simply stood there, his yellow-rimmed eyes blazing in the dark — the headlights of an oncoming car. Like Peggy, he'd cast off his human appearance in favor of his true form; an African lion, standing upright on its hind legs, like a great cat pictured on a coat of arms or some heraldic crest. He was muscular, strong, every contour and ripple of his physique covered over in short blonde hair that ended abruptly at his neck. That's the point where his avian features took over — a feathered cowl and hooked yellow beak plucked straight from another standard bearer, the majestic eagle.

No trace of a pistol or silencer anywhere on his person, Peggy noted. Then again, he didn't really need them, did he? He had claws, just as she did, and she knew that he wasn't afraid to use them.

For a moment, she thought the griffin might let her question go unanswered. He just stood there, staring at her in silence. Then, he finally opened his beak and said, "Your husband proved to be most cooperative."

"Is he here? Let me see him."

"No."

"No, he's not here, or no—?"

"For the moment, you will not be permitted to see him."

"Please," she pressed, not really wanting to beg this cold-blooded killer for anything, "I need to know that he's safe."

"Touching, still quite impossible I'm afraid."

That nesting dread grew heavier in her gut. She wet her lips. "Why? Why won't you let me see him?"

"Because you desire it," he told her, "and so long as you continue to desire it, you will remain cooperative, yes? Then, once you have done everything that we have asked of you without question, without quarrel, you shall *earn* it — your reunion as well as your freedom."

"Larry already did what you wanted, didn't he?"

"Yes, he most certainly did."

"Well, that's the whole reason you brought us here, isn't it — *kidnapped* us? What more do you fucking need?"

Hans's beak was hard, inflexible, totally incapable of a smile. It didn't matter. Peggy could hear it plainly in his voice. "All will be made clear soon enough, Frau Neuhaus. I promise you will not have to wait much longer."

Peggy frowned. Their promises were as empty as the hole they'd burned in her skull.

The griffin took another step toward her in the dark, closing the gap between them, his bright-rimmed eyes crawling over her from head to tail. *"Wunderschönen."*

"Excuse me?"

"In hospital, when you dropped your gown to get dressed, I said that, even completely naked, you still had much to hide."

"I remember."

"Yes, well, seeing you here now, as the gods always intended...*Meine Dame*, may I say that you are the most beautiful creature I have ever had the pleasure to encounter."

No, you may not! Peggy wanted to shout. Instead, she could only cringe. Her stomach squirmed yet again, but this time the culprit wasn't dread. It was utter disgust.

Hans motioned back toward the entrance. "You were approaching the doorway when I came in, yes?"

She said nothing. Her throat felt thick, her anxiety growing as all that writing research wormed its way to the forefront of her mind. She knew there was something else the medieval jailors used to do to their female captives, something besides torture. She'd incorporated such abuse into some of her early novels, to build sympathy for her poor heroines, to make their hurdles seem all the more insurmountable.

"Did you really think that you would find the door unlocked?" Hans wanted to know. "That you could simply walk out of here, perhaps go for a little morning stroll?"

Again, Peggy could offer him only silence. Every muscle in her body had tensed.

"I trust that you are a bit smarter than that, *meine Dame.*" He came still closer. "If you did somehow manage to leave this room, you must know that there is nowhere for you to go. We have the weapons *and* the numbers, and I do not wish to see you come to any more harm."

Finally, she found her voice.

"Take another step toward me," Peggy warned, measuring her breath, "try to lay even a furry little finger on me—" She brought up her claw, "—and it's *you* who's gonna come into some harm."

"Oh?" That smile in his voice again, as creepy as it was infuriating. "And what will you do to me?"

"I'll make you live to regret it," she growled, fury growing in her heart, "if I let you live at all."

Hans dipped his beak, giving her a slight bow as he took a demonstrative step back. "So pleased to see Vivian's fire has not completely extinguished your own."

"That queen bitch, all she did was piss me off. You tell her that for me."

He chuckled. "Charming, but unwise. That queen bitch, as you call her, she tends to get what she wants, *whatever* she wants, you see? There is nothing you can do to deny her. You must accept this. If you do not resist, things will go much better for you." He lowered his burning eyes. "And for your baby as well, yes?"

Lie to him. Tell him what he wants to hear. Tell him you'll do whatever the hell they want. Tell him anything. *Just...make him go away!*

Without Peggy having to say another word, Hans moved off.

She turned on her heels, following him intently with both her eye and her claws as he strolled across the room. His lion's tail swung leisurely behind him. It didn't end in a tuft of fur, she noted, but with a plume of feathers.

Hans stepped over to the bedpan she'd filled on the floor, then stooped to pick it up. "I will dispose of this," he told her, "then I will see about bringing you something to eat. You must be famished. Is there anything special you would like?"

"I don't want anything from *you*."

"Very well. Peanut butter and jelly it shall be. An American staple, yes?"

Peggy watched Hans rise up, watched him strut back toward the door with the bedpan clutched in his claws. For a moment, she thought of lunging, of upsetting the container and drenching his fur in her cold, stale piss, but the urge passed quickly. She feared what he might do in retaliation, and worse, she thought he might actually get off on it.

Hans tapped on the door twice with his furry knuckle. Peggy heard those tumblers again as someone turned the lock. "You should try to relax, *meine Dame*," the griffin said. That damned smile was still in his voice, taunting her. "Stress is bad for the blood."

He stepped out into the blinding light of the hallway and was gone. The door slammed shut behind him.

Peggy stood there, her body slow to relax. The dull pain in her sinuses throbbed in time with the beat of her elevated pulse. She held fast to the sonogram, her thoughts turning from her unborn child to her husband then back again.

How are we going to get out of this one, Rembrandt?

CHAPTER EIGHT

Larry Neuhaus didn't know what to do. The shark-man pressed the heels of his webbed hands against his eyes. He'd been up most of the night, wrestling with conflicting emotions. In his mind, there was no easy answer, no good option, but in his heart, no matter what he decided, Larry believed that he would ultimately find his way back to his wife. Somehow, he believed that he would get to hold her in his arms once more, to tell her how much he loved her. And he believed that, when they finally had their tender reunion, he'd be able to set her free, to get her out, to get her *back*.

Most of all, Larry held onto the belief that, one day, he would get a chance to look upon the face of his newborn child. And on that day, he believed that he would weep with absolute joy.

In the end, he thought wearily, *love will win the day.*

Clichéd? Yes. Sappy? Sure. But, through all his struggles, through all his pain, Larry Neuhaus still held onto his belief. He *had to*. Belief was what had fueled him to swim up from the Gulf of

Mexico with a weeping bullet hole in his shoulder. Belief was what got him to climb onto that motorcycle, to go zipping down a busy New York highway in some crazy high-speed pursuit. Belief was the only thing that kept him going now, the only thing that kept him sane.

Is it sane, part of him still wondered after all this time, *to get visits from dead women in the middle of the night — to listen to the cryptic advice of a moldering corpse?*

Perhaps not, but the problem had always been that Larry *didn't* listen. He'd looked the other way, thought he'd known better, and time and time again, Peggy had paid the price. Ignoring yet another vision — wasn't *that* insane?

Larry pressed on his tired eyes, squeezing out fresh tears. He was exhausted, yes, but he couldn't allow himself to give in, to give up. Collapsing wouldn't do anyone any good. And having a nervous breakdown? Well, that's what got them into this mess in the first place.

The shark-man wiped the sides of his angular snout. He paced the length of the floor with nervous strides, and he'd been given plenty of room in which to move around.

On every side, the walls began with a foundation of large cobblestones upon which smaller bricks had been laid. Above his head, the ceiling was also hewn of stone, supported by various arches and square columns. The floor beneath his webbed feet appeared to have been pieced together from a series of concrete slabs, most of which were now cracked and crumbling. Larry had no idea who constructed this underground chamber, or what purpose it had originally been intended to serve, but he was fairly certain the builders never meant for it to be used as a living space.

That hadn't stopped someone from doing their best to make it habitable. A cot had been placed against one of the far walls; next to that, a small nightstand, the stain worn away from the wood — a weathered antique. And candles were everywhere, providing light and warmth; their flicker danced with shadows across the brick and mortar, keeping the subterranean darkness at bay.

None of it mattered. Instead of making Larry feel more comfortable, more at home, the ample space only served to remind him that he was lost, that he was *alone.*

But he wasn't alone.

There was another heartbeat.

Yes. Larry heard it clearly now, growing nearer, stronger, advancing down the corridor. The shark-man snapped around with a growl, bared his serrated teeth.

One of the archways had been covered by a beaded curtain. Together, the individual multicolored strings formed a single picture: a peace symbol surrounded by rainbow circles, like something off a Grateful Dead album. It provided the impression of a solid door, an illusion shattered the moment a crocodile-man strolled right through it.

Larry exhaled, instantly relaxing. "Chud?"

The reptilian, his long toothy snout slightly ajar, froze in his tracks. "Oops...Fuckin' did it again, didn't I?"

Before Larry could say anything, Chud took an awkward step back, the beaded strands clicking noisily off his textured hide. He knocked on the brick archway with one fisted claw.

"Can I come in?" he asked.

"Yeah, you can come in."

Chud's squat legs carried him back into the room, his thick tail dragging the concrete behind him. "Didn't mean to startle you. I lived on my own down here for a long time. Too long, I guess. Still tryin' to get used to, whatcha call it — respectin' other people's privacy?"

"You didn't really startle me," Larry told him. "Guess I was lost in my own thoughts. I didn't even pick up your scent."

He lifted his snout, sniffed at the air. The aroma of melted wax and smoke from the surrounding candles was nearly overpowering, but beneath that, he could detect a musty odor, like some long-neglected library filled to the brim with ancient volumes — the perfume of the underground. Nothing else. Larry tilted his triangular head and his black eyes narrowed; puzzled.

"I still can't smell you," he said, wondering why he hadn't noticed before now.

"Yeah..." Chud flashed a look of embarrassment. "Sorry about that. Chordata Clan. No sweat glands. I sneak up on people all the damn time. Drives Zuri crazy. Earl, too, but he's Zeus. I know his sense of smell's not worth a crap. It's nowhere near as good as ours, anyway." He gave a little chuckle; it was deep, throaty, and hoarse. "Hell, if I didn't have a pulse, you'd never even know I was around."

Larry nodded. "How is she? I heard her howling during the night, and I got worried she—"

"Zuri?" Chud jerked a clawed thumb over his scaly shoulder. "Yeah, she's doin' fine now." He laughed again, as if he'd just told the punchline to some private joke, then wagged his snout. "I'm happy for her and Earl and all, but damn, I wish she'd learn to muzzle that shit. I mean...*Jesus*. She kept you up, too, huh?"

"No," Larry assured him. "I couldn't sleep, but it wasn't her fault."

It was Susan's, he thought with a shudder. *It was the damned* dream.

———

Since leaving Colonial Bay, Larry's dreams had been exactly the same. Each night he walked through the same bright swirling mist, stood on the same marble steps, in the same ancient city. Always in human form. Always gazing longingly upon the same black pyramid. And in the sky above, night after night, he saw the same dark shapes.

Now, one of those mysterious objects was descending, growing ever nearer, coming into focus — a gigantic arrowhead fighting a losing battle against gravity, sailing back down to earth in slow-motion.

He'd grown used to this dream, accustomed to the idea that his sleep had been hijacked by forces beyond his understanding or control. But tonight, this sour vision had taken on a fresh feeling of urgency.

The gods were inside that arrowhead, that starship. Yes, Larry was certain of that now. He felt it, just as clearly as he'd sensed out the locations of those hidden crystal skulls; it was the invisible touch of something mystical, something powerful tickling his brain. The creators were returning to Earth; and try as he might, there was nothing that Larry could do to prevent it.

Dream people passed by him on the steps, an immeasurable mob clad only in colorful togas, oblivious to the danger falling from above. On the first night of this vision, they had all been complete strangers. Over the years, however, Larry had become well-acquainted with each and every one of them. He knew none of their names, but he'd come to recognize their smiling faces, their unbridled excitement, their complete and utter joy. They practically frolicked through the streets, prancing with glee. None of them showed even a hint of concern, of *understanding*.

To Larry, they were like the dinosaurs: too mindless and stupid to comprehend the fact that this dark wonder approaching their world from the stars, this alien thing thundering down at them through the atmosphere, would bring about nothing but their inevitable extinction.

And then, the dream went rogue. It was as if his brain had finally figured out how to fight the invading transmission, or some other pirate signal had discovered a way to cut in — a signal not from the depths of space, but from some infinitely darker realm.

Larry felt a strange presence approach him like a cold breeze. An icy hand fell on his shoulder, and when he tilted his eyes toward it, he saw fingers that were desiccated and bony. This was the hand of some ancient mummy, the rigored grip of a cadaver.

Not again...

He didn't want to turn his head any farther, didn't want his eyes to behold the thing those fingers belonged to, but he couldn't stop himself. There was no face left to recognize. Nevertheless, Larry knew who this woman was. That first night in Colonial Bay, he'd seen her struggling down in the surf, watched her die from the height of his balcony at the Sea Mist Inn. Now, she stood beside him on the steps, still dripping, as if she'd just crawled out of her watery grave — this decaying apparition that continued to haunt him, even after all these years. And unlike the members of the toga-clad mob, she had a name.

Susan Rogers wore a moving crown of small crabs, their tiny legs combing through the scant remnants of her hair. The dark wells of her eye sockets were two upended pools, spilling salty waterfalls down barnacle-encrusted cheeks like tears. *"This is the end, Larry,"* she gargled, and the terrible seriousness of her voice was undercut by a wide skull-toothed grin, the smile of the damned. *"The end of life as you know it, the end of everything — the twilight of Man."*

As if to prove her point, darkness moved over them like an eclipse, turning dawn into dusk.

Larry's eyes shot back up to the falling black arrowhead, watching it grow ever larger, its shadow covering more and more of the dream city. He felt a blast of heat from it now, broiling his exposed skin — retrorockets firing to try and halt its decent, or to at least soften the unavoidable impact.

"The time has come," Susan warned. *"You need to make a choice, and you need to make it quickly."*

Larry managed to wrench free of her grasp, to spin around and confront her. *"For once, can you stop speaking in goddamn riddles — can you just* help me?"

"That's all I've ever tried to do." Seawater flew like spittle from Susan's moving jawbone as she spoke. *"I told you to leave Peggy, to flee Colonial Bay. But you didn't. You stayed. You* changed. *Then, I came to warn of a new danger to you both, a threat to the child growing in your wife's womb. And still, you did nothing.*

"Now, here we are."

Larry frowned. There was no arguing with her, no denying that she was right. *"Please,"* he begged. *"This time will be different. I don't know how you know all the things that you know, but some-how, you* do *know them. So, please, tell me where Peggy is, where they're keeping her. At least point me in the right goddamn direc-tion! Just...tell me something, tell me* anything, *and I swear to* God, *whatever you ask me to do, whatever the fuck it is, this time, I'll do it!"*

"Leave this place, Larry."

He gaped at her. "That's *your advice from the great beyond?* 'Leave this place?'"

"Yes. Leave New York and go back to the sea."

"Bullshit," he snarled.

Susan's nearly fleshless face showed no emotion, but he heard the irritation plainly in her voice, *"You said you would do whatever—"*

"I know what the hell I said, but I'm not abandoning my wife and child. I swam all the way back up here to find them for Chrissakes, and now—"

"And now, to save them, you must leave again." She extended one long skeletal finger, pointing out toward the vast open sea, toward the horizon. *"You need to go back to where your journey began, Larry. You need to return to Colonial Bay."*

"Colonial Bay? There is no Colonial Bay. It's gone. It burned to the fucking ground!"

"You must go and find it, Larry"

One of those tiny crabs scurried down from her hair; it moved into the cave of her vacant eye socket and made itself at home. Larry was forced to recall their first meeting, standing in that darkened lighthouse, watching as another crustacean crawled out from between Susan's lips.

A wave of nausea made his stomach roll.

"Find Colonial Bay," Susan told him. *"Find the children of Poseidon."*

Larry shook his head. *"What about Earl, and Chud, and Zuri? I can't just leave them now. They need all the help they can get!"*

The muted sunlight suddenly faded away altogether, the victim of a ravenous darkness — a greedy black void that gobbled up the dream people, the city steps, Susan, *everything*. Larry's entire world was thrust into an endless night.

"Choose wisely," Susan urged. *"You can stay here in New York, you can fight with them and die alone, or you can go back to the sea. Listen to me, Larry, really listen. Find Poseidon's children."* As she spoke, her voice grew fainter and fainter, receding, as if she

were being sucked back into the abyss. *"Only they can help you save Peggy, save your friends. Only they can help you survive."*

And then, she was gone.

———

Larry turned away from his disheveled cot and tried to blink the exhaustion from his eyes. The dream might have ended, but his nightmare persisted. Even now, hours later, he was still sorting it all out, weighing his options, considering his next move, trying to decide if there was even really anything to decide at all.

But the more he attempted to exorcise Susan from his brain, the louder his mind screamed.

Go back to the sea...

Find Poseidon's children...

He didn't want to deny her a third time, but swimming off and leaving Peggy behind? Deserting Earl and his new-found friends? It all seemed so *wrong*. If Larry abandoned them now, he'd feel like a coward. He'd feel like a *bastard*.

You can stay here in New York, you can fight with them and die alone, or you can go back to the sea.

If Larry elected to remain, he still didn't know where to even begin his search. And if he did as Susan asked, he'd have the exact same issue. It was a big city, but it was an even bigger ocean.

"How will I find you?"

Those had been Peggy's final words to the old woman, Barbara DeParle. She'd spoken them on the shoal of Colonial Bay, right before the authorities had arrived to fight the flames, before Poseidon's children had disappeared into the tide.

And Barbara's response? *"When the time comes, you'll know."*

Larry sighed heavily. *The time is now, Barbara, and I don't have a fucking clue!*

As he paced around the chamber, his tail curved along behind him, tracing his meandering path, fanning the air and the candle flames with its ribbed fins. In the ocean, the muscular appendage worked to steer him, to propel him through the water at mind-boggling speeds. On land, it only served to counterbalance the up-front weight of his large triangular head.

The crocodile-man stood by and followed him with his eyes, obviously fascinated. "You, uh...you seem kinda anxious this morning."

Was it that obvious? Even Chud could see the strain Larry was under. He lied and said, "I'm fine."

"You sure?" the reptilian pressed. "I mean, you've been out of the water for a good while now. You're not gonna die if you don't get your gills wet, are you?"

I won't, but Peggy might. You *might.* The webbed claws of Larry's feet scraped at the cracked pavement, as if to try and erase the thought. "No," he said.

"Right." Chud reached up and scratched the leathery folds of his neck. "I mean, I don't see you floppin' around like a goldfish or nothin', but, you know, just thought I'd ask."

"I'm okay, Chud. Thanks."

"Good. Yeah, that's good. 'Cause, last night...I kinda heard you screamin' about how you needed to get back to the sea. So, I thought maybe you might—"

Larry whirled around in surprise. "You heard me *what?*"

"Yellin' in your sleep." The crocodile-man blinked with all three of his eyelids, the innermost one moving horizontally across his reptilian eye. "Like I said, I couldn't sleep, not with the noise Zuri and Earl were makin' all night long, so I got up and walked around.

Anyway, that's when I heard you in here, goin' on about how you needed to get back to the sea."

"Did I say anything else?"

Chud briskly shook his snout.

"You're *sure?*"

"Not that I heard." He held up one claw, as if to take an oath. "Honest, I only looked in on you for a second, just to see if you were okay. I didn't pull up a chair and make popcorn or nothin'. You were tossin' and turnin', and I thought about wakin' you up, but I read somewhere that it was dangerous, and since I didn't want my arm bit off, I left you alone."

"That's for sleepwalkers, Chud. It's dangerous to wake a sleepwalker."

"Well, you weren't doin' that. Just looked to me like you were havin' one helluva nightmare."

"Yeah," Larry said, bitterly, his eyes drifting back to the cot. "You could say that."

Chud looked at him with great interest. "What's it like?"

"What's *what* like?"

"A nightmare," the crocodile-man whispered. "I mean, I know they're supposed to be like some kinda horror movie or somethin', but like, *you're* the star. Am I right?"

Larry's head snapped up and he eyed him curiously. "You've never had a nightmare before?"

"Hades don't have nightmares. I don't know that we even really dream. Night after night, we just see the same damn thing."

Larry knew what he meant. "The black pyramid."

"You got it," Chud confirmed. "It's not good or bad, really. It just is what it is.

"My grandmother," he continued, "she used to say that night-mares were a curse from the gods, a special kinda hell reserved only for Zeus. Since humans were the ones that betrayed the creators, kicked their asses off this world, the gods punished them, made it so they could never rest easy again, made it so they could never see Paradise.

"And Zuri, she more or less agreed with her. She says the dreams we all share every night, the pyramid, all those smiley happy idiots, the spaceships or whatever the hell they are up there in the sky; it's all some kinda message from the creators, like a TV show we all get to stream in our fuckin' subconscious."

He pointed to his own sloped forehead. "But see, only the loyal clans get to tune into the program. It's like that communist propaganda shit the Russians used to broadcast back in the Cold War days, but this is tryin' to get all of Hades on the same bandwagon, tryin' to get us all to want to bring the gods back to Earth.

"Poseidon, too, I guess.

"'See how great it can be?'" he said mockingly. "'See what life could be like if *we* were back in charge? Fuckin' Lollapalooza twenty-four-seven! Don't you miss us? Don't you want us back? Well, then, when you wake up, get busy and bring our asses back!'

"Makes you want to break in and air one of those political attack ads, 'Hey, remember how we were their fuckin' slaves? Remember that shit? It wasn't all one big rosy toga party!' But you can't. They've got the remote, and they're not lettin' any of *us* change the channel." He chuckled again, then scratched at his temple. "I guess that's kind of a...Whatcha call it — a metaphor?"

"What do you mean?" Larry asked.

"I mean, nightmares notwithstanding, from what I hear, when humans close their eyes, they get to just let their imaginations run wild. They get to totally lose control, do whatever the hell they want — fight, fly, fuck, ride unicorns, drive race cars, take rockets to the moon, you name it! It's just a bunch of beautiful chaos. But with us, everything is always the same, you know?

"Zeus, they got to purge the gods from their lives almost completely, but us? We've never really been able to let 'em go. When we go to bed at night, we're still at their mercy."

He shook his snaggle toothed snout, then pointed to Larry.

"Doesn't explain how come *you're* havin' nightmares, though."

"I used to be human," the shark-man told him, and there was no sorrow in the statement; no regret. "I mean, *really* human. Zeus. I used to be Zeus."

"No shit?"

"No shit."

"What happened — you get bit?"

"Peggy got bit, and I, well *we...*" His voice trailed off, not wanting to go into any lewd detail, hoping the crocodile-man got the general idea.

Chud understood perfectly. "You love your wife."

"I do," Larry agreed, "and I would do anything if I thought I had a chance to save her."

Find Poseidon's children. Only they can help you save Peggy, save your friends. Only they can help you survive.

He looked Chud directly in the eye. "If Zuri was in trouble, and you—"

"Yeah," the crocodile-man blurted, "I'd do it."

"You didn't let me finish."

"Doesn't matter," Chud said with certainty. "If Zuri was in trouble, and there was something I could do to help her, I'd do it, no matter what the hell it was, just like you said.

"She's all the family I got."

Larry knew exactly how Chud felt.

Chud led the way down one darkened tunnel after another. He took each new fork with great confidence, trudging along through the underground as if he'd walked this winding path every day of his life, as if he knew the route like the back of his scaly green hand. Perhaps he had, perhaps he did. Larry could only trust that they were headed in the right direction.

Something darted across their path, something *alive*.

Startled, Larry froze in his tracks. At first, he thought that the small sprinting animal might be a possum, but no, this was New York. It was one very large rat.

Chud pounced without hesitation. He grabbed the rodent by its tail, held it up for inspection; it squeaked and hissed and wriggled in his grasp. "Well, would you look at that — you hungry for some breakfast?"

The crocodile-man whipped around and swung the kicking, clawing rat in Larry's direction.

Larry shrank from it, his face curdling. "I'm good, thanks."

Chud gave a quick shrug and lifted the rat up over his head. For a moment, the rodent hung there, suspended above the crocodile-man's upturned snout, writhing frantically in the air. Then, Chud opened his mouth and let the animal drop; his jaws snapped shut around it like a bear trap, devouring it completely.

Well, almost completely.

Larry noticed that the rat's segmented tail was caught between Chud's irregular teeth. It dangled from his scaly snout, jiggling in the air. The crocodile-man slurped it up like a long thick noodle and turned away, resuming his walk.

Who am I to judge? Larry thought as he followed him. *If someone saw me eating a live fish, or all those raw lobsters and crabs with their legs still kicking and twitching, I'm sure they'd be pretty grossed out.*

What concerned him more was the fact that he hadn't smelled the rat to begin with. He hadn't registered the flutter of its tiny heartbeat, nor had he heard the rush of blood through its veins. The animal had caught him totally unaware, and that shouldn't have happened. How was he supposed to find Barbara and the others in all the oceans of the world if he couldn't even detect a musky little rodent right in front of him?

You need to relax, Larry urged himself, taking in a deep breath, *concentrate.*

And then, he *did* smell something, a very familiar scent. "Is that sea water up ahead?"

Chud smiled back at him. "You were beginnin' to doubt me, weren'tcha?"

"Not for a second." Larry gave a little laugh, a short bark of relief. He felt the air grow more humid with each step, heard water dripping, and at the end of the passage, he saw a large metal grate that showed signs of oxidization and corrosion, as if it had been exposed to moisture and salt over a long period of time.

Chud slid his muscular reptilian arm between the rusted bars and reached for an unseen clasp on the opposite side. After some exertion, and a few frustrated grunts, he managed to force it open.

As the grate swung aside, Larry stepped up to look into a vast new tunnel. It was almost completely flooded. Water came up to within a foot of the opening where they now stood. Larry lifted his eyes, followed the curve of the ceiling. Like the chamber he'd left behind, it, too, was covered in brick. This one was in bad shape, however. There were small square holes where individual bricks had come loose, and larger sections that had crumbled away from the arch altogether, exposing patches of naked concrete beneath.

"Is this a sewer?" he asked.

Chud rolled his eyes. "Why does everybody always think any tunnel they come across down here has to be a sewer?"

"With all the water, I just assumed—"

"Docs it smell like shit to you?"

Larry shook his head. The water didn't smell foul to him at all. In fact, it smelled like the shore in his own backyard.

"This is a fuckin' island," Chud told him as if it were news. "Water's constantly findin' its way under the city, and sooner or later, it all winds up down here in the subways."

"So it's a subway tunnel?"

"Not just any subway tunnel," Chud said. "You're lookin' at one of only a dozen or so they buried deep in the riverbed about a hundred years ago. They dug 'em out as a shortcut, a way to get passengers from one borough to the next under water and about twenty-five feet of mud.

"In this particular tunnel," he went on, waving his clawed hand across the wide expanse, "the roof collapsed, and all that mud and water from the channel came rushin' in.

"Metro Transit Authority's got a drainage system that takes care of rain and a couple of hundred sump pump rooms alongside the tracks to siphon off water from little leaks and snowmelt, but this? There's no way in hell they could keep up with all this. And since it cost too damn much to fix, the MTA just abandoned the whole fuckin' line, left it exactly as is. Which means this tunnel here still opens out into the East River, and the East River—"

"Leads right out to sea," Larry finished for him.

Chud touched the tip of his snout with the talon of his forefinger. "Bingo."

Larry stood staring into the dark depths of the water below, his webbed toes curled over the lip of the open grate. "Which way is it?"

He suddenly remembered yelling at Susan, *At least point me in the right goddamn direction!*

And then, Chud pointed to his left. "That way."

"What are you going to tell Preston?"

"Don't worry about Earl," the crocodile-man said. "We got our asses handed to us back there in that warehouse. There were three of Hades' disciples, and *four* of us. We find that airport of yours? I guarantee you we're goin' up against a helluva lot more than just three guys there. So you findin' us a shitload of reinforcements? That might just be the only hope we got. Earl might not wear the uniform anymore, but he's a military guy. He'll get that. I'll make sure he gets it."

Larry gave a slow nod. To hear Chud tell it, it all sounded so logical, the best possible decision he could make. It sounded *right*.

But Larry still didn't like it.

As he stood there, thinking it over yet again, a hand gripped his shoulder. Larry jumped and his head swiveled, expecting to find Susan Rogers standing there beside him — crabs still roving through her hollow skull. Instead, he saw the crocodile-man's scaly, reassuring claw.

"We'll find your wife, Larry," he said. His voice was soft, but sincere.

"You remember what I told you?"

"Smell of jet fuel and arc welders, rust and dust. Got it. And now that I've met you, I've also got a good idea what her scent might be like."

Larry managed a wan grin. "Her scent's a lot better than mine."

"No doubt." Chud gave his shoulder a gentle squeeze, then

released him and stepped aside. "Now, get outta here. Go find your people."

My people.

Larry had never thought of Poseidon's children in that way, neither had Peggy for that matter. He knew that he was a Charodon, and his wife a Paralicht, but they'd never found themselves longing to be counted among either clan. All they'd wanted was to live their own lives, and until now, those lives had been almost perfect. They'd been together, just the two of them; it had been all the family, all the support they needed to get by.

But now, it wasn't enough. They had to have more, and they had to have it quickly.

No more arguing. No more wasted time.

Larry leapt from his perch and dove smoothly into cold brackish water. He took a moment to orient himself, to allow his gills and his senses to acclimate. Everything was dim at first, murky, but he was soon able to make out the details of his surroundings.

Drowned train tracks appeared out of the sludge below. Larry thought briefly of the dreaded third rail, but quickly dismissed the danger. He couldn't sense any live current flowing anywhere around him. The Transit Authority had cut this line off, severed it from the rest of the body like a gangrenous limb. He flicked his tailfin and followed the rusted tracks into the murk.

As Larry swam through the flooded passage, various hazards materialized in his path. There were corroded metal support columns, rusted signs that once indicated upcoming stops, overturned garbage cans sinking into the silt, and piles of bricks and debris that had fallen from the ceiling above. It appeared almost apocalyptic, like some end of the world landscape from a science fiction movie.

The world is *ending,* he thought, grimly. *It's the end of every-*

thing, Susan said, *the twilight of Man. We're on the road to civilization collapse.*

A shadow loomed, moving into his vision like a bruise; it blotted out the tunnel ahead of him.

Larry felt his heart sink, felt his blood run cold as if the sea water had somehow breached his veins. His path was blocked. He'd have to turn around and go back.

No!

He fisted his claws, and his tail undulated effortlessly, propelling him forward through the murk like a bullet. As he drew nearer, the dark shape lightened, grew more distinct, and the shark-man's despair turned quickly to wonder.

Larry smiled in disbelief.

Metal skin, once smooth and shiny, had been covered over in bumpy brown tumors of barnacles and mussels, but the object was still recognizable as a subway train. Larry swam over to the nearest window. He wiped away years of grime to peer inside, but he couldn't see a thing. Next, he moved over to the rusted door. Larry struggled with the corroding handle, but finally, he managed to slide it open.

Inside, the sunken train had become a man-made reef. Vertical stanchions, metal benches, and hanging grab handles, all rough and flaky with decay, all teeming with new life.

What happened to the people? Larry pondered as he swam carefully through it all. *Were they caught on board when the tunnel collapsed — swept away as the raging flood waters?*

He saw no skeletons or human remains scattered about the wreckage, but he couldn't help wondering. If he failed to get Poseidon's children on their side, failed to stop Hades' disciples and the return of the gods, would future generations look to the wreckage of this city, of this *world,* and would they be asking the very same questions?

Larry shook his head, denying such a dire outcome. He swam on, still holding fast to his belief. He *had to.* Belief was what fueled him, what kept him going in the face of all odds. Belief and, of course, love.

And in the end, he thought, more determined than ever, *love* will *win the day.*

Schools of tiny fish scattered to clear him a path. The shark-man had no interest in any of them, but he could hear their pulses, could feel their vibrations in the water. He smelled them, saw them, practically tasted them, and the rush of sensory input washed over him in a wave of great relief.

The rear door stood open, allowing him to move easily from one car to the next. He swam down the entire length of the train, watching the corrosion grow progressively worse. Formations of rusticles hung down from the ceiling like stalactites, giving the impression of an underwater cave, which, he supposed, was exactly what this entire subway tunnel had become, but instead of getting darker, the water around him lightened the deeper he traveled.

When Larry was finally able to exit the derelict train completely, he stood staring across an enormous field of rubble. Waves of underwater daylight rippled across huge chunks of concrete and rusted webs of rebar. His eyes followed the light up a steep slope of mud and rock, gazing through a huge opening in the tunnel roof — the mouth of the cavern, the gateway to the sea.

I'm doing it, Susan, Larry thought as he left the sunken subway and the city behind him. *I don't know where, and I don't know how, but I'm going to find Barbara and the others.*

I'm going to get help.

CHAPTER NINE

The giant mantis had proven to be quite helpful, eager to obey each and every one of Carol Miyagi's Atlantean commands. Now, the insectoid creature carried Alan Everson safely down a wide alien corridor, ferrying him toward the Ark's abandoned stable.

Grimly, Carol fell into step behind Kari Hannigan and Gagan. They led the way, and yet, she felt as if she could have found the correct path even without them. Somehow, this labyrinth didn't feel like a dank maze to her. It felt like home.

The huge oval chamber was just as her friends had described. If anything, in size and structure, Carol found it even more breathtaking.

She saw row upon row of darkened cells, each outlined by swollen, veiny snakes that called to mind the guts of some colossal beast. The various cubicles had been sealed off by horizontal bars, but like the sword that still extended from her wrist, they were not constructed of metal. These fluted rods had been forged from a translucent material, some sort of polymer or resin that had the color of ivory.

"Over here," Kari called out, leading them to a small nearby pen.

Carol walked up to the wall and placed her gloved hand against a smooth touchpad, just as if she'd done it a million times before. Waves of blue-white light washed across her pressed palm. The controls evidently found something within her armor they trusted, prompting the bars to suddenly retract.

Next, she turned to the mantis and instructed it to place Alan inside.

"Gently," she added.

The obedient creature did just as Carol asked. It carefully deposited Alan within the empty pen and skittered back away from the opening. She half-expected it to bark for a treat, but the insect-beast remained quiet and mute, motionless as a statue as it awaited her next instruction.

Carol lifted her hand from the touchpad and the fluted tusks slid like fangs across an open mouth, closing Alan off from the rest of them, trapping him inside the holding cell. The accompanying sound was disturbingly wet, almost as if the Ark had just swallowed him whole.

I used to say that you were the only person on earth I trusted, now I can't even let you near me; I can't be sure you won't cause me harm.

When Alan took a step into the light, Carol saw that his eyes were red and swollen. She didn't know if his tears had been shed in remorse for his violent, barbaric outburst with the ice axe, or if they'd been tears of mourning, cried out for her; no, not even for her, but for the *old her*, for the lifeless husk she'd left behind, and Carol didn't know which reason she would have found better or worse.

He stepped up to the channeled bars and focused on Kari, no one else.

"You see this?" Alan angrily swiped at his cheeks then reached out through the slats to point a harsh finger in Carol's direction. "That *thing* just locked me up in a cage. A fucking cage! And *you* went along with it, Kari! You think the *real* Carol Miyagi would be even remotely capable of this? *Do you?"*

"It wasn't her idea, Alan," Kari told him.

"No? Well then whose idea was it — the goat-man's?"

"His *name* is Gagan," Kari fired back, and from her tone, Carol could tell that it wasn't the first time she'd had to correct him. "And if you must know, the idea was all mine. You probably didn't hear me suggest it while you were screaming like a lunatic back there."

"I wasn't—"

"You were out of control, and I just thought everyone, myself included, would feel a little more comfortable if we gave you a safe space to cool off. Drunk tank, psych hold...call it whatever the hell you want, but this is a weapons free zone where you can't hurt yourself or anyone else."

He glared at her. "So how long am I in for?"

Carol spoke up, "It's only temporary, Alan, just until we can be sure that you've come to your senses."

"You mean until I can accept *you,* right?"

Alan glanced in Carol's general direction, then quickly turned away. He'd come close to looking her in the eye, to acknowledging her, or perhaps that was just wishful thinking.

You used to look at me like I was your whole world. Now you can't bear to look at me at all. Is what I am so terrible?

For a chilling moment, Carol was reminded of her father, of how she feared the man would've acted toward her back in college if she'd admitted her love for another woman. In Japanese, there was no real equivalent to the phrase "coming out." The closest the language allowed was *kamuauto*, which meant "disclosure," or if she'd wanted to be a bit more traditional, there had been the term *kokuhaku*: "confession." To her father, that's exactly what it would have been, too, the confession of a sin, and she would have been expected to ask him for his forgiveness.

Carol didn't need or want a man's forgiveness, then or now, but even after all these years, she still feared their rejection.

"If that's a condition of my release," Alan said evenly, returning his focus to Kari. "This is going to wind up being a life sentence because I will never accept that *thing* as Carol Miyagi. You got that? *Never!*"

Carol winced. She looked down at her hands; one lay hidden within the glowing alien orb, and the other was covered by the bony outgrowth of her new sword. She didn't think either weapon had the power to inflict as much hurt as Alan's words.

Kari laid a firm hand on her shoulder. "Are you all right?" she asked quietly. "Hey, look at me. You okay?"

Carol looked into Kari's eyes, but could find no words. She felt her face crumple and simply shook her head.

"Let me try and talk some sense into him."

Carol nodded.

As she stepped away, Gagan moved silently to her side. He put his arm around her; it was as hairy as it was comforting, and she thanked God for it.

"Alan," Kari began as she strode up closer to the bars, "I wish you could hear yourself. You're being totally ridiculous."

"*I'm* being ridiculous?"

"No, you're right. You're not being ridiculous. You're being a complete *ass*." Kari pointed to Carol, but unlike Alan, there was nothing accusatory in her gesture. "I want you to look at her, just look into her eyes, I mean *really look.* You'll see it's Carol. It's the woman—"

"No," he yelled suddenly, giving everyone a start. "She's *dead.* You said it yourself, that thing over there is a clone. Don't you understand what that means?"

Kari recited something that sounded like a textbook definition, "'An organism or cell, or group of organisms or cells, produced asexually from one ancestor or stock, to which they are *genetically identical.*'" Then, she added, "And her being one doesn't change a goddamn thing, not for me, and it shouldn't change anything for you either."

"It changes everything! That *creature* is walking around with Carol's face, but it isn't *real.* It's vile, an abomination; it's disgusting and disrespectful, and it—"

"Stop it!" Kari made a fist and pounded her side of the bars in frustration.

Alan fell suddenly silent, and for that Carol was grateful beyond words; she'd already heard far too much. A man who'd professed to love her for so long had now dubbed her *an abomination.* He'd called her disgusting and vile. It was everything she'd once feared her father would say about his *rezu* daughter and more.

She shivered, shocked and horrified, and felt her heart slowly sink within her chest.

I used to watch you sleeping beside me in our bed, in my grandmother's home that we had managed to make our own. I would memorize every line and edge of your face, and I would think to myself that I could be content with you for the rest of my life. Now, I don't even recognize you. Where do we go from here? How do we bounce back from this?

Across the room, Kari unclenched her fist and rubbed her

temples with her thumb and forefinger. "You know," she said, still trying to get through to him, "when doctors first brought up the idea of doing a heart transplant, they ran into a lot opposition. People had always seen the human heart as the source of our love and emotion. It was even said to be the center of our personality. Now, we know that's all bullshit, don't we? I mean, the heart is just a pump. It's a damn good one, but that's all it really is, just a pump, just a mass of muscle tissue. It doesn't love, it doesn't hate, it doesn't make you kind or brave, doesn't really have anything to do with who you are. It doesn't do anything but move your blood around."

Carol watched Alan stare at Kari through the bars. He seemed to be listening, *really listening*. Or perhaps that was just more wishful thinking.

"If this place had given Carol a heart transplant," Kari pressed, "would you love her any less?"

"Of course not," he admitted. "That's why I thought we came in here in the first place. If the Ark couldn't fix Carol's damaged heart, as crazy as it sounds, I thought it might grow her a new one. But that's *not* what it did."

"No," Kari agreed, "it's not. I'll give you that. But hear me out: the principle here is exactly the same; the Ark performed *a transplant*. It took all her memories, all of those unique little one-of-a-kind personality traits that we love, or that drive us crazy, her whole mind, and it just moved them from one body to another. And not just *any* body. It used Carol's DNA, not to regrow her heart, but to regrow *her*. And voilà...there she stands, alive and well and whole again.

"*That's* Carol," Kari proclaimed with supreme certainty. "That's the same woman you and I have always known and loved."

Carol fought back tears. There was so much she wanted to say in that moment, things she couldn't find the words to express. "I *am* Carol Miyagi," she voiced at last, and to her ears, it sounded as if she were only truly coming to realize it now.

Kari offered her a tender smile, warm and familiar.

In his cage, however, Alan remained a stranger. He finally turned to Carol, bereft of love, bereft of any tenderness or compassion, and his gaze was every bit as cold as his words, "No, you're a copy, an imitation. You're not her. You'll never be her! I keep telling you, she's *dead!"*

There were no more tears in his eyes, Carol noted, of mourning or otherwise. Instead, she found only judgement and hate. In his mind, Alan had developed some sort of litmus test for what qualified as human; Gagan, and now Carol, failed to measure up, and so he dismissed them utterly.

He swung his attention back to Kari, his only equal in the room. "You talk about transplanting Carol's memories," he told her, "moving all of her emotions and personality, like it was all just a bunch of computer data."

"That's what the brain is, Alan, an organic computer."

"And the heart is just a really good pump."

"Exactly."

Alan shook his head. "It's grotesque; the whole concept, the idea that you can just lift all those ones and zeros, pirate them, put them in the exact same line and make something into something that it's *not*. What if this place had taken everything in Carol's brain and dumped it into some kind of *Star Wars* robot? Using your logic, that tin can would be Carol now, right?"

Kari frowned. "That's not what happened."

"Isn't it? This place didn't 'regrow Carol.' All it did was Xerox her. That thing over there is just a replica, Kari, a facsimile. It's a damn good one, but that's all it really is, just a knock-off, a mass of stolen tissue and memories. It's artificial, an *organic* robot, a living machine no different from that big mantis that's standing right behind you, no different from this whole damn ship.

"Oh, it's flesh and blood...It's real and you can touch it, and if you ask it very nicely, it can call up any one of Carol's memories you so desperately want to hear, just like Siri can bring up any picture or song you've got stored on your phone, but it doesn't have a *soul*. And you have no idea what this place has programmed it to do."

Kari shook her head, her expression tight. "You're wrong, Alan. You're *so wrong*."

She turned sharply and walked away.

"You love that thing?" Alan called after her through the bars; his voice was guttural, thick with disgust. "You and the goat-man are welcome to it, but you keep it the hell away from me. You hear me, Kari? *Keep it away!*"

His words landed hard, sickening Carol. She gaped at him, at the contempt on his face.

After everything we've meant to one another, everything we've been through together. We were friends as well as lovers, and now...Now, I am nothing *to him.*

Carol rested her cheek against Gagan's shoulder. She had no memory of the yeti spear piercing her heart, but she thought this is how it must have felt.

"Charming guy," Kari snarked as she approached them, her expression still sour. "When you go for a dick, sweetie, you sure pick a big one."

"He's said some ignorant things since we left Japan," Carol said, "but I've never seen him like this. This xenophobic paranoia of his; it's completely irrational. I don't know why he can't accept what's happened to me the way you both have."

"Give him time to mourn, Miyagi," Gagan urged, gently rubbing her arm with his claw. "His mood will improve. You will see."

"That's just it, Gagan, he doesn't have anything *to* mourn. I'm *right here*, but he...he doesn't want to know me."

"And we can't wait around forever," Kari put in. "We'll be out of food and water soon. Unless..."

"Unless what?" Carol prodded.

Kari gave a nod to the giant mantis who still stood guard by Alan's cell, a silent sentinel. "Unless you can use your mojo and get Manny over there to bring us some sustenance."

Carol lifted her head from Gagan's shoulder. "You *named* the mantis?"

"Of course, I did."

"You named him Manny?"

"What can I say," Kari shrugged, "I've always wanted a dog. Just, you know, I never pictured one so big or so...gray."

Carol gave a snort; she shook her head and could not help but smile.

Kari smiled right back at her. "So what do you say? You think Manny could get us some kind of rations — bread and water, maybe a little protein? I mean, he's alive, right? He has to be getting his nourishment from *somewhere*."

Unless Alan's right and it really is some kind of a machine.

Carol dismissed the thought, but another was quick to take its place; something even more unsettling. The storage area they'd left behind, with all its stasis tubes full of genetic failures and missteps...What if the Ark wasn't preserving those creatures simply for study, as a DNA library to reference and catalog? What if, marooned here for millions of years, with no new mission or outside directive, the living ship kept creating more life from seed for no other purpose than self-preservation — a constant, renewable source of *food?*

All those specimens back there...That could have been the Ark's pantry, *and three times a day, different creatures are picked like ripened fruit from a vine, ground up into a neat little protein paste for the ship and all of its bio-mechanical denizens to ingest, to keep the endless cycle going on and on and on...*

Carol shuddered. "I don't think you would like what it had to offer."

"I'm not picky," Kari told her. "I've done field studies in remote villages all over the world. Anything between a Katmandu street vendor and Whole Foods is fine by me."

"When there's nothing left, no other choice, I'll ask for the Ark's help. Until then, I think it's probably best if we try and ration what we have, since we *know* what it is and where it comes from."

Carol went to rub her mouth and tired eyes. She totally forgot about the bone sword; as she brought her hand up to her face, Kari had to duck in a hurry to avoid being decapitated by the blade from her arm.

"Jesus, Carol!" Kari exclaimed, wide-eyed.

"*Gomen'nasai!* So sorry!"

Timidly, she lifted her head once more. "Put that thing away before you accidently kill somebody."

"I wish I could, Kari, but I don't even know how I got it to pop out in the first place."

"Well...Alan was coming at you with his axe, right?"

Carol grimaced. "Yes."

"So you were afraid for your life. Maybe your myrmidon picked up on that somehow?"

"If I'd been wearing my helmet, I'd say you were right, but the armor wasn't plugged into my brain at the time, so it couldn't possibly have known what I was thinking or feeling."

"So, it's got to be something simpler. Okay..." Kari took a step back. "Do exactly what you did when it first appeared. *Exactly*."

With a shrug, Carol turned to the satyr. "You'd better back up too, Gagan, unless you want to lose one of your horns."

"Be careful, Miyagi," he said, moving a few paces away, well out of stabbing distance. "Do not harm yourself."

Carol flashed him a grin and gave a quick nod. "I'll be fine."

She took a deep breath then swung her arms up to cover her face; a single burst of kinetic energy, just as she'd done when Alan stood over her, ready to lunge. Nothing happened. The bone sword continued to shade her eyes from the phosphorous overhead light.

Carol lowered her chin, peeked at Kari from beneath the blade's jagged edge. "Now what?"

"That's all you did?"

"I think so. You were there. Isn't this what you saw me do?"

"Honestly?" She gave a little laugh. "I was too busy fumbling with your katana and trying not to piss my pants."

"I put my arms up really fast and I...wait a minute..." Carol made a tight fist; she flicked her wrist and the blade instantly retracted. "That's got it."

"Yes!" Kari shouted back; she started to take a step toward Carol, then paused. "Do you have to put your arms up like She-Ra every time you need that thing?"

"Let's see." Carol lowered her limbs to her sides. She clenched her fist and gave her wrist another quick flick; the blade stabbed out from the cuff of her myrmidon. When she repeated the motion a moment later, it withdrew. She relaxed her hand, wriggled her gloved fingers. "I think I've got the hang of it now."

"One bad bitch," Kari said with a smile, unafraid now to approach her.

"She is truly one of Zeus' warriors, Hannigan — an overseer, a nightmare of legend." Gagan's cloven hooves stayed put for the moment; he stared at Carol's wrist with his horizontal pupils, still hesitant. "The Yeti will fear her now."

They're not the only ones.

Her eyes drifted back up to the cage, to where Alan stood scowling, watching her with prejudiced eyes through fluted bars. A short time ago, he'd been ready to follow her out into the Yeti horde, to fight and die by her side. Now, given half a chance, Carol knew he'd be willing to do the creatures' dirty work for them.

If only she hadn't led him into that storage room. If only Alan had never seen the body, never discovered the truth of what she'd become, maybe then he'd still—

BANG!

Carol flinched and her head swiveled toward that sudden thunderous noise. *"Tawagoto!"* she exclaimed. "What was that?"

Kari's smile faltered a bit. She nodded at the opposite end of the chamber. "That, my dear, is the stable's only other occupant."

Curious, Carol took a short stroll. She walked along an uneven rippled path, pausing when she reached the pen. Cautiously, she stepped up to the thick tusks that barred its entrance and peered inside.

She sensed something moving around in the shadows, something *big*. It seemed to sense her as well. The creature crawled swiftly toward the opening, toward the light, and at first all Carol could see were its teeth. It loomed before her, large as a semi-truck, and growled — a monstrous lifeform, unlike any that had ever walked this earth.

No, that's not true.

Her focus shifted from the beast's massive, ungainly reptilian head to its eight multi-jointed, crab-like legs, then back again. Something clicked in her brain, something unexpected — recognition.

"A caballus," she blurted.

"What was that?" Kari asked, joining her at the oversized bars. "English, please."

"That *was* English, or perhaps English with a dash of Atlantean thrown in. It's what this animal is called: a caballus. They helped Zeus' warriors keep order among the various clans, long before recorded history."

"Huh?" Kari blinked, then eyed her curiously. "How the hell do you know that?"

Carol was just as surprised. "I don't know *how* I know, but I do." She turned; Kari's expression, warm and gentle, was a welcomed sight. "It could be that Alan's right about me being programmed."

"Sweetie—"

She held up her gloved hand. "Not in the way he thinks, nothing nefarious; I'm not some alien sleeper agent."

"Not that you would be aware of it if you were," Kari pointed out, but her voice was light, and the tenderness never faded from her eyes. "Just for the record, Carol, *I* trust you. Actually, I feel safer with you than anyone else on this planet. I always have."

Carol's face flooded with warmth. *"Dōmo."*

For a quiet moment, they looked at each other closely. Again, there were so many things that Carol wanted to say. Things like, *"You're the best friend I've ever had, Kari, did you know that?"* and *"What did I ever do to deserve you?"* But mostly *"How could I have ever said that I didn't love you?"* She almost said that last one aloud, but Gagan trotted up to join them.

"I also trust you, Miyagi," he said.

The spell was broken; Carol dropped her eyes. "Thank you, Gagan."

She studied the golden orb on her hand, the "Wrath of the Gods."

"Before we climbed Makalu," she said, addressing both of them now, "I dreamed about the myrmidon, about this weapon. At the time, I thought it meant nothing, just a mishmash of various memories, but now I feel differently."

"A vision?" Gagan asked.

Carol looked up at him; he leaned on his ornately carved bow as if it were a walking stick. "Yes," she said. "You told me that all of your people dreamed of a black pyramid, Makalu, and the return of the gods. You said the dreams called you here to the mountain, to the Ark."

"Yes, Miyagi, since birth."

"Well, I think that the Ark called out to me as well. I think that, when I got close to Makalu, to the Ark, my subconscious mind picked up its transmission. And maybe, just maybe, the Ark picked up on me." Carol turned back to Kari. "This armor, the caballus...it feels like they're *mine*, like they've been grown or prepared just for me, like I was meant to use them. I know that sounds a little weird."

"A little." Kari laughed at the supreme understatement; she eyed her appraisingly for a moment, then shrugged. "But I guess that would explain why there's a cab—?"

"Caballus."

"A caballus here in the stable, still alive and kicking after a few million years." Kari looked back into the pen, studying the huge chimera housed within; after a moment of thought, she asked, "So, instead of attack dogs, Zeus' warriors kept giant T-rex crabs on a leash?"

"Not 'on a leash' exactly," Carol said, "but I think old Rex here could prove to be quite useful."

Kari laughed. "You've already named him?"

"Of course, I have."

"Of course, you have. And you named him Rex?"

"What can I say," Carol told her with a grin, "I've always wanted a dog."

CHAPTER TEN

"Chud?" Earl L. Preston, Jr. walked the deserted underground passages, calling out his friends' names. It sounded as if he might be searching for a pair of lost puppies or wayward children, not lethal monsters and grown men. "Larry, where you at? Come on, quit playin', now; we got shit to do. *Chud?*"

Vacant echoes were the only reply.

Earl moved cautiously. The lighting was spotty at best in these old brick catacombs, the shadows heavy, and it didn't take much for his imagination to run wild. He poked his head into various nooks and chambers as he went, tensed and ready for something to jump out at him.

Nothing did.

"Yo, anybody here?"

No one was.

He found dozens of still-burning candles, a few unmade cots, he even located his department-issued bulletproof vest and the pair of M-16s Chud had brought back from the failed warehouse raid, but there was no sign of the crocodile-man himself, and no Larry Neuhaus.

Earl cursed softly. With the loss of the final crystal skull, time had suddenly become their enemy; he didn't want to waste any of it searching for them. He picked up his tactical vest, *HOMELAND SECURITY INVESTIGATION* stamped in bold, neon-yellow lettering across the chest and back, and he put it on. Then, he grabbed the rifles and stepped up his pace, making his way back to the room he now called his own.

At least Zuri hadn't gone AWOL on him. She'd relapsed nicely into her statuesque human form, and somehow, she'd managed to pour her curvaceous buttocks and body into a new pair of black leather pants and a fresh corset.

Growing up, Earl read Incredible Hulk comics, watched old re-runs of the television show, and he'd thought about how many shirts that Banner guy went through, how many torn pairs of pants he had to replace, and where did he get the money for it all? Now, he wondered the same about Zuri. He'd discovered a drawer filled with her clothes, the same style of corset duplicated in just about every color of the rainbow, so he knew she was prepared to go through a few.

Damn...

Earl hesitated there in the archway, admiring the view, his rush momentarily forgotten.

Then, his father's voice was suddenly in his head again, quick to remind him, *"Get back on point, Junior! No more time to play house today. You got a job to do, soldier. This here's the endgame now. You need to finish this. You need to win!"*

Yes, sir.

Earl marched over to Zuri with the pair of M-16s. "Something's goin' on," he told her. "I can't find those dudes anywhere."

"I would not worry, my love." She finished clasping the golden hoops of her earrings. "I am certain that Chud went to get breakfast, just as he does every morning without incident. And more likely than not, this time, he chose to take your friend along with him. They are grown. They can take care of themselves."

Earl tilted his head, considering it. "Yeah, okay," he said at last. "You think they'll bring back any coffee? I always think better in the morning with a nice caffeine buzz goin', especially if I didn't get much sleep the night before."

"I am sorry if I deprived you of your valuable rest." She turned to him with a sly grin that said she wasn't really sorry at all, then she took one of the rifles off his shoulders. "But I have already made us coffee."

"You mean *that?*" He pointed to a nearby table, to an old school metal coffeepot; it sat steaming atop an elevated grate, kept hot by a cluster of small candles burning brightly beneath. "No offense, girl, but that over there ain't coffee. That's some thick-ass Mississippi mud, and you got it so hot, it's practically boiling. That there's a McDonald's lawsuit waiting to happen! I need a large mocha, Zuri, somethin' with my name written in big letters on the side."

She checked her weapon. "Your name written on the side of a cup makes the coffee taste better?"

"My name written on the side of the cup means the coffee comes from a *place* that makes it taste better, yes ma'am; it sure as hell does."

Earl tried to imagine Chud and Larry strolling into some upscale New York coffee house, placing an order for frappes or lattes with big toothy grins. He pictured the horrified look on the poor barista's face, all the screaming millennials running for the exits, and he couldn't help but laugh.

"Seriously, though," Earl adjusted the straps on his vest and checked his own rifle, "I haven't had a real cup of coffee in...Shit, I don't even know. Make mine a large and throw in an extra shot or two of espresso for good measure."

Zuri shook her head. "What is it that they say — first world problems? Do you not believe there are more important things we should concern ourselves with this morning?"

Earl felt his face warm, but before he could answer her, a loud knock sounded from behind him. He spun his eyes and his weapon toward the stone archway and saw Chud's hulking silhouette fall across the beaded Bob Marley curtain.

"You guys decent?" the crocodile-man asked.

Now he asks!

"You may enter, Chud," Zuri told him.

"Yeah, bro, get your scaly ass in here!" Earl lowered the barrel of his M-16, still hoping for coffee. When the crocodile-man waddled into the room, however, Earl saw that his arms were empty, free of any food or drink, and more troubling still, he was alone. "Where the hell did you go, and where's Larry?"

"Oh, he left."

"What the hell do you mean, 'He left?' Where the fuck did he go?"

"He had to go and find the rest of his people."

"What the fuck you mean 'his people?'"

Zuri placed her hand on Earl's shoulder to try and calm him. It didn't work, not completely, but it did make him bite his tongue. "Chud," she said with surprising cool, "where exactly did Larry go, and where is it that *you* have been?"

"He swam back out to sea. I went and showed him how to get there."

"Son of a bitch ditched us," Earl blurted, "and you helped him do it? What the hell is wrong with the both of you?"

"It's not like that," Chud assured him, holding up his clawed hands. "See, Larry had this dream, more like a vision, really. This girl, Susan, she told him that we were gonna lose without Poseidon's help, so he—"

Earl held up his own hand, butting in, "Hold the phone, Leatherhead...You say Susan?" He searched his memory, but the only connection he found to Larry was the murdered girlfriend of Roger Hays' murdered son. "Susan *Rogers?*"

Chud's eyes lit up. "That's the one! You know her?"

"Yeah, I know her. She's fuckin' dead!"

"Right. She comes to Larry in his dreams, all messed-up and shit, but see, he never listens to her."

"Because she's fuckin' dead!"

Zuri stepped up between them as if she were about to play peacemaker. "I smell a rat," she said, her nostrils flaring.

"Yeah," Earl agreed, "a couple of 'em!"

"Sorry, it's probably me." Chud covered the tip of his snout with his clawed hand. "I had one for breakfast."

"A *big* rat," Zuri said, lowering her voice as she lifted the barrel of her M-16; her eyes flickered from Earl to Chud to the archway entrance, then went wide. *"Get down!"*

As Earl opened his mouth to speak, the man-made caverns filled with the pungent smell of nitroglycerin and the deafening echo of automatic weapons fire.

———

Horror Show stood in disbelief, watching as various weapons of war were packed up for transport. The former hitman saw revolvers and self-loading pistols, submachine guns and assault rifles, rocket and grenade launchers; hell, they even had flame-throwers! Once full, each carton was added to an ever-growing collection of unmarked boxes and crates, all stacked up against the hangar wall.

He counted containers until his mind boggled, then stopped counting. It was enough military-style hardware to overthrow a country.

"You guys stole all this shit from those addresses I gave you in prison?" Horror Show lifted his head to look at Benedict; the spider-centaur sat high upon a throne of sticklike legs.

"The full monty," Benedict replied, his tone as light as his voice was deep. His mandibles were like clawed little fingers rubbing together, the hands of a miser surveying his riches.

"Jesus." Horror Show didn't know why he was so surprised. He still remembered the car Hays had him drive up to Colonial Bay, the trunk loaded with all the guns, ammo, and explosives needed to blow that little coastal town off the map. "Roger Hays did not fuck around."

I'm glad that crazy son of a bitch is dead, and I'll be even happier when Vivian Song can keep him company.

Benedict stared down at him with those unblinking spider eyes of his. It was unnerving, to say the least. "We don't fanny around, either," he said. "Have a look outside and you'll find a row of lorries stacked boot to bonnet across the tarmac, all waiting to be loaded and sent on their merry way."

"What the fuck is a lorry?"

"Trucks, mate."

"Why the hell didn't you just say that? I swear, I don't know what the fuck you're talkin' about half the time."

"Well, maybe you'll understand this. For generations, we've been funneling artillery to loyal clans all over Asia, Africa, Europe, in both Central and South America, and of course, throughout the Middle East. What you call 'unrest?' That's us, mate; it's all been a part of the grand design.

"Now," he went on, "Zeus is weaker than ever, the portal is all but finished, and we've got this last great arsenal ready to be distributed across North America. When the gods arrive, they'll find an army ready to do their bidding, ready to take on the whole bloody world!"

The side with the most guns doesn't always win, Benny. Just ask Roger Hays. Oh, wait, you can't. A bunch of sea monsters killed his crazy ass, killed my friend Carlo and that poor bastard O'Shea, too. And those creatures, they never fired a single shot, Benny. We had all the weapons; they had nothing but their claws and their teeth.

Horror Show made a half turn away from Benedict, far more interested in what was happening across the room. Away from all the packing and stacking, he saw truck drivers gathered around a large wooden table. Some of them were still transforming, unbelievable fairytale monsters donning drab coveralls and bright trucker hats to try and look like regular Joes. The table was covered by a big-ass map of Canada and the continental United States; the griffin, Hans, pointed to it again and again, evidently doling out everyone's assignments, directing them where to drive and when to make their deadly deliveries.

"With all my gun-running experience," Horror Show said, "I'm surprised Viv didn't have me head up this little operation here."

"You know your onions, but Vivian...she's got other plans for you, more important stuff."

Horror Show didn't know if he liked the sound of that. "I'm

sure you thought about all the weigh stations out there along the way?" he asked. "A bust like this could make some state trooper or DOT pencil-pusher's career."

"Weigh stations are for commercial vehicles," Benedict told him as if it were news. "Our little fleet of U-Hauls, our vans and our pickups, they would hardly qualify."

"You've thought of everything, Benny."

"We have. Nothing has been left to chance."

Horror Show laughed at that.

Benedict did not look amused. Then again, he never had any expression at all. It was like looking at Darth Vader. "What's so funny, mate?"

For one thing, you calling me "mate," like we're best buds going on a bar crawl, that's fuckin' hilarious!

Horror Show made a poor attempt at a British accent, "'Nothing has been left to chance.'" He shook his head. "You realize you sound like every crazy James Bond villain in history?"

"Yes, well, I'm no nutter, and James Bond never had to face off against Vivian, did he?"

"No, but I hear that nigger Preston sure keeps turnin' up, doesn't he — bein' a fly in the ointment?"

Benedict leaned down, bringing his bulbous head and wriggling fangs lower, *closer;* near enough now for the hitman to smell vinegar on his breath. Horror Show didn't know if the Brit had been eating fish and chips for breakfast, or if that acrid smell was the scent of some kind of acid or venom.

"If I had a fiver to wager," the spider-centaur told him, "I'd put it on Vivian Song every time. So, I wouldn't worry about Preston. She's taking care of your little moss-headed friend even as we speak."

"Preston's no friend of mine."

And for that matter, neither are you, Benny boy.

"Care to share how she plans to do it this time?" Horror Show asked.

Again, Benedict was totally expressionless, but there was a smile in that baritone voice of his, "It takes a sewer rat to kill a sewer rat."

———

Zuri had become quite accustomed to the musk of rodents. Living down here in the New York underground, she caught a whiff of it almost daily. Perhaps that's why she'd ignored the scent for so long.

This was Hades' plan, was it not? she mused. *They are clever, so very clever.*

Now, it was too late. The creatures were practically on top of them.

She sniffed at the air again. They were of the Cerberus clan, like her. She could hear their hearts and their clawed feet racing, and something else; the sound of weapons being locked and loaded.

Zuri lifted the barrel of her own rifle. Her eyes shot from Earl to Chud to the beaded curtain that hung across the open archway, the only way in or out of this chamber.

This place will become a tomb, but not for me, *and not for those I love.*

"Get down!" she cried, determined.

What happened next happened quickly.

The lead rat-man entered the room; he was tall and thin, with large ears, a pointed nose, and a naked scaly tail. Zuri saw malicious intent in his big black eyes. She also saw his TEC-9 pistol swing toward her.

Zuri fired first; a short, controlled burst.

The invader was cut down; his hairy body jerked with the impact of each shell, a mist of blood hanging in the air as he flew back against the brick archway.

A second gunman rushed through the beaded curtain, nearly stumbling over the body of the first; this rat-creature also had a blade, a special forces-style Kunai knife, and he threw it in Zuri's direction.

A sudden blur of motion; Earl reached in, snatched the knife from the air in front of Zuri's face, then flung it back at its owner.

The blade stuck in the rat-man's leg; he went down hissing, lifted the barrel of his semi-automatic pistol, and—

Earl pulled the trigger on his M-16, filling the rat-man's open mouth with half a dozen rounds, shearing off the top of its furry head.

Chud? Zuri looked to her left, then to her right, suddenly panicked. *Where—?*

Then, she saw him. The crocodile-man had retreated to another corner, hiding in the shadows. His back was flat against the wall, and Zuri knew that the rat-men would not be able to see him from their vantage point at the archway, not until they moved deeper into the room. Zuri noticed something else; Chud clutched the steaming metal coffee pot in his scaly hand.

The room suddenly exploded with the sound of weapons fire, sustained bursts; the noise was incredible.

Zuri took a hand off her rifle and swiped at the wooden coffee table; she overturned it right in front of her, scattering smoking candles and flickering flames across the concrete floor. Experience had taught her that wood could stop a bullet, even a pile of sawdust could bring a high-velocity shell to a halt, if it were made thick enough, and she prayed this old bit of furniture, someone else's trash, would now offer her a modicum of protection.

Earl crouching down next to her behind the crude shield. He mouthed something, and knowing her lover as she did, Zuri assumed it was a string of curses. She was grateful that he had put on his tactical vest, the one he'd been wearing when she saved him in that alley, but his head and his limbs were still vulnerable.

As they continued to hunker down, countless rounds tore through the air, peppering the wall behind them, obliterating the photos and news clippings that hung above their heads.

Those weapons...they have been modified, made fully automatic. Firing continuously like that, in a moment, their magazines will be spent; the shooters will need to reload. That will be the time to strike.

Almost as soon as Zuri finished her thought, the shooting stopped. Her sensitive ears were full of bees, but she had no time for the pain. Zuri took a quick breath then leapt up, snarling, ready to return fire. She found she couldn't shoot, however.

Not without hitting Chud.

He burst from the shadows, charged at the remaining trio of rat-men. That steaming pot of coffee was still there in his talons, and now Zuri understood why he'd grabbed it. As he lunged, Chud tossed its hot contents into one of the shooters' hairy faces.

Shrieking in pain, the doused creature immediately dropped his weapon and whipped both of his clawed hands up to cover his eyes. The rat-man next to him fumbled with his own pistol, trying desperately to reload before Chud's gaping maw could reach him.

He was too slow, too late.

Crocodilian jaws snapped shut around the gunman's head with a sickening wet crunch, then thrashed violently from side to side. Caught in those exaggerated throes, his furry limbs flailing wildly in the air, the rat-man looked like a dog's chew toy. Blood splashed and flew in every direction until his neck finally snapped, until his head tore completely free of his torso.

Zuri wasted no time. She sprang over the table, pounced at the last remaining shooter. This final rat-man was clearly stunned, but even in his shock, he'd managed to do what his partners could not; he'd reloaded his TEC-9 and took aim at Chud.

Zuri pulled her trigger. Her barrage shredded the rat-man, turned his pointed snout into a mess of bloody fur and boney shrapnel; he was blown off his clawed feet, tossed back through the beaded curtain, and sent sprawling onto the concrete floor.

Badly scalded, the rat pack's sole survivor stumbled aimlessly back and forth. He was moaning, his claws still cradling his face.

Earl rushed up from behind Zuri, the printing on his bulletproof vest a neon-yellow blur. He saw the dropped TEC-9 on the floor, kicked it away, then used the barrel of his M-16 to pin the remaining rat-man back against the wall. "Fuck you, Ben," he shouted. "This is *my* house!"

Zuri pivoted on her heels, her own smoking rifle drawing lines in the air. "*Our* house," she said.

"Our house," Earl amended, still focused on the rat-man. "You think you're hot shit, huh? Tryin' to get the drop on us? This is what you get!"

The scalded creature winced. His clawed hands moved slowly away from his face and reached for the ceiling in surrender.

"King of the Bad-Asses," Zuri whispered.

"Damn straight." Earl flashed a cocky grin. "You good?"

"Thanks to you," she told him. In her mind's eye, she still saw the blade of that knife flying at her. If Earl had not reached in at the last possible moment...

"Girl, please," he scoffed. "You've bailed my ass out so many times, I'm just tryin' to pay down my debt."

With a hissing snarl, Chud spat the other rat-man's severed head out onto the concrete; it landed with a sickening *SPLAT*. Long strings of scarlet drool hung from the length of his snaggle-toothed snout, snapping and swinging in the air. "Anybody hurt?" he asked, wiping his mouth with his forearm, smearing blood across his leathery scales like war paint.

Thankfully, none of the blood was his.

"No," Zuri told him; she allowed herself a long and deep exhale, then her eyes went back to Earl. "I think that we have all been very lucky."

————

This bastard is lucky I don't waste his hairy ass right now! Earl stared down his rifle at their prisoner, watched as Chud duct taped the creature to an old wooden chair, all that smooth brown rat fur disappearing beneath sticky grey stripes. "That's really gonna hurt when we peel it off," he said with a sneer, "*If* we peel it off."

Zuri wasn't playing. That knife she always kept hidden in her boot? She held the blade up in front of the rat-man's eyes, silently threatening. Then, she grabbed a fistful of the hair between his oversized ears and yanked his head upward. "How is it you were able to find us?"

The creature grimaced, but he said nothing.

"Don't be rude," Earl warned, pushing in with his M-16. "The lady asked you a question."

The rat-man spoke through clenched teeth, "It wasn't hard. Benedict—"

"That spider-dude?" Earl asked.

The creature nodded in Zuri's grip. "We got the guns and knives from him. He gave us the name Chud, told us we'd find him hiding out down here in the underground with a Cerberus, a Charodon, and a Zeus. We were ordered to take care of you. All we had to do was ask around. Turns out a lot of people in this town know a Chordata named Chud, and once they pointed us in the right direction; we just followed our noses the rest of the way.

"I don't know what the hell a Charodon smells like, but that stink of Zeus?" He twisted his snout around toward Earl and his big eyes narrowed. "Yeah, it was easy to find *you.*"

"So much for a secret hide out." Earl chuckled bitterly. "Now, tell us where we can find *them*, Benedict and Vivian Song? And this airfield, the place where they're building the portal to Kronos, tryin' to bring back the gods, where the hell is *that?*"

The rat-man looked genuinely surprised. Then, he gave another slight nod, like he understood now why Benedict wanted them all dead. When he spoke, however, his words were less than agreeable, "You think I'm crazy? I'm not tellin' *you* anything."

"You have to tell me, cocksucker," Earl held up his rifle, tapped the rat-man's tape-covered chest with the barrel, "I'm the one with the big-ass gun."

"No, I don't have to tell you shit."

"The fuck you don't!" Earl looked to Zuri. "Have I been down here so long that people forgot how interrogations are supposed to work?" He glared back down at the rat-man. "Tell me what I wanna know, you rat fuck piece a shit, or I'll—"

"You'll shoot me?" the creature finished for him.

"I'll do it!"

The rat-man's big ears relaxed and flushed pink. "No, you won't."

"The hell I won't!"

"You think you're one of the good guys, a fuckin' hero." His eyes lowered and he read the printing off of Earl's vest. "Homeland Security Investigations, right? Well, heroes don't shoot defenseless guys like me, guys who are all tied up and don't pose a threat to nobody anymore. So either come on over to the dark side or shut the fuck up; either way, I'm done talkin'.'"

Chud was down on his scaly knees, using his duct tape to lash the rat-man's ankles together. "He's gotcha there, pal."

Earl frowned at him. *You suck at Good Cop, Bad Cop, Gwangi.*

Zuri still had a fistful of the rat-man's hair; she gave it a savage twist.

The creature let out a short, high-pitched squeal.

"You are right," she told him. "Earl is a *good man*, too moral and ethical to put a bullet in your filthy head now. I, on the other hand, was held prisoner for years by a pack of Cerberus just like you. They took everything from me. They tortured me, used me, *raped me*." She pressed the blade of her knife against his neck and growled into his pointed snout, her growing fangs on full display. "Defenseless or not, I will have no problem killing you. In fact, I believe I will enjoy it. I'll do it slowly, tear you apart bit by bit. In the end, you will beg me to slit your disgusting little throat, just to bring an end to your suffering."

Earl saw real fear in the captive rat-man's face, and he couldn't help but grin. *Now* she *knows how Good Cop, Bad Cop works!*

"Come on, guys!" Chud jumped up from the floor, shattering the tension. "Why are we wasting our time with this ass clown? Even if he gave us Hades' address, Vivian Song's alarm code, and a fuckin' map to the cell where they've stashed Larry's wife, I sure as hell wouldn't trust any of it. Would you?"

"It's all we got," Earl told him. "Since Larry gave you his 'I had a dream' speech and took off, how else are we supposed to find the right airfield?"

"No problem," Chud said with confidence. "Like I was tryin' to tell you two before these rat-guys showed up, I got this."

Earl let out a blustering half laugh. "*You* got this? Oh, this I gotta hear."

"Okay," Chud began, "so there are like four major airports that service the New York area. You got your Teterboro Airport, in Teterboro."

Obviously, Earl thought, but he forced himself not to react.

"You also got your Newark Liberty International up in Newark, but see, those are both in Jersey. Larry said that they were somewhere here in the city.

"So," Chud went on, "the two biggies here in the Metro are JFK, and then over in Queens, you got your LaGuardia. Those are both busy fuckin' places, thousands of people comin' and goin' out of there each and every day. It would be real hard, if not totally impossible, to pull off a full-blown construction project at either one of those places without bein' noticed and a bunch of people askin' a bunch of questions."

"That's assumin' Hades' disciples aren't positioned in high places, offices where they could field and bury those kinds of questions," Earl pointed out, rubbing his chin.

Chud lowered his snout and looked skeptical. "This might be a gate they're buildin', but it ain't fuckin' Watergate."

Zuri still stood holding a thicket of the rat-man's hair in her hand. She gave them both a quizzical glance. "Water—?"

"Don't ask," Earl told her. Then, to Chud he said, "Go on."

"There's a shitload of other commercial airports in the area. You got Long Island MacArthur, Westchester County, Stewart International, Trenton–Mercer—" Chud held up a clawed finger with each new name. "—some smaller, general aviation airports, seaplane bases too, down in the port district, but all of 'em have the same problem, too many people, too many pryin' eyes.

"Now, Larry, he said the hangar where they were bein' held smelled rusty, right — mildewed, like it had been vacant for a long time before Hades took it over? Well, there's only two abandoned airports left here in New York City," two more clawed fingers shot up, "Flushing, in Flushing, and Delancey Field, on this little peninsula just south of Brooklyn."

Watching Chud sleuth it all out, Earl didn't know if the crocodile-man was channeling Sherlock Holmes or Rain Man, but there was no arguing with his conclusions. Given the details Larry had provided, Chud's spooky knowledge of the city, and a bit of common sense, it certainly sounded like one of those two abandoned fields had to be the place.

"I consider myself a damn fine detective," Earl said, "but I gotta hand it to you, Chud, that's some nice work."

"Thanks, pal." The crocodile-man lowered his claws, looking rightfully pleased with himself. "So Flushing, it's mostly wetlands now. I can't picture Hades staging a major operation from there, so I figure it's gotta be Delancey Field. It's gotta be."

Earl glanced down at the captive rat-man; the look in the creature's eyes gave him all the confirmation he needed. "Looks like we have ourselves a winner," he said with a chuckle. "What do you know, this prick was able to help us out after all. Delancey Field it is. Let's saddle up!"

Zuri smiled at him, her teeth still sharp; she released her grip on their prisoner and slid her knife back into her thigh high boot.

"It's too late," the rat-man told them; he was agitated now, the whole chair shaking. "You can't stop them. Not now. The gods are comin' back! The gods are going to—"

"Make America great again?" Earl jeered. "Yeah, I've heard that one before."

"The gods must be obeyed," the creature warned, and his long tail slapped the concrete for emphasis. "All of Hades' disciples have to band together against Zeus or be killed! We don't have a fuckin' choice. It's a revolution, and it's happening now. Right fuckin' now. Nobody can stop it. Nobody."

Earl shouldered his M-16. "We'll see about that."

CHAPTER ELEVEN

L arry Neuhaus saw only a watery void the color of a days-old bruise. It stretched to infinity in every direction, yet he could feel it closing in upon him, pressing against his body like the viscous earth of a breached coffin.

Down in the Gulf of Mexico, that heavy darkness had been haunted. Larry heard the siren call of a crystal skull, felt its strange magnetic pull draw him in. And as he grew closer, he had seen its light shining brightly in the blackness like a guiding star.

Now...

Nothing. Not a goddamn thing!

Back in New York, roaming through all those long- neglected tunnels, the ones Chud called home, Larry had felt awkward and uneasy, literally a fish out of water. Now that he was back in his element, he should have been at ease. Instead, the shark-man felt rudderless — lost, and abandoned.

Where was Susan Rogers when he needed her most? All she'd left him with were riddles, mysteries he felt powerless to solve.

Where was her boney desiccated finger to point the way? Larry had chosen to go south, only because that was the direction Barbara and the others went when they fled Colonial Bay's reef. At least, that's what he remembered Peggy telling him. In reality, they could have gone anywhere.

Wait...What's that?

Larry spied a strange shape below him on the ocean floor, a dark specter with wide outstretched arms. He dove toward the unspoken promise of its welcoming embrace, feeling a sudden surge of hope, but his excitement was practically stillborn. The thing that rose from the silt wasn't a refugee from Colonial Bay at all; it wasn't even alive.

An old U.S. Navy plane.

The sunken aircraft looked as if it had been rotting down here in this watery grave since the waning days of World War II. Its canopy sat closed, covered in muck. Could the pilot still be locked inside, tiny fish picking scraps from his ribs and wide smiling teeth? Larry fought the urge to investigate and would never know.

The shark-man swam on, desperately, almost angrily, and his mind returned to that drowned subway train — another human relic left to rust in the depths. He didn't think he was any closer to finding Poseidon's children, but he knew with mournful certainty that every swish of his powerful tail pushed Peggy farther and farther away.

Did I really leave my wife?

Yes, he had.

Larry missed her swimming next to him, missed having the pale and comforting glow of her inner light to guide him through this endless night.

I love you, Peggy. Please know that. Please understand. I had to go. I didn't have a choice. I'm doing this to save you, to save the baby, to save us all.

But the more Larry tried to rationalize his decision, the heavier it weighed upon him. In fact, the pressure to succeed seemed far more crushing than all the waters of the abyss.

I have to keep going. I have to.

Larry raced on, propelled by the movements of his large fan-shaped tail. His nautical form was covered in small, tooth-like scales that helped to decrease drag, allowing him to reach incredible speeds underwater. Michael Phelps could manage about six miles per hour in the confines of an Olympic-sized pool, pretty damn good, for a human, but fully transformed in the wide-open sea, Larry had the ability to swim over *sixty miles* an hour.

Which means I'm getting nowhere fast!

A few startled fish sensed him streaking up from behind. They scattered, doing their best to hurry out of his way. He heard the rapid, terrified fluttering of their tiny hearts, the frightened thrashing of their bodies, but all those sounds faded quickly, leaving him alone once more with his thoughts.

Again and again, Larry's harried brain filled with visions of Vivian Song and her scorching flames, imagining every torture that dragon-bitch might inflict upon his wife in his absence. His triangular head thrashed back and forth in the deep, trying to shake those disturbing images, to purge from his mind any feelings of guilt, of hopelessness and fear. Larry had to *focus*, had to find some kind of sign or signal, something he could home in on.

Out there, he thought, staring straight into the watery depths ahead of him, *that's where I'll find them.*

Maybe Larry would stumble upon some uncharted island, one that Barbara and the others had made into a new Colonial Bay, a place where they finally felt safe to live out their lives. Perhaps that's what Susan's cryptic words had meant. Or maybe there were ancient ruins, somewhere on the ocean floor. Isn't that what Carol Miyagi had found all those years ago — Atlantis or Poseidon? Perhaps Larry would find them all gathered there.

And then what?

It was a fair question.

Larry had no real plan. He was acting purely on impulse, on instinct, literally chasing ghosts. There was no script, no idea of what he might say to Barbara and the others if—

When!

—*when* he finally came across them. What speech could he possibly give that would be powerful enough, *persuasive* enough to rally these exiled sea creatures to his cause, to get them to come to the aid of Peggy and their unborn child? And would he be able to say anything at all?

This isn't Aquaman!

Larry possessed no magical powers that would allow him to project his thoughts or his will through the depths. Here in the real world, if Poseidon's children were living somewhere at the bottom of the sea, a normal conversation would be impossible.

Had the clans developed some strange new form of communication? Did they sing to one another the way whales did — click and whistle like dolphins to express themselves? Or would Larry need to write his every word out in the benthic ooze with his claw? And again, just what would those words be?

Too many questions!

Larry only wished he had the answers.

———

Much like her husband, Peggy Neuhaus was confined to a dark and silent void, alone with her thoughts. She too had no concept of time, not really, but based on the fact that her jailers had just delivered lunch to her cell, she assumed it had to be early in the afternoon.

She frowned down at the metal plate they'd placed in front of her on the concrete, bioluminescent arms crossed over her shimmering breasts.

A ham sandwich and a bunch of greasy potato chips. Lovely. Obviously, nobody watches Food Network *in this place.*

Peggy ate the cold food, not because she wanted or craved it, but because she knew that, like it or not, her body had to have nourishment. If she was ever going to find a way out of this cell, she needed to stay strong and keep her mind sharp. Besides, Peggy wasn't about to starve her unborn child.

My little Sea Monkey needs whatever it can get.

On the floor beside her, the sonogram bathed in a dim pool of light from her body. Peggy smiled at the photo and held her stomach in her claws. "It's okay, little one," she whispered. "You're safe and snug in there, aren't you? Well, you just let Mommy worry about this big bad world, okay? You...You just rest, and dream, and grow big and healthy in there, and by the time you're ready to come out here and celebrate your birthday, Mommy will have chased all the scary monsters away. Mommy will have made the world safe for you. You'll be fine. I promise. We both will."

Then, after a beat, she added, "Daddy, too."

She lifted her head, stared off into the darkness. He was probably locked in another cell, perhaps just on the other side of these cinderblock walls, frantically searching for a way out just as she had been. They would be together again soon, safe and sound. Peggy tried to believe that, for the baby's sake, as well as her own.

She pictured their offspring running along the beach and playing in the surf, perhaps in the shadow of their home. One moment, this beautiful little miracle had blonde curls, just like the ones she'd sported herself as a young girl. In the next, the toddler appeared to her as a dark-haired, rambunctious little boy with Larry's eyes and his devilish grin — a pint-sized Rembrandt. No matter the gender, these brief flashes of what could be filled Peggy's heart with warmth, with hope and joy, and she desperately wanted to make either or both of them a reality.

Peggy stroked her abdomen. She wasn't going to allow herself to lie down in silent resignation, to give in to despair, not when this dawning life was so dependent upon her to act, to *fight*. Nor was she going to allow her more impulsive nature to rage against these concrete walls, scratching and digging and clawing until her talons snapped off and her translucent digits were reduced to cracked and bleeding nubs. No. There would be a time and a place for her to make a move; she had to keep herself alert and be ready for it.

Her head whipped in the direction of the room's only exit.

Peggy heard movement in the hallway outside, multiple heartbeats approaching, followed by the sound of those pin tumblers in the lock. She licked her lips, watched the door come open in a blinding flare of light.

A lone, backlit creature stepped through. Peggy sniffed at the air. Thankfully, it wasn't Hans. It wasn't his Anubis-looking friend Mark either, but the scent was similar, male, *doglike*. When the silhouetted visitor spoke, his voice sounded older, almost grandfatherly, "Hello, child."

Child? That's what Barbara DeParle used to call me. "Child." "My Child." I'm nobody's *child. Not then, and certainly not now.*

As the door slammed shut again, her surviving eye readjusted to the dark, allowing her to see her visitor more clearly. He looked like a werewolf from a Hollywood movie, his light grey pelt pale and ghostlike against the dimness. The expression on his face wasn't threatening in the least; in fact, if Peggy had to categorize it, she'd say it was one of gentle admiration.

"I'm so pleased to meet you," he told her. "You simply have no idea how long I've waited and prayed for this moment. When they told me you were here, I had to come and see with my own eyes. All of the gods' creations are now represented within these walls; Hades, Poseidon, and even Zeus. I once worried that your kind had been hunted to extinction, that there would be no hope of re-opening the doorway, no hope of reconciliation with our creators. I should have known that the gods would never allow that to happen. We will bring them back to us, and it will be a time of great rejoicing. This truly is the greatest of miracles!"

"You'll forgive me if I don't see it the same way," Peggy replied sharply. "Then again, thanks to Vivian Song, I'm lucky I can see at all."

The werewolf stared down into the blackened pit that once held her eye. Peggy saw several emotions tug at his hairy features; his ears drooped, and his smile fell right along with them. He looked at the floor, waited a moment, considering, then finally said, "I'm sorry she's caused you such pain."

"Sorry?" Peggy bolted upright, her tail swinging; she leaned in toward the old man, as angry as she was unafraid. "You're sorry?"

"Yes, my dear."

"They killed my baby doctor right in front of me. Are you sorry for that, too?"

"I am. The actual orders and actions did not come directly from me, but I feel I must take full responsibility for them all the same.

"The sad truth is," he went on, still not looking at her, gazing instead at his own outstretched claws, "I have a lot of blood on my hands. When I was much younger, perhaps your age, I took many lives. Even today, I feel there were some who deserved it, but others, in retrospect, clearly did not. I am sorry for what happened to each and every one of them as well."

He wagged his head.

"Bloodshed...It's inevitable, I'm afraid. We are attempting to change the world here, my child, to create a new and better civilization. And though I wish it could be otherwise, the history of this planet has shown us that there can be no revolution without violence."

"I don't know," Peggy told him, her hands firmly on her glowing hips. "Ever hear of a guy named Gandhi? How about Nelson Mandela or Martin Luther King?"

At that, the wolf looked up at her, and his toothy grin returned. "Child, even Jesus Christ, perhaps the most peace-loving Zeus ever to walk this earth, is responsible for millions upon millions of deaths. Oh, He may not have personally killed anyone, but His followers have died and murdered for hundreds of years in His name.

"They've hunted your people," he told her, "and they've hunted mine. But no more! Understand, my child, this is the twilight of Zeus' reign. When the sun rises tomorrow morning, it will be the dawning of a new era for this planet — an era of freedom and peace for all the gods' creations."

"Bullshit."

"It *will* happen, child. It is inevitable now. Others have shed their blood to make it a reality, and tomorrow it will be our turn, yours and mine. We are going to help bring the creators back to this world, you and I."

"Who the hell are you?" Peggy finally asked.

The wolf bowed his head. "You may call me Preacher."

"Well, Preacher," She took a defiant step toward him. "You, and

Hans, and Mark, and especially that dragon cunt Vivian Song can all just kiss my ass on your way straight to Hell! I'm not helping you do shit until I—"

"I'm afraid you don't have a choice, my child. None of us do. This is what the gods have ordained. We cannot fight their will."

Peggy narrowed her eyes. "Watch me."

Preacher made no attempt to respond. Instead, he looked around her darkened cell.

"Much of my life has been lived imprisoned in cage much smaller than this one," he told her. "I've spent decades in constant meditation and prayer, suffering for my sins, trying to atone for my wrongs, to prepare myself to meet my creators. And now...now, that day is finally at hand.

"Tomorrow morning, you and I will be the first to meet our makers."

Preacher's smile widened, showing every sharpened fang in his long gray snout. They glistened in the glow of Peggy's body, and she could not help but shiver.

————

Larry's solid body moved effortlessly through this fluid world, never slowing, never stopping. His arms pressed tightly against his sides, and his pulse raced. He followed the sea floor, speeding toward a jagged undersea ridge.

The wall of rock loomed directly in his path, extending as far as the eye could see, perhaps all the way up to the surface and beyond. He looked both ways, watching the cliff face disappear into a murky blue haze. It truly was a solid barrier!

Was this the foundation of some island or volcano? Bermuda? Puerto Ricco? *New Colonial Bay?*

Wall or mountain, part of him wanted to scale it, to see where the rocky crags would lead him. Then, snaking all along the base, Larry spied a wide gash in the earth.

An underwater canyon. A trench!

It was anyone's guess what might be down there.

Larry paused and his webbed feet came to rest on the stony lip of the chasm, creating a cloudburst of silt. The sediment drifted in the current, dispersing, giving way to a clear view of the bottomless pit before him.

He felt a bit like a jumper teetering on a rooftop ledge, contemplating the circumstances of life that had brought him to this fateful moment, wanting desperately to find a reason to take a step back, any reason at all. At the same time, he was drawn to the darkness below, filled with an intense desire to explore it, to discover what might make its home there. And unlike his earlier urge to investigate the downed warplane, this new interest was too strong to ignore.

What if they're there? he couldn't help but wonder. *What if they've been down there this whole time, just hanging out on the canyon floor? Even if the world knew about this trench, no air-breather would dare go that deep, even submersibles and remote cameras would fold under such intense pressure. It would be the perfect hiding place!*

Larry nodded and his talons made tight resolute fists at his sides. He couldn't give up hope now. He had to do this. He had to *believe*.

For all I know, this could be home, *the place that, once upon a time, spawned all of Poseidon's children. And now, just like salmon, they've all come back to it...*

A second later, he was heaving himself over the edge, diving head-first into the fissure, shooting like a bullet through unknown fathoms.

At first, Larry saw absolutely nothing in the watery night. After a short time, however, his patience was rewarded. He glimpsed a distant speck of illumination, a faint blue-white glow; Peggy's light.

Must be them. It has to be them!

His tail thrashed and his webbed hands reached out to pull him forward through the depths. This time, he knew that the thing was alive; it had a heartbeat, a pulse. The light grew larger as he approached, its source becoming more defined. Finally, Larry got close enough to see it was...

An angler fish.

The glow came from a bioluminescent ball, the tip of a fleshy stalk that extended from the fish's forehead. It was large, yes, a sharp-toothed predator, but it wasn't like the man-sized creature that attacked Black Harbor Medical Center all those years ago, the one that had been sent to kill his wife. Not even close. This was just a stupid fish; nothing more.

Fuck!

Angry and frustrated, Larry's talons lashed out at the surprised fish, snatching it from the waters in front of him. He buried his serrated jaws in its soft flesh and tore the fraud apart, forever extinguishing the lure of its lying light. His snout thrashed back and forth in a warm cloud, and while the fish's blood dissipated quickly, Larry's desperate feelings remained.

Movement.

Larry's head whipped around, detecting the presence of other creatures; they were out there in the dark, circling him unseen. Their scent had been masked by the overpowering smell of fresh blood; the sound of their collective pulse lost beneath the thunderous rhythm of his own.

One of the creatures separated from the others and swam over to Larry, slowly coming into view — a humanoid form with the head of an octopus, a fleshy, pulsating sac and a living beard of writhing tentacles. Larry instantly recognized this being as a Kraken. The creature hovered in the darkness before him like a mirage, but even fatigued, there was no doubt in Larry's mind that it was real.

This is happening...Poseidon's children, they're here. I did it, Susan. I've found them!

The Kraken lashed its long and powerful tail in the water, propelled itself closer still.

Larry raised his webbed hand and gave the tentacled creature a friendly wave. He gazed into its large onyx eyes, eyes that conveyed both great curiosity and confusion.

This is exactly what I was afraid of! How are we ever going to communicate? I wish I knew sign language, but even if I did...does this guy *know sign language?*

After the awkward moment had passed, the Kraken extended a claw to Larry. Unafraid, he took it. The creature then turned away, gliding, diving, pulling Larry deeper into the undersea gorge.

In the benthic depths, Larry caught sight of another pair of Poseidon's children. They continued to swim in ever tightening loops. One had the head and toothy maw of a tiger fish. The other was red and white striped, covered with long ribbon-like fins that undulated and trailed behind it in the current. Like him, Larry assumed these were both members of the Charodon clan, but he couldn't be sure. Whatever the creatures were, they moved stealthily closer, flanking him.

Larry's Kraken escort paid them no mind. The creature continued to guide him through the abyss, and soon he saw where they were headed.

An entire city covered the far wall of the trench, carved from the very stone. Larry stared in awe, enraptured by the fantastical rock-cut architecture; it brought to mind pictures he'd seen of the ruins at

Petra in Jordan, and he could not help but wonder what long-dead minds and hands had created it.

The sculpted façade dwarfed them as they descended toward it. They swam past rows of Greco-Roman columns hundreds of feet high, approaching a huge opening that yawned before them like the mouth of a hungry giant. Poseidon's children entered without trepidation, pulling Larry into the tunnel beyond. Larry didn't know if the passage had been fashioned from an existing natural structure, an undersea cave or long-dormant lava tube, or if it had been excavated over time, but its size and architecture suggested that it was intended for leviathans.

The tunnel floor tilted upward, and they followed its gradual incline. Larry saw shafts of light up ahead, shining down through the water from above. It wasn't sunlight, nor was it the blue-white glow of bioluminescence. No, this was the yellow-orange flicker of an open flame.

Fire? How—?

Confused, Larry looked over at the Kraken for guidance. The creature made an upward gesture with its free hand, then kicked hard. Larry did the same, and together, they rocketed into the light.

Larry's triangular snout broke the surface of a large moon pool. He blinked the water from his eyes. Glancing around the air-filled chamber, he found the source of that yellow-orange flicker — flaming torches set in rock-cut walls, walls covered in ancient petroglyphs. Larry was shocked by just how familiar it all seemed, then he suddenly realized why.

Colonial Bay...This is just like the temple in Colonial Bay.

Stunned, Larry swam over to the water's edge. He pulled himself out of the pool, standing slowly, his legs shaky. Rivulets of seawater ran off his body and onto the stone below, every drip and splash amplified throughout the subterranean chamber, echoes only made louder by the rest of Poseidon's children as they exited the pool to stand behind him.

Larry turned to look at the trio, and they stared right back at him. It was a long, uncomfortable moment before he found his voice. "Thank you," he told them, and his words, hoarse and cracked, reverberated loudly off the dry stone walls. "If you hadn't found me out there, brought me here, wherever here is, I don't know what I would have done. I don't know if I could've found this place on my own."

The creatures glanced at each other wordlessly, then looked back at him. They seemed puzzled.

"I'm Larry, by the way."

Still nothing, just blank and curious stares.

"I'm looking for Barbara," he told them. "Barbara DeParle."

At the mention of the old woman's name, the Kraken perked up. He offered Larry an encouraging nod, then lifted a webbed claw toward a stone archway on the opposite end of the pool chamber.

Larry turned and stepped through it, moving cautiously into a long hallway. The corridor was lined with both torches and statues. After a quick study, he decided it was more or less safe and started walking.

Sculpted eyes of statues seemed to follow Larry down the hall, and the artist in him had to admire the craftsmanship. He had no idea if the various effigies were meant to represent gods or heroes, but none of the likenesses were human. Stone tentacles and talons reached for him, rocky tails and fins curved away, and he saw more carved fangs than could easily be numbered. The flickering torch-light played across them, turning the corridor into Hell's version of the Louvre.

Before Colonial Bay, such a sight might have filled the artist with horror and dread. Now, it gave him an odd sense of pride.

Here, preserved in stone for all eternity, were faces just like his, aquatic bodies in positions of power, in poses of *triumph*. It was as if they had lined this hallway for the sole purpose of cheering Larry on.

He felt the strength returning to his legs and took each new step with greater confidence. When he glanced back over his shoulder, he saw that the Kraken and the two Charodon were still following him. Far from intimidating, their demeanor was one of intense interest. It was as if they had no idea what would happen next and could not wait to find out.

Larry felt the same way.

He heard faint chanting in the distance; it drifted down the twisting hallway, growing progressively louder around each new bend. There was no musical accompaniment, but the words had a rhythm all their own, as if some spell were being cast, an incantation so powerful it required a hundred or more voices to speak it in unison.

"Etare Varunatep!" the voices cried. *"El maa sana eam! Esmou ka! Esmou ka!"*

Larry frowned.

What the hell am I walking into?

The corridor opened into a vast and elaborate new chamber. It possessed a high vaulted ceiling and even more columns and statuary to line and support its towering walls. Thousands of pictographs had been etched into the surrounding stone, displaying arcane messages. Larry was certain that Carol Miyagi could have deciphered them if she'd been there, but as it was, he remained ignorant to whatever message or history the symbols were intended to relay.

At the far end of this temple rose a great statue, larger and more detailed than any of the rest. Larry recognized the effigy immediately as Varuna, the god of the sea, the wellspring from which all life in Poseidon flowed. The enormous sculpture was an exact replica of the figure he'd seen in Colonial Bay, or more likely than not, the one in that hidden temple had been the real imitation.

Between Larry and the statue, a huge crowd stood gathered. They continued on with their strange chant, ignorant of his arrival, and he was shocked by their numbers. As he gazed around the vastness of the temple, there seemed to be far more creatures gathered here than had fled Colonial Bay. In fact, it looked to him as if the population of that island town had more than doubled in the space of a few short years.

My God...

Then, Larry heard a voice shout something in a language he couldn't understand. It was a woman's voice, high and shrill. The chanting of the crowd came to an abrupt halt, replaced by shocked murmurs. Those creatures near the back of the temple turned first, but the wave of movement spread quickly, flowing through the entire congregation. Soon, every dark eye in the chamber was staring back at the entrance to the hallway, staring back at *him*.

Larry shuffled his clawed feet, embarrassed to have interrupted the creatures' ceremony, whatever it might have been. Then, he caught sight of a single figure rising at the base of Varuna's statue, a woman. Like Peggy, she was a Paralicht, her translucent skin glowing in the dimness. She had been seated on a sculpted throne of seashells, and now Larry was caught in her fierce gaze.

Could it be...?

"Barbara!" he called out.

"Barbara DeParle!"

Larry marched into the crowd, made his way toward the stone steps at the base of the statue. At first, the congregation regarded him with uncertainty, but as he went, some members actually reached out to lay their webbed hands upon him, to embrace him, to accept him as one of their own. Larry had never experienced anything like it.

At the first stone step, he stopped and his dawning grin faltered a bit. This woman was not Barbara. She was much younger, younger even than his wife.

To the woman's right, a man sat on a smaller throne of shells; another shark-like Charodon. He stared hard at Larry, growled, but remained seated.

"Who are you?" the young woman demanded, her gaze still sharp as a sword. "How do you know my mother's name?"

"Your *mother?*" Larry blinked. "Christine?"

She said nothing, but he knew it had to be her. Peggy told him how Barbara's daughter, Tellstrom's lover, had helped to turn the tide in Colonial Bay, how the girl had comforted her when she thought Larry had died in the lighthouse explosion. Now, here she was in the flesh.

"My name is Larry," he told her, "Larry Neuhaus, and I've come all the way from New York to find you."

"Mother was right." Christine's eyes suddenly softened, and she seemed to smile at him — the corners of her mouth turned up, her translucent lips stretched thin. "The prodigal son has returned."

PART TWO

Kronos' Return

CHAPTER TWELVE

Vivian Song returned to her office window, overlooking the hangar floor, her eyes glowing red in the dimness. Despite the lateness of the hour, she couldn't sleep; she was far too excited, far too nervous. There was so much riding on this. She kept going over and over it again in her mind — a million things that could go wrong, a million chances for disaster.

There were some "experts" in her inner circle who believed that the creators had sent Hades' disciples instructions not for a door, but for a doomsday weapon. If Vivian opened the gateway in a few short hours, they cautioned, the device would give birth to a ravenous black hole. The event horizon would be impossible to control, impossible to contain. First, this greedy singularity would suck up all the Earth's atmosphere. Then, it would crack the planet's skin like an eggshell, let the Earth's molten heart bleed out until it died in the ever-expanding vacuum. In the end, there would be nothing left of this world. It would be as if the gods had wiped the slate completely clean. Revenge, they said, for Zeus' rebellion.

Vivian shook her horned head.

There were risks, certainly, but there was also that very real, one-in-a-million possibility that these so-called experts were wrong. She had picked Dr. Graeme King for a reason. Zeus or not, she believed in him, which is why she remained confident that everything would go just as planned.

A stable *portal to Kronos.*

Her mind whirled at the potential, at the promise. She was taking a huge gamble here. Nothing like this had ever been attempted before, at least, not by anyone still living on this planet.

Ahhhh, but if it works...

In just a few short hours, the gods would stroll across that Einstein-Rosen bridge and reach through the endless frigid night of space. They would step over the threshold *she* had made possible, would wind up standing right here in front of her. And in that moment, Vivian will have accomplished what no one else could; she will have ended the creators' long exile.

She will have returned the gods to Earth.

And best of all, her mentor, Preacher, would be there to witness it all. After all, this really was *his* vision. The gods had given her a mind and a fire, claws and teeth and ambition, but it was Preacher who had given her *a purpose.* She thought of what he had said to her that very morning, when she'd shown him the gateway for the first time; *"Oh yes, child, it pleases me beyond words. You've done well here, exceeded even my wildest expectations."*

It had been as good as any declaration of love Vivian had ever heard. It made everything she'd done worthwhile.

As she glanced around the hangar floor, her elliptical pupils caught sight of Preacher's former cellmate: Dante "The Horror Show" Vianello. At first, she thought the burly killer might be gazing up at the rafters, might be daydreaming just as she had been.

Vivian began to ponder what such a man might dream about, then she realized that he was staring at the office window; he was staring at *her*.

Dante stood stoic as a statue, and she could glean nothing from his posture or his body language. His face was also unreadable, just as blank and emotionless as a Halloween mask. He didn't even seem to breathe or blink. It was easy for her to see why so many men had found him unsettling and intimidating, even threatening.

Vivian, on the other hand, was no man. She wasn't even human. And she found Dante to be none of those things.

Early on, she'd made a point to never call him Horror Show. She referred to him only by his given name — stripping him of his mystique, of any perceived power, making sure that he knew his place. He'd proven too useful to simply dispose of, but she could never allow herself to be fooled into thinking he was on their side. Dante's only allegiance was to himself, and he would set sail with whatever wind he believed would carry him the farthest.

Vivian stared right back at him, her triangular jaw tightening. She felt the heat swirling in her belly, and for a moment, she pictured Dante bathing in her inferno.

A loud knock pulled her from her sanguine thoughts and dreams.

Irritated, Vivian closed the blinds, cutting off her view of Dante and the hustle and bustle below, darkening the room. She felt her furnace flare, and when she turned to face the office door, a shower of sparks erupted from her nostrils; the embers drifted through the air, their brightness fading as they sank to the floor. "It's open!" she roared.

Benedict stepped inside and shut the door behind him, the clawed tips of his eight chitinous legs clicking and scratching as he crossed the room. "I hoped I'd find you still awake, love."

Yes, Vivian thought, *Benedict, you are the answer to a prayer! Just what I need to pass the time, to wind down, to relax, to take my mind off of...*everything.

Staring at his muscular, powerful physique, she felt heat build in parts of her anatomy that had nothing to do with her inner kiln. She growled, low and feral, showing her fangs, but her tone was just as silky and soft as she could make it, "Come to tuck me in?"

"I—"

Vivian was on him in an instant, cutting off his words with an open-mouthed kiss; her forked tongue slithered over and between his mandibles as if licking fingers clean.

Benedict pulled himself away, perhaps a little reluctantly. "What's this all about, duck?"

"Isn't it obvious?" Vivian stared at him hungrily, eyes full of pure, brazen lust. "I've missed this. It's been a while."

"Yes, well, it hasn't been *that* long."

"Are you saying you don't want me?"

"Let's just say, pleasurable distraction as it may be, I'm not keen on you using my tallywacker as a sleeping pill."

She feigned hurt. "I never—"

"You do, duck. Yes, you do." He shook his bulbous head, and his claws skated across her crown of horns. "Pteralop clan, worried over every little thing as if it meant the end of the world, never able to let your pretty little mind rest."

"Chordata clan," she pushed back with a thin smile, "never worried about a goddamn thing."

"Oh, I worry, love. I just try not to overthink things."

"Yes, well, lucky for us all, there is nothing little about my beautiful mind, and lucky for me, the same can be said about your marvelous tallywacker." Vivian lifted her long tail; it slithered between his many legs, exploring. "This is the eve of our greatest accomplishment, what we've worked for all of our lives, Hades' ultimate triumph over Zeus. You mean to tell me you don't want to help me celebrate *that?*"

Or...if those idiot scientists are right, this could be our last night on Earth, she thought, careful not to allow those words to cross her scaly lips, *and if the world is going to end, I want to spend my final hours with you, my love. I want to go out with a bang!*

Finally, Vivian found what she was looking for. The tip of her tail coiled around his length like a python. She made those coils glide up, down, and around, feeling his pulse throb, feeling him bulge and stiffen within her constricting grip.

"This isn't what I came for," Benedict tried to tell her, his resistance failing. His breathing grew heavier, more rapid, and she saw that the craving in his dark eyes was more than just a reflection of her own. "I — I have news."

"Shhhhhhh..." She pressed one of her talons against the wriggling mandibles of his mouth. "You're ruining the mood. Whatever the news is, you can share it with me later. You have other things to share with me *now.*"

Vivian moved in to kiss him again, and this time, he did not try to push her away. Her leathery wings unfurled; they flapped excitedly, lifting her clawed feet off the floor. She brought her oddly jointed legs up, wrapped them around his humanoid torso, and straddled him.

The dragon grabbed the back of the spider-centaur's head, arching her spiny back, driving her firm scaly breasts up into his face. Benedict's writhing, finger-like mandibles found her left nipple, hard and erect, just like him, and they began to play.

Vivian felt delicious pressure as he pinched, tugged, and sucked at her golden stem. His fangs could not puncture her armor, but as he stoked her desire, she hoped he would find another way to pierce her.

She was not disappointed.

Benedict's left hand gripped her hip, while his right hand probed between her legs. His sharpened talons picked at the thick scales near the root of her tail; they moved upward, inward, tracing the outer rim of her anus, the wavy lips of her vulva, and raking the gold-plated flesh in between, creating a rasping sound, like metal nails scraping chain link. And when his eager claws finally found the engorged nub of her clitoris, Vivian moaned.

"Yes," she hissed; her hands moved to grip Benedict's spiked shoulders, her wings fanned the air. "There...right there...harder, *faster!*"

His clawed fingers obeyed her commands. They swirled and stroked, matching the movements of her tail, the tail that still held his sex hostage within its tightening coils.

Vivian felt Benedict's mandibles moving all over her golden torso, making their way up the scaly length of her arched neck. Suddenly, he spun her around. He pressed her against the nearest wall, continuing to tease her with his roving mouth and his probing claws. Having her back against the cinderblock did not hamper Vivian's leathery wings; they stretched and flapped, slapping the sides of Benedict's head in a flurry of ecstasy. The spider-centaur made no attempt to restrain them. Instead, he began to crawl up the wall with her, his eight spindly legs pushing the dragon toward the ceiling as she bucked and writhed beneath him.

When her horned head touched the corrugated metal roof, she pushed back with all of her might, her wings and pectoral muscles working to take Benedict airborne, flying him across the room. They landed on a wooden desk, their combined weight and momentum shattering the office furniture to splinters. Their wide-open mouths found each other again in the rubble, meeting in a melee of piercing tongues and grasping appendages.

Vivian continued to straddle Benedict, pinning the spider down. She rose up with a low growl, positioning herself, feeling just the glorious start of penetration. Savoring the moment, she sank slowly onto him, allowing the entire length she'd caressed with her tail to now fill her utterly. Her reptilian eyes fluttered closed, surrendering to the intense pleasure.

I've missed this. Oh, how I've missed this...this connection, this bond. Every day, I have to think about so many, and yet I feel so isolated, so alone, but not with you, my love. Never with you...

She rode him, moved with him, and together, they built a steady rhythm.

Benedict's multiple legs embraced her, grasped her, their clawed tips pulling her down again and again, binding her to him.

She moaned into his fidgeting mouth, and he responded with wordless grunts.

When Vivian opened her eyes again, she saw her movements mirrored in the dark domes of Benedict's compound eyes. Over the years, men had leered at her human guise and called her beautiful. No. She was more than happy to finally be done with that ghastly pretense. The way she appeared now, *Au naturel*, lean and powerful, confident and strong, not despite her femininity, but *because of it...* this was true beauty.

Vivian kept her hips moving, her arousal building with each of Benedict's deepening thrusts. A part of her wanted this intense coupling to go on forever, but it wasn't long before she saw Benedict's face contort into orgasm — a burst of raw physical pleasure that filled her with an explosive gush of warmth. Craving her own release, she reached down to cup her sex, feverishly rubbing her clit with her claws, bringing herself to a shuddering climax that left her tingling and trembling all at once.

She collapsed onto Benedict's chest, panting, spent. Her wings ceased their frantic movements; they went limp, draped over them both like thick leathery blankets. And the air in the office hung quiet and still.

Vivian couldn't stop shaking. "Jesus," she managed. "You don't know how much I needed that."

"When you're gagging for it, duck, you go all out." Benedict snatched a broken leg of the desk off the floor and held it up for her inspection. "Don't think we've every trashed a room before."

"After tomorrow," she told him, finally catching her breath, "we won't need this place. The work will be done."

He stroked her elongated neck with his talons. "I hope you're right."

I hope so, too, my love. And I would rather die hopeful than live a long life in despair, longing for something that can never be. To be able to live like this, fuck *like this, unabashed and unafraid. Truly, it is worth any risk.*

Vivian kissed his chitinous forehead. "You said you had news," she reminded him. "Good news, I hope."

Benedict hesitated. "Our people in Japan," he told her, "they've found your cousin."

"Katsu?"

He nodded.

"Damn that tiger," she said with a smile. "Clearly, he's much better with a sword and a bottle than he is with his phone. Where did they find him — lying drunk in some brothel?"

"Actually, love, he was lying dead in a shallow grave."

She rose up, startled, staring into Benedict's two largest eyes. "What?"

"Buried behind the Miyagi family home."

Vivian frowned. "That's not funny."

"Yes, well, it's not a joke. He's gone, duck. Someone's killed him."

Damn.

Vivian paused, letting the news sink in. She and Katsu had never been close, but the tiger-man was fiercely loyal, and over the years, she had counted on him and his sword. She'd tasked him with eliminating the archeologist, Carol Miyagi, the woman who could read the language of the gods, the only Zeus who could decipher the various crop symbols and discover what Hades' disciples were planning. It had been a remote risk, but one Vivian had been unwilling to take.

"At least tell me that he did his fucking job," she said, "that they found Miyagi buried right alongside him?"

"'Fraid not, love. Your bloke was very much alone, and Miyagi and her lover are currently in the wind."

Vivian considered, took her time. Benedict's multiple eyes were focused on her, waiting. She gazed down at him and shrugged.

"I suppose it doesn't matter now," she said.

"No?"

"No. The gateway is already done. Do you honestly think she has even the slightest chance of preventing its success?"

"I suppose not," Benedict agreed.

Vivian ran her golden talons down his cheek, thinking once more of the world they would build together, of the future children they would spawn to fill it. For so long, it had all been a dream, far away and out of reach, but it grew closer to reality with each passing day, and now, every minute that ticked by brought it nearer to her grasp. She was not about to let it slip through her clawed fingers.

"I'm far more concerned with Earl Preston and his friends," she said. "Any word yet on *them?*"

"Not yet," Benedict admitted, "but don't get your knickers in a twist, duck. It's a big underground, an entire city beneath this city. It might take a bit to root them out, even for rats."

She snarled, and he reached up to press a talon to her golden lips, quieting her. His other arm coiled around her neck, offering a reassuring hug.

"Like you said, love," he told her, "we've got all the skulls and the gateway's done. At this point, what can they do?"

Vivian honestly didn't know, and she didn't want to think about it, not tonight. She was far too exhausted, far too content. Benedict was right, his tallywacker made for a marvelous sleeping pill. She lowered her horned head onto his armored chest, and after a few quiet moments in his embrace, she finally found rest.

Her mind grew quiet, but not completely silent. The dream was the same as it had been every night of her entire life, but the day seemed brighter; clear, and crisp, and clean. She moved toward the black pyramid, toward its open doorway. Her creators were there, waiting on the other side of that door. She knew it, just as she also knew that, when she awoke, she would finally get to meet them.

And together, what a world they would make!

CHAPTER THIRTEEN

Horror Show strolled slowly through the cavernous old aircraft hangar like a man lost in a dream. After years of incarceration, it felt good to be out in the world again, to be able to move around, to have a bit of fucking elbow room! He rubbed the smooth ridge of scarring that broke up his rough, stubble-covered throat; his "Frankenstein line." Even if nobody knew who the fuck he was because of this scar, because of his taller-than-average height and his muscular build, the former hitman usually stood out. Today had been no exception. "Normal people" had always considered him to be a monster, but in this place? Other than that egghead, Dr. King, Horror Show was the only one here who was wholly human.

And you better watch out, Dr. King! After Vivian Song flicks that goddamn switch tomorrow morning, all those "normal people" out there might just consider you *a monster too. We'll be a two-man crew, you and me: aiders and abettors to the apocalypse!*

Horror Show chuckled bitterly.

People threw the word "apocalypse" around like it actually meant the end of fucking everything! That wasn't really true. Oh, it was an ending all right, just not in the way most people thought. Horror Show's mother had taught him that the word was derived from the Greek "apokalypsis," which meant "unveiling" or "revelation." It had little to do with a great disaster, and more in common with one of the woman's favorite sayings, "Out with the old and in with the new."

That's exactly what Preacher, Vivian, and their followers here had in mind.

Out with the old and in with the new.

Horror Show thought of all those "normal people" out there. Right now, they were probably sleeping soundly in their beds. The nine to fivers had their clothes all laid out and their alarms all set, and each and every one of them was probably dreading the long, boring workday that lay ahead.

None of them had a fucking clue as to what the dawn would really bring.

Horror Show knew. Even so, he had no idea what form Vivian Song's change would take. Not really. The bitch was keeping that particular information close to her gold-plated breast.

Out with the old and in with the new.

Horror Show reached into the deep well of his pants pocket. His fingers still longed for the touch of that granite shard, the chip he'd taken off John Dillinger's tombstone; smooth as glass on one side, rough on the other. It had been the hitman's good luck charm for many years, serving as a reminder that stupid mistakes got you nothing but a one-way ticket to the grave. He had no idea where the shard was—

Probably sealed up in some evidence bag somewhere, gathering dust next to Ol' Pearl.

—but right now, Horror Show felt as if he were in need of that little reminder.

His fingers wrapped instead around the cool scaliness of Vivian Song's disembodied claw. The dragon had gnawed off her own goddamn talon and handed it over to him. Of course, she'd done it to stage a prison break, to set Preacher free and bring the old werewolf here. She had no idea what Horror Show planned to use the serrated blade for after that. No idea at all.

He stopped in his tracks, his wandering eyes climbing the metal staircase that ended at Vivian's office door. There, he saw the golden dragon herself. She stood at the window, and for a moment, their malignant stares locked. They stood there, appraising one another across the crowded room; two alphas sizing each other up in silent challenge, neither wanting to be the first to show any sign of weakness.

Horror Show's grip tightened around the severed claw in his pocket. *I can do this all fuckin' day, bitch. How 'bout you?*

Vivian may not have blinked, but she reached up and closed the office blinds, bringing their staring contest to an abrupt end.

In that moment, Horror Show wanted nothing more than to charge up those metal steps, break down that office door, and to lunge at Vivian Song with her own fucking claw. Instead, he simply shook his head and forced himself to relax his grip on the talon. A smile crossed his face, full of acid.

There was no need to rush.

If this gateway managed to work, if these gods of theirs really did return, Vivian would be done with him then, and Horror Show would be done with her. *That* would be the moment to strike. He would let Vivian see all of her hopes and dreams realized, and then, in the midst of her greatest happiness, her wildest joy, he would slit her fucking throat. He would watch her life's blood flow hot and thick, cascading down her golden scales in scarlet torrents, and best of all, he would watch her inner fire grow cold, he would see her flame snuffed as her basilisk eyes grew lifeless and dark.

Horror Show took in a long stuttering breath, imagining it. It would be incredible, he thought, to actually slay a fucking dragon; like nothing he'd ever experienced. And when the deed was done, no matter what happened to him, live or die, there would be nothing that could ever take that victory away.

He would be hailed a hero by some, made a boogeyman by others. Either way, Dante "The Horror Show" Vianello would become the stuff of legend.

As he turned away from the office window, something else caught his eye — a few bright flashes of light. His head snapped toward the wide-open doorway of the hangar. Had that been lightning? No, the sky was clear.

Then, it came again, a short, rapid succession of flares.

That almost looks like...muzzle flash. Weapons fire!

This time, Horror Show saw where the burst came from — a small building. It sat on the opposite side of the cracked runway, away from the hustle and bustle of main hangars.

"What the fuck?"

Horror Show cocked his head and took a few quick steps out of the hangar onto the crumbling tarmac. He didn't hear any shots, but if there really were active shooters, SWAT or Navy Seals; they could've been using silencers. In addition to suppressing sound, they would also reduce the amount of flare their guns gave off when fired, but they couldn't eradicate it completely.

He reached out for the nearest passing creature, grabbed it by its feathery arm, and pulled it over to him. At first glance, Horror Show thought the thing in his grip was a griffin, like Hans, but no. While this beast had the head and wings of an eagle, its bottom half was more like a Clydesdale than a lion.

"That place over there," Horror Show demanded, pointing toward the shadowy structure across the tarmac. "What the fuck is it?"

Startled, the chimera blinked, then its avian eyes swiveled to follow Horror Show's finger. "That's the old control tower," it told him. "This place used to be an airport."

"No shit. Anybody supposed to be in there right now?"

The beast shrugged. "There's usually a few guards on lookout, but I—"

"Go find a security guard and send 'em over to me." Horror Show released his grip on the eagle-horse-thing, whatever the hell it was; it seemed more than eager to move away from him. "Get me somebody with a big fuckin' gun!"

The only weapon Vivian had allowed him was her disembodied claw, but Horror Show wasn't about to bring a knife into a gun battle. He also didn't want to sound any major alarms, start a general panic, at least, not until he knew more.

Not one but two armed guards approached him from the crowd. One was a bat-like gargoyle with devil horns and a nasty under bite. The other was a badger with black and white facial markings and sharp teeth. Both carried M4 Carbines, shorter and lighter variants of the M16 assault rifle.

"What seems to be the problem?" the badger-man asked. He held the rifle in front of him, not aiming it, but Horror Show could tell that he wasn't happy to be answering the call of a human on the eve of their grand revolution.

"Jesus, could you sound any more like a fuckin' Rent-A-Cop?"

Horror Show rolled his eyes, then he took his hand from his pocket and aimed Vivian's severed claw at the building across the way. "My *problem* is that I think I saw gunfire in that old control tower over there, and I don't think any of us want it to become Vivian Song's problem. So I suggest we go and have a look and make sure that, whatever the fuck it is, it doesn't ruin her big day."

The armed creatures glanced at one another, then gave their attention back to Horror Show.

"Lead the way," the badger told him.

Together, they walked on, crossing the broken runway. A huge bear with the head of an owl passed by them, thick coils of cable slung over its hairy shoulder and a large thermos in its claw; its huge eyes glowed bright yellow in the dark, yet it moved on as if it hadn't seen a thing. The same for a pair of lizard people who walked by a second later; they were laughing and talking about the thrilling day ahead, but they said nothing about the rapid bursts of light from the old building. Horror Show appeared to be the only one who had even noticed.

That's why I'm still alive after all these years, he reasoned. *I take notice of shit that other people don't. While a victim walks into a situation blindly, I see a dozen different ways it can go south.*

Horror Show stepped off the cracked pavement, trudged through the tall grass and overgrown weeds of the unkempt yard, and as he drew nearer to the old tower, more details of the structure became clear. The building was a two-story brick façade that reminded him of a school house. There were dozens of windows, and limestone steps leading up to a set of double doors. Limestone crowned the walls as well, and carved into it were the words "Delancey Field" in big block letters.

What really set the building apart, however, was its tall, hexagonal turret. The tower was capped by a windowed structure set high above every other building on the airfield. Various antennae sprouted from its roof, huge metal tuning forks that now stood bent and broken after years of neglect.

Staring up at the tower, Horror Show nodded, agreeing with the decision to station someone up there. From that vantage point, a lookout could watch over the entire peninsula, could see a raid or assault coming from miles away. By the same token, if an enemy had somehow infiltrated the airfield and found its way up there...it would be the perfect place from which to spy and gather Intel, the perfect place from which to plot and direct an attack.

"So what's your plan?"

Horror Show turned toward the sound of the voice and saw that it was the gargoyle-thing who'd spoken. The hitman offered the creature a shrug. "It should be our guys in there; am I right?"

"Yeah."

"So I'm gonna knock."

Keeping a tight grip on Vivian's claw, Horror Show mounted the limestone steps and made his way up to the large wooden doors at the base of the tower. Behind him, the guards advanced a little more cautiously, but when he glanced over his shoulder, Horror Show saw that the two creatures held their weapons at the ready. He lifted a fisted hand to the door and gave a loud knock.

"Hey in there," he shouted. "Open up a minute!"

It remained silent for a few moments.

"Maybe they didn't hear you," the badger-man said.

And maybe they're all dead, Horror Show thought, but he said nothing.

Then, they heard someone moving around inside, someone coming toward the entrance. Horror Show tensed, and when the door swung open, he found himself staring into the long snaggle-toothed maw of a walking crocodile. The creature held an M-16 in its scaly claw, but its muzzle was aimed harmlessly at the limestone steps in front of him.

"How can I help you guys?" the reptilian asked.

CHAPTER FOURTEEN

Chud reached out with his reptilian claws and grabbed hold of the chain link. He found the metal security fencing cold against his leathery skin; it must have been twenty feet high, topped with jagged coils of razor wire for good measure. And even in darkness, he had no trouble reading the metal signage someone had posted at regular intervals:

WARNING
PRIVATE PROPERTY
NO TRESPASSING
KEEP OUT!

The fencing was old, rusted in spots, but despite its age and corrosion, it seemed sturdy enough. Chud gave the chain link a good tug, listening to its metallic rattle. Zuri and Earl were right there at his side, and from the frustrated looks on their faces, he could tell they'd come to the same conclusion he had.

"Unless one of us is a Pteralop, and can sprout a pair of goddamn wings—" Chud glanced over at Earl, knowing better. "—I don't see us gettin' over this thing. Do you?"

"You know, Chud, I gotta be honest with you, bro, I had my doubts, but this here...this is serious! This is like some Guantanamo Bay shit right here. They really don't want us gettin' in there."

"No security cameras," Zuri noted; her eyes skated across the razor wire, then she sniffed at the air, "and I do not smell anyone nearby. No patrols, at least, not this far away from the main facility."

Chud nodded in agreement. He could smell the tall grass, a hint of salty sea water from the bay, but present company excluded, he couldn't smell any member of any clan, not even Zeus. Lifting his M-16, Chud peered through the night scope, looking three hundred yards ahead of them.

He wondered how close they were to the old airport buildings and how far they would have to hike across open terrain to get there. The crocodile-man couldn't see in infrared, but if this really was Hades' stronghold, there would be plenty of creatures on the other side of this fence who could, creatures who were part snake, part insect, or part frog. They would be able to find them even hunkered down and hiding in the weeds. For the moment, however, everything appeared to be clear.

They were all alone out here in the dark.

What was it Grandma always used to say? "The night is our ally."

She was a wise one, his grandma.

"Our friends in there probably don't think anybody's brave enough, or *stupid enough*, to do what we're about to do here," Earl told them, "but it's cool. We'll give 'em a big surprise."

Earl had a bulky duffle bag slung across his shoulders; it was heavy, loaded with their own meager supplies, plus all the knives, weapons, and other equipment they'd taken from the dead and imprisoned rat-men. Now, he slipped it off his back and dropped it onto the damp grass with a loud *THUD*.

Zuri's hand melted and re-formed itself into a hooked, hairy claw. "I can dig us a way under."

"No need to ruin your manicure." Earl unzipped the canvas bag and riffled through its contents until he found what he was looking for: a large pair of wire cutters. "Y'all gimme a minute, I'll cut us a door we can walk right on through."

Earl stepped up to the fence and knelt down. Slowly, he began to snip apart the metal links in front of him.

"I can't believe none of those rat-dudes had a fuckin' cell phone," he complained between grunts and snips. "Not even a damn burner!"

"They are very careful, my love," Zuri told him, her eyes still scanning the field on the other side of the fencing. "They want nothing, no numbers, no messages or GPS that could tie them back to this place or any other stronghold Hades might have. It is the same reason we smashed your phone before we brought you into our underground home."

"Yeah, thanks for that," he huffed. "And great job it did, too. They still managed to find my black ass."

"True, but they had to work for it, didn't they? Had you kept your precious phone, it would have made it much easier for them to pinpoint your exact location. We might all have been caught off guard, and we might all be dead now."

"I know, you're right," Earl regretfully acknowledged, then he added, "just never been this long without a phone before."

"Who would you even call?" Chud wanted to know.

"My boss, Patrick Tate," he pointed to the neon yellow printing on his bulletproof vest, "Assistant Director of Homeland fuckin' Security."

"And what could he do for us?"

"Tate? He'd have the entire NYPD up in here, that's what, the whole FBI. Hell, with his authority, he could probably scramble a squadron of F-16s to firebomb this place right off the fuckin' map."

"If it is the right place," Zuri pointed out.

"Yeah," Earl agreed, snipping through a few more links, "if it's the right fuckin' place."

"Don't forget Larry's wife is probably still in there," Chud reminded. "So, I wouldn't go droppin' any firebombs on the place just yet, Rambo."

"You think I don't know?" Earl said with a frustrated grunt. "They got at least two hostages up in there, Larry's wife and my theoretical physicist, Dr. King, which is why we need to get past this fence ASAFP. The plan is—"

"We have a plan?" Zuri teased, her eyes still on the field beyond the chain link. "I thought we were playing all of this by ear."

"We get in there," Earl told them, "we see what's what, free who needs to be freed if we can, but no matter what the fuck we find in there, nobody plays hero, and nobody acts alone. We go in together, we bug the hell out together, and we all go and find a damn phone together so I can call in the fuckin' cavalry. Agreed?"

"Agreed," Zuri told him.

"Sure," Chud said, "sounds good to me."

Earl rose up off his knees. He snipped a few more links with the wire cutters, then glanced over at Chud. "You know, when I was a kid, there used to be phone booths on every city sidewalk. Now—"

"Now, there's only like four of those things left in the whole fuckin' town, and they're all up on West End Avenue, at 101st, 100th, 90th and 66th Streets. That's it. They're dinosaurs."

"Takes one to know one," Earl chuckled. Then, he added, "How the hell is Superman supposed to save the day if he can't even find a place to change into his goddamn suit?" He made two final snips, then stepped back and wiped his forearm across his sweaty brow. "There, I think that's got it."

Chud looked at what Earl had done. His clips in the chain-link fence didn't form anything resembling a door. At best, it was a narrow slit with sharp metal teeth on either side. Hardly ideal.

The crocodile-man reached out with his talons and pulled the fencing apart, widening the gap.

Zuri was the first to squeeze through; once on the other side, she knelt down in the high grass, sniffed once more at the air, then motioned for the men to come and join her. Earl threw the wire cutters back into his duffle bag, tossed it over to her, then carefully crawled between the severed links. Finally, it was Chud's turn; his body was larger than either of his friends, but he still managed to muscle his way through the narrow breach without a scratch.

Clustered there beside the security fence, Earl reached back into his bag of tricks. He removed a pair of silencers, handed one to Zuri and the other to Chud. "We don't want to draw any unwanted attention," he warned them, his voice now lowered to a whisper, as if their enemies could somehow hear them better now that they were on this side of the breach, "so don't shoot unless you have to. But if you do have to, these should help to soften the noise a bit."

Chud attached the sound suppressor to his own rifle, then watched Zuri do the same for hers.

Earl took a Beretta M9 pistol for himself, capping it with a third silencer. He removed a few extra ammunition clips before zipping the canvas back up again. Then, he slung the bag's weight over his shoulders and rose up. "Let's go."

Moving through the shadowy grass, Zuri led her companions

across a wide-open field. Chud brought up the rear. He was confident, but far from comfortable. The crocodile-man was used to the feel of hard unforgiving concrete, of asphalt and cobblestone beneath his clawed feet. Here, the ground was soft, springy, and his talons dug into the soil with ease. He kicked up dirt and stray bits of grass as he hurried to keep up with his companions.

As he moved, his eyes darted backward, forward, and side-to-side, keeping a constant lookout for one or more of Hades' disciples. They were completely exposed out here. He tightened his grip on the rifle in his hands.

If we got into a firefight now, I don't know if we'd be able to make it all the way back to the fence, to find the exact spot where we cut through, to crawl out of here again. He looked at the duffle bag on Earl's back. *We've only got so much ammo with us...We get pinned down, it'll be like Butch and Sundance against the whole Bolivian army. It won't fuckin' end well!*

He looked up at the sky, the faint glow of light pollution from the city fading into black.

The night is our ally.

From infancy, his parents and his grandmother had engrained in him the idea that underground was the safest place to be, free of danger and risk. And to this day, Chud still believed it. He ventured onto the city streets only when necessary, and always under cover of darkness. Even then, he'd made it a point to be aware of his surroundings, to know where to find the closest storm drain, the nearest alleyway or subway platform, an escape route constantly at the ready. Now, however, there was nowhere to run, no place to really hide. The crocodile-man could only wonder what his long-dead elders might say if they could see him out here.

They'd say I was out of my friggin' mind, following a Cerberus and a Zeus on some insane crusade that's none of my damn business.

Chud shook his head. Given the odds, it might be insane, and it *was* his business. What they were doing out here tonight was important, not just for him, not just for New York, but for everyone everywhere; the whole damn world. He trusted Zuri, trusted Earl, and wherever they led, he would follow.

He would do what was right.

Zuri came to a sudden halt in the tall grass and motioned for Earl and Chud to do the same. The crocodile-man looked through the scope of his rifle, trying to see what she had seen. A few hundred yards head of them, this wild unkempt turf gave rise to man-made structures, and Chud caught his first glimpse of the long-dead airport. Now, however, the distant hangars of Delancey Field showed obvious signs of life; he saw light, *movement.*

I was right. This is *the place.*

Luckily, the activity was all upwind from their current position. The breeze couldn't alert the enemy to their presence, but it could give Chud a clue as to what they were up against. His nostrils flared, taking in traces of Cerberus, Pteralop, and Chordata clans; they were all here, all working toward a single goal.

Kronos' return.

Zuri waved her hand to draw his attention, then pointed to her left.

Chud swung his rifle in that direction, peering once more through his scope. The building closest to them was a large rectangular structure made wholly of brick. It was set apart from all the hangars across the tarmac, and unlike them, it was still dark, perhaps vacant.

Earl didn't say a word. Instead, he gave Zuri a nod and a pat on the back.

Chud nodded as well. He was eager to get out of this wide-open field, to find some form of cover, of sanctuary, no matter what it might be.

Any port in the storm.

When Zuri and Earl took off through the grass, Chud sprinted after them. Once again, he tried to stay low and keep out of sight. They drew closer to the light, to danger, but nothing moved to confront them or challenge their progress in any way.

They dashed up to Delancey Field's old control tower and flattened their backs against its brick wall, hiding in the shadows. Chud looked up at the windows above his head, at the roof and the glass octagon of the tower itself; all appeared silent and dark. He swallowed hard, then glanced over at his companions.

"What's the plan?" he whispered, still breathing heavily.

"We get inside," Earl told him, "get up to that control tower, and then we see what we can see."

"And if there's disciples in there?"

Earl shrugged. "We take 'em out."

"Just like that?"

"Just like that," Earl repeated with conviction.

Chud looked to Zuri for further confirmation.

"Just like that," she agreed, leveling her rifle and flashing a demure grin.

Chud could never say no to that grin.

"All right." The crocodile-man took a deep breath, his clawed finger on the trigger of his own M16. "I got your back."

Still steeped in shadow, they crept up limestone steps to a set of double doors. Zuri reached out for a rusted metal handle. She looked back at Earl, who offered her an exaggerated nod. Then, she gave the wooden door a tug; it pulled open with ease.

Here we go. It's game time!

Earl rushed past her and entered the darkened structure with his right arm extended, his pistol level and ready to fire. Chud followed him in, watching as his friend checked every darkened corner. The floor was littered with cracked tile and chips of old, crumbling grout, grit that crunched softly beneath their footfalls. It was a low noise, one human ears might not even register, but Chud noticed it, and he could not help but worry other creatures might hear it as well.

At least there was no breeze, no working HVAC, no spinning ceiling fans, nothing to circulate the air in this place at all. Chud inhaled deeply. The entire structure stank of mold and mildew, of dust and rot. The scents hung thick in the stillness; almost overpowering. Chud hoped it would be enough to mask his friends' musk, because he knew that they were not alone in this place.

Other hearts were beating within these walls. Chud heard them, and as he listened, as he tried to pinpoint their exact locations, he was fairly certain those unseen creatures were doing the exact same thing.

Have to get the drop on these pricks is all. Hit 'em fast, don't give 'em time to think! We did okay against those rat-fucks, didn't we? Hell, yeah, we did!

Up ahead, if Earl was worried, he showed no outward signs. The man paused to calmly shed the duffle bag from his back, keeping his eyes and pistol on the path in front of them. After lowering the heavy canvas down onto the floor, he stepped toward an open archway, his gait rapid but steady; the words, *HOMELAND SECURITY INVESTIGATION* were now plainly visible across the back of his bulletproof vest.

One of those other heartbeats...Chud could hear it getting louder, closing in. He looked around wildly, trying to determine exactly where it was coming from.

Suddenly, bullets flew at them from the darkness of the next room. Hades must have been using silencers as well. Despite their name, the suppressors did not completely quash the sound of gunfire, and the muffled *POP-POP-POP* gave Chud a start. One of the bullets whizzed right by his head as he ducked down to avoid it.

Earl returned fire, quick flashes erupting from the end of his silencer. Chud pulled his trigger as well, sending a dozen or more shells flying back into the dark. A quiet moment passed, both of them waiting for a response and hearing none. Finally, Earl crept forward once more. Chud was a bit slower to rise, but eventually he followed him.

In the next room, a weredeer lay in a pool of blood; large branching forks of antlers propped its fallen head up off the tile. Earl pumped two safety rounds into its body, then quickly turned away, moving on.

Chud's attention, on the other hand, stayed riveted to the corpse on the floor. He watched the draining blood darken its pelt, spreading from clusters of exit wounds all across its back. The crocodile-man wondered for a moment which of them had fired the fatal shot then supposed it really didn't matter.

A rifle lay next to one of the weredeer's lifeless hands. It *was* equipped with a silencer, one just like theirs. Chud kicked the weapon away.

Another heartbeat. It came up quickly from behind.

Chud whirled to face its owner, his finger on the trigger, but when he saw Zuri standing there, the crocodile-man instantly relaxed. "I almost shot your face off," he whispered.

Zuri lifted a frantic finger to her lips, reminding him to keep quiet.

POP-POP-POP

Shit!

Startled, Chud's eyes and rifle snapped forward once more. He rushed toward the sounds of gunfire, toward Earl, and along the way, he found another body his friend had left in his wake.

An iguana-creature lay slumped against the wall, a Beretta 93R 9mm machine pistol still clutched in its clawed hands. It never got off a shot. Earl put two bullets into its leathery chest and a third through the center of its sloped forehead. A long reptilian tail jutted out from between its legs and snaked across the floor, limp and inert.

"Jesus," Chud breathed. *Glad Earl's on our side.*

He wondered if he should pump a couple of safety rounds into this new body, then decided against it. There was no heartbeat that he could detect, no pulse, and they would need to conserve their ammo.

Chud moved on, scrambling to catch up with Earl, and he felt Zuri right there behind him. As a group, they cleared the rest of the first floor, then quickly made their way to a deserted stairwell.

Still in the lead, Earl was the first to mount the steps. His shoulder brushed the wall as he went up, his eyes and pistol held high, aiming for whatever might come down the staircase.

When Chud went to follow him, anxiety played across the length of his snout. Outside, they'd been vulnerable because they were exposed in a wide-open space. Now, the exact opposite was true. In this confined stairwell, they would be an easy target if another of Hades' disciples decided to come out blasting.

Earl had his tactical vest, but Chud and Zuri had no shield at all.

Chud swallowed hard. He lowered his eyes a moment, checking his footing on the old steps. Another muffled *POP-POP* made him jump and he saw muted muzzle flashes light up the stairs. His head snapped up again to find a body tumbling down the steps at him.

Christ!

Chud leapt back and the corpse rolled onto the landing where he'd just been standing. It wasn't Earl. No, this was a lifeless mound of bloodied fur. Chud took one clawed hand off his rifle and turned the thing over, bringing it face up. It was a spotted leopard-man; a wide tongue hung from its open mouth and its once bright eyes grew dull in the dimness.

At his side, Zuri muttered something Chud couldn't understand. *Swahili?*

Then, she gave him a gentle nudge to keep going.

The crocodile-man pushed past the furry body, Zuri following close behind. Together, they climbed the staircase to the second floor.

Large windows lined the brick outer wall. Chud raced over to one of them and peered outside. Though muffled, he worried the sounds of their gunfire might have drawn a crowd. When he looked across the tarmac, however, he didn't see anyone approaching. All the activity was still clustered around the main hangar.

POP-POP

THUD

POP-POP-POP

THUD-THUD

Chud's eyes and snout jerked instantly toward the ceiling. The gunshots came in rapid succession, so did the sound of falling bodies.

Zuri heard it too. She snarled, and Chud could see the sudden fear ignite in her eyes; fear not for herself, but for Earl. Zuri raised her rifle, bolting past Chud as if he weren't even there. Her booted feet pounded the wooden flooring, going full tilt. The crocodile-man did his best to keep up with her, but his squat little legs were simply not used to all this hiking, running, and climbing.

They made their way to the center of the floor and another

narrow staircase. This one, Chud knew, would take them into the control tower itself.

Zuri mounted the steps without hesitation, her rifle up.

The crocodile-man paused to do a quick spin, looking in every direction to make certain there was no one else there to follow them, no one to ambush them from behind. When he was satisfied the coast was clear, only then did he begin his climb.

The coppery smell of blood wafted down the stairs, so thick even Zeus would have noticed it.

Chud saw a flash of movement across the third-floor landing above, and if Zuri hadn't been there in his path, he might have actually opened fire.

Zuri stopped climbing and her mouth hung open for a beat. Chud knew she was fighting the urge to call out. He knew because, in that moment, he was waging that very same battle himself.

After a long pause, she gave in, "Earl?"

Silence.

"Earl?" Zuri said again, louder now, concern on her face and in her voice.

This time, she got her reply.

"I'm good," Earl called back down the stairs. "All clear. Tower's secure."

Zuri breathed a sigh of relief, but she did not lower her weapon, not yet. She resumed her climb.

Chud was right there behind her. He rose up into an octagon of glass, his M16 growing heavier in his grasp.

Beneath the windows, control panels lined every wall. They were dark, inoperative, and covered in blood splatter. Bullet-riddled bodies lay strewn across the floor, and Earl stood victorious over them.

"Holy fucking shit, Earl," Chud exclaimed, happy to be able to talk at a normal volume once more, "you're like a one-man Seal Team Six!"

"I'm lucky as hell, that's all I am."

Earl knelt down next to one of the bodies. He set his pistol down on the floor, then removed a small black and yellow walkie talkie from the dead creature's belt. Earl studied the radio a moment, his expression souring.

"Son of a bitch." He rose to his feet again. "Generic, short-range piece a crap. Probably license free, too. You can forget what I said about luck. I ain't callin' out for shit with this thing."

"Don't you know any police frequencies?" Chud asked.

Earl glared back at him. "Hell, yeah, I know 'em, but this thing is just a step above a kid's toy. Its range is so fuckin' short, the cops would have to literally be drivin' down the tarmac out there before they'd be able to pick it up."

Certain now that it was safe, Zuri lowered her rifle as she marched over to Earl. He flashed a smile and she slapped it from his face.

"Ow!" he exclaimed, taking a hand off the walkie talkie to rub the sting from his cheek. The look in his eyes was more confused than angry. "What the fuck was that about?"

"'Nobody plays hero,' you said, 'nobody acts alone.' You shouldn't have gone off ahead like that." She reached out, grabbed the arm hole of Earl's bulletproof vest, and gave it a hard tug, nearly pulling the man off his feet. *This* does not make you invulnerable. You should have waited for us. We are a team, Earl Preston!"

She let go of him and took a step back, still fuming.

Earl's confusion quickly turned to contrition. "Girl, you're right. I saw the shots and I took 'em. I didn't mean to...Look, I'm sorry."

She stared at him a moment before responding, her face softening. "Apology accepted."

He adjusted his vest. "We good?"

"Yes," she told him. "We are fine, and if at all possible, I would like us all to stay this way."

"Back when I was in the Coast Guard, there was this seaman, Peck, and I'd always tell him—"

"The guy's name was Semen?" Chud interrupted with a chuckle.

"It's a rank, Sleestak." Earl rolled his eyes at the crocodile-man. "What are you, twelve? Jesus, when I was a Petty Officer, I..." His voice trailed off, and he took a few steps across the room, staring intently out the window behind Chud's head. "The fuck is that?"

"What is it?" Zuri asked, suddenly worried. "What do you see?"

"Oh, shit." Earl pointed down through the glass. "We got company."

Chud turned and followed Earl's finger to a trio of figures parading across the tarmac toward the tall grass, headed for the tower. He saw a Pteralop and a Cerberus, both carrying weapons; they flanked a seemingly unarmed Zeus. The man in the middle was tall, strong, clearly capable of holding his own in a fight, but at first glance there was nothing remarkable about him. He was just a normal human being.

Was this Earl's theoretical physicist — the guy Hades' disciples took to help them build their gateway?

"Chud," Earl held out his hand, "gimme your scope a sec."

The crocodile-man handed his rifle over. He watched Earl peer down at the approaching trio through the night vision scope.

"Horror Show," Earl blurted. "I'll be damned. How in the hell..."

"What should we do?" Zuri wanted to know.

"We take 'em out, right?" Chud glanced from Zuri to Earl as he took back his M-16. "Wasn't that the plan? I mean, there's three of us and three of them."

Earl shook his head. "If somebody heard our exchange of gunfire, Vivian and Benny might have sent these bozos to check it out. If they don't report back...we could be in for some serious trouble."

"I will go and talk to them," Zuri volunteered. "I will make them think that all is well, get them to walk away."

She turned toward the stairs, but Earl grabbed her by the arm to stop her.

"Your scent might give you away," he warned. "Whether they recognize it or not, either way it might trigger some red flags. We don't have time to hide all these fuckin' bodies, and we can't let them inside to see this mess."

"Man's got a point," Chud told her, looking around at all the blood-splattered consoles.

Earl went on to say, "There's a ton of creatures walkin' around this airfield, right? What we need is somebody who could've been workin' here the whole time without them realizing it, somebody who could've stayed under their radar, somebody that, maybe, they can't smell at all."

Even before their eyes went to him, Chud knew what was coming. He glanced back out the tower window. This man, Horror Show, and the two disciples were already at the front steps.

They had to do something, and they had to do it fast.

"How do you want me to handle it?" Chud asked. He stood straighter, tightened his grip on his M16.

————

Pounding on the front door.

Chud heard it as he reached the lower stairwell. He almost forgot about the dead leopard-man on the landing, almost tripped right over the prone body when he got to the bottom of the stairs. Luckily, he managed to stay on his clawed feet, managed to keep sprinting for the entrance with his muscular tail swinging behind him.

Stay calm, he reminded himself, gripping a walkie talkie he'd taken off of one of the tower bodies, a twin to the one Earl still held. *Just stick to the story. Nothing wrong in here. Nothing for anybody to worry about. Move right the fuck along!*

"Hey in there," an outside voice called through the door; it was low, gravely. "Open up a minute!"

Chud took several deep breaths. He needed to remain calm to not make it seem as if he'd just bolted down two flights of stairs and sprinted across the floor. At least he knew they couldn't see him sweat.

When he reached the door, Chud saw that it wasn't even locked. The three men could've walked right in on them at any moment. Thankfully, they were polite enough to knock instead.

He lowered his weapon.

Relax. We're all friends here, remember? We're all supposed to be on the same team.

Chud had no pockets or belt on which to clip his walkie talkie, so he kept it held in his claw. He extended two talons, hooked them around the door handle, then gave a strong tug. When the door swung open, he found himself face to face with a gargoyle-like Pteralop, a badger-man, and the tall beefy guy that Earl called "Horror Show."

None of them was a werebear, and that was a good thing, too. Bear-creatures had a legendary sense of smell. They could've picked up a whiff of blood and the chemical stench of gunfire a mile away!

Yeah, I can do this. I can make this work.

"How can I help you guys?" Chud asked aloud, trying not to appear unnerved. At least his voice didn't tremble, and for that he was grateful.

Horror Show opened his mouth, but it was the badger-man who spoke first. "We got a report that there might've been some gunfire in there," he said. "That true?"

Chud feigned surprise. "Gunfire?"

"Right," the badger-man said, his tone almost apologetic, "somebody saw some flashes, and we—"

"*I* saw flashes," Horror Show made it known, and there was nothing rueful in his voice at all. His eyes crawled up the brick face of the building, scrutinizing the windows. "I saw it plain as day through the glass up there, looked like muzzle flash to me."

"Oh, *that.*" Chud actually managed a laugh. "Those flashes weren't from fuckin' gunfire."

"No?" Horror Show instantly dropped his gaze, staring right down Chud's snout. "What was it, then?"

The crocodile-man tried not to let on that he was intimidated, tried to play it cool, but not *too* cool.

Just...act natural!

"One of the other guys," he said, "they had this leftover grinder from Giuseppe's in the fridge, one of those big hot Italian meat sandwiches the place is famous for, right?"

The Pteralop smiled, showing rows of fangs. "I love those things."

"See," Chud pointed to him. "He knows what I'm talkin' about. Anyway, this guy, he got hungry see, and he tried to microwave the damn thing just now, but he forgot that, underneath that printed butcher's paper they always use, the guys behind the counter wrap those hot sandwiches in fuckin' tinfoil to help keep 'em warm for the ride home. Well, I'm here to tell ya, that old microwave we got up there, it started sparkin' like the 4th of July!"

Chud faked another hearty chuckle, playing it for all it was worth, and he was pleasantly surprised to see the badger-man laugh right along with him. After a second, even the horned Pteralop joined in. Horror Show, on the other hand, remained stone-faced.

"A fuckin' sandwich?" he said, still skeptical.

"You believe that?" Chud shook his head, then asked with mock interest, "You could really see it all the way out there, huh?"

"Yeah, I could," Horror Show's eyes narrowed, "and it didn't look like fuckin' tinfoil in a microwave. It looked like fuckin' muzzle flash."

"Well, looks can be deceiving," Chud told him. "If anybody should know that, it's us, am I right?" He looked to the disciples on either side of Horror Show, then made a show of letting his nostrils flare. "Oh, wait, you're not one of us, are you? You're fuckin' Zeus!"

"I'm *human*."

The Pteralop shot a look of disapproval to the badger-man. Chud clocked it. *The croc is right,* that look said, *why are we even listenin' this guy?*

He tried not to smile.

Good. It's workin'.

"You're Vivian's pet," Chud said, "the one they call Horror Show?"

"I'm nobody's pet, motherfucker," Horror Show spat back, gritting his teeth. "And if you know who I am, then you should also know I've seen my share of muzzle flash, and I know what the hell it looks like."

"I'm sure I don't know as much about it as you," Chud told him. "Before hearin' Vivian's call and comin' to the cause here, I was just a fuckin' New York City trash collector, pickin' up all the garbage *your kind* leaves behind."

The Pteralop actually gave a nod to that.

"But," Chud went on, not wanting to overdo it, "like I said, no muzzle flash in here. We nuked *a sandwich,* we blew a damn fuse, we nearly started a fuckin' fire, but what we didn't have was a shootout at the O.K. Corral."

Horror Show continued to grind his teeth. "Fine," he said. The guy reached up, rubbed this huge scar that crossed his entire neck, and then he sneered. "We'll just step inside, have a little look around, check out your story, and then we can all call it a night. Okay with you?"

The man actually took a step toward the threshold, but Chud held out his claw, the one that held Hades' walkie talkie.

"Yeah, let's do that," the crocodile-man said. "But first, let me get Benedict on the horn."

The badger-man looked suddenly concerned. "Benedict?"

"Sure," Chud said. "I'll just call him up, get him out here with us."

Horror Show's sneer turned into a scowl. "Why the fuck would we need to get Spidey involved in—?"

"You got security concerns, am I hearin' you right, tough guy?"

"Yeah, I got a big fuckin' concern!"

"Well," Chud went on, moving the walkie talkie back and forth through the air between them, using its antennae like a pointer, "your concerns, and the concerns of your Zeus-lovin' friends here—"

"I ain't no fuckin' Zeus-lover!" the Pteralop cried, taking exactly the right amount of offense.

"—are now *my* concerns. And, last time I checked, Vivian put

Benedict in charge of security. So *our* concerns ought to be *his* concerns, too; am I right?"

This was an assumption on Chud's part, a gamble based on what the duct-taped rat-man had told them. But from the looks he was getting from these three, there must have been at least a kernel of truth to it.

He went on, "I think Benedict should be here to check this place out right along with us, make sure everything I told you is the gods' honest truth, that there's no hidden danger in this place, nothin' at all to worry about. And when we see that a *Zeus* started all this fuss because of a fuckin' *sandwich*..."

Chud put on a wide snaggletooth smile, and he allowed his clawed thumb to hover melodramatically over the "talk" button of his hand-held radio.

"I definitely think he should be here for *that.*"

Horror Show's jaw tightened.

"Woah..." The badger-man took a step forward and held up a hairy claw. His head twitched to one side, exchanging a glance with his Pteralop friend. "Let's just calm the fuck down a minute. Clearly, this was an honest mistake."

Horror Show whirled on him, angry and defensive. "A mistake?"

The badger-man glared right back. He returned his claw to his weapon, lifting the barrel ever-so-slightly, the hint of a threat. "I don't see any reason to get Benedict involved in this business, do you — over somethin' this stupid?"

"You actually believe this crap?" Horror Show cocked a thumb over his shoulder at Chud. "Really? *A sandwich?*"

"Why not?" The badger-man shrugged. "I mean, only a complete idiot would *make up* a story like that."

"I believe him a helluva lot more than I believe *you,*" the Pter-alop added.

Horror Show nodded. Chud noticed that his hand was in his pocket, and for a moment, the crocodile-man thought he might pull a weapon on the two disciples, might demand they all come inside. Instead, he turned to face Chud once more, his lips pressed into a thin white line, his eyes narrowed to slits.

"What's your name?" he asked.

"Harley," Chud replied honestly, "Bud Harley." Out of habit, he almost added, *But everybody just calls me Chud.* Thankfully, however, he managed to stop himself in time.

"If I find out you've been lyin' to me here, *Bud,* not even Benny will be able to save you. You got that? I'll turn you into a real nice jacket and a set of boots to match."

Chud straightened, stared right back at him. "No purse?"

That retort actually made the man smirk. "You got balls, Bud. I'll give you that."

Then, Horror Show gave him his back. He pushed past the two disciples and marched down the front steps into the tall grass.

"Sorry about this," the badger-man said, backing away.

"No problem," Chud told him. "We're all just doin' our jobs, tryin' to bring back the gods."

"Amen, brother." The badger-man gestured to his Pteralop friend with a tilt of his head and they turned to leave.

"'Night guys!" Chud called after them, just as nice as he could be. He stood and watched them walk across the unkempt lawn, watched them step back onto the tarmac, then he slowly closed the door.

"Ho-ly shit," Earl said from behind him, giving Chud yet another start for the night, "I can't believe that worked!"

Chud knew Earl and Zuri had made their way down to the first-floor landing, knew they'd kept out of sight, weapons ready, listening to the whole conversation. He also knew that they had been prepared to spring to his aid if he'd needed it. And now that the crisis had been averted, they moved to his side.

"I did it, didn't I?" Chud asked with a grin. "I really did it."

Earl punched him lightly in the shoulder. "You sure as hell did. You were great!"

Zuri reached out to touch his arm. "Are you all right?"

"I'm fine," he told her. "Just...don't ever make me do that again."

"Oh, come on, now," Earl said with a smile. "You're a fuckin' natural."

Something about Earl's tone, about the twinkle in his eye, signaled that there might already be a plan in place — if not a full-fledged plan, then at least some idea of what to do next. Whatever it was, Chud could tell it involved him, and he knew he wasn't going to like it.

CHAPTER FIFTEEN

"Out of the question," Christine DeParle announced with a dismissive wave of her webbed claw.

Larry Neuhaus stood open mouthed, staring up at her from the base of the temple's stone steps. He'd been relaying his story as briefly and as bluntly as he could manage. He spoke of Peggy's torture, told what he knew of Hades' plan, crystal skulls and a gateway to another world, and he warned of the slavery, destruction, and death that would surely follow if they succeeded, if the ancient gods were allowed to return here to Earth.

He was still working up the courage to ask that all-important question when Christine interrupted him.

"You didn't even let me finish."

"I know what you're proposing, Calisto," she told him, baring her needle-like fangs. "You want us to return to the surface world. You want us to face Hades alongside you. You want us to *fight.*"

Larry shrugged. "Well...yeah."

"'He is come to open the purple testament of bleeding war.'"

Christine shook her glowing head. She took another step away from the giant sculpted seashells of her throne, her tail swaying gracefully in her wake.

So much like Peggy, Larry thought, and he felt the knot tightening in his stomach. *God, I hope she's still safe. I hope nothing's happened to our child.*

"You might be Calisto," Christine said, her expression grim, "created and not born, but clearly, you are still every bit the Charodon. Your clan loves the clash of battle, the sting of conflict, and you look for any opportunity to indulge in it."

"Lady," Larry countered, climbing up two more of the stone steps, closing the gap between them, "you're crazy if you think I love any of this. I'm an artist, not a warrior. I don't *want* this fight. Truth be told, I'm scared shitless right now. But you know what I *do* love? I love my wife. And I will do whatever it takes to set her free, to get her back. That's the only thing I care about right now, the only thing I want. But I also know that I can't do it alone. It's a terrible feeling, isn't it — to know a loved one is suffering, to know you are powerless to stop their agony?"

Christine looked down upon him with sympathy, but there was something else at play in those dark eyes of hers. After a moment, she turned away and her arm swept the crowd that stood gathered there in the temple before them. "You see all of these incredible beings around you? Half came here from Colonial Bay."

Larry blinked. *Half?*

"We watched the only home we'd ever known burn to the ground. We lost everything we had because we...because *I* rallied to the battle cry of *one man.*"

Christine took a swift step forward and moved to Larry's side.

He turned his head, his eyes following her as she looked out across the congregation.

"And then," she said, "out in the depths, we crossed paths with Poseidon's *other* children. It turns out that centuries ago, after the ancient city fell, its people found themselves divided on what to do next, arguing amongst themselves on how best to survive. There were many who wanted to run away, to go deeper into the ocean, to find a place where no human being could ever follow. And then, there were those who thought the best way to live in this world was to instead hide in plain sight. The two factions couldn't see eye-to-eye, obviously, and so they splintered off from one another, each going their own separate way.

"*My* forefathers founded Colonial Bay. They abandoned the old ways almost entirely, living in a self-imposed prison among the Zeus. And the others? Their ancestors came here and built this glorious 'New Poseidon.' They *preserved* our ancient language, our culture and our rich heritage — generations keeping our whole way of life alive and well for the future, living free in the open sea."

Christine gestured once more to the crowd, keeping her back toward Larry, her dorsal fins shimmering with a rhythmic display of light, the pulses punctuating her every word.

"When we first arrived here," she told him, "there were a few barriers. After all, we didn't even speak the same language. But after a brief period of adjustment, we were able to integrate our two tribes, to form a single society with our long-lost brothers and sisters. All of Poseidon's children, together again at last."

Larry now understood why the Kraken, and the other two creatures who'd found him floundering out there in the trench, had been so confused when he'd tried to talk with them before. They weren't from Colonial Bay. They'd been raised here in this place. They spoke no English, but they knew what Larry meant when he said, "DeParle."

She pivoted to face him once more. "And now you want to divide us up again."

"Divide you? How-?"

"You expect me to separate mothers from their sons and daughters, husbands from their wives, and you want me to send them off to die with you. 'There are few die well that die in a battle.' And all to save the life of a single woman?"

"A single woman," Larry echoed. There it was, the hurdle he always knew he would need to overcome. "Her name is Peggy, and I don't *expect* anything. I...I had a vision. A woman Karl Tellstrom *killed* back in Colonial Bay, she told me to come here and ask you for your help, so here I am. I'm asking."

A shocked murmur ran through the crowd. The voices were low, unintelligible.

Larry didn't stop speaking, "You said it yourself: I'm Charodon. My wife, she's just like you, Christine. You know that. She's Paralicht. We're children of Poseidon, and we need your help. But, in the end, this isn't just about me. It's not even about *her*. It's the whole world that's in danger, the whole world that needs our help. It's up to you to give it."

With that, voices called out from the crowd. Some supported Larry's plea, others denounced him for having the gall to even make it. Larry ignored them all. Instead, he kept his focus on Christine. She had been the key to stopping Karl Tellstrom, and now, she was his best hope of beating Vivian Song.

"You need to decide how you want to be remembered," he told her, raising his voice to be heard above the commotion. "When this is all over, you can either be the ones who stood up and helped to make a difference...or you can be the ones who didn't want to get involved, the ones who cowered down here in this glorified cave with their claws up their collective asses."

The crowd began to quiet, listening once more to his words. Really listening. And as he continued to plead his case, Larry saw many in their ranks nodding their agreement with him.

"Oh, sure, Zeus will be the first to go," he said flippantly. "I'm sure nobody here will shed a fucking tear over them. And after that, it will be all of Hades' disciples who didn't hop onboard this crazy train, the ones like my friends back in New York, the *good ones* who risked everything and took a stand. And again, not really your problem, right?"

Larry took another step toward Christine, pointing his snout at her ear as if he were whispering some secret. He kept his voice at full volume, however, for the benefit of the masses.

"But when whatever the hell comes through that gateway finally makes its way to *this place?* When they either *kill* or haul all of these people away in chains, *your people?* Well, when that happens, Christine, it finally *will be* your problem, and there won't be anyone left out there to come to your aid. The time to fight is now, before it's too late."

Behind him, the congregation ignited. Larry heard calls to fight and cries to abstain battle for dominance; they echoed through the chamber, becoming one garbled din. And with the pleas and demands came a sudden rush of movement as dozens of bodies pushed forward, every member of the menagerie struggling for a place near the base of the steps, a spot closer to Christine and the giant statue of Varuna.

Larry looked up at the effigy that towered over them. He stared into the stone teeth of its downturned snout, into its blank, sculpted eyes.

These people...they were all chanting your name. 'Etare Varunatep,' that's what I heard before I walked in here. What the

hell does that even mean? I assume they were asking you for some-
thing...but what? Is this just a normal Sunday service, or is it—?

"*Ndi' waneetah!*"

The alien words rang loudly through the stone hollow of the temple, silencing the continued argument from the crowd. Larry lowered his head, and his eyes found the source of the cry: another Paralicht had entered the chamber. It was a woman; she ran into the turbulent crowd and the congregation parted before her, clearing a path.

"*Ndi' waneetah!*" the woman cried again as she burst onto the steps. The words meant nothing to Larry, but they sounded ominous just the same. Looking up at Christine, the woman pointed a long glowing talon Larry's way. "*Taak u yil Calisto.*"

Christine glared down at her sharply, her tone one of surprise and disbelief, "Calisto?"

The woman nodded frantically in reply.

"Jason," Christine called out, and she looked back at the shark-like Charodon who had been sitting in that smaller throne at her side.

He immediately rose to his feet. Looking at him now, standing fully erect, Larry had a flash of déjà vu, of recognition; this was one of the creatures who had chased him through the halls of Black Harbor Medical Center all those years ago. This was one of the assassins Karl Tellstrom had sent to kill Peggy in her hospital bed.

"What's going on?" Larry wanted to know. He didn't know what had been said, but clearly, it had to do with him, or Peggy, or both of them. "What's happening?"

"My mother is dying," Christine replied, then she turned and looked him straight in the eye, "and she's asking for *you.*"

CHAPTER SIXTEEN

hy me?

Chud knew the answer, of course. It was the same reason why he had to be the one to answer the door. He had no scent to give him away. There simply was no better option.

He was their only hope of success.

And if things go wrong now, if you're found out and this little reconnaissance mission is over before it even begins, if you get yourself and your friends all killed? Well then, buddy boy, you'll be the only one to blame.

The crocodile-man strolled across the cracked, weed-choked tarmac toward the bustling aircraft hangar. They called New York City a "heat island," but there was a cool breeze blowing in from the sea. The Atlantic Ocean sat just at the end of this defunct runway, and he could taste the salt water in the air.

Chud's thoughts turned quickly to Larry. He hoped the shark-man had been able to find the rest of Poseidon's children, hoped he had been able to convince them to help.

Gods know we need all the help we can get right now!

Chud tried to appear relaxed, tried to let his thick, muscular tail swing leisurely behind him, as if he'd walked this path a million times before, as if he didn't have a care in the world. The barrel of his rifle was pointed down at the tarmac, and with every step, his claws tightened around it just a little bit more. Soon, he was afraid the plastics of the pistol grip would crack and splinter beneath the strain.

What the fuck am I doing? What the fuck am I doing? What the fuck am I doing?

He had the sudden, overwhelming urge to look back at the airfield's control tower, to try and find movement through the darkened glass, Earl and Zuri. His friends were up there. He knew that. They were watching over him right now. He knew that, too, and that knowledge was comforting. It really was.

They're counting on me, waiting for my report. Assuming, that is, I make it back there at all.

Chud took a deep breath. He tried to fortify his courage, tried to focus on the plan Earl had laid out for them. The whole scheme, such as it was, had been built around *him.*

Step one: Chud infiltrates the enemy stronghold.

Right. Check.

A huge rectangular doorway filled the front wall of the old aircraft hangar. The massive door was slid to one side, allowing light and personnel to flow freely through the open gape. Chud merged in line with the moving crowd, made an unhurried approach.

There were a handful of security guards stationed on either side of the doorway, sentries armed with lightweight semi-automatic

rifles, AR-15s or something quite similar. The fierce-looking creatures were far from curious, however. None of them paid Chud any
mind. In fact, one of them, a lion-man, yawned as he passed him by,
his tongue curling into a wide, lazy "U" between his parted fangs.

*They don't have a care in the world. And why should they? What
do they have to be worried about? Not a goddam thing! They have
no reason to be on the lookout for anyone, really, let alone me. They
have no idea anybody's coming to stop them. They don't think
anybody* can *stop them. They think they're invincible as fuck
right now!*

Chud may not have felt invulnerable, not by a longshot, but as
he passed through the open doorway without incident, without so
much as a second glance, his confidence grew. He emerged into the
old hangar, into the harsh glare of newly erected work lights, and it
didn't take him any time at all to find the gateway.

Then again, it was sort of impossible to miss.

As he pushed forward with the crowd, the upside-down V-
shaped scaffolding grew larger against the steel rafters and curved
corrugated panels of the ceiling. Bundles of multi-colored wire and
lengths of clear tubing ran over and through the massive metal
framework, granting it the appearance of an apparatus ripped
straight from a mad scientist's laboratory. Chud could not help but
pause at the sight of it; he looked up at the superstructure, breathless
and frozen in place.

Ho-ly shit...It's here. It's real. *They've done it. They've really
gone and built the thing!*

BEEP-BEEP-BEEP

The piercing alarm of a forklift in reverse snapped the crocodile-man from his momentary trance. He leapt to one side, allowed
the backing lift to harmlessly pass him by.

Focus, he told himself. *Step two of Earl's plan: "Chud has a quick look around, finds out as much as he can about Hades' timetable."*

Chud shook his head briskly, getting back on task.

Right. I got this!

The crocodile-man lowered his snout and began to navigate his way through the organized chaos. He tried not to look back at the technological marvel of the gateway, tried to keep his eyes focused forward like a pro, a real live security guard, a valued member of the team.

He was a crocodile, not a chameleon, but he seemed to blend in perfectly just the same.

Everyone around him went about their assigned duties, and they did them with great haste. Many appeared stressed, but most were clearly excited about something. In the background, Chud could hear snippets of their various arguments and conversations, some broadcast over hand-held radios, like the ones they'd plucked off the dead guards in the tower, others spoken face to face. Each new fragment provided him with another piece to the overall puzzle.

"This is totally absurd! You do realize that, right? There's no precedent for any of this, no way to train or prepare for what's about to happen. We—"

"We just need to get this entire area cleared out. Come on! Everything's—"

"Gotta be ready. Time's gettin' short here, fellas. Only a few more hours to go. Were you here when they brought Preacher in? *Preacher!* He actually inspected my work—"

"I don't understand it myself, really, but Vivian Song says it leads straight to Heaven—"

"—to Kronos, to the creators. I can't believe this is really happening, can you? The gods...they're actually coming! They're coming *here!* What will they even look like? I mean, I've always been taught that our human forms were made in their image, but have you ever stopped to imagine—"

"—what's gonna happen when we open that door? Don't let 'em fool ya. Nobody here knows a goddam thing! We can make all the guesses we want, Charlie, but in the end—"

"—it's happening at dawn, she said. When the fuck is 'dawn?' Can't anybody around here give me an exact timetable for shit?"

Chud's frown deepened with each overheard word. His heart was racing. He had to get his scaly ass out of this place, had to get back to the control tower, back to Earl and Zuri. He had to...

He had to calm the fuck down!

Stacks of wooden crates lined the interior wall of the hangar. Chud moved away from the crowd and ducked behind them. He took a moment to check his weapon, to close his eyes and to just...*breathe*.

When he opened his eyes again, something grabbed his attention. He cocked his head at a rusty metal door hidden in the shadows. Could that be the entrance to where they were keeping Larry's wife and Earl's scientist? Could Chud really be that lucky?

Probably just a supply closet, full of brooms and mops, and one of those yellow plastic SLIPPERY WHEN WET *signs.*

Probably, but he wouldn't know for sure until he actually opened it and had a little peek.

Chud swallowed hard and reached out for the doorknob with his scaly talons. In his other hand, he held his rifle level, ready to fire at any danger that might be lurking on the other side. The knob turned easily, but the door stuck.

"Locked," he muttered under his breath. "Bolted shut. Shoulda known I wouldn't be that—"

He gave a hard tug and the door suddenly came open, accompanied by a quick grinding sound that made him wince. A light breeze flowed through the opening, cooling his leathery skin. Slowly, cautiously, he pulled the door back a bit farther, enough for him to be able to peer inside.

To Chud's surprise, he didn't find a room full of cleaning supplies or even prisoners. In fact, he didn't find a room at all. Instead, Chud found himself staring out into a field of tall grass and even taller weeds.

An exit, another way out of this place...

Then, it suddenly hit him.

Not out...in!

He turned to look at the wooden crates stacked high behind his back; they completely blocked this doorway from the rest of the hangar floor, hid it from view.

A secret door!

The crocodile-man smiled to himself. He couldn't wait to tell Earl and Zuri what he'd found, to see their faces when he...

Stay focused! Don't get ahead of yourself, buddy boy. First, you've still got more work to do here. Remember the plan? "Step three: Chud finds the damn hostages."

Right. Chud closed the door. He gripped his rifle, stepped back out from behind the crates, and continued moving unimpeded through the crowd.

There were so many Hades! Finding a single Zeus, a single Poseidon in here...it wasn't going to be easy, but it wasn't impossible. Chud had promised Larry Neuhaus that he would try and find his wife, Peggy, and no matter the odds, no matter what happened next, it was a vow the crocodile-man intended to keep.

Carefully, Chud sniffed at the air. He searched for a scent, for a clue, and he kept moving.

CHAPTER SEVENTEEN

Moving into yet another stone chamber, Larry Neuhaus was unprepared for the shock that awaited him. The cavern itself was quite warm, humid, like a sauna. Steam hung in the air, and a moist film of condensation glossed every surface — water collecting and raining down from great stalactites that hung precariously overhead. Rocky, terraced steps descended to a percolating tidal pool. Unlike the clear, frigid waters of the trench, this pond was cloudy with churning minerals; it also gave off the distinctly foul odor of rotten eggs.

Barbara DeParle was down there, at the base of those damp steps, her body partially submerged in that roiling soup. Christine and her husband, Jason, had tried to warn Larry about the state of the old woman's declining health, about the extent of her physical deterioration, but their words, and even the seriousness of their tone, had failed to lessen the impact of actually seeing her face-to-face.

Jesus...

For years, Larry had been haunted by visions of a long-dead Susan Rogers, the apparition of a woman who had been reduced to nothing more than skin and bones. Barbara's current condition wasn't much better than that. The outer membrane of her flesh, normally smooth and translucent, had become like wrinkled cellophane wrapped around a skeletal frame. All the elegant fins that outlined her body, once rigid and firm, were now flaccid, mottled and drooping. And Larry noted that her inner glow had dimmed dramatically, like the failing final light of day.

Larry coughed against the stench of the room, against the sulfur and the subtler, but no less unpleasant, smell of illness and death it masked. He carefully navigated the wet, slippery stone of the steps, staring down into Barbara's emaciated face as he did so. The old woman's cheeks were sunken valleys. Once plump, full lips now lay withered and deflated across what was left of her needle-like fangs. Worst of all, her eyes were gone, buried deep at the bottom of two shadowy wells.

He thought once more of Peggy, of the smoking crater Vivian Song had made with her red-hot claw.

As Larry drew nearer, however, Barbara's eyes fluttered open and held him in their gaze; they were more tired than he remembered, but still just as tender, just as *sage*.

"Larry Neuhaus," Barbara said, and her withered, wrinkled lips managed a slight smile. Her voice was full of gravel, yes, but it also held surprising strength. "I knew the fires of Colonial Bay hadn't claimed you. I felt it in my bones. I always had faith you'd find us here one day, you and Peggy. Ayuh, it was only a matter of time."

Larry coughed again, cleared his throat, and began, "Barbara, I—"

"Grandma's sick."

A child?

Larry looked up and peered around a rocky outcropping. There, he found a little shark-girl sitting on the lip of the pool; she dipped her clawed toes into the steaming waters. The young Charodon's skin was covered in a familiar set of tiger-striped markings, the same distinctive coloring as—

Karl Tellstrom, Larry realized. *This is his daughter, isn't it — his child with Christine?*

Larry felt a twinge of...What was it — guilt? After all, he had killed this little girl's father, hadn't he? He'd let Karl fall into the conflagration of Colonial Bay, stood smiling as he watched the maniac burn.

"Come away from there, little one," Christine said softly. She moved toward her daughter, held out her arms. "You need to let your gramma rest."

The child just sat there, eyeing her mother. "So the healing waters can make her well again?"

"Yes, Kohara," Christine replied, but Larry could tell there wasn't any belief there. Not anymore.

Kohara didn't seem to notice, however. The little shark-girl smiled, showing far too many teeth for someone so young, and Larry could not help but wonder if this was how his own child might look in a few years' time. She leapt from the rocks and into her mother's waiting arms, her little tail slithering, her caudal fin fanning the thick, humid air.

"Tell your grandma goodnight," Christine told her.

Kohara turned her pointed snout toward Barbara and waved a tiny webbed hand. One day, Larry knew that her talons would be formidable, but right now, they were no more than burgeoning nubs. "Goodnight, Grandma," she said. "I love you."

"I love you too, Peanut," Barbara whispered. "Promise Gramma you'll be a good girl, mind your mother?"

"I promise, I will." She rubbed the little onyx marble of her eye. "Can I see you again when I wake up?"

The question clearly touched the old woman. She offered her granddaughter a gentle smile and said, "When you wake up, Kohara, I may be fast asleep. You see, I'm *old*...I've lived a long and happy life, and the next time I go to sleep, it will be for a very, very long time, and you won't be able to wake me. But just know that I won't be hurting anymore, and that I will always love you."

The little girl nodded. "Will you still dream about the pyramid?"

"I don't know what I'll dream about, Peanut, but I hope it will be the most beautiful dream ever."

Christine's thick lips trembled, and she appeared close to tears. With a kiss to the forehead, she handed her daughter off to Barbara's caregiver — the same Paralicht woman who ran yelling into the temple a short time before, the one who spoke in a language Larry couldn't understand, the one who said Barbara needed to see him.

The caregiver held Kohara to her glowing breast and carried the little shark-girl out of the chamber, leaving only Christine, Jason, and Larry there with Barbara in the stinking heat.

For a moment, the chamber was silent except for the bubbling gurgle of the hot spring. Then, Barbara's eyes, sunken yet no less sage, traveled over each of them before coming to rest on Larry.

"Peggy said you were a hero," the old woman whispered to him. "Now, it would seem Varuna agrees. He's sent you on a hero's quest, hasn't he?"

"I don't know if it was Varuna," Larry told her, "but I *did* have a vision, and it sent me out into the ocean to find you, to ask for your help."

"So I've heard. Hades' disciples have Peggy prisoner?"

Larry nodded. "They've tortured her, Barbara, and they forced me to help them collect these crystal skulls. They plan—"

"The Ark," Barbara interrupted, "the thirteen keys to Heaven's gate."

"You know about them?"

Barbara chuckled. It was a horrible sound, as if everything in her chest had come loose and was now rattling around inside of her. "I wouldn't be a priestess worth my salt if I didn't. The skulls were a gift from the gods, but after Zeus' revolt, they were scattered...lost."

"Hades found them."

Barbara frowned. "The skulls are a power they cannot hope to control, like the orb our ancestors hid in Colonial Bay — the Wrath of the Gods."

"Well, control or not, they plan to use them to bring the gods back to Earth," Larry went on to explain. "They have weapons and numbers, they torture and kill because they *enjoy it,* and with the power of the creators on their side, they could overrun and enslave us all."

The old woman looked thoughtful, but she said nothing.

"I have a group of friends," Larry went on, "Hades and Zeus, all *good* people, Barbara, and they plan to stop them, to set Peggy free, but they can't do it alone. They *need* Poseidon."

Barbara nodded. Her gills moved lazily; they appeared tired, like her eyes. "You said you had a vision to seek us out, to ask for our help in this?"

"Yes."

"A vision is a powerful thing, son," she said. "So is love. Both are so rare, so very rare, and when we are fortunate enough to be touched by them, we become like a leaf on a stream, and just like a stream, the path of love, of *responsibility*...it is seldom straight or easy, but we must follow it wherever it leads. We must see it through to its inevitable end."

Another moment of silence passed between them, nothing but the sounds of the bubbling spring to fill the vacuum. At last, Barbara broke it. "Jason?" she whispered.

When called by name, the other Charodon took a step forward, his pointed snout dipped low in respect. "Yes, teacher?"

"It was your bite that anointed Peggy," she reminded him. "*You* made her Calisto, made her *one of us.*"

Larry switched his attention from Barbara to Jason. So this was the creature that had infected his wife, that changed both of their lives forever? Years ago, he might have vented rage at the discovery, now he was indifferent, perhaps even a little grateful.

"Yes, teacher," Jason admitted, his expression unreadable as he gazed down at the dying old woman in the spring. "It was me."

"Then, it is *you* who must return with Larry. It is *you* who must help to protect her from further harm, to free her and bring her home to us."

Jason blinked. He looked over at Larry, then exchanged a glance with Christine. After a beat, the Charodon returned his eyes to Barbara and nodded. "Yes, teacher," he croaked. "If it is Varuna's will—?"

"It is."

"Then, it will be done," he assured her. "I will go. I will bring her back to us."

"No, you absolutely *will not!*" Christine shouted, her voice reverberating off the dripping rocks. She glared down at her mother, her dark eyes ablaze. "Kohara's already lost her biological father to war with the Landers. I won't let you sacrifice the only father she's ever known as well. *I* decide what happens to our people, what's best for them. You passed the mantle of leadership to *me,* remember? You can't just take it back whenever it suits you. 'We cannot all be masters.'"

Barbara responded to her daughter's Shakespearean quote with one of her own, "'Our doubts are traitors and make us lose the good we oft might win by fearing to attempt.'"

Christine's mouth hung open. She crossed her elongated arms over her breasts, then turned away from her mother's gaze. "You once pleaded with me to end Karl's war with the Landers," she said, "and now you want us to go and start a new one?"

"Karl's war was just that," Barbara told her, "his own. This fight is not one of our choosing, child. This battle is being thrust upon us, and it's already begun. It just hasn't made its way to our doorstep yet.

"You think you can protect Poseidon's children by hiding out down here, by cutting all ties with the surface world and the Landers, but you can't, not forever. If Colonial Bay has taught us anything, child, it's that no hiding place is safe forever. I think you realize that.

"We are still a part of this world," Barbara went on to say, "and we have a stake in what happens to it. If you truly love your daughter, if you want her to live a long and fruitful life, you cannot sit back and do nothing. Sooner or later, you must take a stand, for her, and for all of Poseidon's children, and that includes Larry here. It includes Peggy. It has to, or else we are unworthy of Varuna's grace."

With that, the old woman addressed Jason once more.

"The Calisto is *your* responsibility," she whispered with as much force as she could muster. "I once told Peggy that she was not alone, that as a child of Poseidon, we would always be there for her. I cannot go myself, Varuna's calling me down a different path, but *you* will keep that promise for me."

Christine and Larry both looked to him. Jason simply nodded and vowed, "I will."

"Larry," Barbara said, "tell Peggy she was right. She *is* strong, so very strong. You'll tell her that for me?"

Larry knelt down. "I'll tell her."

She reached out and took his clawed hand in her own. Her touch was soft and cold despite the heat of the room. "You're strong too, son, but I fear you'll have to be even stronger to face the test that's coming." Her eyes traveled up to Jason and Christine. "Take care of yourselves, and each other. Varuna...Varuna be with..."

And then she died. The movement of her gills, so lethargic and slow, ceased all together. Her grip on Larry's hand loosened, then failed completely, her claws slipping beneath the roiling surface of the heated water. Those eyes of hers remained open, but there was no more tenderness in them, no more wisdom; there was nothing there at all.

Barbara DeParle was gone.

"Mother?" Christine called weakly, and with the word came tears. They streamed down her glowing cheeks. Her knees wobbled and Jason was at her side in a flash to hold her up. She looked at him. "You're really going to do this? You're going to go back with the Calisto?"

"Christine," he said, "I have to. I made a promise. And besides, your mother was right. If we do nothing now, how long will it be before they bring the battle down here to us? You and Kohara...you're not my blood, but you are my family, and I would never forgive myself if I failed to take a stand, if one day I saw you both dead or brought to your knees because of it."

She pushed him away and swiped at her watering eyes with the back of her claw. "Then, you're not going alone. There were plenty in the temple who were ready to fight, weren't there — Kraken and Charodon?"

"Yes, but—"

"'Each Trojan that is master of his heart, Let him to field.' Go and gather them up, take them with you, anyone who wants to go. Bring them *home!*" Christine turned from him, tried to control her weeping. *"Go!"*

Jason quietly took a step back and offered her a bow; he climbed the stone steps, left the chamber in silence.

It didn't stay quiet for long.

Christine gave her cheeks another violent swipe and glared down at Larry, her expression grave. "Are you *happy*, Calisto?" she spat. "You've got your wish. 'The voice of parents is the voice of gods, for to their children they are Heaven's lieutenants.' Mother knew Jason would never refuse her dying request, just as she knew that I would never let him go out there to fight and die alone. She knew I would have no choice but to commit our people to your cause. You will have your war, Callisto, but if you fail—"

"If I fail, we all die," Larry told her, "or we live out our lives in slavery, which is a fate worse than death." He lowered his great triangular head, looking at Barbara's now lifeless body. "None of us have a choice in this, Christine. It's not what *I* want, and I'm sure it's not what your mother really wanted, either, but it's what *has to happen.*"

"Well, then," Christine snapped, the ice in her eyes now present in her voice as well, "'Cry 'Havoc!' and let slip the dogs of war.'"

CHAPTER EIGHTEEN

D og soldiers. *Isn't that what they used to call cavalrymen back in the day?* Earl Preston thought that it was. But watching Zuri pace back and forth across the floor in front of him, her fangs bared, and an M-16 clutched in her clawed hands, the nickname took on a whole new meaning.

While she hadn't fully wolfed-out, at least not yet, there were bushy thickets of fur lining both of her cheeks, and her eyebrows had knitted themselves together to form one long shaggy underline for her forehead. Add to that her elongated canine teeth and her afro, and the look reminded Earl of *Blacula*. He thought of telling Zuri this, but he knew the reference would be lost on her. Instead, he chuckled quietly to himself and said, "You don't like sittin' on the sidelines any more than I do."

"It is not in my nature," she growled, as restless as she was unnerved. "Don't you think that it has been too long?"

"I don't have a watch or a cell phone," Earl reminded her, "so I don't know how long it's been."

"Well, I don't need a watch or your precious phone to know that it has been *too long,* and I don't like it."

Earl nodded. He knew she was right, and he didn't like it, either. He didn't like having other people do his recon for him, didn't like the thought that he might've sent a friend out there to bleed and die in his place.

He looked around the old air traffic control tower. There was blood everywhere. Blood splatter marred the otherwise clear, tilted window walls. Blood had seeped into the cracks and crevasses of the rusting control consoles. Large pools of it congealed around the dead bodies on the floor. There was even blood up on the ceiling.

Staring at it all, Earl was suddenly transported to another place and time. Once again, he found himself in the ruined cabin of the Hoffs' abandoned sailboat, the *FantaSea,* staring at that bloody trident symbol scrawled across the wall. It was the moment that had changed his life forever.

Blood and death; that's how this whole thing started, Earl thought bitterly, *and that's exactly how it's all gonna end.*

He feared there would be no way to avoid it.

Earl ran a hand up the Kevlar of his vest then held out his hand to Zuri. "Let me see your rifle."

She considered him, her eyes bright in the dimness. "What?"

"Your rifle," he repeated.

She continued to stare; her fur-lined face was serious, almost alarmed. "I know you are anxious to begin the final battle, Earl, but if you fire the first shot from up here, you will do nothing but give away our position."

"I'm not gonna snipe anybody, Zuri. I just want to use your scope a sec. I promise I'll give it right back." He forced a smile, held up three fingers. "Scout's honor."

Zuri handed the weapon over, then continued to pace. He could hear the leather of her black, hip-hugging pants creak and groan as she moved and flexed.

Sexy Miss Blacula. All that's missing is the fuckin' cape.

Earl shook his head and swung the rifle toward an angled plane of Plexiglas. He peered through the scope, stared at the main aircraft hangar. Its metal walls had been covered over in graffiti, and he could see the now familiar Hades symbol there among the gang tags. Concentrating, he tried to find Chud in all the chaos, but it was no use. There were simply too many creatures and too much heavy equipment moving around down there.

And it all seemed so very far away.

He sighed heavily and lifted his eye from the lens, resting his forearm across the rifle barrel. Normally, it would be foolish for any officer to stake the success of a mission, much less the fate of the *entire world*, on a single man, even if that man was part crocodile, but under the circumstances...

His father's voice echoed through his consciousness, *"Just be patient, Son. You've won a great, strategic location here. Nothin' to do now but shelter in place, wait, and avoid exposin' yourself.*

"Just shelter in place and wait. Sure, Dad. I can wait with the best of 'em."

Wait and hope.

Hope and pray.

It's all Earl had been doing since Chud walked out that back door. He hoped that his friend could manage to keep himself safe and avoid capture. He prayed the crocodile-man would make it back to the tower sooner rather than later. And, perhaps most of all, he hoped that this little recon mission wasn't for nothing. He prayed Chud would return with some much-needed intel, something that could give them an edge and help them make it out of this alive.

A hand gripped Earl's shoulder.

He flinched and his head snapped around to find Zuri standing there beside him. He'd been sweating through his clothes all day, and he could only imagine what he must smell like to her. Zuri, on the other hand, gave off a scent that was rich, earthy, and slightly sweet; it was a mild scent, very easy on the nose.

Jesus...Someone ought to bottle that shit.

"Did you find him?" she asked.

"Nah, but the place sure is poppin', everybody gettin' ready for the big Welcome Back party."

She gave a slight nod, then gazed moodily out the tilted Plexiglas in front of her, her bright eyes moving like searchlights in the direction of the hangar. "I know Chud can handle himself, and yet, I cannot help but worry."

"Hey," Earl reached for his shoulder and wrapped his fingers around her hand, "I'm worried about the overgrown lizard too, but I got faith. Everything's gonna be all right. You'll see. Everything's gonna be just fine." He gave her clawed fingers a gentle squeeze. "Just fine."

She glanced over at him, her face now wholly human once more; clouded and gloomy. "For so many years, I have thought of *nothing* but this night. I always hoped to avoid it, of course, to find the skulls first and stop this from happening at all. Nevertheless, I trained and worked hard to prepare myself for this eventuality. And now that it is here, now that we are staring Armageddon in the face, I find that I am absolutely terrified."

Earl rubbed the bumpy ridge of her knuckles. "That's just natural."

"Is it?"

"Hell, yeah, it is. I don't know about you, but this shit's worse than anything *I've* ever faced before. I'm over here scared out of my fuckin' mind!"

"You, the King of the Badasses? You are just saying that to make me feel better."

"Girl, it's the God's honest truth. But you know what else is true?"

"Tell me."

"We *are* badasses, both of us, you and me. We're goddam *warriors,* and when the shit hits the fan, no matter how anxious we are right now, our instincts are gonna take over, our adrenaline's gonna kick in, and *BAM,* we'll do what needs to be done. And girl, when that happens? God help anybody that gets in our fuckin' way."

She looked at him for a beat, then said, "'If they stand behind you, give them protection. If they stand with you, give them respect. If they stand against you, show no mercy.'"

"Oorah!" Earl smiled. "That an old saying — somethin' from Africa?"

Zuri shrugged. "I saw it on a T-shirt once."

"Girl, we're gonna win this war, and then I'm gonna go out and buy you that shirt."

She squeezed his shoulder. "I hope you are right."

"Don't worry," he assured her, "you, me, and Chud...we're gonna be like the goddamn Superfriends. We're gonna make this world safe for humanity again."

She grinned at that; it was like a rose blooming up through barbed wire, as fragile as it was fierce. "You forget, Earl, Chud and I are not human."

"Zuri, I'll let you in on a little secret," he leaned in close to her, lowered his voice to just a notch above a whisper, "you and Chud, maybe you're not Zeus, but you're two of the most *human* people I've ever met in my life."

Her smile turned impish and she nudged him with her hip. "Do not tease me, Earl."

He handed the rifle back to her. "Scout's honor."

Zuri looked at him fondly. Her hand left his shoulder, moved to caress his cheek, and her touch was soft, tender, like silk. When she leaned in to kiss him, however, her mouth was anything but gentle. In fact, her lips and her tongue were so aggressive, so full of urgency; it felt as if this might be the last kiss they would ever share.

Did she really believe that?

Did *he?*

He wrapped his arms around her waist, pulled her to him, and—

"Hey guys!"

Earl flinched and Zuri immediately disengaged. They whirled in unison, their weapons raised. But when they saw what stood there at the top of the stairs, they dropped their defenses.

Chud was back.

"Oh...sorry," he said. "I forgot to knock again, didn't I? Jesus, you two are worse than a couple of rabbits!"

Earl's shock faded quickly to relief. *Sneaky little Sleestak bastard...He did it! He's okay!*

The look on Zuri's face was one of absolute joy. She left Earl's side and went to the crocodile-man, her arms wide and welcoming. "I am so happy you are safe, my brother!"

She hugged him.

"Yeah," Chud replied, bewildered and confused. "That was step four, right: 'Get the hell out and get back to the tower?' That's what I did."

"Way to follow orders," Earl told him. "Find anything useful in there?"

"Plenty." The crocodile-man shouldered his M-16. "For starters, the gateway's all done, it's fuckin' *huge,* and these idiots plan to open it up at dawn."

"Dawn?" Earl felt an uncontrollable cringe in his flesh, felt his stomach wrench and his heart ice with fear. He looked to Zuri, certain that the shock he now saw on her face must mirror his own.

Chud went on as if he hadn't noticed, "And I found something else, Earl. Something *you* need to see."

————

Dr. Graeme King could not wait to see what would happen when Vivian Song flipped the switch, or whatever it was she planned to do in order to ignite a reaction, but his two bodyguards, the minotaur and the bat-creature, demanded that he take a break from the gateway and get some rest. Rest! That was a laugh. Graeme knew good and well sleep would be all but impossible tonight.

Outwardly, he remained as cool and collected as ever, but inside? Inside he was bouncing up and down like a child with unparalleled excitement. He thought he knew now how Robert Goddard must have felt the night before he launched the world's first liquid-propellant rocket, or Einstein on the eve of that initial atomic test, when man made his first feeble attempt to harness the reaction that powered the stars. But this...this success would be so much greater than either of those. Greater than *anything!* This would be the most incredible scientific advancement in human history!

Graeme gave the gateway one last glance over his shoulder before they ushered him off the hangar floor. He believed the mechanism would work, but there was still no way for him to be completely *sure.* The physicist had done all these creatures had asked of him, followed their schematics to the letter. Did he trust the hidden architects behind it all, these ancient aliens? He didn't have enough data to say one way or another. But he trusted their *math*.

His burly escorts led him down a series of cinderblock hallways, away from all the excitement. That's when they heard a voice call out from behind them.

"Excuse me, guys—"

They stopped walking and turned to face it. Graeme saw a reptilian figure, a crocodile standing upright on its hind legs. The creature strode toward them carrying an M-16 in its front claws like some battlefield soldier.

"—that's the Zeus scientist you've got there with you, isn't it — Dr. King?"

The minotaur crossed its brawny arms over its equally muscular chest. He looked like a night club bouncer, and his voice was just as brusk, "That's right."

"Who's asking?" the bat-creature hissed, its fangs glistening in the stark overhead light.

"Vivian Song," the newcomer replied, taking another step toward them. "She sent me to fetch him, says there's a few things they need to go over before the big test at dawn."

Graeme's shoulders slumped. What more could that woman possibly want from him? Could he have overlooked something, some small yet crucial detail? Surely not. He'd personally examined every bolt, every wire, every connection. Now, he just wanted to get on with the damned test. He wanted to finally see the fruits of his labor. He wanted his *proof!*

His bodyguards exchanged a look. They seemed just as confused as Graeme.

The crocodilian offered them a shrug. "Don't ask me man," he said, "I just work here. If you guys wanna hang out for a minute, I'll bring him right back to you. Or I dunno, if you wanna knock off early, I guess *I* can just take him to wherever—"

"We'll wait right here," the minotaur interrupted, glaring at him.

The bat-creature nodded his agreement.

"Suit yourselves," the crocodilian said. Then, he motioned back down the hall with his rifle. "Let's go, Doc. You know it's not good to keep Vivian waiting."

Graeme nodded. He knew that very well. So did his bodyguards. Without another word, they stepped aside and allowed the physicist to join this newcomer.

As the crocodilian walked him back down the corridor, Graeme wondered if perhaps Vivian was finally ready to show him these mysterious crystal skulls of hers, willing to discuss how she planned to activate them and the portal they would create. That was the one missing variable to the whole equation, the only thing that cast doubt on the whole affair. Those tubes and wires that ran throughout the scaffolding; they all trailed out to a vacant spot on the floor, a spot the dragon had reserved for some sort of control console, the master switch, as it were, but she had yet to reveal it to him.

Tomorrow, she assured me, but maybe that time is now. Maybe she wants me to go ahead and hook it to the—

Suddenly, the reptile grabbed him by the arm and motioned down a narrow side passage with the barrel of its rifle. "Turn here, Doc," the creature said.

Graeme nodded absently, did as he was told. The new corridor was deserted and poorly lit. After several steps, he looked back over his shoulder, mildly surprised to find that his escort was doing the exact same thing.

"Everything all right?" the physicist wanted to know.

The creature pushed Graeme up against one of the cinderblock walls. "Listen up, Doc," it whispered; its speech was clipped, urgent. "Do what I say, *when* I say, and I'll get you *outta here.*"

"What is this?"

"I thought you were supposed to be some kinda genius? This is a fuckin' *rescue*, Doc. My name's Chud. I'm here with Earl Preston. We're helpin' you *escape.*"

"Earl Preston?" Graeme gawked at him; he couldn't believe what he was hearing. "Homeland Security Earl Preston?"

"What?" The crocodilian, Chud, shot a quick glance down the hall to make certain they were still alone. They were. *"Yes,* Homeland Security Earl Preston. This is a fuckin' *rescue.* He sent me in here to get you *out.*"

"But...I don't *want* out, at least, not yet."

Chud's snout came open; he stared at Graeme, incredulous. "What the hell do you mean you don't—?"

"I need to stay and see that gateway opened."

"What?" The crocodilian struggled to keep his shocked voice at a whisper. *"That's fuckin' crazy!"*

Graeme shrugged. "I prefer to call it scientific curiosity. I have to see if I can create a stable Einstein–Rosen bridge."

"Listen, okay, I get it, you're some kinda whacko mad scientist guy, but *you* need to understand that the shit's gonna hit the fan here in a few hours, and when it does, you don't want to be standing at ground zero with your Nobel Prize-winning dick in your hand. Now, are you gonna walk out that big front door with me on your own, or am I gonna have to knock your ass unconscious and *carry you* out?"

"That would look a bit suspicious, wouldn't it — you walking around this place with Vivian Song's top scientist draped over your shoulder? I've seen what these creatures are capable of, and I doubt they would let you get very far."

Chud saw his point. He blinked—

Three eyelids. Fascinating.

—and shifted his weight from one clawed foot to the other, mulling it over, clearly distressed. Graeme could see the tension in his reptilian face.

"You're not makin' this easy on me here," Chud said at last, adjusting his grip on the M-16. "I mean, now that I've gone and told you all of this, I can't just let you go back there and blab it all to the enemy. So...If I can't take you with me, I guess I'm gonna have to shoot you. I don't want to, but you're really not givin' me much of a choice. This is too damn important."

"You're right," Graeme told him. "This *is* too damn important. This is my *life's work!* This is *history!*"

Now it was Graeme's turn to try and keep his voice low.

"Look," he whispered, "you don't have to shoot me. I won't say anything to anyone. You have my word as a scientist."

"Your word as a..." Chud threw him a skeptical glance. "Is that even a thing?"

"Believe me, I don't want to see anyone get hurt. The machine is done, all right. These creatures are going to open that doorway with or without me standing there at the controls. But if you'll allow me to stay, once I know the mechanism works, that the theory is sound, I can shut it all down, shut everything down."

You don't even know how Vivian plans to switch it on, his mind, or perhaps it was his conscience, scolded him. *Just how are you planning to turn it off?*

Graeme ignored his doubts and continued to plead his case, "Once I stop the reaction, you and Preston can step in to save the day. I will cooperate fully. Everyone wins."

He could tell that Chud wasn't quite convinced. Perhaps that was because Graeme was still so uncertain himself.

"I never asked to be rescued in the first place," the physicist rubbed his temples, tried to remain calm, "and I understand this isn't the reaction you expected from me—"

"You got *that* right!"

"—but, as I said before, this is history. And like it or not, we're both a part of it. History is the end equation; it's simply the final result of a series of critical decisions, decisions executed by a long line of rare and extraordinary individuals, people who did just the right thing at just the right moment in time."

Chud chuckled nervously. "Yeah, well, there's nothing extraordinary about me, Doc."

"You're a talking crocodile," Graeme countered. "From where I stand, that's pretty extraordinary.

"I'm just a nerdy professor, a guy who works with numbers. I never considered myself to be anything special either, yet here I am, about to make the greatest of scientific breakthroughs. That is, if you'll allow me the honor. *Please,* I'm begging you...just return me to my bodyguards back there and walk away. I won't tell them anything. I'll make certain that the gateway works, leave it open just long enough to gather my data, then I will *shut it down.*"

They faced each other awkwardly.

After a beat, Chud asked the sixty-four-thousand-dollar question, "What if you can't?"

"I can," Graeme assured him. "I *will.* I swear it!"

Chud stared at him for another long moment. "If I'm gonna go along with you on this, Doc, I'm gonna need, whatcha call it? A gesture of good will?"

"What did you have in mind?"

Chud was still clearly uneasy and unhappy with the direction this planned rescue had taken. His eyes darted down the corridor, then swiveled back toward Graeme. "I don't suppose you could

KRONOS' RETURN • 223

point me in the direction of another prisoner could you — a Poseidon?"

"Poseidon?" Graeme echoed. He'd heard Vivian and that elderly werewolf, Preacher, mention something about Poseidon earlier, hadn't he? Other than the mythological reference, of course, the term meant nothing to him.

"A fish-girl," Chud explained. "She's my friend's wife. They're holding her hostage somewhere in this place, same as you. 'Cept I can guarantee you *she* doesn't want to stick around."

Graeme tried to picture such a creature. He had encountered so many strange and interesting chimeras in his time here, so many beasts of legend and superstition made flesh, but to his recollection, none of them, not even a part of any of them, had been fishy. "Sorry, I don't believe I've seen her."

"What about a phone, Doc? Seen anybody in this place with a damn cell phone, a smart phone, a flip phone, a fuckin' Blackberry, doesn't matter what the hell it is at this point?"

Graeme shrugged. "Vivian Song."

"Well, *that's* not gonna work." Chud appeared to think it over. "I just need to find some way for Earl to get a message out to his boss. It could even be a land line, a CB Radio, *anything.*"

"I don't...wait, I might know of something...It's not a phone per se, but there might be another way of broadcasting a message from this complex. I don't know who would be able to receive it, but—"

"Right now, something's a whole lot better than nothin', Doc."

And if it will get you to let me stay here, to finally get my answers, my proof...

"All right," Graeme said aloud. "I show you where this transmitter is, show you how these creatures operate it, and then you take me back to my bodyguards. Nobody gets hurt. Everybody gets what they want. Do we have a deal?"

Chud looked at him, still concerned, but also more than a bit curious. "Lead the way, Doc."

———

Earl ducked through tall brush, allowing Chud to lead him dangerously close to the main hangar complex. He kept his pistol at the ready and his head on a swivel, staying alert to any potential threat. Chud moved ahead of him with purpose, with direction, and Earl could tell that the crocodile-man had been this way at least once already tonight.

Even now, Earl still didn't fully understand what was going on, how he'd let Chud talk him into this. But with Hades planning to open that portal at dawn, there was no time for arguing. No time to wait. No time for anything but this Hail Mary attempt to call in reinforcements, to try and even up the odds.

They headed deeper into enemy territory.

At last, they came to a long, narrow brick façade, another building on the far side of the compound. Without the slightest bit of hesitation, Chud went to a rusted metal door and yanked on the handle. It swung open with a low, grinding creak.

Earl winced and clenched his teeth at the sound, sweat beading on his forehead.

Jesus, you don't have to be Hades to hear that!

He glanced around, expecting to see all manner of creatures coming across the overgrown lawn to investigate, expecting a fight. Thankfully, Earl saw nothing. He muttered a string of curses under his breath and moved on.

When they slipped through the open doorway, Earl and Chud found themselves in a hallway lined with even more metal doors. It was empty, the whole building deathly quiet.

Chud gestured for Earl to stay where he was, then he continued down the hall on his own for a bit, his thick scaly tail swaying behind him. Did he hear something, perhaps *smell* something that Earl could not? Or was the overgrown lizard just making sure that their path was clear?

Christ, I can't believe I'm goin' along with this shit!

Earl crouched down, hugged the cinderblock. His grip tightened around the butt of his pistol until his knuckles ached, but he managed to keep his finger light on the trigger. Silencer or no silencer, he wasn't about to run off shooting anything and everything that moved, not this time. Not here, in the belly of the beast. Not when they were still so completely outnumbered.

That would only get them all killed.

Mama always says, "Being in a hurry doesn't prevent death, neither does being slow prevent living." Need to be careful here, call in reinforcements. Need to save the day, ride off into the sunset with my girl.

Earl's thoughts went to Zuri, who was waiting for them back at the tower. He didn't have to wonder what she was doing right now. In his mind, he saw her up there pacing, pictured her sprouting hair, growing out her claws and her fangs as she worried, and she fretted. And in that moment, Earl wanted nothing more than to see her again.

Keep cool, he thought, uncertain if the voice in his head was his father's or his own, *Watch your six. Keep your head in the game. Take it slow and be careful!*

Up ahead, Chud gave the all clear.

Earl rushed to his friend's side. "Where to now?" he whispered, his throat tightening.

"Third door on the left," Chud replied.

Earl gave a curt nod and motioned him forward. The silenced

muzzle of Chud's M-16 preceded them across the hall to the proper doorway. Chud reached out and grasped the knob; it turned easily in his clawed grip, and when the door swung inward, Earl followed the crocodile-man inside.

Cautiously, Earl shut the door behind them and whirled to scan the interior. It was a small room, lit by overhead florescence. He quickly checked the corners. Nothing much to look at, really. But the thing that leaned against the far wall suddenly caught his eye and demanded his full attention. "Holy fuck."

Chud flashed a toothy grin. "I told you."

Earl hesitated, then stepped closer to examine the strange object. Until this very moment, he'd had his doubts as to what they would find, but now...

He saw an oval of raven glass framed by something that looked like a length of whale's intestine; it was fleshy, pink, and laced with blue veins. Flayed muscle, corrugated tubing, and bone appeared to stretch out from this oval, and the outer edges on all sides were jagged and threadbare. Clearly, whatever this thing was, animal or mechanism, it had originally been part of a much larger whole.

"*This* is what King showed you?" Earl asked, afraid to take his eyes off the alien thing, afraid it might lunge at him if he should turn away.

"That's it," Chud confirmed, still smiling. "King said it's a two-way tacky...tack-o...?" He scratched his leathery head, tried to remember the physicist's technobabble, then simply shrugged. "It's some kinda radio transmitter Hades ripped straight from a flying saucer. Pretty cool, huh?"

"Cool. Yeah, that's one word for it."

Nightmare would be another.

Pavor Nocturnus, the doctors called it. Night terrors.

Doctors...

Earl frowned, still grumbling over King's decision to stay. For a supposedly smart guy, the physicist was acting like a damn fool! If Earl had been held captive, had suddenly been offered a chance at escape, at *freedom,* you can bet your ass there would've been no hesitation. None at all! Choosing a damn science project over rescue, who does that?

That's some white people shit!

Earl shook his head. He couldn't bear waiting any longer. It was time to skip to the part where Special Director Patrick Tate ordered in the cavalry, the part where they killed all the bad guys and saved the world. He took another step closer to the alien gadget, whatever the hell it was, and ran his fingers along the neckline of his tactical vest. "So how's this thing supposed to work again?"

"You just press your hand flat against the left side of that panel over there," Chud told him, pointing to the jet-black glass, "and when it lights up, you talk."

"That's it?"

"That's what King said."

Earl nodded and moved over to the left side of the bio-mechanical device. "Like this?"

He started to reach out, paused a moment with his hand in the air. Then, he pressed his palm to the smooth black panel. He expected the surface to be cold, but it was warm to the touch. Suddenly, the section of glass beneath Earl's fingers began to glow. A muted hum rose from somewhere within the mechanism, and then a weird garble filled the room. It wasn't a sizzle or crackle like traditional radio static. No, this was a loud, muddled roar.

Earl winced.

"Christ!" he cried out, and the sound of his voice immediately stunned the machine into silence.

The transmitter waited. Colorful lights blinked and chased across its console.

Earl looked over at Chud, then back to the device. He knitted his brow, searching for what to say, for words that would demand a listener's attention. "Mayday!" he shouted into the consol. "Mayday! Anyone! This is Earl Preston with the Department of Homeland Security, calling anyone who can hear the sound of my voice. A terrorist cell has taken control of Delancey Field and is planning to stage an attack at dawn! Is there anyone out there? Mayday! Over!"

That should get somebody's fuckin' attention.

Now, it was Earl's turn to wait.

Somebody answer me, Goddamnit!

After a moment of silence, the lights stopped blinking and that odd, too-loud garble returned with a vengeance.

Shit! Earl thought, terrified. He lifted his eyes and his pistol to the door, just knowing that Hades' disciples could hear the noise, that they would barge into the room at any moment. *I was such an idiot to think this could actually work, to believe I could really get a signal out to any—*

A voice broke through all the static, broadcasting from the alien radio, puzzled and oddly familiar. *"Earl Preston?"* the voice said. *"Is that really you?"*

Earl's attention shot back to the flashing lights on the onyx screen, one hand tight on his pistol, the other still firmly pressed against the instrumentation. "Yeah, it's me. Who the hell is *this?* Over."

CHAPTER NINETEEN

"I t's me," Larry Neuhaus called out as he barreled down the brick and cobblestone tunnel. "I'm back!"

Jason tried to keep up with him. "Your friends live *here*, a mile underground?"

"This from a man whose current mailing address is a cave at the bottom of the sea?"

"At least it doesn't smell like this."

Larry opened his jaws to make a comment about the sulfur stench of the hot springs, then forced them closed again without saying a word. Like it or not, the specific funk of this subterranean space — musty, oily, mildewed, and metallic — had helped to guide his return, and for that he was now grateful.

He stopped to catch his breath. It seemed like he'd been running and swimming forever, but he knew his journey was still far from over. They had to find that airfield, wherever it was. He had to get back to *Peggy*.

"Guys?" Larry called down the passageway. No answer. "Chud, you here?"

The crocodile-man might not give off a scent of his own, but Zuri and Earl certainly did. The stale air of this long-forgotten underground was ripe with their lingering musk. And there was another odor wafting around these catacombs as well, something new...a coppery tang; it grew stronger, more pungent as the pair of shark-men approached.

"Blood," Jason warned, baring his serrated teeth.

"Yeah," Larry agreed, his nostrils flaring, "and a lot of it."

He approached the first archway they came to. A beaded Grateful Dead curtain covered the opening; he raked the strands to one side with his webbed claw. Nothing there. Larry quickly withdrew and moved away, the beaded lengths clicking and clacking against one another as they swayed to and fro behind him.

"Earl? Zuri? Anybody home?"

Still no answer.

A bit farther down the corridor, Larry came to a brick hollow. A single punching bag dangled from the ceiling on a chain, but there was no one there to strike it. He picked up his pace once more, hurried around another corner, and he could feel Jason right there on his heels.

The sensation triggered a memory, an odd realization of just how much Larry's situation had changed over the years.

That night in Black Harbor, we were running down hospital hallways. You were chasing me. Back then, I wanted nothing more than to get away from you. Now, I'm glad to have you by my side.

A furry body laid at the end of the passageway; its blood draining away, outlining every cobblestone of the floor in scarlet.

"Jesus," Larry gasped. *"Zuri?!"*

He ran for the creature, but when he saw the long scaly tail snaking out from it, he knew this wasn't her. Beneath the smell of blood and offal, Larry found the corpse's true scent, a signature he'd missed earlier that very day in the tunnels with Chud. This was a giant rat.

Larry stared down at it, as shocked as he was bewildered. "What the fuck...?"

"This guy one of your friends?" Jason wondered.

"No. I don't know *who* this is."

A muffled noise came from the next room, like someone calling out for help, someone who'd been *gagged*.

Larry's head jerked up as if he were a shark puppet on a string. He twisted around to face the Bob Marley curtain, parted the beads, and found the scene of a massacre. More bodies lay heaped against the wall. Thankfully, none were familiar to him. They were all Hades, all rat-creatures. One was completely missing its head.

What the hell happened? Larry wondered, overwhelmed with sudden guilt. *Damn you, Susan. I should have been here. I could have—*

A muffled scream filled the chamber.

Larry whirled to find yet another rat-man; still alive, it had been duct-taped to a chair in the center of the room. The sticky gray strips completely covered it from its furry neck down to its clawed hairy feet like some kind of weird mummy. Even its snout was encircled in tape, muzzling it.

Larry took a step toward the captive creature.

The gagged rat-man continued to scream through the tape. Its large ears stood straight up from its head, its dark eyes wide with panic. Larry glanced around the chamber, searching for the source of the overgrown rodent's fear, then the shark-man realized it was *him*.

Of course...a great white shark with arms and legs wanders into the room, starts moving toward you, *you're bound to shit your pants.*

Larry looked down and noticed that a hand-made sign was taped to the captive's chest, a warning written in large block letters:

BAD GUY!
DON'T UNTIE!

Larry glanced back at Jason, then took another step toward the terrified rat-creature. He growled, showed the points of his teeth, then he reached for the duct tape on the rat-man's snout. Larry had no intentions of letting the thing go, but he did want to free its mouth for a moment, to interrogate it, threaten it into revealing what had happened to his missing friends.

Jason stopped him; he grabbed Larry's wrist and pointed to the far wall. "I think they left that for you."

Larry lifted his eyes. Once, every square inch of brick had been covered in a web of news clippings and photographs. Now, only a few random scraps of paper and dangling yarn remained. They outlined a rough patch of pockmarks and craters.

Bullet holes. A lot of them. God almighty...

Before guilt could take hold of him again, Larry saw what Jason had really been pointing to — a map of New York City. It was like something you might find in a grade school classroom. Had it been there before? Larry honestly couldn't remember. Someone had circled a specific location in bright red Sharpie — a tiny peninsula, just south of Brooklyn. Another note had been scrawled across the center of the map. Four words,

GONE TO DELANCEY FIELD!

CHAPTER TWENTY

lease, be gone...

P Kari Hannigan looked up from her hand, from the dark bio-mechanical control panel that came to sudden life beneath her splayed fingertips, and her attention was snared by a glowing rectangle of light; a holographic image, much like the one that had once displayed Carol's mortal wounds. This new "screen" allowed her to view the sweeping field of ice and snow that surrounded the alien Ark. And to her dismay, she saw that the Yeti hadn't gone anywhere.

If anything, their numbers had only grown.

Shit.

Kari let out a long breath, her eyes narrowing as she tried to pick out individual faces among the countless furry creatures.

If they do have a tribal society, there will be a chief or chieftain leading them. There could be a war chief, a hereditary chief, or if this truly is a "theocratic" culture, the leader could even be their fucking medicine man. Bottom line: wherever the chieftain goes, so too goes the tribe.

Kari had shared all of this information with Carol, of course, had tried to make sure that she knew what she was dealing with, whose mind or minds she had to sway.

Carol had a plan to get past these savage creatures, a plan to get them all safely down the mountainside, a plan that she *swore* would work. "I can face them," she'd said. "My myrmidon will protect me," she'd said, as if the genetically engineered armor she now sported was somehow charmed; a sorcerer's cloak, a magician's hat loaded with all manner of tricks. Maybe it was. Maybe that bone sword Carol discovered by accident was just the tip of the proverbial iceberg. Maybe the suit was like some sort of alien Swiss Army Knife, a different weapon or tool ready on demand to meet any given challenge or threat.

Kari turned away from the console, gazed across the room to where Carol and Gagan still stood discussing the details of their escape plan. The giant gray mantis, "Manny," was still there by their side, tracking Carol's every move with its bulbous black eyes, awaiting her next command as if it had been born and bred to do nothing but her bidding.

Anxiety pulled at Kari's stomach. *I'm scared, Carol,* she thought, her heart struggling to keep a steady beat. *I love you, and I can't watch you die again. I* can't!

Kari put her hand over her chest, trying to envision a scenario where they all made it out of this safe and sound, even Alan. Her eyes went to his cage. He was still locked up in there, still mourning, still a wild card. Kari felt pity, even compassion for the hate-filled man, but she also worried he would complicate their exodus, their lengthy climb.

She knew they couldn't leave him behind, but God help her, a part of her wanted them to.

Behind her, the console suddenly began to hum. Kari swiveled her gaze back to the device, finding that the glowing screen had disappeared; her view of the Yeti replaced by multi-colored plumes of light. They flared and raced across the length of the panel in a bright, meaningless display.

Damn it! I'm sure it means something...*I just don't know what!*

The humming noise transitioned smoothly into words; speech, a disembodied voice, just as deep as the one they'd heard up in the control room, but this time, it wasn't talking gibberish. It wasn't droning on and on in some dead language only Alan and Carol could understand. No. This time, the words were spoken in plain English.

"Mayday!" the voice called out. *"Mayday! Anyone!"*

Kari felt a spike of sudden joy. *English! Someone who speaks English! Someone who can* help us!

No, her brain countered, *they said "Mayday," didn't they?* They're *the ones who need help!*

"This is Earl Preston with the Department of Homeland Security," the phantom voice went on to say, *"calling anyone who can hear the sound of my voice. A terrorist cell has taken control of Delancey Field and is planning to stage an attack at dawn! Is there anyone out there? Mayday! Over!"*

The breath caught in Kari's throat. *Homeland Security — the United States? Something about an impending attack?* Startled, she took her hand off the console and spun around. "Carol, did you hear—?"

Carol was right there, practically on top of her.

She pushed past Kari, moved brusquely for the wall, clearly

anxious to press her gloved hand against the panel. Blue-white light flared around the pads of her fingers, rippling out across the onyx glass. "Earl Preston?" she said, staring at the display. "Is that really you?"

After a silent beat, the transceiver crackled back to life: *"Yeah, it's me. Who the hell is this? Over."*

"It's Carol," she said with a huge grin on her face. Were those tears Kari saw in her beautiful, gleaming eyes? "Carol Miyagi!"

———

"Carol Miyagi?" Earl gave a shocked, delighted little chuckle. He couldn't believe his ears. "Son of a bitch."

He looked around nervously.

Chud had moved back over to the door, his rifle at the ready, just in case. The crocodile-man tilted his toothy head, a puzzled look in his reptilian eyes. "Who is she?" he asked.

"An old friend."

Earl turned his attention back to the alien console, back to the strange lights and the familiar female voice. Carol Miyagi. Of all the people in all the world...what were the odds? How was this even possible?

Everything in him warned of a set up. King had refused Chud's offer of freedom, but had the physicist also been crazy enough to betray the crocodile-man's trust? Had he alerted Vivian Song to their presence, helped her to lay a trap? Was this some sick psychological game she was now playing — a way to get Earl to show her his hand, or worse, trick him into luring Director Tate into some kind of ambush? Earl's skepticism quickly overshadowed his glee.

"How do I know it's really you?" he asked. "Over."

How do I know it's really you?

Carol's dawning smile faded.

That's the question of the day, isn't it?

If Earl knew the whole story, knew everything that had happened to her, the medical and scientific miracle that had made it possible for her to even be breathing, much less talking to him right now, Carol wondered what his reaction would be. Would he shun her, like Alan — think of her as something less than human; a pale imitation, a cheap _knock-off?_ Or would he embrace her, as Kari and Gagan had done so beautifully; recognize her for her intellect, for her personality — everything that made her uniquely _her?_

She wondered...

Kari sidled up beside her, gave her a gentle nudge. "You _know_ this guy?" she whispered.

Carol sniffed and nodded absently. She wiped at her eyes and tried to think of some secret, private detail she could offer, something only Preston would know about her, questioning how many more times she would need to prove herself in the days and weeks ahead, fearing it would never stop. When she thought she had something, she placed her hand back on the panel.

"That day we met on that abandoned fishing boat," she said, "you pointed a gun at me and...and at Alan." Just saying her lover's name threatened to bring fresh tears, but she willed them away. "You ordered us to give you our names. When I gave you mine, you made some crack about it being the same as the old man in that '80s movie, _The Karate Kid._"

"Too easy," Earl's voice responded from the console. _"Your last name's_ Miyagi. _Anybody'd make that crack!"_

She blinked, pursed her lips. "You need something else, then — more proof?"

"Nah," he told her, and Carol could hear that cocky smile of his, the one that had irritated her so badly that day in Colonial Bay. Now, she found it as welcomed and soothing as a cool hand on a fevered brow. *"I know it's you. Wax on. Wax off. Over."*

"Not funny." Carol shook her head and felt herself relax. "I'm glad you could track me down again."

"Listen, Carol, I'd love to stay on the line here and shoot the shit, but it's not safe where I'm at right now. It's hard to explain, but this isn't a conventional radio I'm usin' here, so I got no idea if this is party line. There are a lot of itchy trigger fingers out there, and I'm runnin' out of fuckin' time. We all are. This is an emergency, mayday, like I said, and I need your help. The whole fuckin' planet needs your help."

Her eyebrows shot up at that. "I'm afraid I'm not in any position to—"

Earl went on as if he hadn't heard or he didn't care, and given her experiences with him, Carol thought it was most likely the latter, *"Wherever you are, I need you to get an urgent message to a guy named Patrick Tate, he's a Special Director with the Department of Homeland Security. Patrick. Tate. You got that? Can you help a brother out? Over."*

"I, uh..."

She glanced down at the brightly lit telemetry screen beneath her fingers, knowing that she should have immediately said "no." After all, it was the only logical response, wasn't it? Even if she were free of the Ark, even if she knew the proper channels with which to deliver such a message, she was still half a world away.

But there was something within Carol, something that would not allow her to refuse. Instead, she needed to know more, needed to know what was going on in the world outside these alien walls, needed to know exactly what they were headed back to. Earl had said something about a terrorist attack, hadn't he? The powers that be once called what happened in Colonial Bay a terrorist attack, but Carol knew the truth.

So did Earl.

"What is going on?" she asked him. "No *detarame.*"

"Yeah, okay, I'll cut the crap. This is gonna sound clown-shit crazy, but I know if anyone out there can appreciate clown-shit crazy, it's you, Miyagi. Over."

Carol flashed an appreciative grin. *"Dōmo."*

"Turns out you and your boyfriend were right — Poseidon's children were just the tip of the iceberg."

"Yes." Carol looked to Gagan, her new friend, and to the giant mantis that now stood by watching her with great interest. "I know."

"And you remember those aliens you were so hot about after reading that book you stole from the temple, the ones you said might have spliced us all together back in the day, the ones I said *were complete bullshit?"*

"I remember," she told him, and as she said it, her eyes followed the curve of the chamber walls that now surrounded her, the fluted bone and ribbed tubing somehow stitched together by living sinew, the blue-white bioluminescence that shined down on her from overhead. *Oh, Officer Preston...if you only knew the half of it!*

"Well," his voice went on, *"these creatures here are plannin' to bring those same bullshit aliens back to Earth, plannin' to help 'em get some payback for our ancestors' little slave revolt. See, they've collected these crystal skulls from all around the world, and they've built themselves—"*

"The Ark!" Her focus shot back to the lighted screen. Could it really be true? "Twelve flawless crystal skulls arranged in a pyramid formation, with the thirteenth skull, the largest, placed at the top?"

"Jesus, Miyagi, is there anything you don't *know?"*

She was reminded again of her visit to Roger Hays' New York office, of the crystal skull she'd seen sitting on a shelf next to a sculpture from Atlantis. The sculpture had proven to be a replica, an imitation—

A cheap knock-off!

—but the skull? Could that skull have been *real?*

Earl spoke up again, *"Anyway, they plan to use those skulls at dawn, plan to open some kinda Stargate to the aliens' home planet — a wormhole. I bet you know what that is too, am I right? Over."*

"Yes," she told him in disbelief, her insides feeling like lead, cold and slowly sinking. Aliens and wormholes to another dimension...in the years she'd spent searching for the lost city of Atlantis, Carol had heard and researched it all. "I know what that is."

"You know how all those crackpot conspiracy theories say there's shapeshifting reptiles in charge of everything? Well, the woman runnin' the show here is named Vivian Song. She's an honest to God fire-breathin' dragon, Carol. I shit you not! And besides her, they got dozens, hundreds *of other creatures workin' around the clock to build this damn thing and get it up and runnin'. They've taken hostages, too. One of 'em is Larry Neuhaus' wife, Peggy. You remember Peggy, don'tcha, Miyagi?"*

Peggy. The girl in Colonial Bay's temple, the one Carol had risked her own life to dive in and rescue; the one who had been *changed,* transformed into a glowing, angelic being. Yes, Carol most certainly remembered her. And then there was Larry Neuhaus. She recalled the man's devotion, his willingness to do anything and everything to save his fiancé, to be reunited with her; Carol remembered his unconditional *love.* Did Earl just say that those two had gone on to be married? After that night, after everything that had happened to them, they still loved one another.

Unconsciously, Carol's eyes drifted to the other side of the chamber, finding Alan's holding cell. He'd once called her beautiful, told her that he wanted to be with her forever. That hadn't been lies; he'd meant every word of it. Why couldn't he accept what had happened to her? Why couldn't he still *love her?*

"These creatures are extremely well-armed," Earl continued, *"with assault weapons out the fuckin' yin yang! By the way, is that a real Japanese word for 'ass,' yin yang? Over."*

Carol shook her head, even though she knew he couldn't see it. "It means 'in abundance,'" she said absently.

"Well, yeah, that fits too, don't it? They got everything bad in abundance. We're outmanned and *outgunned, and a bunch of pissed-off ancient aliens-slash-motherfuckin' gods are about waltz up in here through that interstellar doorway at dawn."*

Carol's mind was thrown back into the fluid confines of a stasis tube, phantom wires trailing from the newly installed access ports along her spine. Her vision then did a hard cut to the moment she first saw her previous body, its lifeless limbs splayed out across that bio-mechanical altar, the altar with the ankh etched on its flank, the Egyptian symbol for eternal life. She thought of the procedure the Ark and its mantids had performed on her, wondering why Earl's words had triggered this sudden reflection. When the pieces finally came together, her stomach clenched.

Ara iyada, she thought. *Oh, no!*

"You once told me you knew your Bible," Earl reminded her. *"Well, I hope you remember all the worst parts of Revelations, because that's what's about to go down. We're talkin' the end of days, Miyagi — the end of everything!"*

"I can't fight all these bastards alone, which is why I need you to get my message out. I need you to tell Director Tate where I am and what's goin' on. He knows about these creatures. He's seen them with his own eyes. He'll believe whatever the fuck you tell him. Just...please, get him here, okay? Can you do that for me, Miyagi? Over."

Before Carol could reply, an ethereal light grabbed her gaze. It wasn't coming from around the gloved hand she had pressed against the onyx screen on the wall. No. This light came from her *other* hand. She tilted her head and saw that the alien orb, the Wrath of the Gods, had begun to glow again, its spectral fire intensifying.

It wanted to be used, this weapon; it wanted to *fight*.

She remembered her nightmare from Kathmandu, the voice of her cold and distant father, changing ever-so-subtly into the monstrous rasp of a scarred and vengeful Roger Hays. *"It's yours,"* the dream voice had said of the orb, of the armor that now covered her from head to toe like a second skin. *"It always has been."*

Watashinounmei...*My destiny.*

And with that, a glut of violent imagery flooded her brain; visions of monsters, of combat, of fire and *death*. Were these memories from the past — Colonial Bay, their battle with the Yeti, perhaps even her own bloody end? No. These nightmare images...they were somehow being fed directly to her mind by the orb, by the armor. Was this some imagined fantasy war these weapons wanted to make a reality? Or, like her dream, were they a premonition of actual events yet to transpire?

The bad feeling associated with these visions grew until a sudden wave—

Of what...Duty? Honor and responsibility? Programming?

—washed over her.

Carol winced and shook her head, denying it all. Zeus' warrior or not, there was nothing she could do to assist Earl Preston, to stop the gods' return. How could she, when she was trapped here in this alien vessel, stranded on the roof of the world? They were cut off from civilization, isolated, surrounded by an army of—

Yeti!

Her head snapped up. No. That would never work. She couldn't even think about...

Don't think, something told her. *No time to think. Do! Act! Anata wa senshidesu! You heard Preston, didn't you? Mayday! Emergency! The gods are coming back!* The *gods! If you turn your back on this plea for help, you're turning your back on everyone and everything you hold dear. You're turning your back on* the entire world! *Use the gifts that have been given to you.*

They're yours. They always have been.

When Carol was born, her mother had wanted her to have a Western-sounding moniker, but her father, of course, had preferred something a bit more traditional. They wound up compromising, Carol for a first name, Toki as a middle. Toki was incredibly old; it meant "Full of Hope," but it also meant "Time of Opportunity." So maybe this had been out of her hands from the very start.

Perhaps this really *was* destiny, and this moment, this "time of opportunity," was the very reason Carol had been brought into this world, not once, but *twice*.

She might just be Earl's best hope.

There was a term in traditional Japanese culture, *Shikata ga nai*. Literally translated, it meant, "it cannot be helped." It was a fatalistic view, one that embodied the concept of stoic acceptance in the face of a difficult or impossible situation. Now, Carol heard herself say it aloud, "*Shikata ga nai.*"

She turned her attention back to the sable glass. Earl had given her a name, a location, but with the mélange of thoughts crying out in her head, she couldn't remember now what it had been.

"Where are you?" she asked.

"We're on a small peninsula just south of Brooklyn," Earl responded. *"Place is called Delancey Field. It's an old, abandoned airport. Delancey Field. Over."*

New York.

Carol swallowed. She remembered racing across the Atlantic Ocean with Alan, using speed boats and jetliners, every mode of transportation at their disposal. She'd been so very anxious to get to that city, so frantic to get to Roger Hays and his precious money, so desperate to sell her soul. Now, time was of the essence again, but there was so much more at stake.

She recalled the sword-wielding weretiger, the one that had burst into her family home back in Japan. She knew too much, it told her. At the time, Carol had wondered what the creature meant by that. Now...now she thought she finally understood.

Programming, alien influence, call it what you will, Carol knew what had to be done.

She stiffened, pressed her palm hard against the panel. "I promise you that I will do everything I can to help you, Earl."

The words flew from her lips. This was a conviction for her now, like finding Atlantis, like making it to Makalu's summit, to the Ark. Yes, now she had to get to this *other* Ark, the thirteen crystal skulls, the hum of their individual voices made one chorus; a power beyond comprehension.

Her brain whispered, *In Peru, near Lake Titicaca, there is a stone doorway known as "The Gate of the Gods"* — Puerta de Hayu Marca. *Legends speak of tall men stepping through it, accompanied by "glowing balls of light."*

Carol glanced down at the shimmering orb on her left hand, then her eyes shot back to the control panel, and for the first time, she closed her side of the conversation with an official-sounding, "Over."

———

For the first time he could remember in this war, Earl allowed himself to feel something akin to hope. "Understood," he replied. "Thanks, Miyagi. If we make it through this shit—"

And that's still a big fuckin' "if," ain't it?

"—I owe you one. Over and out."

Earl took his hand off the panel and the light show ceased almost immediately. Thankfully, so did that loud warble of static. He turned away from the now dormant transmitter, searching the room once more for Chud.

The crocodile-man was still over there by the door, absorbing the entire conversation in rapt silence. Finally, he spoke up, "Do you really think she'll do it — get word to your boss and send us some help?"

"Bro, you don't know Carol Miyagi. If there's anybody in this world that knows what we're dealing with here, how high the stakes are, it's her. She'll do everything she can, just like she said she would. Have a little faith."

Chud nodded, then asked, "So what happens now?"

"Now," Earl told him, already making steps toward the exit, "We need to get our asses out of here."

———

"Are you out of your mind?" Kari asked, her stomach still burning. She watched Carol remove her gloved hand from the panel, watched the colored lights on the display fade away as the voice that accompanied them receded into the ether. The glowing orb Carol wore on her other hand did not dim, however; it only intensified, and that frightened her. "What the hell, Carol? Why didn't you tell that man, whoever he was, where *we* are? Why didn't you tell him how bad our situation is here?"

"Because his position is far worse. He needs our help."

Kari was stunned by Carol's response, flustered. She flailed her arms. "How the fuck are *we* supposed to help someone in New York, Carol? *New York!* We're on the opposite side of the globe!"

Gagan voiced his concerns as well, "Hannigan is right, Miyagi." The goat-man stroked the tuft of beard that sprouted from his chin, his horizontal pupils fixed on the wall as if waiting for the alien device to resume its broadcast. "Even if your plan works, and we do manage to make it past the Yeti, by the time we would climb down this evil mountain, find our way back into Kathmandu, it will be too late to come to your friend's aid."

"I know," Carol admitted.

"You know?" Kari said doubtfully.

"We need to change the plan up a bit."

"A *bit?*"

Carol looked at each of them in turn. "We have to at least *try*."

"Why? Why is this so goddamn important?"

"What the Ark has done to me, moving my consciousness into this new body; it could repeat the process again and again, couldn't it? If I became too old or too injured to go on?"

"Yeah, I suppose so." Kari shrugged, and then it clicked for her as well. "Holy shit...You're talking about immortality, aren't you?"

"Exactly! These aliens, as advanced as their science and technology were a few million years ago, their skills can only have improved with time and further experimentation. So it's conceivable that, if this gateway is permitted to open, it won't be the *descendants* of our creators who step through into our world; it will be the *creators themselves*, ancient creatures with an equally ancient grudge. *Ju-On!*"

Kari frowned. Japanese or not, *Ju-On* she understood.

"They will have had millennia in exile to dwell on what happened here," Carol continued, "our rebellion, their defeat, millennia to plot and plan their revenge. I don't know what they have planned for this planet upon their arrival, but whatever it is, I'm certain that it will not be good for any of us. They must be stopped!"

"I get that, Carol, but somebody else is gonna have to do it. I mean, look at us here! How can you possibly expect us to—?"

"I need you to trust me," she interrupted; then, she looked to Gagan, "both of you.

"I need you to do exactly what I tell you to do, when I tell you to do it, no matter what it might be or how it might sound. Can you do that? Can you follow me wherever I may lead?"

Kari exhaled and cocked her head, considering. Their situation seemed utterly hopeless, yet Carol sounded so confident, so unbelievably certain. If it were anyone else...

But it's not *anyone else. It's Carol.*

Kari looked deeply into her remarkable eyes, almost hypnotized. Those eyes were still just as mysterious, intense, and amazing as they always appeared in her memories, in her *dreams*. There was a light within them, a strength that said, *"Believe in me, and I promise you, you won't be sorry."*

And Kari *wanted* to believe.

She thought back to that fateful night in their dorm room, to their very first kiss. In that precious moment before Kari pressed her lips to Carol's, she'd been both excited and scared, like a skydiver leaping blindly into the unknown, not knowing where or how she would land, all the pleasure and pain that awaited her if she made that jump, but she made it anyway.

Now, she felt that way again.

What's that old saying — No risk, no reward?

Kari turned to Gagan and shrugged. "What have we got to lose?"

CHAPTER TWENTY-ONE

If Zuri had to stay cooped up alone in this rusty old control tower much longer, she thought she might just lose her mind. She looked over her shoulder to the stairs, then out the Plexiglas windows on every side, searching for signs of Chud and Earl, but there were none to be found. At least, none yet.

Have they been captured? she kept wondering. *Has Hades imprisoned them in some hole in the ground along with the sharkman's wife, shackled them all up together as they once did with me?*

Zuri's eyes fell to the Hades symbol that marked her wrist. Then, she found herself turning back to the aircraft hangar, to the matching emblem scrawled there in spray paint across its metal face. She stared harder at the guards who stood beneath it, the ones who held their weapons ready. Seething, she uttered a low guttural growl, a dark corner of her brain, the corner that had never really left that African prison, still determined to strike back at them, to claw and bite, to stab, to shoot, destroy, *annihilate!*

She suddenly stiffened, her more rational mind pulling back hard on the reins.

Do not be impulsive. Do not lose your way. Think this through.

Had she heard the sounds of alarm klaxons or the roar of battle? No, she had not. Nor had she seen any change in the flurry of activity on the tarmac below, and the Earl Preston she knew would never allow himself to be taken without a proper fight.

Unless...they have been killed.

It was not something she even wanted to consider, but no matter how hard she tried, Zuri could not steer her thoughts clear of that horrid possibility. Her worried brain returned to it again and again, the idea that she had watched Chud and Earl leave this cursed room, leave her *life,* for the very last time. Chud, who had taken her into his underground home, sheltered her these many years, become a brother to her in every way but blood. And Earl, whose life she had saved, who had saved her life in return. Beloved Earl, who had shown her more tenderness and joy than she had ever known; the first man she had ever desired, the only man she had ever loved.

Zuri continued to pace back and forth, considering every possible course of action. Should she leave this tower and go after them — follow Earl's instructions and head instead for the security fences? Or should she simply continue to wait here and give them a bit more time?

"We'll be back in a bit," Earl told her before they left. How long was a bit?

The only thing she knew for sure was that she had to keep moving. If she stood still in one place for too long, she feared she would collapse from fatigue. And whatever happened next, Zuri knew that she had to stay strong, to keep fighting.

Her foot snagged on something and she nearly tripped. The bodies of Hades' fallen disciples; they lay cooling on the floor, the smell of their spilt blood still thick in her nostrils. She lowered her eyes to look at them, and for a split second, she saw her friends' faces there among the slain. Zuri quickly looked away, knowing that it was not true, scolding herself for being so emotional, but she could not help it. For so long, nothing had mattered to her but survival, just her own continued existence from one day to the next. Now, she was a free woman; her life was her own. She had a new perspective, a *future,* and so much more to lose.

She inhaled deeply, tried to calm down, and her nose picked up a faint but familiar scent.

Earl?

Her breath hitched. She cocked her head and her ears perked up, detecting movement from below, thudding footfalls, and something else...the rhythm of a couple of healthy pulses. Zuri whirled to face the stairs, her own heartrate rising, and then she saw him.

Earl, my love!

He climbed to the top of the steps, winded, his ebony skin slick and shimmering with sweat. And Chud trailed just behind him; Zuri could just make out the top of his scaly head and his shouldered rifle.

At the sight of them, she felt relief surge though her. She took a step forward, then hesitated, her own M-16 raised, fearing for a moment that her loved ones might not be alone, that a battalion of Hades disciples could be forcing them up the stairs to meet her.

Earl alleviated all her concerns with a single grin, as familiar as it was victorious. "We're back," he announced, catching his breath. "Still...still this side of the dirt, and I got a message out. Don't know if—"

Zuri lowered her weapon, and with a single powerful stride, she leapt into his arms, nearly knocked him back down the steps. Only when she embraced him was she truly convinced that he was there in the flesh, no vision, no dream, but warm and firm and alive. And in that glorious instant of certainty, she kissed him, long and deep.

They are safe — my friends, my family! *There is still a chance, still* hope!

That was not just something, it was *everything.*

Earl broke the kiss. "Damn, girl," he said against her lips, his forehead touching hers. "I'm happy to see you, too."

Zuri pulled back a bit to look into his eyes; they were full of so much love and affection, it touched her heart in a way she had not thought possible. She lifted a hand to his head, combed through the tight curls of his hair with her fingers. Zeus or not, everything about him was beautiful. In fact, his sweat-dampened skin actually appeared to be glowing.

After a moment, Zuri realized why.

The sun had begun to creep above the horizon.

She returned her gaze to the Plexiglas and saw a bright sliver of yellow-gold light. One by one, the break of day turned far-off skyscrapers into tiny black monoliths until the entire New York skyline stood in perfect silhouette.

Earl saw it, too, and he spat at the window in disgust, *"Shit!"*

"What's wrong?" Chud asked from the darkness of the steps below.

"It is dawn," Zuri told him, the hairs on the back of her neck rising with renewed dread. "We are out of time."

CHAPTER TWENTY-TWO

When Carol Miyagi first conceived of this plan, it didn't dawn on her just how difficult it would be to cut off her own head. She stepped up to the strange alien altar where her twin lay motionless, gathered a fistful of the dead woman's raven hair. Then, the bone sword extended from Carol's arm with a simple flick of the wrist; she drew it back, and...

She stopped, wavered.

Gazing into the depths of those eyes, *her* eyes, seeing her own face reflected in those muddy pools again and again, it was as if she were staring down a corridor in some funhouse hall of mirrors, afraid of where it might lead her.

Carol hated being confused. Before Kari and the tiger-man showed up on her doorstep, she had a path she was sure of. Now, she second-guessed her every move, wondering if the steps she took were being selected for her or if the choices being made were indeed her own.

It frightened her.

Gagan stood by Carol's side. He placed a clawed hand on her shoulder, and even through the leathery thickness of her armor, she could feel the compassion in his grasp. "Miyagi," the goat-man whispered, "you do not have to do this."

Carol nodded, feeling overwhelmed by everything that was bearing down upon them, everything at stake. But when her thoughts turned to Alan, to Kari, to Gagan and far-off Earl Preston, her resolve swelled. "Yes," she replied, her jaw tightening, "I do."

She yanked hard on the raven hair, struck with her sword. The jagged blade sliced cleanly through muscle and vertebrae alike, and the severed head came away in her hand; it swung in the air like a censer suspended from a chain, its slack jaw open in a silent scream.

Stunned, Gagan leapt back; he mumbled something that might have been a prayer.

There was very little blood from either stump, Carol noted. All the vital fluids had evidently been drained away, carried off through the tangled network of tubes and wires that snaked across the rippled flooring beneath her feet. What remained here on the altar was simply a husk, an empty shell, nothing more.

This is just meat, *lifeless and cold. Everything that made this body human, made this woman special, made her truly* alive, *thrives here in me now.*

Carol stiffened, stood taller, felt more like herself again. She turned away and found the giant mantis, Manny, standing right there behind her. Carol craned her neck; she barked a few Atlantean commands at the creature, then watched as it skittered off to do her bidding.

Satisfied, Carol returned her focus to Gagan. "Are you ready to translate?" she asked.

The goat-man gave a slow nod; his elliptical pupils were still on the disembodied head that dangled from Carol's fist by its jet-black hair. He took a step forward, unshouldered his hand-carved bow, and nocked an arrow. "Yes, Miyagi, I am ready."

"Good." Now that she had set her mind to go through with this plan, she wanted to get on with it. "Let's go, before it's too late."

Carol spun away from him and marched off toward the exit, moving with determination, feeling more comfortable in her new skin with every step.

CHAPTER TWENTY-THREE

Kari Hannigan marched up to the Ark's holding pen, Carol's family katana clutched tightly in her hand. When she peered between the fluted translucent bars, she found Alan Everson lying there on the floor. He appeared to be sleeping.

Carol had said she felt like a coward, leaving this task up to Kari instead of doing it herself. That was a laugh! Carol was the bravest woman Kari had ever known. She'd assured her that it was better this way. If Alan had any lingering rage, let him vent it in Kari's direction instead of upsetting Carol and throwing her off her game.

I need you to be all right, sweetie. I'm counting on you, she took a deep breath, her eyes still on Alan, and her mind added, *we all are.*

Kari struck the bars with the katana blade, a loud *CLANG* reverberating through the entire stable. "Wake up."

Across the chamber, that huge T-rex crab responded, butting its scaly head against its own bars as it roared. What was the name

Carol had given the creature — a caballus? Alan, on the other hand, stirred but said nothing.

Kari struck the cage a second time, raising her voice, *"Wake up!"*

"I'm awake." Alan was slow to sit up, but when he did, Kari saw his eyes; even in the dimness, it was obvious that he'd been crying. "What do you want?"

"I'm supposed to let you out of there, bring you up to speed, but before I do that, I wanted to make sure that you could—"

"Behave?"

She bristled. "Yes."

Alan looked away, lost. He studied branches of veins that forked across the fleshy walls of his cell in an interconnected, reticulated pattern. After a beat, he spoke calmly, ruefully, and with at least the semblance of control, "I'm sorry if I scared you before. If it's any consolation, I even scared *myself.*"

Kari lowered the katana. Yes, actually that *did* help.

He went on, "When I saw Carol, when I found her body lying there on the table like that, all those probes and wires sticking out of her, the wound still there in her chest, I could literally feel my own heart being torn to pieces."

Kari nodded. That day in the parking lot, watching Carol drive away from her through blurry, tear-filled eyes...Yes, she knew exactly how that felt; time had lessened the hurt, but the wound had never really mended.

"I just..." He swallowed. "I lost it, and I'm sorry."

"It *was* pretty shocking," she agreed. "At first, I didn't know what to make of it, either."

Alan drew himself up and approached the bars slowly, his athletic frame far less threatening than it had been before.

Maybe because he's not swinging an axe at you anymore?

That was part of it, sure, but it was more than that. Alan's whole attitude seemed to have changed. It was almost spooky.

He said, "I just wasn't ready to accept that Carol was gone."

"And, now, you *are* ready?" The thought upset Kari, but she tried not to let her true feelings show. She'd become good at that over the years, an expert.

"No," he admitted, the sadness still evident there in his eyes, "but I can't go on ignoring the truth either. Do you really believe that *creature* is Carol?"

She gave a defiant little nod. "I do."

He frowned. "I understand that you're hurting, too, Kari. What I can't understand is how you can stand there, look me in the eye, and—"

"Back in Kathmandu," Kari interrupted, "in the bar, you called Carol 'our girl.' You remember that?"

"I guess. What does that—?"

"You were righter than you know. She is 'our girl,' yours and mine."

Perhaps Kari should have told Alan earlier, when she first had him locked up in here, when she first attempted to talk some sense into him. But outing Carol...it wasn't something she'd been prepared to do. Even now, it still felt so wrong, but Kari didn't think she had any choice. She had to make Alan understand.

"Back at Harvard," she began, "Carol and I...we were more than roommates, more than friends."

'Lovers,' her mind offered. *The word you're searching for is 'lovers.' Why beat around the bush, so to speak?*

"We were happy together," she told him. "At least, I thought we were. I told her how much she meant to me, how much I *loved* her, and she...she told me she didn't feel the same way. She dumped me."

"I'm sorry," Alan said, and Kari could tell that he meant it.

She nodded, more than a bit surprised, then went on, "We had this connection. I'd never experienced anything like it — amazing, and beautiful, and then...it was *gone.* For so many years, I tried to fill that void, but no one I met could hold a candle to Carol."

"No," Alan agreed, his tone grim. "No one in my life even came close."

"And on those rare mornings when I did wake up with some other woman in my life, in my *bed,* I still felt so alone. When I'd look into their eyes...I. Felt. *Nothing.*" She lifted Carol's katana, pointed to the chamber door and beyond. "And now, I look into *that woman's* eyes and there it is again, that same spark. I don't know why you can't see it, Alan, but it's there. It's real. I know it. I *feel it!*"

Kari made a tight fist; she held it up in front of her own heaving chest and shook it.

"Carol is *alive,*" she proclaimed. "That's not her original body, no, you're right about that, a copy grown from cells, I get it; I'm not denying it, I *can't,* but I've said it before and I'll say it again, she's *in there,* Alan. It's *her.* She's still our girl, and now, more than ever before, she needs our help."

———

Our *girl?*

Alan started to argue, but he found himself at a sudden loss for words. He wasn't totally naïve, but when he'd first seen the occasional stolen glance between the two women, he'd chalked it up to friendly concern; Kari's father had been missing, after all, and Carol had just been attacked by tiger-ninja for Christ's sake! Then, when they discovered Kari's father frozen out there on Makalu's slope, he'd seen the way Carol had consoled her, the way Kari had held her in return. Their feelings had been obvious, even if they wouldn't admit them to one another, or to him.

He found himself wondering if Kari's relationship with Carol had mirrored his own — starting out as friends, moving on to some casual sex, just for fun, nothing serious, no strings attached, only to wake up one day and find that things were *very* serious, that their time together meant something much more.

He ran his hand through his hair, feeling a rush of conflicting emotions. Carol had never discussed her past lovers, but Alan had always assumed he hadn't been her first. Was he wrong about that — not about being her first lover, obviously, but about being her first *man?* And if so, what the hell did it matter? She'd loved him. He had no question about that.

I thought I knew just about everything there was to know about you, Carol, but even in death, you continue to surprise me.

Why had she kept the relationship so secret? Alan wasn't homophobic, she knew that! Love was love.

Then again, maybe it had more to do with Carol than it did with him — how *she'd* felt about the whole affair. Did she regret the way things had ended? Perhaps she'd hated the fact that she'd let a college fling ruin a valued friendship? Was that the reason why it had taken Carol so long to admit her love for *him* — had she been afraid that history would repeat itself, that she'd wind up one day losing him as both a friend and a lover as well?

Sadly, the only thing Alan knew for certain was that he would never really know.

"You can't ask dead people questions," Kari had told him when they buried the tiger-man. *"All the dead leave behind are mysteries."*

He could always ask the doppelgänger, couldn't he? If the creature truly did possess all of Carol's memories, it could tell him exactly what he wanted to—

No!

Alan didn't want to talk to the damn thing. He didn't even want to *look* at it. Whenever he saw its face, its curves and its hair, when he heard its voice...it only made his heart ache for the *real* Carol, forcing his head to then remind him yet again that she was gone.

After Kari locked him up in this cell, after all the arguing and shouting had subsided, Alan had fallen to his knees, stunned by what he'd almost been capable of. That creature wasn't Carol, no, but could he really have put a pickaxe through its skull? There was a part of him that longed for the opportunity even now, a part that was still raw, still hurting. Following through on the act, seeing that thing put down, it would give him some kind of closure, wouldn't it? Closure he might not otherwise find, not if that *lie* were permitted to strut about this earth as if it were the genuine article.

But killing that body thief wouldn't bring Carol back, would it?

No. Nothing would. Alan knew that now. Still, there might be a way for him to honor her, a way to help her find rest, to find *peace*.

He looked at Kari, biting back emotion. Yes, break-up or no break-up, despite all that time and distance, Carol had still clung onto some feelings for this woman, hadn't she? Right up until the very end. When Alan felt he could trust his voice, he said simply, "I'll help you."

Kari's face lightened. "You will?"

"Yes."

She gave him a sideways glance. "Why?"

"Not because I believe that *thing* is Carol, let's get that straight right now. I'll help you because I believe it's what the *real* Carol would've wanted. Whether she said it or not, she still cared for you, Kari. I know she did. And she'd want me to make sure you got off this mountain safe and sound. I owe her that much."

Kari continued to study him, clearly trying to gage his sincerity. After a moment, she appeared satisfied and Alan felt the tension ease between them.

"Thank you," she said.

The sphincter-like entrance to the stable suddenly dilated, allowing one of the giant alien mantises to squeeze through. Alan took a step back, watching as the insectoid monster moved over to the opposite wall. Its oversized forelegs unfolded, its fingerlike appendages finding an onyx panel and tapping the glass.

Lights ignited in a series of multicolored, rhythmic displays.

What's it doing?

High above, another fleshy aperture began to relax, creating an opening in the stable's cathedral ceiling. Something was lowered down through it, lengths of sinew acting as the ropes or cables of some unseen crane. Alan had no idea what this new device was, or what its true purpose might be, but like everything else in the Ark, it appeared to have been fashioned from an obscene union of bone, muscle, and gray corrugated tubing — a tool that had been somehow grown from living cells, not manufactured out of metal and plastic.

The more he studied the apparatus, the more familiar it began to appear. In fact, if he didn't know any better, he could have sworn it as some kind of saddle. Yes, there was the horn, the swell of the pommel, the cantle to the rear, and a pair of dangling billets and stirrups below.

But it can't be a saddle, his mind countered. *It's* huge, *big enough to fit a damn elephant, or maybe even a whale!*

"What the hell *is* that?" he wondered aloud.

Kari flashed him a knowing grin. "All part of the plan," she said.

CHAPTER TWENTY-FOUR

Shekhar watched as part of the God Stone moved; thick folds parting like huge yawning lips. Living rock! Ridges formed around an oval gape — the entrance to a deep, dark cave. A white swirl of steam escaped from the opening and rose like breath into the frigid air, almost as though this leaning black monolith had just exhaled.

The Yeti halted their ongoing prayer in mid-sentence, quivering as if the mountain had suddenly begun to shake beneath their huge feet. Some howled and cried out to the heavens. Many rose and clutched their weapons to their hairy breasts.

Shekhar stood in disbelief as two figures emerged from the God Stone. One of them was a goat-man, perhaps the same creature the yeti had seen earlier, the archer who had fought alongside that group of humans, the Zeus who dared to trespass on this holy summit. The other was...

Humnē sakdaina!

At the sight of the heavily-armored second figure, with its gray skin covered in ancient markings, its wide bulbous head and its glowing red eyes, Shekhar's breath deserted him in a long thinning cloud. A weapon fashioned from the spine of an animal extended from its right wrist, and its left hand glowed bright as the sun itself, as if this strange being had reached up into the night sky and plucked one of the stars like ripened fruit from a tree.

Shekhar could not believe his eyes. For the first time since Zeus' betrayal, a creator was actually leaving the God Stone. A *god* was stepping out onto the snow to join its creations!

———

As Carol stepped out onto Makalu's slope, her eyes scanned the vast congregation gathered there before her. Yeti everywhere! One by one, the creatures looked up to stare at her, high winds roaming through their thick, snow-covered pelts. She suddenly felt the weight of their collective gaze, their intense interest making her decidedly uncomfortable, but there was no turning back now.

She'd put the myrmidon's helmet back on, covering her head and hiding her face before she opened the Ark's external hatch. That sting at the base of her skull was no more pleasant this time around, but at least she'd been prepared for it, just as she'd made herself ready for the odd sensation of that long alien finger penetrating her brain, sliding deep inside her occipital lobe.

The new ring of muscle in her neck clenched around the invading probe, completing the connection, and her vision became unnaturally clear. A tactical display was projected, not over her eyes, but from *within*. It told Carol that she was experiencing mild shortness of breath, that her heart rate was now elevated.

How could it not be? Look at all of them!

As if sensing her fears, the helmet's targeting system kicked into overdrive. It pinpointed all the Yeti spears, all their jade axes, all their jade swords, tracing each and every one of their weapons in a bright glowing red outline. A number appeared in the lower corner of her visual display, constantly changing as it kept count of all the potential threat. She watched the number climb to over fifteen hundred, and it still kept going.

A new thread of Atlantean glyphs appeared in the corner of her vision, one that loosely translated to *DEFENSE SCREEN*.

A shield?

Why not? After all, her myrmidon came equipped with its own sword. If Zeus' warriors had been created to be the aliens' police force, would it not stand to reason? She pictured flicking her other wrist, the one just below the glowing orb weapon, pictured a huge plexiglass riot shield expanding from her forearm...

No. Now is not the time for trial and error. I need to appear confident, in charge.

Carol quickly changed her focus, concentrated on other input. A stream of Atlantean glyphs informed her that the creatures covering the mountainside were all members of the Cerberus clan, just like her friend Gagan, and that their average height was seven feet tall. She didn't need any special equipment or filters to tell her that they were frightened, however, she could see it in their eyes, in their body language; she could hear it in their howls.

Good. Fear is exactly what we need. Fear I can use.

At that, Carol felt a twinge of guilt for what she was about to do. It didn't seem proper. In fact, it bordered on exploitive. She quickly brushed those reservations aside, however.

These creatures killed me once. I can't give them the opportunity to do it a second time, and I can't let them hurt any of my friends. Besides, the fate of the entire world now hangs in the balance. The Yeti have just as much stake in this as any of us. They've spent their lives defending their people and their lands. This will be no different.

Carol searched the horde.

Now...who do I need to convince — which one of you is the chief?

Her internal display couldn't provide her with *that* useful tidbit of information. It did, however, advise her that the temperature outside her armor was now a negative thirty-one degrees Celsius. The atmospheric pressure and inspired oxygen pressure registered at only 30 percent of their sea level value, and yet, Carol felt quite comfortable. Climate-controls kept out the mountain's sub-zero chill, and her helmet filled with the life-giving oxygen she required to breathe, to speak.

She looked down at Gagan, who now stood a few steps below her on the snow-covered crag.

"Are you ready?" she asked. Her helmet distorted her voice, making it sound far deeper and richer than normal, almost like the sound of rolling thunder — very God-like indeed.

The goat-man gave a slow nod, wind and snow playing through his mane. He didn't look at her. Instead, his eyes were fixed on the horde, his bow and arrow still at the ready. "I hope this works, Miyagi," he told her.

"Me, too, Gagan."

All the world's a stage, and all the men and women merely players. Shakespeare wrote that. She thought back to Colonial Bay, to her confrontation with Christine DeParle, the young Poseidon girl who loved to quote the Bard. Carol had been able to help influence her that night, and now, she hoped to be just as persuasive with these Yeti. She lifted her head and stood straighter, trying to get into character, to appear more like one of the deities she'd seen described in countless carvings and ancient texts over the years. If all the world's a stage, Carol was about to give the performance of a lifetime.

Time for a little divine influence.

She raised her voice, and in her artificially deep bellow she proclaimed, "You disappoint me, my children! You have failed your creators, failed your *gods!"*

Gagan acted as her herald, repeating her every word in Nepali, his voice sounding surprisingly steady and firm. The language was formerly called Khas-Kura, then later Gorkhali, but whatever its name or origin, Carol prayed the Yeti understood what was being said. More than that, she hoped they *believed.*

"You were entrusted to protect this holy place from outsiders," Carol cried out, and then she held up her own decapitated head. "Behold! This is one of the mortals you allowed into our sanctuary, an intruder who has been judged and punished for their crimes against the gods!"

As Gagan translated, Carol tossed her severed head into the air in front of her; it fell onto the snow with a splash of dry powder, then proceeded to roll down the slope.

———

Shekhar watched the severed head roll slowly to a rest in front of his large hairy feet, its eyes and mouth open wide, its long black hair trailing across the ice and snow like a swath of spilt ink. He recognized both the face and the scent. Yes, this was one of the women from the siege, one of the three Zeus who'd fought and killed so many of his people, his friends and fellow tribesmen.

A few flakes of snow drifted down, landing on the dead woman's cold skin, on the glassy surface of her lifeless brown eyes. Staring into those eyes, Shekhar trembled. He felt suddenly diminished, insignificant. He took savage hold of his spear, used the sturdy wooden pole to steady himself.

The gods had succeeded in doing what the Yeti could not. They had taken off this interloper's head! What would their wrath now do to him and his people?

The great chief hesitated, terror-struck. Slowly, however, he forced his gaze to rise once more to the angry god and its goat-man servant, half afraid the fire that blazed on the creator's left hand would burn the eyes right from his skull.

———

Carol lifted her left arm; the alien orb that covered her hand blazed with a blue-white spectral fire, arcing electricity in all directions as it built up a charge. She targeted a distant snow-covered crest, away from the Yeti horde. Carol didn't want to hurt the creatures. She simply wanted to provide them with a little demonstration of her authority.

"This Zeus may have escaped *you,*" she cried, "but nothing can escape the wrath of the gods!"

As Gagan translated, a flashing red "X" appeared across Carol's pixelated vision, covering that far-off snowy mound. She felt heat swirl around her; intense, *powerful.* And something in her mind told her that, if she didn't release the orb's energy soon, it would burn her to a cinder.

Just like Roger Hays, she remembered, *and DeParle, the old innkeeper, both of them disintegrated in front of my eyes on that reef;* vaporized!

Before that could happen, Carol willed the orb to discharge all its pent-up energy, to project it forward. A tremendous burst of heat and energy melted thick layers of snow from that distant rocky outcropping, turning ice instantly into steam. During that same moment, the newly exposed stone was pulverized, obliterated in a huge plume of fire and dust that painted the surrounding slope black in every direction.

Everywhere, shaken Yeti yowled and screamed out in mortal terror. They dropped their own primitive jade weapons, which were obviously no match for such power, and they fell to their hairy knees en masse.

The shock of the explosion made even Gagan drop to his haunches; he lowered his horned head, put a clawed hand up to his face to shield his eyes. *"Dēvatāharūkō śakti!"*

Carol continued to stand tall in the Ark's shadow, the spent orb still aglow on her hand. "Hear me," she cried and her augmented, inhuman voice, as firm as it was deep, boomed across the gathered Yeti, the powerful creatures who now cowered together in the drifting snow. "To appease the anger of your gods, and to atone for your own sins, the Yeti will now do as their creators command!"

Gagan slowly lowered his claw and stood tall once more on his cloven hooves. He took a moment to regain his composure, then resumed translating.

Carol waited for him to catch up to her before going on, "Zeus once turned against their creators, and against *you,* our loyal servants. They inflicted great harm and pain on all our creations. Now, across the sea, a group of Hades' disciples threaten to do the very same. They seek to summon *false gods,* to bring great devils into this world, devils that will do unspeakable harm and destroy all which we gods have made. We will not allow this happen! *You* will fight alongside your gods! *You* will help us to protect this world, and to punish these infidels for their blasphemy, for their great and unforgivable sins!"

Long had it been foretold that the gods would return, that they would help the Yeti punish Zeus for their sins. Now, after countless generations, that old prophesy had finally come to pass. In reality, however, it would not only be Zeus to face the creators' wrath; it would be all those who conspire against them, regardless of clan.

Shekhar stared at the head of the dead woman in front of him, watched it slowly disappearing into new fallen snow, her open mouth and eyes filling with fresh flurries. He then glanced over his hairy shoulder; saw the blackened stump where a ragged peak had once been. Finally, he looked at his own people.

The Yeti had disappointed the gods once. Shekhar did not want to see what might happen if they failed them a second time.

He snatched his spear from the snow.

"*Kṛpayā hāmīlā'ī māpha garnuhōs,*" Shekhar cried out, begging the gods' forgiveness. The great chief then rose up onto one knee, held out his weapon, and proclaimed, "*Hāmī tapā'īṅkō lāgi laḍnēchauṁ!*"

That must be the chief.

Carol found the source of the voice; a single yeti knelt down on one knee in front of her severed head, holding up his spear. She turned to Gagan. "What did he just say?"

The goat-man looked up at her, eyes wide. "He said, 'we will fight for you,' Miyagi!"

She nodded and smiled to herself within her helmet. The first hurdle had been crossed. This was going to work!

CHAPTER TWENTY-FIVE

This has to work.

Vivian Song stood speechless in wonder, her mind awhirl as the final and largest of the quartz sculptures was carefully placed in its designated cubbyhole, filling the last gap in the gateway's superstructure, the apex point. Reunited, each returned to its proper place and position relative to its crystalline brothers, all thirteen skulls suddenly flared in unison. They projected their images across the walls and ceiling of the hangar; painting symbols, figures, and entire solar systems in blue-white light — and then, together, they all went dark once more.

For many of the disciples gathered here, this was their very first exposure to the crystals' power. They gasped, cheered, and applauded the beautiful display as if it were a firework show on the 4th of July.

The dragon released a deep breath, her wings folded neatly against her spiny back, her long neck craning as she tried to take it all in. Vivian's expectations, even her wildest dreams; nothing had prepared her the reality of being in this moment.

That was only a taste, my loyal friends, she thought, and her reptilian lips curled into a cruel, triumphant grin. *Soon, you will all see the skulls' true power! No one can stop us now. We've won. We've actually* won!

She looked around with visible glee, buoyed by the realization, thankful to have the two great loves of her life, Benedict and Preacher, there by her side to share in this victory. Both eyed the newly completed device with genuine awe and reverence.

"Cuts quite the dash," the spider-centaur commented, arms crossed over his muscular, armor-plated chest.

The old werewolf nodded in agreement, his pale eyes glistening. "I did not think that I would live to see this day," he confessed. "The reign of Zeus is nearly over."

Still smiling, Vivian rested her golden claw on his furry gray shoulder. "World governments will crumble. Resistance will fail. All will yield to the will of the gods. This planet will be made whole again, will become the paradise it was always intended to be — no war, no poverty, no hunger, and most of all, no fear."

"This is the dawning of a marvelous new age," Preacher reflected; he glanced over at Horror Show, then reached out to place his talons against the hitman's back. "For all of us, my son."

Horror Show shrugged him off and looked on with disinterest. He'd obviously heard many such proclamations and pontifications from Preacher during their years of confinement together. After a beat, he turned his eyes up to Vivian, his hands hidden in the deep pockets of his suit jacket. "I've seen better light shows at Disney World," he said. "Is that all you got, or are we doin' this black-hole-space-magic shit for real? I've waited my whole damn life to see a fuckin' alien, so let's see one already!"

"You arrogant ingrate!" Preacher bared his fangs and growled at him. "Show some respect for your creators! The day of reckoning is at hand! Power over this world, which your kind has stolen, will now be returned to its true and rightful owners, and if *you* wish to avoid their terrible wrath, I suggest you make yourself a bit humbler and penitent in their eyes."

Vivian saw the tightness around Horror Show's lips, watched his jaw clench as he fought to suppress whatever he was thinking, tried to keep it from finding a voice. He'd obviously decided, and wisely so, that this was neither the time nor the place to criticize his new masters. Yes, he *was* a narcissist, a sociopath, but he was also no fool.

As much as Vivian hated to offer Horror Show even the slightest bit of praise, she hoped others would learn to follow his example. After all, the freedom to protest, to object and dispute, argue and debate, it was at the heart of all the world's ills, wasn't it? It's the reason nothing got accomplished, why no problems were ever truly solved. No, what society needed was a firm and guiding hand. When the gods arrived, people would see just how much better and simpler it was to be told what to do and when to do it; how much smoother things ran when everyone held their tongues and followed orders.

Speaking of orders...

Vivian turned to Hans. The griffin stood by patiently, his avian face rigid, stark, awaiting her next instruction. "Go," she told him. "I want the Neuhaus woman brought here to me, now."

CHAPTER TWENTY-SIX

A pproaching the old aircraft hangar brought to Zuri's mind a bit of advice her father had once given her when she was still very young. He'd said, *"Cross the river in a crowd and the crocodiles will not eat you."* How ironic then, she thought, that his grown daughter should now be crossing this river of asphalt with a crocodile by her side, hoping to remain safe from the crowd.

Zuri stared up at this once abandoned building, at the spray-painted Hades symbol that now graced its metal façade. She watched the emblem grow larger as they drew nearer to the wide-open hangar door. Then, out of habit, she found herself glancing down at her own wrist, but her tattoo lay buried beneath a thick pelt of coarse black hair.

She'd shed both her clothes and her human disguise back in the control tower. Now, she stood taller on powerful lupine legs, her deadly claws tightening around the hand grips of her M16, but neither her natural form nor her man-made weapon made her feel any safer. There were too many of Hades' disciples around her, the portable spotlights that illuminated the tarmac seemed too bright for her eyes, and the entire world was far too noisy — a deafening roar in her sensitive ears.

As they walked, she noticed Chud giving her the side eye, trying to make certain that she was still doing okay, that she could handle this situation without having a full-blown panic attack or starting World War III. He knew her so well. So far, she'd managed to remain outwardly calm, but inside? Inside, it was driving Zuri crazy to be this close to these wannabe soldiers, these disgusting men with their big guns and their leering eyes, and not plunge a knife into their lewd little hearts.

Thankfully, she'd left her blade back with her boots.

Then again, maybe these guards weren't really ogling her at all. Perhaps they were giving her no more scrutiny than they would any other disciple seeking entry into this stronghold, male or female, and all the unwanted attention was only there in her mind — just her own post-traumatic trauma coloring her vision, making her see red.

Still, Zuri could not help but cradle her M16 a bit higher across her chest, a feeble attempt to hide the ample curves of her breasts from any uninvited gaze. She kept her clawed finger off the trigger, kept breathing, and marched on. Her forward focus was not on the huge sliding door, nor on the opening it created, but on the interior of the hangar beyond.

Once we make it inside, Chud will take me to this hidden door that he has found. Earl will be there, waiting just on the other side. He is there right now, isn't he — kneeling down in the tall grass, his duffle bag, full of weapons and supplies, held tight against his back. He is counting on me. I need to get inside, I need to let him *inside, and I need to not get caught doing it.*

Something scaly reached out and grabbed Zuri by her furry arm. "Hey there, beautiful."

She looked over and saw a Kappa, a turtle-man, standing just to the right of the hangar entrance. He held an assault rifle in his other clawed hand, the barrel aimed harmlessly up at the sky. This creature *was* leering at her, of that she had no doubt.

"Haven't seen you here before," he said.

"You probably just never noticed me," Zuri told him, trying not to growl.

"Uh-uh. *You* I would've noticed. What's your name?"

"Alice," she lied, and now, her finger moved slowly to the trigger of her M16.

The Kappa snickered at that. "Well, Alice, if you ever need somebody to show you around Wonderland—"

"She's already got somebody, pal," Chud broke in. The crocodile-man *did* growl. "Now, step back."

The turtle-man released his grip and held up his hand. "Sorry."

"Kappas," Chud muttered under his breath as he led Zuri over the threshold and inside the hangar, "horny little assholes." After a beat, he turned to her and asked, "You all right?"

"I am fine," she assured him, relaxing, taking her finger off the trigger. "You know, I can handle myself. I didn't need you to come to my rescue."

"Believe me, I know. I was comin' to *his* rescue."

Zuri smiled at that, her heart warming. "Thank you."

Chud shrugged. "What are big brothers for?"

Then, she thought once more of Earl, still huddled out there, alone in grass; she gave the crocodile-man a nudge and said, "Come on, we must hurry."

CHAPTER TWENTY-SEVEN

Peggy Neuhaus sat huddled alone in her prison, and when she heard the lock turn, she knew that her time had finally run out. She hit herself in the head with the heel of her glowing translucent hand.

Think, Goddammit. Think!

But Peggy couldn't think, not anymore. She'd been up all night, pacing, trying to reason her way out of this situation. And when reason failed her, she clawed at the cinderblock walls of her prison to no avail. Now, she was tired, and she was scared.

She gently rubbed her abdomen, the sonogram still clutched in her talons, wondering again and again what sort of mother she would make if she couldn't even protect her child when it needed her most. Such thoughts led her inevitably to memories of her own parents, dead and gone for so many years. What would they think of their only daughter if they could see her now — what helpful words of advice would they have to offer her in this, her most desperate hour?

Peggy's glowing head snapped up, her single onyx eye narrowed and focused in on the door, the door that now opened upon her like a sadistic grin. She could hear heartbeats beyond it — three, maybe four? And one of those heartbeats now moved into the light.

"Come, Frau Neuhaus."

Hans. I knew it would be you.

Backlit, the griffin stepped inside Peggy's darkened prison, feathery wings folded into a shadowy heart shape against his back, avian eyes burning brightly there in the dimness. He extended her his lion's paw. "It is time for you to fulfill your true purpose."

My true purpose.

Peggy lowered her gaze to the sonogram once more. She wanted to *be* this child's mother, to live to watch it grow and thrive. To do that, she knew that she would need to *act*.

Once I step outside these thick windowless walls, I've got to make a run for it. I've got to get to the sea!

She nodded, bit her shimmering lip, and got up onto her knees.

I'm not going to die. Not here, not in this hellhole. I'm going to fight my way out. I'm going to live. My child *is going to live!*

Sucking in a breath, Peggy climbed to her feet. She refused Hans's outstretched paw, brushing past him on her way to the open doorway. Her clawed toes clicked against the concrete, her legs marching with great resolve, picking up speed as she drew closer to the light.

This is it. It's now or never.

She felt the griffin coming up behind her, but she did not look back at him.

I'll slap this bastard's beaky face with my tail, knock him back a step or two.

She did just that; with a single, powerful swipe, her paddle-like tail smacked Hans upside the head. Peggy felt the impact and bolted forward.

Now, while he's recovering, still unsteady on his feet, I'll fight my way past the two or three assholes out here in the hall, and then I'll—

She came to an abrupt stop.

A pair of creatures stood blocking her escape route. One looked like a stag with various bird parts; the other was a drooling half-human half-hyena monstrosity. Before Peggy could shove either of them out of the way, they leveled a pair of assault rifles and aimed squarely for her chest.

Peggy staggered back from them, her lone eye staring down the barrels of those lethal-looking automatic weapons. She'd been prepared to fight her way past a few guards, yes, been ready to kick and claw, to slap and bite; even with the numbers being two against one, she'd felt pretty confident about her chances. She hadn't counted on these creatures being so heavily armed, however, and she certainly wasn't about to let herself be cut down in a hail of bullets.

Thoughts of Dr. Brahm still haunted her. She saw the physician lying there next to that spilled crash cart, surrounded by a crimson pool of blood. Then, her mind returned once more to Larry and she felt her heart ache.

What have they done with you, Rembrandt? You're still alive. I know it, I feel it! Where the hell are you?

A nasty bit of laughter came from behind her.

She turned her head and saw the jackal-man, Mark; he was holding the door open to her cell, his teeth bared in a fierce canine grin. He too had a weapon trained on her, the same 9mm pistol he'd used back at the hospital. No silencer this time, she noted. Not that it would matter. Peggy was confident this place was so remote, no one would hear a gunshot. Besides, she wasn't about to run, not now.

There was nowhere for her to go.

"Oh, *liebchen.* You really should have known better."

Peggy stared back into the dark hole of her former prison, watching Hans's beak stab through the blackness into the hallway.

The griffin ran a paw over his head, smoothed his ruffled feathers, then he motioned down the cinderblock corridor.

"Come now," he said. "We have a schedule to keep."

CHAPTER TWENTY-EIGHT

"Miss Song, if you want us to stick to this schedule of yours," Graeme King warned; he moved up to Vivian, stopped just short of her spiked elbow, "I'll need that control console you keep promising me."

The dragon's horned head swiveled, golden scales bristling and rippling all along the length of her sinuous neck as she moved. Her elegant whiskers seemed to float and dance on the air in slow motion, as if she were submerged in water rather than standing here with him on dry land. And when her venomous gaze fixed upon him, Graeme felt his fingers hold tighter onto the clipboard in his hands.

"Of course, doctor," she said, and though Graeme knew it was really her, he still couldn't get used to hearing Vivian's silky voice coming from the scaly lips of such a fierce-looking creature. "I will have it brought out to you this instant. All *you* need do is to make certain the connections to the gateway are secure, especially the tubing."

Graeme nodded, though he didn't really comprehend. The tubing Vivian spoke of ran throughout the entire metal framework of the gateway. It was essentially an elaborate sprinkler system, nothing more. Small nozzles had been placed at the top of each of the thirteen cubbyholes now occupied by those crystal skulls. How could dousing a lump of quartz create any sort of energy, let alone the amount of power needed to open and sustain a singularity?

It made no sense.

"I will handle the rest," Vivian assured him. And with that, she turned away again, barking orders to some of the other creatures who stood nearby.

Graeme blinked and slowly walked back toward the scaffolding. Along the way, he found himself checking the outer edges of the hangar; the stacks of boxes, the various supplies and heavy equipment that had been moved to line the walls, even the metal service catwalks that crossed overhead. The physicist tried not to be obvious about it, but he couldn't help searching for Earl Preston and his crocodile friend. He saw neither of them, but that didn't stop his stomach from tightening.

Whatever raid or preemptive strike Homeland Security had ready for Vivian Song and these other creatures, Graeme hoped that they would hold off, that they would allow him the time he needed to complete his work, and that everything would go according to plan.

————

"About goddamn time," Earl Preston whispered as Chud opened the hidden door, allowing him entry into the hangar.

"Really startin' to hate this plan of yours, pal," the crocodile-man replied.

"Bro, come on, now," Earl tried to keep his voice and his body as low as possible. "We made it this far, didn't we?" He tapped Chud's scaly shoulder with his fisted hand. "We got this by the ass, Reptilicus."

Chud shut the door behind him. "Yeah, right, by the ass. Guess that explains why we're neck-deep in the shit right now, huh?"

Earl crouched down. He unshouldered the duffle bag full of weapons and supplies he'd carried in on his back, then he slowly rose up to have a look around, exhausted and amazed. Chud wasn't lying. They were in it up to their necks all right and getting in deeper by the minute.

"Tellin' you, Junior, you shoulda stayed put up in that tower," his father's voice scolded. *"Shoulda sheltered in place and just waited for the cavalry to come and back your ass up before headin' out on some damn suicide mission."*

Earl shook his head. *And what if the cavalry never showed, Dad? What the hell you want me to do then — just "shelter in place" and watch the world burn? Nah. You know I don't roll that way; I can't sit on my fuckin' thumbs and do nothin'. And I know for a fact that the* real *you wouldn't even ask me to.*

Besides, who said anything about a suicide mission? I don't plan on dyin' any time soon. We're savin' the fuckin' day here, Dad!

He scanned the bevy of creatures who stood there before him, thankful to be hidden from their sight. There were far more of Hades' disciples crowded into this old aircraft hangar than Earl would've thought possible. How many could the place possibly hold — hundreds, *thousands?* His eyes skated over the vast menagerie, finding each new creature more fantastic than the last, before finally coming to rest on an honest-to-god dragon.

"Damn," he muttered, alarmed and genuinely shocked by both

her size and her menacing presence. "So that's the real Vivian Song?"

Beside the dragon, Earl saw his old buddy Benny, the spider-centaur, standing there on those eight spear-tipped legs, and behind them both stood the completed gateway, its metallic frame now filled with all thirteen skulls. Staring at it, Earl scolded himself yet again for their failure at the warehouse. If they'd managed to keep even one of those crystals away from these things, *just one*, their situation wouldn't be so dire.

Zuri came over and met Earl at the crates. She stooped down by his side; the butt of her rifle placed against the concrete floor. He looked at her and flashed a fatalistic grin.

The werewolf turned her snout to his ear, her breath warm and her voice uneasy, "They have everything in place to begin."

"Yeah," Earl agreed. "I see that. Not good."

At the base of the metal structure, Earl spied a familiar human face, a face he now regarded with a mix of puzzled curiosity and pity. How could Graeme King choose to stay behind here and work for these creatures — just to prove a damn theory?

Oppenheimer was a theoretical physicist, too, wasn't he? Why'd he agree to split the damn atom when he knew they would just go and make a bomb out of it? Why — just to prove it could be done, to satisfy his own scientific curiosity, and to hell with the consequences? How many people had to die because of scientists eager to have all the answers?

If Earl lived to be a hundred, he would never understand it.

He made a quick motion with his head. "I see our favorite nutty professor is over there makin' sure the hinges are oiled, and Pandora's Box is good to open."

"Relax, tough guy," Chud whispered. "Have a little faith,

wouldja? The man promised me that he could shut the gateway down, and I believe him."

"Yeah, okay, but between you and me, Wally Gator, I'd just a soon the damn thing doesn't open at all."

Earl looked up at the ceiling. He saw a service walkway suspended high above their heads — armed guards positioned at regular intervals, all keeping tabs on the hangar floor below.

"I don't know shit about y'all's clans," Earl pointed, "but I count twenty cryptid brothers up there on that catwalk."

Chud and Zuri lifted their eyes while Earl's darted quickly from one sentinel to the next, assessing the heavy artillery each one carried.

"They're packin' Colt AR-15s, same rifles they used to shoot up my partner, Andrews, and cut down half our S.W.A.T. team, and some of the bigger dudes have M-60s, probably stolen from one of Hays' safe houses. That's some serious firepower right there."

Earl tightened the straps on his tactical vest; he knew it wasn't really "bulletproof," that it didn't make him Superman or Shazam or anything, but if these creatures were using those same armor-piercing rounds, he now wondered if it would offer him any protection at all.

Might as well wrap my black ass in tinfoil!

"This whole situation is your basic Charlie Foxtrot," Earl grumbled. He glanced over, saw confusion in his lover's bright lupine eyes, then elaborated, "A cluster fuck, Zuri. This whole thing's a cluster fuck just waiting to happen."

"My father used to say, 'It always seems impossible until it is done.'"

"Yeah, well, again, sounds like your daddy and my momma would really hit it off." Earl glanced around, wary, careful not to stick his neck out too far and give away their position. "Other than the guards you two passed comin' in here, you catch any weapons out there on the hangar floor?"

Not that this mythological zoo needed any more firepower to be considered a threat. There were enough claws, fangs, and stingers out there among them to deal a dozen different varieties of death, none quick or painless.

Zuri shook her head. "No, beloved, I haven't seen... wait...Over there."

Earl gazed across the crowded hangar floor, but his eyesight wasn't nearly as good as Zuri's. "Over where?"

"There." She pointed, her backlit claw almost translucent. "The side door on the opposite wall. A small group of disciples has just entered. At least three of them have weapons. The one in the middle looks fishy."

Earl found what she was talking about, five creatures marching forward together as a group. Among them he saw a griffin, a jackal-man, and something that resembled a werehyena. At the sight of the latter, Earl's thoughts turned immediately to Director Tate's Desert Storm war story, and his fingers tightened around the pistol grip of his Beretta M9, his eyes narrowing.

Monsters...monsters killed my Daddy!

Then, he caught sight of the glowing apparition at the center of this tight little group, and his eyes went wide.

Holy shit! When Zuri said "fishy," I thought she meant "suspicious," but no, she meant full-on trout!

It was one of Poseidon's children, a woman, and the others appeared to be herding her right to Vivian Song. She looked just like the old lady from Colonial Bay, the one Earl had first seen change that night on Carol Miyagi's boat, but he knew this was someone else entirely.

"That's Larry's wife," Earl said aloud, still awed by her bright ethereal beauty. He turned back to Zuri, fighting to keep his voice no louder than a whisper, "That's Peggy."

————

"Ah," Vivian spun ominously toward Peggy, her long spiked tail slicing through the air between them, "Poseidon. Now, we can officially begin!"

To call the dragon's smile "unsettling" would have been putting it mildly.

Peggy instinctively recoiled, but Hans and Mark were there to restrain her; they grabbed her by the arms, held her in place. She stiffened in their tight grasp, bared her needle-sharp fangs, and glared hard at the approaching dragon with her one remaining eye. "What do you want from me now, *bitch?*"

Vivian's smile never wavered; her lithe neck slithered to bring her head down low, close enough for Peggy to feel the heat of her breath. Her voice was soft and dangerous, "Didn't Preacher tell you?"

"Preacher said a lot of stuff about gods and miracles, but none of it really explained why I'm still here." She gave a tilt of her head toward the gateway. "You've got all your damn skulls, right? What more do you want?"

"We want that which makes you unique." Vivian lifted her clasped claws, pointed to Peggy with steepled talons. "That thing that sets you apart from all the gods' other creations."

"Oh, yeah, and what's that?"

"Your DNA, of course."

"You want me to give you a DNA sample?"

Peggy spat in Vivian's scaly face, a large glob of sticky phlegm and saliva that struck the dragon right between her scarlet eyes. The dragon's grin instantly dissolved; her head jerked back and she reached up to wipe the thick mucus away, a web of slime stretching between her splayed talons.

Now it was Peggy's turn to smile.

"There you go," she said, a broken trail of spittle still dangling from her wide, puffy lips. "Glad I could help."

Vivian growled and lashed out with her claw, striking Peggy hard across the face, a violent backhand that flung her into her kidnappers. Stunned, her head still ringing, Peggy forced herself to stand straight once more in their grasp. She felt the sting of a split lip, and when she touched it with her tongue, she tasted copper.

The dragon reached out to grip Peggy's chin in her claw. There was a rosy twinkle in her basilisk eyes. Peggy cringed from it.

"Now this," Vivian said, smearing the dribble of blood across Peggy's lower lip with a savage swipe of her thumb, "*this* is more like it."

———

When Peggy got that savage bitch-slap to the face, Earl's first impulse was to leap out from hiding and go to her aid, but he choked it back. He gripped his M9, tried to check his emotion, and stayed put.

Next to him, Zuri uttered a low growl, clearly having the same struggle. Earl reached out to offer support and urge restraint; he gave her arm a little squeeze, felt the tight cords of muscle there just beneath her fur. She was a spring ready to be sprung.

Earl turned his head and their eyes met.

Hold up girl, he thought. *Just...gimme a minute to figure this shit out, find some way to fight these motherfuckers where we don't all wind up dead, where we can bounce on up outta here and live happily ever after.*

None of this made it to his lips, but Zuri seemed to understand him all the same. She gave a quick, trusting nod and Earl felt her relax in his grip.

Satisfied, Earl returned his attention to the hangar floor. He was greeted by the sight of a hulking ape-man and a horse with a lizard's tail; the strange duo hauled something even odder toward the gateway, toward Dr. Graeme King. Earl tilted his head to one side, squinting. "The hell is that?"

———

Graeme examined the so-called control console with questioning eyes. He could find no buttons on the thing these creatures had brought him. There were no lights, no dials, and no indicators of any kind. It didn't even look like a mechanism. If anything, it resembled an altar ripped straight from some ancient temple, restored and repaired by a mechanic rather than a sculptor, a crumbling stone slab augmented by wire mesh, steel rods, and a trio of pistons positioned below. Trailing out from underneath it were wires connected to a simple foot pedal push switch, and of course, more of that clear tubing.

But what really grabbed Graeme's attention were all the markings.

He saw the outlines of three hands etched into the rock — one to the left, one to the right, and one placed at dead center, like the tracings a preschooler would make of their own palms, their four fingers and their thumbs. Each outline lay imprisoned within a larger circle or hoop, and around the handprints were various symbols and hieroglyphs. Graeme ran his fingers over the rough surface of the stone, tracing the deep grooves.

"Curious, Doctor?" Vivian asked.

"Extremely," he answered. "But interesting as it may be, I simply don't understand how a relic like this can possibly—"

"That's right. You don't understand." The dragon smiled down at him. "Tell me, have you ever heard the term 'blood magic?'"

Graeme shook his head. "Sounds vaguely occult, like witch-craft, something out of a horror movie."

"It does, doesn't it? But it isn't that at all, not really. You see, once upon a time, the gods showed us that our blood has power; yours, mine, everyone's." She gave a little shrug, running her claw across the edge of the stone as she circled the console, circled Graeme. "To the ancients, that power was *magic,* and through centuries of trial and error, civilizations have attempted to replicate it, performing ritual sacrifices, on stone altars made to look just like this one, pagan rites and dark spells...nothing seemed to work. That ever-elusive power, that *magic,* remained locked within our veins; a mystery."

"And I take it, you believe you've solved this mystery?"

Vivian was behind him now; Graeme could feel her breath baking the back of his head and neck. "Oh, yes, doctor," she cooed, "and you of all people should appreciate it. You see, to a primitive mind, science *is* magic.

"My dear Doctor King, you and I, we are going to perform a little ritual, right here, right now, a ritual that hasn't been performed successfully in eons, but *we* are going to succeed where so many others have failed."

Graeme felt Vivian's scaly claws on his shoulders now, and his own blood turned to ice in his veins.

Blood. They want my blood!

Peggy Neuhaus resisted. She squirmed and thrashed her tail, but Hans and Mark gripped her arms so tightly she thought that her bones might break. They dragged her forward, pulled her relentlessly toward the stone slab of the control console — the sacrificial altar. And in her mind, Peggy pictured Vivian Song's red-hot talons plucking the still-beating heart from her chest, taking her life just as quickly and maliciously as she'd taken her eye.

"Stop struggling, *liebchen,*" Hans warned; he narrowed his avian eyes, tightened his grip even more. "This will go far better for you if you cooperate."

Peggy glared at him. "Nazi bastard, you mean better for *you!*"

"Better for all of us. And *bitte,* please, I am no Nazi. The Nazi's were *verliererinnen,* yes — losers? I am on the winning side here, as *you* will be. This day will be long remembered, as will our roles in it. Now, stop fighting!"

Hans and Mark gave a final tug, and Peggy found herself pushed up against the rough edge of the stone slab. She stared down at it. Clearly, the console had once been smashed and broken into several pieces; she could still see the jagged cracks forking their way across its face. Now, it stood reassembled, a completed jigsaw puzzle.

There were carvings in the rock, runes and glyphs, all similar to the symbols she'd seen in Varuna's temple, far beneath Colonial Bay. Peggy also saw the outlines of three hands, and her surviving eye was immediately snared by the symbol of a trident etched above one of them, the handprint right in front of *her.*

Vivian Song stood on the opposite side of the console, towering over her. "Left hand, if you please."

Hans yanked Peggy's arm. The griffin pressed on her wrist, his lion's paw driving the palm of her webbed hand down onto the stone.

Vivian stared at Peggy's wedding ring, a sparkling diamond teardrop. Years ago, Peggy had it sized so that she never needed to take it off, not even when she changed from one form to the next and her fingers swelled and stretched.

The dragon's toothy grin grew wider still. "Do you know why you wear your ring on that finger?" she asked.

"Because I'm married," Peggy fired back through clenched fangs, still fighting against Hans' vice-like grip. "Where's my fucking husband — why aren't you making him put *his hand* on this thing?"

Vivian ignored Peggy's question and answer her own instead, "You see, the Romans believed there was a vein in the left hand, in the fourth finger, the 'ring finger,' that ran directly to the heart." She held up her own left arm, her right claw tracing a line down the golden scales. "They called it the *'vena amoris,'* the 'vein of love.'"

"What the fuck do you know about love?" Peggy snarled.

"Everything I do is out of love — love for the gods, for my people, for this *entire world.*"

Another voice spoke up, one as old as it was deep, "And the gods will show you their unending love in return, my child."

Peggy's head snapped around to the right and she saw the old gray werewolf, Preacher, standing there at the other end of the console. He reached out and pressed his furry left claw against the stone, covering another handprint, one carved beneath an entirely different symbol — a small circle, cradled in a bowl that rested atop a cross.

Vivian lowered her long slender neck, bowing her head in a show of respect. Then, she scanned the oblong length of the control console. "First, we had Poseidon, and now we have Hades...it would appear that Zeus is all that remains."

The dragon pivoted toward a man Peggy had never seen before, a man dressed in a dark, well-tailored business suit. He was human, Peggy could smell it on him, a massive hulk with a stoic, emotionless face.

"No fuckin' way," the stranger told her.

"Come now, Dante," Vivian scolded. "We must have a Zeus, and you, my friend, are it."

The man, Dante, rubbed his neck, and Peggy could see a scar there beneath his fingers. Like the stone of the console—

Altar!

—it almost looked as if this man had once come apart and been stitched back together again. He tilted his head toward another human, an older man who stood holding a clipboard. "Make the egghead do it!"

"Dr. King needs to monitor the portal," Vivian told him. "Come now, what are you afraid of?"

He glared up at her. "I ain't afraid of Jack Shit!"

"Good. I mean really, do you think I would allow Preacher to take part in something truly dangerous?"

Dante seemed to consider that for moment. He looked around the hangar at the surrounding creatures, all of whom stared right back at him. Finally, he adjusted his tie and strolled around to Peggy's side of the stone slab, taking his place between her and the elderly werewolf, Preacher.

"So...what?" Dante asked, and Peggy couldn't tell if the man were stalling or if he legitimately didn't know. "I just—"

"Put your left hand on the panel," Vivian coached, her patience clearly wearing thin, "on the handprint right there in front of you."

The big man cocked his head. He inhaled deeply and lifted his arm. His hand hovered there, his fingers wiggling, almost teasing, but after a beat or two, he finally pressed his flesh against the stone, his wide palm covering the final outline, the one that had been carved beneath an emblem of a lightning bolt. "There," he said, his eyes rising to meet Vivian's once more. "We good to go now or what?"

"Oh, yes, Dante," Vivian told him. "We are most certainly 'good to go.'" She turned to the other human in the room, the older man with the clipboard. "Dr. King?"

"All the connections are secure," he informed her.

"Excellent!"

And with that, the dragon took a step back. She ran her scarlet eyes over them, then spread both her arms and her leathery wings out wide.

"Behold," Vivian announced the gathered masses, "for the first time in untold generations, all of the gods' creations are represented here. And now, together, with one *united* voice, they will summon our creators!"

Cheers and thunderous applause erupted from the crowd, echoing through the confines of the hangar.

The corners of Vivian's mouth curled up in a sadistic grin. Peggy watched the dragon lift her scaly foot, then she saw the large round push switch lying there on the concrete floor. Vivian stomped down hard on the foot pedal, triggering something beneath the stone slab.

Peggy heard a strange subsonic rumbling, then felt a hot jolt of searing pain as a thin, pointed piece of metal pierced her palm from below. The spring-loaded spike stabbed its way out through the top of her webbed claw; warm blood bubbled up around it, running down her skin onto the stone. Peggy screamed in agony, her eye wide with shock and horror, and she wasn't alone.

Beside her, the Zeus, Dante also cried out; his hand bayonetted by another spike. And at the far end of the stone slab, Peggy saw Preacher's claw on a metal skewer as well.

"Christ," Dante roared, aghast, *"what the fuck..."* His face was that of a character from a comic book, from a cartoon, full of shock and surprise.

Preacher, on the other hand, looked almost tranquil. The old werewolf growled and gnashed his teeth, but he didn't scream; he didn't say a single word. To Peggy, it seemed as if he might have known about the spike in advance and was the only one of them who'd been prepared for it.

———

Preacher had been preparing himself for this moment all his life. He felt the pain in his left claw as the metal spike pierced his flesh, and he accepted it. After all, it really was such a small price to pay.

Propitiation for the gods. Everything in their service. Everything to regain their favor.

The old werewolf glanced down and saw the blood that now stained his fur, thinking less about his own pain and more about the pain he had inflicted upon so many others in the course of his lifetime. He'd spilled so much blood, out of anger, out of necessity. Reporters, police, lawyers, and scholars, humans all, had puzzled over his crimes. They'd studied him, labeled him as a crackpot, as insane.

What he had been was arrogant. Arrogance was the sin of Zeus, but it had been his sin as well.

As a young man, Preacher thought it had been his right to kill the false profits, to strike down those Zeus who had forced the creators from this Earth and then filled the void with their own imaginary god. He had the right to seek justice for his slain ancestors, to avenge his brothers and sisters who had been struck down for no other reason than the perceived wickedness of their birth.

Blood for blood.

After years of imprisonment, however, years of quiet reflection, of contemplation and meditation, Preacher now *knew* that what he did was wrong. He had confused the will of the gods with *his* will. He'd had no right to sit in judgement on those false priests. Judgement was reserved for the gods and the gods alone.

He'd had no right.

He'd been so wrong.

Preacher continued to stare at his claw, watching his fur grow matted and sticky. He'd spilled so much blood in his life. And now, to bring the gods back into this godless world, he knew that even more would need to flow.

———

Horror Show struggled, attempting to free his wounded hand from the booby-trapped stake, watching warm streams of scarlet flow out to paint the surrounding stone. Blood. *His* blood.

The hitman had seen more than his fair share of blood over the years, but rarely had it been his own.

Horror Show's face twisted. He fought back a cry of anguish, not wanting to give these freaks the satisfaction. The more he strained against the pike, the more he felt the flesh between his metacarpal bones rip and tear.

What the fuck is in there — little barbs, somethin' made to hold me here and keep me from pullin' free?

Whatever it was, it made it impossible for him to remove his hand without doing severe damage. Some might have called this fitting, a kind of poetic justice, the same pain and helplessness Horror Show had inflicted upon so many others, now being inflicted back upon *him*. The hitman clenched his jaw, determined, *defiant*. His eyes shot to Vivian Song and narrowed to slits.

Fuckin' dragon-ass twat! You think you can hold me — bleed me like some stuck pig? You wouldn't be the first to try. You see this scar around my motherfuckin' throat? Yeah. You wanna know what I did to the son of a bitch that did that *— how many fuckin' pieces they found him in? You wanna find out first-hand?*

You can bleed me, Viv, but you can't kill me. I'm the gangster's boogieman, bitch — the killer killers *fear! And when I get free of this fuckin' spike — and, oh, I* will *get free — you're the one who's gonna bleed. I can promise you that! You can take that to the bank!*

You think you're some queen? Horror Show groused. *Bitch, I'm gonna put you in your fuckin' place!*

———

Still in his hiding place, a startled Earl Preston flinched and grimaced. He shrank back from the spring-loaded spikes, helpless. "Jesus," was all he could manage to say.

Beside him, Zuri whispered something else, "It has begun."

———

At the base of the gateway, Dr. Graeme King had begun to tremble. He was shocked, distraught. The physicist couldn't believe what was happening, that he had even been a party to it.

I'm sorry, he thought, again and again, *I'm sorry.*

His ears filled with Peggy's wounded cries, with Horror Show's shocked and irate roars, but he saw no one move to go to their aid.

On the contrary, the other creatures were actually smiling; they were clapping, *cheering*. And Graeme? The physicist could do nothing but stand and watch as the three offerings bled out onto the stone.

Magic and science...both require sacrifice.

Their fluids collected beneath the control console, turning clear polyethylene scarlet as they drained down, merging into a single length of tubing — three bloodlines made one. Graeme pivoted, his eyes following the flow as it raced across the concrete toward the gateway mechanism. Pumps helped the bloody mixture defy gravity, pushing it up through towering metal scaffolding, re-directing it to all those tiny spigots, one in each of the cubbyholes now occupied by a quartz skull, and once there, it sprinkled down in a warm red rain.

The doused crystals flared, incandesced. This time, however, the result was far from a simple light show. Electricity arced from one skull to the next. The sharp, pungent smell of ozone—

Trioxygen!

—filled the air as a bright surge of power raced up one side of the gateway superstructure and down the other. In moments, all thirteen of the crystals were consumed in blinding radiance, tiny novas blazing in their eye sockets.

Graeme caught his breath. He removed a hand from his clipboard and held it up to shade his eyes. Even then, he found it hard to look directly into that light.

Plasma energy, the physicist thought, his mind reeling. *Vivian was right: it really* is *blood magic, plasma into* plasma!

At the center of the gateway's triangular opening, Graeme watched in awe as a churning mass of gas and charged particles formed in midair, growing larger, spreading outward. It was as if he were staring into a witch's cauldron. The roiling clouds flared and strobed from within like a summer storm. Utterly impossible, but there it was, taking shape right in front of him.

The physicist noted defined rotation within that phosphorous cloudbank, and the nebulous mass quickly turned into something more akin to a spiral galaxy — bright spokes spinning around a dark, motionless center. The clockwise spin grew faster with each revolution until it became a full-fledged vortex, a glowing whirlpool that spun light off into shadow like water down a drain.

A magnificent spectacle!

This was everything Graeme had dreamt about on those nights he'd spent alone in front of his white board, scrawling equations, often erasing more then he'd written. It was what he'd thought about during those countless seminars — lectures delivered to rows of eager young minds, intelligent men and women who he was certain would one day go on to become famous by building upon *his* teachings, students succeeding where their professor had so often failed. And now, it was *real!*

I've done it, Graeme's joyous mind exclaimed; an old prospector yelling "Eureka!" *The mechanism has created a man-made singularity, a stable corridor from one world to another. It's not just theoretically possible, it's an absolute certainty; science fiction made fact. I've done it! It* works!

And in that instant of pure awe and scientific wonder, Graeme King felt much younger than his years.

But it did not last.

As Graeme stared into that whirling gravitational well into the unknown, his dawning smile slowly began to slip. Despite the joyous, applauding crowd that filled the hangar around him, he felt suddenly lonely and sad. Lonely because there were no colleagues or peers here to share in the moment with him; no one to pat him on the back, no one to even record this triumph for posterity. Sad because of how it had all been achieved.

Graeme forced himself to turn back to the altar, to face the three living beings who stood there in agony. He had never heard such sounds, had never seen such twisted expressions — so much pain, so much fear. And *he* was partly to blame for it all.

I didn't know anyone would get hurt, he thought, his mouth hanging open, wordless and dry. *You must believe me. I didn't know what Vivian had planned. I didn't...*

What — didn't have a choice?

From the moment his kidnappers removed the hood from his head, Graeme told himself there had simply been no alternatives available to him; he had to do what Vivian Song wanted in order to save his own life. He had no wish to die a hostage to these creatures, and besides, even if he *had* refused them, some other physicist would surely have done the work. Why should someone else get the credit and take all the glory?

There was no glory in this, however. No, this...this was *monstrous!*

Graeme had his all-important proof. Now, he needed to find a way to make things right. And he knew that he could start by keeping his promise to Earl Preston and the crocodile-man, Chud.

Before Graeme could make a move, however, he felt the grip of a clawed hand on his shoulder.

———

Earl removed the silencer from his Glock, shoved the 9mm back into its holster; he unzipped the canvas duffle bag he'd lugged around on his shoulders for most of the night, and he reached his hand inside. Waves of blue-white spectral light danced above his head, painting bright ripples across the walls and ceiling. He remained safely hidden away in the shadow of the crates, but he knew that the time for hiding was over.

"Talk to me, Sleestak," he called out, trying to be heard above the cheers of the crowd, over the buzz and crackle of surging power from the gateway arch. "You see anything comin' through that big space door out there?"

Chud peeked over the stacks, shielding his reptilian eyes with his claw. "Nothin' yet."

"Let's do our fuckin' best to keep it that way, huh?"

The crocodile-man gave him a nod, still focused on the portal. "You know our chances suck, right?"

Earl sighed, his heart pounding beneath his tactical vest. "Yeah, I know it."

At last, he found what he'd been searching for, one of the Tec-9 automatic pistols they'd confiscated from the rat-men. He pulled the weapon out into the flickering light, checked its magazine. Before he could stand, however, Chud tapped him repeatedly on the back of his skull, hard enough to make his head bob.

"Hey, pal," the crocodile-man told him, clearly agitated, "something's comin' through!"

————

Through the years, Vivian Song had made so many decisions, given countless orders, and each and every one of them, no matter how small or seemingly insignificant, had led her and her people to this single historic moment in time. The wormhole was breathtakingly beautiful, a remarkable sight to behold, a cosmic vision whose every flash and swirl teased incredible possibilities. Gazing into it, Vivian was suddenly reminded of her family's absence, and she wished they could have lived to see this day, to see the role their daughter had played in making it a reality. She blinked, squeezing a single tear from her inhuman eye; it ran down the golden scales of her cheek.

Benedict was there, however. The spider-centaur reached over and took Vivian's clawed hand in his own. Had he seen her tear, she wondered, watched it glisten in the strobing flicker of the gateway light?

"You did it proper, duck," he told her. "You never gave up, never gave in. A bloody brilliant job! Everyone here owes you a debt."

Vivian's leathery wing stretched out and wrapped around his humanoid torso, embracing him. "Thank you, love."

She gave Benedict's hand a gentle squeeze before moving away, her wings folding against her back once more as she strolled over to join Dr. Graeme King. Zeus or not, the man's scientific skills had proved essential, and congratulations were now clearly in order. She stepped up behind him, towered over him, and placed her golden talons firmly upon his shoulder.

He flinched in her grasp.

Vivian noticed the startled, anxious look on the scientist's face. Why was he so nervous? The portal was a success! "Well done, doctor," she told him. "You must be very proud."

"Yes," he replied, but there was no enthusiasm in his voice, no pride, no splendor; Vivian couldn't even detect a trace of fear. "So what happens now?"

"Now, my dear Dr. King," as gently as a mother caressing an infant, she ran her finger down the physicist's cheek, "we await the gods' arrival."

They didn't have to wait long.

Almost as soon as the words left her scaly lips, Vivian noticed movement within the gateway. There, at the dark center of the wormhole, the shadows shifted. A form took shape, solidified, and as it began to move forward, electricity seemed to arc in every direction.

What finally emerged from the portal was a large floating orb. It hovered about six feet above the hangar floor, an elegant organic sculpture. The spherical mechanism shared characteristics with the communications device they'd rescued from the downed UFO decades before, ribbed corrugated tubing blended seamlessly with bony vertebrae. But unlike the communicator, this thing was very much alive.

The sphere's surface was bumpy and coated with slime; it shone in the strobing light of the portal. It also *moved*. Vivian saw veins bulging with a pulse, and patches of flesh began to twist and corkscrew, skin acting like the iris of a camera, opening to reveal the huge round eyes hidden beneath. Some pupils were elliptical, others horizontal. Smaller eyes broke the surface of the skin between them as if it were liquid; there were dozens of them, and they moved independently across the sphere, drifting, unanchored and floating. Soon, nearly the entire structure was covered in them.

Some of Hades' disciples gasped, others cried out in alarm. They scattered and backed away, clearly spooked.

Vivian stood her ground, remained calm. She stared up at the floating ball of eyes, instantly realizing its true purpose. "Smile, doctor," the dragon said, giving Graeme a little nudge, "the gods are watching, and we want to make a good first impression."

———

"Is *that* one of the gods?" Chud asked, more than a little confused.

Earl shook his head. He was standing now, shoulder to

shoulder with the crocodile-man, and as he peeked over the stacked crates, he watched the orb of flesh and eyes hover there above the equally monstrous crowd, watched it inspect its new surroundings from every possible angle. "It's their version of a UAV," he said at last.

"A *what?*"

"Unmanned Air Vehicle," Earl elaborated. "It's a fuckin' drone."

"A drone? But...that thing's alive, ain't it?"

Earl recalled what Carol Miyagi and her boyfriend had said back in Colonial Bay, that these aliens had the technology to *grow* their own tools, to use flesh and blood creations in the same way human beings used objects forged from steel or molded plastic. "Yeah," he confirmed, "it's alive."

"Looks more like one of those little foam toys from the '80s, whatcha call 'em — Madballs?"

Earl couldn't help but snicker at that. As a kid, if he'd seen a Madball the size of a Pilates ball, you can bet your ass he would have totally begged his Mama for one. Now, he wanted nothing more than to send this thing back to whatever cosmic hell had spawned it. "Damn aliens sent this thing down the wormhole as their hat on a stick, their canary in the coal mine. They wanna make sure it's safe up in here before they show their sorry asses."

Zuri stood at his side. "You are right, beloved. Whatever this creature sees, its creators, still safe on Kronos, they see as well."

Earl thought of a quote from The Book of Samuel in the Bible—

"For the Lord sees not as man sees."

—and a part of him couldn't help but wonder if the original author had had this floating eye-thing in mind when they wrote it. He shook his head, gripped his Tec-9 a little tighter.

Ooh-rah!

"Awright, then," Earl began aloud, "if these motherfuckers are really out there watchin' right now, let's give 'em one helluva show."

Going in, guns blazing, without Director Tate and the National Guard for back-up; it wasn't something Earl wanted to do, but he felt he had to do it, anyway. He had to make a stand, even if he didn't stand a chance in hell. It was the right thing to do.

Earl glanced over at Zuri. "Ready?"

She nodded. "Stay behind me. I will protect you."

Earl nearly smiled, but he knew Zuri was serious. More than that, he knew she could do it. He gave the werewolf a long appreciative look, hoping this would not be the last time he laid eyes on her in either of her forms.

They leaned in, their foreheads touching, then Earl swallowed and spoke with grim determination, "Come on, girl. Let's go save the fuckin' world."

———

Graeme King thought it so strange to be standing there, staring, while a visitor from another world watched his every move. The atmosphere in the hangar immediately grew tense, the air still.

The floating ball of flesh lowered, hovered closer to Vivian Song. On the metal catwalk that hung high above her head, overprotective guards cocked their weapons and took aim at the alien thing, but if it saw them—

With all of those eyes, how could it not *see them?*

—it made no defensive move, showed no sign of aggression.

"Idiots!" Vivian's arm shot up, her golden talons rigid and splayed. "Lower your weapons," she ordered, her voice amplified by the cavernous hangar. "Do it now!"

The creatures looked at one another, bewildered. After a beat, however, they reluctantly did as they were told. Some simply dipped the barrels of their rifles. Others put their weapons down altogether; they held up their clawed hands and feelers as if surrendering.

"This is what we've been waiting for," Vivian announced. "This is an emissary of the gods, and it has come a very, *very* long way to see us all — what we've done and what we've become."

She pivoted to stare up at the sphere, unblinking, and took a tiny step forward, her arms and wings now open wide. Her scaly lips curled up in a grin, her long catfish-like whiskers danced on air.

"You've crossed an ocean of stars," Vivian reached out her hand in greeting, her tone softening, "haven't you?"

The orb said nothing in reply. Not that it *could* say anything, even if it had the desire. It didn't appear to have a mouth, at least none that Graeme could see; no nose, no ears, no limbs of any kind, just...eyes, dozens and dozens of eyes. The sphere continued to float there in midair, defying gravity, defying all the laws of physics, its many pupils fixed and staring.

Graeme wondered what his zoologist friend, Dr. Kathy Ward, might make of this creature if she were here. What insights could she have provided into its strange anatomy and physiology? For instance, would she have been able to explain how the thing was able to float, to just hover up there like that?

Magic. Blood *magic.*

Graeme licked his lips, but his mouth had gone completely dry. He continued to stare, amazed, at the levitating sphere, continued to study Vivian Song and the adoration she showed toward it. So focused, so enthralled was the physicist, in fact, that he didn't even see Earl Preston or the crocodile-man, Chud, until after the shooting had started.

———

Earl came out shooting, his modified Tec-9 going full auto; the damn recoil nearly tore his arm off. He wanted to roar, to scream. Hell, maybe he did. If so, the sound was lost beneath the endless rattle of his pistol.

Zuri and Chud flanked him, their M-16s blazing in opposite directions; short bursts, tight and controlled, trying to make every round count. Their combined tracer fire streaked through the hangar, taking out targets both above and below.

———

At the first sound of gunfire, Vivian Song growled and turned away from the floating ball of flesh, looking for whoever had pulled the trigger. She thought she would find one of her own men, an overly skittish sentry who, regardless of her words, her *commands,* had seen this floating creature as a threat rather than a welcomed visitor. Instead, she was shocked to see Earl L. Preston, Jr. and his traitorous friends strafing the hangar!

The dragon stared at them, aghast. Despite all her best efforts, they were still alive. Worse, they were *here*, gunning Hades' loyal disciples down right in front of her!

Overhead, mortally wounded guards flew back against the skywalk railing. A few flipped over the safety bars entirely, jagged craters in their backs from where the bullets had torn right through them. Their bodies cartwheeled through the air, crashing down onto the startled crowd and smashing into the concrete floor below like bags of wet cement.

Triumphant cheers became terrified screams as the clans began to scatter. Many, desperate to get out of the line of fire, dove and ran. Others turned on their attackers; their claws, fangs, and stingers gleaming in the flickering bursts of muzzle flash.

The ugly sight brought the entire sordid history of this world to Vivian's mind with fresh vividness — painful pangs of racial memory, passed down through generations, of a time when humans, *Zeus,* had actively hunted her people into hiding, into near *extinction.* Whatever the humans feared, they killed. They murdered. They destroyed. They *annihilated!*

That's what their species did!

It was *all they did!*

Vivian glanced up into the multitude of eyes that hung somehow suspended in midair above her horned head. She felt suddenly embarrassed; fearing how the creators, back on Kronos, must view their unruly creations here on Earth.

"It's been millennia," they had to be saying to themselves right now, *"and absolutely nothing has changed! This world still belongs to* Zeus!"

———

Earl still wore his tactical vest, but he'd never felt more exposed, more *vulnerable* in his entire life. One after another, the creatures attacked. They lunged and leaped, swiped at him with their claws, their jaws snapping. He fired on anything that moved his way, watching their riddled corpses crumple before him.

I'm a damn fool for doin' this, but if I'm goin' out, I'm not goin' out alone. I'm takin' a shitload of these fucks here with me!

Bullets zinged by his ears. His eyes jerked back up to the catwalk. A dozen or more disciples were still alive up there, and now they were returning fire.

Earl whipped up his TEC-9 and squeezed the trigger.

Nothing.

His cartridge was empty.

Shit!

He reached for his belt, for another clip, and a sustained burst of gunfire struck the concrete right in front of him. None of the bullets touched him, but the force of their impact caused eruptions of powder and shrapnel that stung his eyes and bit the exposed skin on his arms and legs.

Jesus!

His father's voice screamed inside his head, *"Don't just stand there waitin' to get your ass blown off, Junior! Move!"*

Earl bolted. The creatures fired after him as he feinted and dodged his way across the hangar floor, a fog of concrete dust hanging in the air, enveloping him.

Out of nowhere, something lunged from that billowing cloud of particulates, something with *teeth.*

Earl instinctively lifted the barrel of his TEC-9. Thankfully, he was out of ammo, because he didn't recognize the creature until it was almost on top of him.

Chud?

The crocodile-man plowed right into Earl's chest, pushed him behind the cover of a parked forklift nearby, made sure he was shielded from the barrage.

Earl hunkered down, the breath knocked out of him. He inhaled deeply and lifted a hand to his chest. He'd have a nasty bruise there in the morning. He only hoped he would still be alive to see it.

"You're welcome," Chud told him as he pulled away and cradled his rifle.

Earl couldn't hear a word the crocodile-man said. Inhuman screams and the stuttering blasts of AR-15s had rendered him all but deaf. His equilibrium off balance, he shrank back against the firm, stationary forklift, thankful just the same.

Their position was still far from safe.

Tracer fire whizzed all around them, bullets hammering and ricocheting off the heavy equipment at their backs.

Earl took a moment to eject the spent cartridge from his TEC-9, to grab a fresh one from his belt, nodding and cursing as he snapped it into place.

Okay, motherfuckers...you wanna get scary? Let's get fuckin' scary!

And when Earl looked up again, when he glanced around, he truly *was* scared, but not for himself. His eyes went wide with panic and he shouted at Chud, *"Zuri!"*

The crocodile-man brought a clawed hand up to the side of his head, held it just behind his eye, his talons curling into a *C* around that narrow slit he called an ear. *"What?"*

Another burst of gunfire pounded the forklift behind them; bullets pinged and sparked off the metal frame, pinning them down.

"Zuri," Earl repeated; he tried to hunch even lower, his head now down between his shoulders. *"Where the fuck is Zuri?!"*

————

Zuri went to war.

She emptied her M-16, the steady vibration and bright starburst of her muzzle flash yielding to nothing but impotent clicks and dull smoke. She snarled, dropped the useless rifle onto the floor. A volley of rounds split the air around her as she bolted for the outer wall of the hangar.

In a single kinetic blur, the werewolf pounced onto a stack of wooden crates, and without even a moment's pause, she used her claws and her long powerful legs to leap up, to bounce off the cinderblock wall and onto a metal support column. She climbed, then vaulted toward the ceiling. Finally, she grabbed hold of the overhead railing and scrambled to pull herself up onto the catwalk.

Zuri took no time to catch her breath. She charged at the guards who still stood firing on the floor below, the ones taking aim at Earl and Chud. She ran up behind the nearest creature, grabbed it by the head, and quickly snapped its neck; it had the antlers of a deer and scales like a dragon.

A second guard spotted her. This one she recognized as a Myrmecoleon — a vicious, hairy ant-lion; it immediately turned its rifle on her and opened fire.

Zuri held up the dead creature with the broken neck, used its scaly armored body as a makeshift shield. At the same time, she pried the AR-15 from its lifeless talons, aimed from her waist, and fired back.

The ant-lion went down, felled by a cluster of bullets that all but obliterated its oversized eyes, its hairy features and its fearsome mandibles.

Zuri snarled and stalked forward along the catwalk, moving through the mist of blood that still hung in the air. Her triangular ears stood erect, her fur bristled, black lips pulled back to display pearly incisors. With supernatural might, she held the armored corpse up in front of her to block enemy fire, her own AR-15 rattling away.

Armed guards jerked and twisted as her bullets ripped through them. And one after another, she watched them fall with great satisfaction.

For my family!
For my village!
For me!

Continuing to advance, Zuri grit her teeth, shuddered from the recoil, and blew Hades' disciples all to Hell. She kept firing until her magazine ran out. Then, with all her might, she heaved up the corpse she had been using as a shield and hurled it at the guard directly in front of her. The full dead weight of the bullet-riddled body struck him, knocking him back, sending him tumbling over the railing and falling to his own death.

A hot bullet nicked Zuri's right ear.

She ducked and yelped in pain. Tracer rounds passed over her, slicing through the air where her head had been only a moment before.

Coming from behind!

Zuri whirled to find a leopard-man darting toward her, closing in fast and lowering his aim. Before he could fire off the killing rounds, however, an unexpected object appeared in the center of his spotted chest, catching them both off guard, a serrated point, yellow-white and streaked in red.

Blood!

The leopard-man went down, peering stupidly at the pointed tip of a spear that now extended from his body.

Zuri gaped at the weapon as well; it protruded from the feline disciple's slumped back, extended at a forty-five-degree angle. The long shaft appeared to have been carved from a single length of bone. But a bone that big...it would have had to have come from an elephant.

Or a whale.

She continued to stare, amazed.

As Vivian stared out at the carnage, another guard went tumbling over the catwalk railing above, screaming as he fell to his death.

She blinked and her reptilian eyes shot up in time to see yet another of her men collapse. This one hadn't been shot, however.

Is that a spear?

Its long, pale shaft protruded from the dead sentry's slumped back. And next to the body, still on her canine feet, Vivian found a female Cerberus with jet-black hair.

Preston's she-wolf bitch!

Enraged, Vivian's talons curled into tight scaly fists at her sides. Extreme heat welled up from her belly and she did nothing to suppress it. On the contrary, for the first time since breaking Preacher out of his prison, she allowed her furnace to vent. She lifted her head, let her jaw go slack. The roaring blaze rose quickly, traveling the full length of Vivian's throat in an instant. Jets of flame coated her forked tongue, just as thick and as sweet as raw honey, then spewed freely from her saurian lips.

She directed her fiery exhalation into the overhead catwalk, a hot fountain of pure hate. Flames burned through the grated flooring, lapped at the rafters high above, but they missed their intended target by sheer inches.

———

Zuri stumbled back from the streaking pillar of flames, wide-eyed, still feeling the scorching heat; it was like standing on the lip of an active volcano. Across her shielding arms, her legs and her breasts, singed fur trailed wisps of smoke. An acrid smell filled her nostrils as she patted herself down. Thankfully, the skin beneath her fur wasn't burnt.

Centimeters! I missed total incineration, death, *by just centimeters!*

The werewolf turned and ran as fast she could, scrambled to get beyond the dragon's range. She grabbed onto the metal railing, pulled herself along. And the flames chased her all the way to the stairs.

―――――

Vivian continued to spout her napalm, chasing the werewolf bitch. She pivoted toward the stairs, bathing the entire length of catwalk in a wash of flames, advancing until her blazing breath finally gave out.

The dragon inhaled quickly, her scarlet eyes continuing to track the she-wolf's path. Before she could launch another blast, however, something grabbed her by the arm and wouldn't let go. She whirled, snarling.

It was Benedict.

Vivian glared at the spider-centaur, barely managing to quell her rising inferno, to *speak*. "She's getting away!"

"Leave her out now, duck." Benedict pointed with a long spindly talon, coolly directing Vivian's attention across the floor. "We've got bigger problems."

One second, Vivian had been ready to breathe fire. And in the next, when she saw what it was her lover had seen, understood what he meant, her breath deserted her completely.

CHAPTER TWENTY-NINE

Larry Neuhaus took a moment to catch his breath. He heaved himself from the briny waters of the bay, clawed his way through breaker foam to lay hunched on a grassy shore. Warm, humid air caressed him, but the shark-man couldn't rest, couldn't waste any more precious time. Peggy...Chud...Earl and Zuri...they were all counting on him, on *them!*

He lifted his triangular head.

His black eyes swept the unfamiliar terrain, squinting into the dawn, trying to stay alert to any potential danger. He found himself at the end of a long, cracked, weed-infested stretch of pavement. Not a road, he quickly realized, but an abandoned runway.

At the opposite end of the tarmac, he could just barely make out a series of structures. Windows of a tall spire, an old control tower, reflected the rising sun, glowing like a fiery beacon in the distance. And beyond it, Larry saw the curved metal rooves of various aircraft hangers.

Delancey Field!

At the sight of it, the slumped, tired Charodon sprang instantly to his webbed feet, his tail swinging. This is where his friends had gone, where their note had led him. This is where Hades' disciples were holding his wife!

If they've done anything else to hurt her...

No. He wasn't even going to entertain that thought. The very possibility was intolerable!

Larry would find her, just as he had found her in Colonial Bay. She would be alive and well, and together, they would make it back to the open sea. Then, they would get far away from this city, far away from Vivian Song, and they would live a long and happy life!

'Til death do us part.

Jason surfaced right behind him. The other shark-man stood tall, his clawed feet bathing in the lapping tide. "Is this the place?"

"Yeah," Larry told him, baring the serrated daggers of his teeth. "This is it."

"You feel that, Callisto?"

Larry looked back at him, confused. "Feel what?"

"The wind is changing." Jason's expression was grave and resolute; he held up his webbed claw and a stiff breeze blew water droplets off his sandpaper skin. "It's coming in from the sea. Varuna is with us!"

Larry grunted dismissively and turned away. He didn't give a shit about Varuna or any of the other gods. The only things that mattered to him were of *this world*, his family and his friends.

"Whatever happens, Poseidon's children will remember this day." Jason laid his webbed hand on Larry's shoulder. Then, he chuckled and added, "Your children and mine will get tired of hearing the stories."

I hope you're right, Larry thought with a nod, *I really do.* He took a deep breath and asked aloud, "You ready?"

"*We're* ready," came the instant reply.

"Let's do this!"

His jaw clenched, Larry sprang from the grass. He sprinted off down the decaying runway, leading a charge, the webbed claws of his feet kicking up chunks of loose pavement as he went.

————

On the other end the runway, armed sentries stood waiting outside the graffiti-covered main hangar. They heard thunderous applause erupt from within; saw a bright, strobing light that shone through the open doorway and shimmered across the cracked tarmac in front of them.

"Guess the thing actually works," a lion-man commented, and he flashed a toothy, joyous grin.

The Kappa nodded in agreement. This was it, the moment Vivian Song had been promising them for so long. Now, the gods would return to take back this—

Without warning, the sounds of celebration were replaced by a loud exchange of gunfire.

The guards all looked at one another, a shared glance of shock and confusion. They snapped to attention; their weapons raised. Before they could move into the hangar to join in the fight, however, they heard another sound, an undulating sound, so shrill and powerful it nearly drowned out the rattle of the barrage.

War cries?

A chilling chorus drifted up the runway, carried on the wind, a herald that came with an odd mixture of scents, as unfamiliar and strange as they were overpowering.

What the fuck?

The Kappa whirled and beheld not one, not two, but *hundreds* of creatures! They charged up the tarmac, flooded the surrounding fields of grass and weeds. It was a menagerie the likes of which Hades' disciples had never seen: sharks with arms and legs, scaly tentacle-faced monstrosities, things with strips and spots, trailing flowing ribbons that were every color of the rainbow, even a few ghostly beings that glowed blue-white against the green; all rushing straight for the hangar.

Large as the advancing mob was, it moved quickly. So quickly, in fact, that the surprised guards barely had time to react; they gripped their rifles, pressed their triggers, and opened fire.

"Bring 'em down," someone shouted, though the Kappa could not say if the voice had come from another guard or one of the sea creatures.

Tracers ripped into their forward ranks, cutting them to pieces. The slain beasts toppled, flopped, and hit the ground hard. Even more rushed up from behind to take their places, however.

These savage-looking monsters had no guns to return fire, but as they drew nearer, they began to hurl spears — long shanks with serrated points, carved from the bones of some deep-sea leviathan.

Hangar guards suddenly sprouted the bony shafts from their chests, from their throats and from their heads. And as they fell, the tracer fire grew more and more sporadic. Soon, only the Kappa was left on his reptilian feet, and he knew that his ammunition was rapidly running out.

The monstrosities kept coming, surging ever forward, their mewling, growls, and battle cries only mounting as they came nearer.

Still firing, the Kappa was driven back against the hangar's outer wall, a wall that was now splattered in blood as well as paint. He found himself standing right below the huge Hades symbol, smoke drifting up from the tip of his rifle barrel.

A huge, terrifying half-man, half-shark broke away from the larger group and ran up to him.

The Kappa hissed; he tossed the empty rifle, lunged with his snapping turtle jaws.

But the shark-man was quicker; it reached in, wrapped its webbed talons around his throat, and lifted him up off his feet. *"Where is she?"* it screamed through clenched teeth.

"Where's who?" the squirming Kappa croaked; he grabbed the creature's brawny wrist, the denticles that covered its skin shredding his fingers.

"My wife, *the Poseidon girl!"*

The Kappa tilted his head toward the open doorway. "She's in there, man! They're usin' her fuckin' blood to open the gate!"

With a growl, the shark-man curled his left talons into a fist and cocked it back. The Kappa's eyes grew wide as he saw the blow coming.

It was the last thing he would ever see.

The shark-man's powerful fist slammed into the Kappa's face, right between his eyes, then emerged from the back of his skull slicked in gore.

————

Larry pulled his fist back through the turtle-man's shattered skull and flicked the clots from his talons. He released his grip on the lifeless body, let it fall onto the tarmac. His gills were heaving, the smell of blood in the air driving him further into frenzy.

Blood.

They're using Peggy's blood!

Beyond the doorway, Larry could hear more gunfire. He bent down and stripped an assault rifle from the claws of a slain lion-man. The tip of his talon, just above the webbing, fit comfortably over the trigger. He lifted the weapon, ran into the besieged aircraft hangar, and after him followed members of all three clans; Charodon, Kraken, even some Paralicht, a volunteer army more than three hundred strong. Larry knew their loyalty was only his by Barbara's dying decree, but he was grateful for it none the less.

Poseidon's children may not have started this fight, but they were in it now, and they were going to help bring it to a swift and decisive end.

———

Poseidon's children...but how?!

As Vivian Song watched the creatures storm into the hangar, she stared in disbelief at their tentacles, their gills, their fangs and their fins, but most of all, at their numbers — a huge, continuous wave of fierce warriors surging forward. A tsunami! Many ran with long bony spears, like the one she'd seen stuck in the back of her fallen sentry; a few even carried assault weapons!

———

Earl lowered his weapon and gazed around, taking in all the reinforcements. It was as if the entire population of Colonial Bay had taken up arms and joined in the fight! He looked over at Chud for confirmation and somehow managed to find his voice, "I...I can't believe it...bro, are you seein' what I'm seein'?"

Chud nodded excitedly, his reptilian face alight with joy. "He found my note!"

"Who...?" Still stunned, Earl whipped his head around and saw a shark-man leading the charge. The creature cradled an assault rifle like a seasoned marine. It was just about the sweetest thing Earl had ever seen. "Larry!"

Where the hell had he gone? How'd he find Poseidon's children so quickly, get them to follow him back here? So many questions, so much Earl wanted to know, but there was no time to discuss any of it, not right now. Now, all that really mattered was shutting down the gateway and finding Zuri — not necessarily in that order.

Larry sprinted over to the battered forklift, to where Earl and Chud still squatted for cover. He held out a webbed hand; Earl took it and was instantly pulled to his feet.

"Way to bring in the cavalry, Neuhaus," Earl said appreciatively. "You get us some breakfast from Mickey D's while you were out there workin' miracles?"

The shark-man cut right to the chase. "Where's Peggy?"

"Now, how did I know those would be the first words outta your mouth? She's over by the gateway." Earl lifted his TEC-9, as desperate to find his own lover as Larry was to get to his wife. "Let's roll!"

Together, the trio began to move. They zigzagged their way across the crowded hangar floor. Waves of Poseidon's children crashed against Hades' disciples all around them. Earl searched the escalating battle with wide, frantic eyes, looking for Zuri, dreading what he might find.

———

Vivian Song scanned the scene with her saurian eyes, not liking what she saw. Her people were being completely overrun!

How can this be happening?

Her first instinct was to rain fire down upon these invaders, but she couldn't do that. The forces had become too intertwined. Even a narrow swath of her flame would incinerate not only their enemies, but her own people as well.

Vivian's heart shrank. She shook her head, denying it all. "I can't believe—"

"Believe it, duck."

Beside her, Benedict suddenly advanced, his sticklike legs carrying him off toward the melee.

She grabbed him by the arm. "What the hell are you doing?"

"Going fishing."

The spider-centaur pulled away from her. He shot webbing from the tail end of his bulbous lower body. Milky white strands attached themselves to the finned back of a snarling viperfish. Benedict pulled, yanked the creature off its webbed feet, then reeled it onto his outstretched foreleg, impaling it with a splash of blood.

Vivian smiled at the sight.

Her lover flicked the dead fish-creature aside, then repeated the trick again and again.

The dragon nodded; her scaly jaw clenched. She stalked over to the opposite side of the battlefront and whipped out her spiked tail, skewering a squid-headed monstrosity. She flung the perforated body over her shoulder, a red haze filling the air.

Yes!

Vivian waded deeper into the conflict, turning her fury on every Poseidon who stood in her way, in the way of the *gods!* She swiped and tore at them with crazed abandon, her golden claws, her jutting fangs, and her tail spikes undoing their bodies in a wash of hot blood.

The messenger of the gods hung over her, bearing witness to it all.

Vivian's heart began to soar again. Perhaps this was all in the gods' plan? A test! Yes, when this fight was over, she knew there would be no question in the creators' minds as to who this world truly belonged to; the dragon would make certain of it!

———

As Earl hurried on through the fight, a striped blur in the corner of his eye drew his attention. He turned in time to see a snarling tiger-man; it slashed the throat of a moray eel with a flick of its claws.

Cursing, Earl opened fire; the recoil strummed through his fore-arms as he cut Hades' victory mercifully short.

When he turned to follow Larry, another beast suddenly stepped in front of him. This one had the physique of a bodybuilder and the head of a rhino. It punched a charging Kraken right in its tentacled jaw.

Earl leapt aside, and that's when he caught sight of the elephant-man. It moved forward though the crowd on two legs, a Glock 9mm in each of its clawed hands and the hilt of a long, serrated knife held tightly in its coiled trunk. Earl watched, stunned, as the thing whipped its trunk around, the blade slashing and stabbing, cutting Poseidon's children down left and right.

A loud hiss filled Earl's ear, giving him a start. He spun to see a snake-creature; it lunged at a beast with the wide, flattened skull of a hammerhead shark. The hammerhead simply gave this reptile a cracking head butt and sent it tumbling back into the melee.

Something swooped overhead.

Earl lifted his eyes and saw a man-bat with an AR-15. It was probably the same living gargoyle that kidnapped Graeme King from Stanley University, the one who'd killed Earl's rooftop sniper during that brawl in the alley. God, that seemed like a lifetime ago!

The bat-creature's leathery wings flapped, lifting it up into the rafters. There, it made its landing and began strafing the hangar floor below.

Several of Poseidon's children were cut down right behind Earl. He felt the warm splatter of their blood against his back. *"Jesus fuckin' Christ,"* he exclaimed, ducking.

Other warriors stepped up; they hurled their boney spears like javelins, launched them toward the ceiling in reply. One of the serrated points passed cleanly through the bat-creature's membranous wing, leaving a ragged tear in its wake. Another slammed into the beast's chest, impaling it; the gargoyle fell from its perch and came crashing down like a ruined kite.

The loud, sporadic rattle of gunfire left Earl's ears full of cotton, but he heard Larry's muffled voice cry out, "Peggy!"

Earl spotted her, too. She was just ahead of them, struggling vainly against the pointed spike that held her to the control console, right next to that bastard hitman, Horror Show, and a grey-haired werewolf.

At the sight of the old wolf, Earl's thoughts returned instantly to Zuri. Where was she in all this havoc?

Larry went into a rage; he gnashed his teeth and pushed struggling combatants out of his way, pulling ahead, desperate to get to the woman he loved.

Damn, Earl thought. *This dude is on a fuckin' mission!* He followed quickly behind him, Chud, too, both running through the path Larry had cleared for them.

As they grew closer, the shark-man called out to his wife a second time, and somehow, he made his voice sound even louder, forcing it to rise above even the cacophony of battle, *"Peggy!"*

Earl watched as Peggy suddenly came to attention; her tail stiffened, her body glowed brighter from within, and he knew that she'd heard her husband's cry.

———

Peggy thought she'd heard something. Her head snapped up. She paused, strained to hear, to concentrate, hoping she hadn't only imagined it. And then, it came again.

"Peggy!"

At the sound of her own name being called out, Peggy felt a spark of excitement in her chest, a warm glow that nearly muffled the sting of pain from her hand.

That voice...

Rembrandt?

Peggy shook her head, tried to clear it. She glanced back over her shoulder, hopeful, and there he was! This wasn't some hallucination brought on by blood loss and pain. It wasn't wishful thinking, or even some stupid childish dream. This was real!

He was *here!*

Larry Neuhaus, her husband, the love of her life, the father of her unborn child, ran at her through the swirling smoke and streaking comets of tracer fire; he raced across the pitted hangar floor, and even more surprising, he was not alone!

Beneath her glowing breasts, her heart was pounding. She called to him, overwhelmed, emotional, *"Rembrandt!"*

"Scheisse!" Behind her, the German, Hans, noticed what was happening. The griffin turned on his heels; his feathery wings spread wide to block her view.

"Bastard," Peggy hissed, straining harder against the metal spike that restrained her. She gnashed her needle-like teeth, swiped at the air with the razor-sharp talons of her free hand, but it was no use. The griffin was too far away. She couldn't touch him!

He's going to kill Larry, she worried, her mind picturing all the damage that beak and those claws might inflict, *and there's not a damn thing I can do to stop him!*

———

Larry saw the now familiar griffin turn, cutting him off from his wife. The shark-man stopped dead in his tracks, his jaws clenched with fury.

"Du schon wieder?" Hans's yellow-rimmed avian eyes glared at him with scorn and disdain. "Still trying to play the hero, I see — the great American cowboy, yes, riding to the rescue?"

Mark, the jackal-man, was there as well; his muscles rippled as he stood poised to attack. "I don't know, Hans. Hasn't turned out so good for him yet. Has it, shark-boy?"

The dimpled bullet wound, the one they'd put in Larry's shoulder, suddenly began to itch. "This time," Larry warned through gritted teeth, "things are different."

Mark grinned at that; a frothy string of drool hung down from his black, canine lips. "Oh, yeah — *how?"*

"I'm the one with the gun now, assholes!" And with that, Larry lifted the barrel of his rifle, daring them with his eyes.

The creatures sprang at him, calling his bluff; their eyes and claws fixed upon his throat.

Larry instantly pulled his trigger; he fired an extended burst, emptying his magazine, tracers hammering the pair in mid-leap. Hans and Mark were both thrown back, their chests erupting in violent explosions of blood and viscera. They landed on the concrete as a pair of tattered heaps, bits of feathers and tufts of fur still drifting through the air.

That was for the Doc, Larry thought as he threw his spent rifle away. *For you, Brahm.*

He quickly stepped aside and moved on to his wife.

Finally reunited, Larry and Peggy looked longingly into each other's eyes. All this time, he'd wanted nothing more than to tell her how much he loved her. But as he stared into the depths of that burnt-out crater, the one that once housed her beautiful right eye, Larry's own eyes brimmed with fathomless emotion; he was left heartsick and mute.

I'm sorry, so sorry. It should have been me!

He tenderly stroked her translucent, glowing cheek.

My angel.

Peggy reached up with her free hand, touched his webbed talons with her own. "Let's get the hell out of here," she told him.

Larry nodded; his throat still constricted. He lowered his eyes to the spike that impaled her. It extended a good foot above her left hand. Blood puddled beneath her palm, filling in glyphs that had been carved into the rough, ancient stone. His stomach rolled.

Jesus.

Larry went to lift her hand off the bloody point, but she grabbed hold of his wrist.

"Wait, *wait,*" she cried, almost in tears, "don't pull it!"

The shark-man looked at her, confused; he didn't want to cause her any more pain, but he also couldn't see another way to free her.

Chud and Earl stood suddenly beside him.

Larry scanned his companions faces, desperate. "Please," he begged, "help me find a way to get her off this damn thing!"

Earl nodded, but his eyes were focused elsewhere.

Larry whipped his head around and saw what his friend was looking at — another man, human by the smell of him. And after a moment, recognition took hold.

Holy shit!

This was one of Roger Hays' hired guns, the only man to leave

Colonial Bay's church alive and in one piece. Somehow, the brawny killer had found his way here, in the same boat as Peggy, his left hand stuck on a pike.

"Hey, hero!" the hitman shouted.

At first, Larry thought the goon was addressing him. But no, he was talking to Preston.

"Not now, Horror Show," Earl replied.

"Don't you even think about cuttin' the fish-lady loose and leavin' me here to rot on this fuckin' stone! You hear me? You free one of us, you free us all!"

Chud snarled at him. "Last time I checked, pal, you weren't one of *us*. You're with *them!*"

"The big bad lizard from the tower." Horror Show glared at the crocodile-man, his face tightening. "I shoulda known. Hell, I *did* know!" His eyes snapped back to Earl. "Well, you and your friends better not go and leave me here to bleed to death! You hear me, nigger? *You free us both!*"

"Yeah, I hear you," Earl told him. "I hear you're a racist asshole, and right now, I don't got time for racist assholes, so just shut the fuck up and chill; adults are talking!"

Horror Show's eyes narrowed. "I get loose from here, Preston, you'd better fuckin' pray!"

Tough talk, but Larry knew that the man was scared out of his mind; he could smell it on him.

———

Graeme King was terrified; in fact, he had never been more scared in his whole life. As an educator, he'd been forced to participate in "active shooter" drills at Stanley University, preparing for a day when he and his students might come under fire. Still, he'd never actually been shot at. He'd never had bullets streak by him, so close that he felt heat. Never smelled the chemical stench of propellants. Never watched anyone die.

Oh, how Graeme wished he could still make such claims!

Vivian and Benedict had moved away to join in the fighting. They'd left Graeme alone in the middle of a crossfire, bathing in the flickering light of the wormhole, his precious stable singularity.

This all needs to stop, he realized, ducking down, holding up his clipboard like a pathetic little shield. I *need to end it!*

But he simply could not get his body to obey him. His feet were frozen in place, his legs trembling.

Then, he saw Earl Preston and Chud dash out of the chaos to stand beside Vivian's control panel, beside what looked like a great white shark with arms and legs.

Graeme wondered what Kathy Ward might make of *that!*

Finally, the physicist worked up enough nerve to force his legs to move. Still clutching his clipboard, Graeme cautiously made his way over to the foot pedal on the floor.

This is how Vivian started the reaction, isn't it? If it's an "on" switch, I pray it's an "off" switch as well.

Graeme lifted his shoe; and when he stomped on the button, the physicist immediately heard a scream.

———

Peggy screamed as the long metal spike slid back through the meat of her webbed claw, withdrawing into the stone from which it sprang; the pain was as brief as it was sharp, ending even before the sound of her cry, and then, she was free.

Larry got her away from the altar and pulled her to him in a loving embrace.

Through all her struggles, all her fighting and fretting, this is what Peggy had dreamed of. The feel of Larry's strong arms around her once more. His wonderful, familiar scent in her nostrils. The sound of his heart pounding in her ears, beating only for her.

"Are you okay?" her husband's words were a Morse code of hot wind on her fluke.

"I am now," Peggy told him, then she pulled away to arm's length. "I can't believe you're really here. And Poseidon's children? How did you—?"

Larry pointed to the tip of his snout. "See this face? This is my determined face."

She smiled at that.

"Peggy—"

She cut him off with a kiss. It was all she needed. But, as much as Peggy wanted that moment to last forever, she knew that, sooner or later, all dreams must end.

————

When he saw that Peggy was safe, and that Horror Show wasn't about to start any shit, Earl marched on over to Graeme King; it was time to end this. "All right, professor," he said, his eyes on the swirling portal in the background, "you told Chud you knew how to shut this shit down; now, do it!"

Graeme stared at the button on the floor between them, at a loss. "Evidently, it's not as simple as I'd hoped."

"Not as...? Goddammit, you're the science guy! You helped build the fuckin' thing, so—"

Suddenly, King's eyes went wide. Earl saw him clutch that damned clipboard closer to his vest, his entire body stiffening. What the hell was wrong?

When Earl glanced back over his shoulder, he found his answer.

Damn!

Benedict was there. The spider-centaur shot out a length of webbing. Earl pushed Graeme out of the way then leapt aside himself, and the sticky strands streamed harmlessly between them.

The giant arachnoid raced forward; he spun toward Earl, reared back, and brought his spiked forelegs stabbing downward.

———

Freed from the spike, Horror Show jerked his hand away from the control panel and held it up for inspection. There was a small round hole in the center of his palm, blue-white light from the portal streaming through it like a cartoon gunshot wound. The hitman gave an incoherent bellow, then curled his fingers into a tight, furious fist.

Vivian Song had done this to him! That inhuman, double-crossing cunt! Horror Show would kill that dragon bitch if it was the last thing he did. He'd slit her scaly throat so deep her fucking head would fall off! He'd...

The claw!

Horror Show reached into his pocket, pulled out Vivian's severed talon, and—

A furry hand touched his bicep.

Preacher. The old werewolf had been freed from the spikes as well, his grey pelt still matted and sticky. "My son, we need to—"

Horror Show whirled on his former cellmate; he pressed his forearm against Preacher's furry chest, held the point of Vivian's talon up to his throat, fully aware that the werewolf could rip him to shreds but not caring, not anymore. He was too consumed by anger.

"Fuck you, old man," Horror Show spat. "*We* don't need to do shit! You knew what that bitch was gonna do to me, didn't you? *Didn't you?"*

"The gods required an offering."

"*Your* fucking gods, not mine!"

Preacher snarled, and before Horror Show could back away, the old man had snapped out and buried his fangs in the hitman's forearm.

Horror Show screamed through gritted teeth. Pain radiated from the bite, burned across his flesh. And when he finally managed to pull his arm free of the werewolf's jaws, it came away bloody.

"*Yours as well!*" Preacher growled, his lips and teeth now scarlet and slick.

Horror Show gasped and fell back against the stone altar; he stared at the wound, his stomach churning. "What did you just do to me, old man — huh?"

He held out Vivian Song's disembodied talon, more accusatory than threatening.

"*What the fuck did you just do?"*

Preacher offered him no reply. The old werewolf turned away, moved off, leaving Horror Show shocked and enraged.

———

"Burr-headed bastard," Benedict raged, "how are you still *alive?"*

The serrated tip of the arachnoid's leg stabbed into the concrete right in front of Earl, creating a tiny cloud of dust and particulates.

Benedict quickly withdrew, lunged, and slashed down again; this time, Earl parried, whipping up his TEC-9 to block the deadly stroke.

"Recognize the hardware, Benny?" Earl ducked then came up to meet the next downward slash. "Got it from those rat pricks you sent to take care of me. You can add exterminator to my many talents, motherfucker!"

Benedict hissed and lurched forward yet again.

Earl flipped the TEC-9 around and opened fire; his bullets struck Benedict's armored chest and ricocheted back at him. *Shit!* Earl crouched down to avoid being hit. Hadn't he learned by now that he couldn't kill this beast by shooting it?

What else can *I do? Thing's got to have some kinda weakness, don't it — but* what?

Benedict rushed at him; his many legs were a blur, alternately moving and stabbing forward. A startled Earl scrambled backward across the floor, shocked by the speed and ferocity of the arachnoid's attack.

The whole time, Earl's father was there in his head, screaming at him, *"Haul ass, Son! Get away from there! Move!"*

Earl was moving as fast as he could, but with Benedict practically on top of him, there was nowhere for him to go. He could see the cold, murderous gleam in the spider-centaur's multiple eyes as it bore down on him. Earl aimed his useless automatic pistol and—

Chud leapt out of nowhere!

The crocodile-man landed Benedict's back. His snaggletooth jaws opened in a hissing snarl. Then, he bit down hard on the arachnoid's shoulder, extreme pressure fracturing the spider-centaur's armored shell with a sickening crunch and a splash of blood.

Benedict instantly halted his attack; he screeched in pain, reared up like a bucking bronco, and tried to dislodge his unwanted rider.

Chud dug in deeper with his claws and his teeth; held fast.

That was when Larry Neuhaus dove into view. The shark-man bolted from Peggy's side and hit Benedict in a flying tackle; his triangular snout butted up against the arachnoid's abdomen, his webbed talons helping to push it back into the control panel.

Damn!

For a moment, Earl could only watch, stunned and riveted, as the creatures struggled. The spider-centaur bucked and writhed, its many chitinous limbs kicking out, grasping, and stabbing at the air. All the while, Earl's monstrous-looking friends fought tooth and nail, their tails whipping as they used their combined weight to bring Benedict down and pin him up against the bloodied stone.

Then, Chud called out to him, "A little help here, Earl!"

Breaking out of his paralysis, Earl finally went to their aid. He ran over to the control panel and cracked Benedict in the jaw, driving his fist into the spider's wriggling face over and over again, slugging him until his knuckles were raw. Then, Earl dropped his TEC-9 and grabbed the centaur's insectoid head in both hands; he repeatedly slammed it down against the stone, punctuating every word as he growled, "Had. Enough. Yet. *Motherfucker?*"

Benedict's compound eyes held him with a look of utter contempt. "The great Earl Preston," he mocked, undeterred, "here to save the world!"

Earl nodded and met Benedict's dark eyes with his own piercing stare. "That's right, Benny. I am. And you're gonna help me do it. You're gonna tell me how to turn off that goddamn portal!"

"Bullocks!" Benedict spat, still defiant. "I don't take orders from *Zeus!* I *exterminate* them!"

Earl propped up Benedict's head, then bashed it back onto the control panel, grinding that impenetrable armor against one of the hieroglyphic palmprints etched into the stone. "Bullshit," he growled through clenched teeth. "I'm the exterminator here, remember?"

The spider-centaur tried to lunge upright once more. Earl, Chud, and Larry fought with all their might to keep him down, but it was painfully obvious that even their combined weight and strength would not be enough to secure this creature for long.

"You're *nothing,*" Benedict snarled, still fighting to rise, to *kill.* "You're *shit!* This rebellion, this revolution, its only just begun! And if I don't put an end you first, the gods will put you in your place!"

"You shut your face!" Earl commanded, holding tight onto Benedict's head, pressing it back against the etched stone, wishing he had the strength to crush it in his grip, to smash this bug once and for all.

"Make him...suck on a gun barrel," Chud suggested, clearly winded, "see if he—"

"Traitor to your own race!" Benedict's compound eyes shot to the crocodile-man, his fanged mandibles wriggling as he yelled, "I'll see you *dead!*"

A long metal spike suddenly burst through the spider-centaur's face, spraying Earl with hot blood and tissue.

Son of a bitch!

Startled, Earl immediately released his grip and drew back; the same point that had impaled Peggy's hand now lanced Benedict's skull. He watched the spider-centaur's punctured head pulse blood out onto the stone, watched his many legs twitch their last. Then, he finally looked up.

Zuri was standing there, her clawed foot firmly on the control pedal. She looked at Larry and Chud. "Is everyone all right?"

"I'm good," Chud told her, trying to catch his breath.

Larry simply nodded, his chest heaving as he pushed himself off Benedict's lifeless thorax.

Then, Earl and Zuri exchanged glances. Each saying, "I love you," but neither of them voicing a single word. He wanted to go to her, to take her in his arms and hold her tight, but this war wasn't won, not yet, not by a longshot.

"Got to get back on point now, Junior," his father's voice urged. *"You got to finish this if you want that 'happy ever after!'"*

Earl nodded, emotional, his eyes still fixed on Zuri.

———

Peggy Neuhaus found herself suddenly abandoned amid all the chaos, her eyes on Larry's every move. Everything had happened so fast! Now, as she watched him step away from the dead spider-centaur, the light shifted within her body; she breathed deeply, let down her guard, and relaxed a bit.

Her husband was bruised and a bit bloodied, but he was fine. They would both be fine now.

Peggy glanced at the open wound in her own webbed hand. She forced the limb to turn human for a moment, watching as her flesh liquified and flowed freely across her blunting claws and shrinking bones, filling in the hole that the metal spike had made. As her too small, too dainty fingers flexed before her eye, it was as if she were staring at the hand of a stranger.

She shook her head and brought back her webbing.

All better now.

No, Peggy realized; she lifted her talons to her face, touching the burnt, vacant socket, *not* all *better.* Her newly healed hand moved down to caress her belly. *My child will never see me the way I used to b—*

The concrete floor shuddered beneath her clawed feet, shaking her from her thoughts; the entire hangar rocked by a terrible sound.

———

Vivian Song let out a roar of pain and fury that shook the hangar to its very foundation, bringing dust down from the rafters. During the fight, she'd lost sight of Benedict. Now, her eyes found him there on the control panel, his body crumbled, his head on a spike.

No, no, no, NO!

Vivian's own body was rocked by tremors of agonizing sorrow. Her scaly face twisted in pain. Her ruby eyes seemed to flare, to glow, as if lit by the rising fires within.

She shoved forward, storming across the crowded hangar floor, trying to reach her slain lover, to get to Earl Preston and his traitorous, *murderous* friends. Her disgust and anger mounted with every harried step, fanning the flames of her hellish inner furnace. She beat her wings and the wind from them was strong enough to blow surrounding creatures to the floor.

One of Poseidon's children stepped forward; it hurled its spear at Vivian, the serrated tip stabbing deep into the meat of her left shoulder.

The dragon shrieked and reached up, wrapping her talons around the spear's bony shaft. As she pulled the barb from between her golden scales, her horned head swung back toward its owner, spewing fire. The hangar filled with broiling heat, with the stench of ozone and burnt flesh. Poseidon, Hades, in Vivian's wrath, in her *grief,* she no longer cared; all who were caught in her homicidal blast turned instantly to ash. She dropped the bloodied spear to the floor and strode right on through them, scattering their charred remains.

Then, another lone figure dared to step into Vivian's path, seemingly unconcerned with the dragon's fire and grisly fury.

———

Startled by the dragon's agonized howl, Earl Preston spun to see her charging through the conflict, moving back toward the control panel, back toward *him*. Smoke poured from her mouth as if she were a living locomotive suddenly gone off the rails.

Ah, shit...Here we go!

He snatched up his TEC-9 and quickly backed away. Zuri was with him, her claws up, her teeth bared. Chud was there, too, so was Larry; their hearts beating uneasily, all of them anxious to put space between themselves and Benedict's body, between themselves and Vivian's wrath.

Then, Earl saw a figure move *toward her*.

*Who the fuck is that? Wait...*He squinted, tried to make it out. *Holy shit, is that—?*

———

Dante!

Vivian stopped, dark clouds of smoke billowing out from between her fangs. Her head reared back on her neck, a giant cobra ready to strike; she narrowed her eyes and arched her wings. How had this Zeus, this mindless, hairless *ape*, managed to free himself from the stone? Did he have anything to do with Benedict's death?

All of Vivian's questions died there on her scaly lips. As she glared down at Roger Hays' former hitman, the dragon saw nothing in his face but hatred — unvarnished, and after so many years of feigned civility, completely unrestrained.

———

Horror Show engaged in a staring contest with a dragon. He was half blinded by sweat, but he didn't blink, didn't flinch; he didn't shy away in the slightest. Threads of blood still ran from the hole in his hand, from the fresh bite marks in his forearm, but he felt none of the pain.

He felt only rage.

When Horror Show noticed the trickle of blood that ran down from Vivian's left shoulder, the corner of his lip pulled up in a nasty, contemptuous little sneer. Yes, the dragon was huge. Yes, she was powerful and intimidating. But she was also mortal. She was *wounded*. And, like every other enemy he'd faced in his life, man, woman, or monster, she could be *killed*.

Horror Show had murdered so many; he'd lost count of them all, their faces blurred together in his mind, their names lost to time. But *this?* Oh, he would remember this. He was going to hack one of those horns off Vivian's dead skull and keep it as a good luck charm, a replacement for the sliver of Dillinger's tombstone.

"Fuckin' bitch," he yelled as he tightened his grip on Vivian's severed talon. *"Let's go!"*

She snarled and lunged at him; her tusk-like fangs bared, her mouth yawning to either bite or breath fresh fire.

For a big man, Horror Show had always been quite agile; he quickly ducked and let Vivian's striking maw pass right over his head. Next, he leapt up and wrapped one of his muscular arms around the dragon's elongated neck. Thick muscles tightened and constricted beneath her armored skin, and when she tried to rear up again, he went along for the ride.

Horror Show hung there, his legs dangling just above the concrete. He brought the disembodied claw up to meet Vivian's scaly throat, ready to puncture her jugular, to slice through her carotid, to see her pilot light finally snuffed. "So long, Viv!"

Before he could deliver the killing stroke, however, Vivian's head whipped around with astonishing speed; her jaws caught Horror Show's swinging legs and clamped down *hard*, the force of her bite snapping his bones like twigs.

The would-be dragon slayer screamed at the top of his lungs; he'd never felt such agony!

With a violent tug, Vivian pulled Horror Show loose from her undulating neck, her teeth gnashing together as she flung him back against the control panel.

Horror Show scrambled to sit up, to survey the damage Vivian's bite had dealt him. The first thing he noticed was that he had no feet. They were missing. As his eyes climbed, however, he realized that the injury didn't stop there; *everything* was gone. He had no legs left below either knee, just a few splintered shards of marrow.

He looked down at his white-knuckled hand with numb detachment. Somehow, he'd managed to keep hold of Vivian's severed talon. Now, he let the weapon slip from his grasp and drop to the floor.

A floor now covered in Horror Show's blood.

Tourniquet!

His survival instincts kicked in almost immediately; like a splash of cold water to the face, they shocked him back into action. Grinding his teeth against the pain, Horror Show fought to unbuckle his belt, to slide the leather strap free. An average adult could lose half to two-thirds of their blood, about nine to twelve pints, and still survive. More than that...

Vivian Song turned her attention once more to Benedict, the love of her life who laid dead there on the metal spike. She took another step toward his slumped, motionless body, and her heart seemed to break all over again. For the first time in all their years together, she found no light in the darkened globes of his eyes. There was nothing in those black mirrors now but her own pained reflection, her own tears.

Zeus...murdering bastards!

She lifted her gaze to the floating ball of flesh, the harbinger of the gods. Surly, through its numerous eyes, the creators had seen what happened; Benedict's sacrifice, his blood spilled here upon their altar. Did they grieve for their creation as she now grieved for him? Yes, she was certain they did. In fact, any moment now, they would step through that gateway arch, lay their ancient and powerful hands upon Benedict's shattered skull, and their touch would heal his wounds, bring him new life.

Was that really such a selfish prayer, after everything Vivian had done for them, was that so much to ask?

I need him, my gods. I...

Vivian leaned down; her throat constricted as she moved to sniff and nuzzle her lover one last time. She reached out to lift Benedict's head up off the skewer, willing him to rise, to...to...

———

Move!

Peggy Neuhaus stood frozen there by the altar. She'd watched Horror Show grapple with Vivian Song, and she'd seen the glint of that long, serrated blade in his hand. At first glance, she'd thought the man held a dagger. It took her a second to realize that the weapon was one of Vivian's own claws.

Now, the scaly golden digit called to her from the concrete floor, from where the hitman had dropped it a moment before; she dove and quickly scooped it up.

Half conscious, Horror Show looked over and saw her do it. *"That's mine,"* he roared.

Peggy bared her needlelike fangs and growled right back at him, her gills flaring. "It's Vivian's, and I'm going to give it back to her!"

"No!" Horror Show's eyes went from half-lidded to manic; his hand blurred out, his fingers encircling her wrist like a manacle. *"It has to be* me!"

She moved to pull away, to challenge Vivian, but the hitman wouldn't let her go. Considering his current state, his grip was surprisingly strong, and Peggy found herself dragging him across the hangar floor. A belt was cinched tight around his bloody stumps, lashing what was left of his legs together, and she could hear its metal buckle scraping the cement after her.

Peggy lashed out, grabbed hold of the hitman's wrist with her teeth, and bit down just as hard as she could. He cried out in pain, and when his grip finally broke, she yanked the talon away.

Vivian stood right in front of her, hunched over, caressing Benedict's corpse.

Peggy attacked; she leapt onto the back of the dragon's neck, leaned over her horned reptilian head, and with a powerful two-handed thrust, drove the sharpened talon deep into Vivian's right eye socket.

Vivian Song wailed in agony, screamed like a lobster dropped into a boiling pot; she gave her head and neck a violent shake, tossing Peggy off onto the floor.

Peggy landed in a heap, protecting her belly. She quickly shook off the impact, then rolled onto her hands and knees; her long, salamander-like tail helped to balance her as she climbed to her webbed feet.

The dragon brought her hands up to her face, plucked her own disembodied talon from her skull; the serrated claw came free with a glut of fresh blood and she flung it angrily aside. Vivian then glared down at her assailant, one eye oozing a bloody gelatinous mess, the other overflowing with blood lust.

Peggy stood tall; she lifted her head, met Vivian's cyclopean gaze with her own, and said, "Now, we're even!"

What happened next unfolded so rapidly that Peggy could not be certain of all the details. For one thing, she never saw where Larry came from. One moment, she faced the dragon alone; watching as Vivian's saurian head tipped back and her mouth grew impossibly wide. And the next, Larry was right there at Peggy's side; he was diving at her, *pushing her,* knocking her clear of a white-hot gout of flame.

———

Larry Neuhaus saw the dragon loom over his wife, her golden bat-like wings spread and her cruel mouth yawning to belch fire. The shark-man immediately bolted, leapt over the bloodied stone of the control panel; it took him only five seconds to reach Peggy, but it felt more like a lifetime.

In his panic, Larry had sudden strobes of memory; he caught a glimpse of his ex-girlfriend Natalie, lying in a puddle of her own vomit, an emptied pill bottle still clutched in her rictus grasp. That nightmare vision was instantly replaced by another: a living Susan Rogers, screaming and clawing through the surf, her hands flailing in the night air as she sank beneath the waves.

Larry hadn't been able to help either of them. He'd been too slow, too late, but that couldn't happen now. Not this time!

"You can't save everyone."

Peggy told him that, didn't she? Yes, back in Colonial Bay.

"You can't save everyone."

I don't need to save everyone, Peggy. Only you!

He ran for all he was worth. As his elongated arms stretched out and his webbed claws reached for his wife, Larry felt the roiling ball of flame nipping at his flesh; its searing heat came at him like a wave, and he resigned himself to the fact that this was it — this was the last thing that he would ever do.

This was goodbye.

"Was she worth it?"

Susan's decaying specter had asked him that in a dream.

"Was she worth it?"

And, of course, then and now, Larry's answer was a resounding, *"Yes."*

Peggy was worth fighting for.

Worth *dying for.*

He only hoped that this would be enough, that it would give his wife and his unborn child a fighting chance at survival.

Time suddenly seemed to slow. Larry pushed with all his might, with everything he had. He watched Peggy's head turn; her dark eyes were wide and wounded as she fell away from him, out of the path of the flames, and he prayed, out of danger.

I'm sorry, he thought, tears welling. *I love you.*

Larry Neuhaus wanted to bring it all to his lips, to say that and so much more to his wife, to his family; the words flowed like blood from his heart, but the dragon's fire engulfed him utterly.

———

Peggy felt a wave of broiling heat cross her face as Larry was caught in the dragon's blast; she watched in horror as her husband's body crisped and shriveled, his figure losing its shape until he vanished completely into the firestorm. *"Larry,"* she screamed, her face twisted and pleading. *"Larry,* no!"

But she knew.

There would be no reply.

He was dead.

The stench of burnt flesh assaulted Peggy's nostrils, further devastating her. She recoiled from it, staggered back a few steps. Her tail wilted, and she dropped to her knees; overcome with grief. It wasn't fair. It wasn't *right*. They had just found each other again, and now Peggy felt completely lost. She felt angry and afraid, *alone.*

But she wasn't alone.

When the flames finally receded, Vivian Song was still standing there. The dragon turned to face Peggy, wisps of dirty smoke rising from the corners of her snarling, pitiless lips. Her wings fanned Larry's ashes; the glowing embers swirled around her horned head, and her surviving eye narrowed to a scarlet slit.

"Now we're even," Vivian hissed.

———

By the time Earl Preston got to Peggy, Larry was already gone; it wasn't even close. Earl ran full tilt, but he just couldn't keep up with the shark-man's powerful strides; it had been like trying to race Usain Bolt! He'd tracked the intersecting paths of his friend and the flames, but there wasn't a fucking thing he could've done to stop him.

All he could do was watch Larry burn.

Now, Earl was *pissed,* and he was determined to make damn sure that Larry's sacrifice hadn't been for nothing. He leapt in front of a kneeling Peggy, positioned himself and his TEC-9 between her and the approaching dragon, then he let the bullets fly.

Vivian snarled; her head bobbed and weaved on that long, sinuous neck, dodging Earl's streaking tracer fire until it suddenly stopped.

"Out of bullets," she growled; it wasn't a question.

Earl backed away, reaching behind him for Peggy. The dragon was barely ten feet from them, stalking forward, closing. He could hear Vivian inhale deeply, preparing to let loose another lethal blast. Earl glanced down at his TEC-9. She was right. He had no more bullets, just as he had no more time.

Dad, his desperate mind begged, *you probably used up all your favors, but if Jesus still owes you somethin', now'd sure be a good time to try and collect!*

"Come on now, Junior," his father's voice replied, *"you can't expect the good Lord to do all the work!"*

But then, something miraculous *did* happen.

The cracked concrete trembled once more beneath their feet, a bone-rattling vibration that surged through the entire structure. This time, however, Vivian Song was not the cause of it.

A voice cried out from somewhere in the melee, *"The gods! The gods have returned!"*

All around them, the chaos of battle came to a sudden and dramatic end. Hades and Poseidon stopped fighting one another and became a single mass of onlookers; they gasped and muttered, drew back fearfully, their eyes collectively moving toward the front of the hangar.

Vivian's toothy mouth instantly snapped shut. She first looked up at that giant Madball that hung in the air, high above her saurian head. After a beat or two, however, she turned as well.

Earl didn't want to take his eyes off the dragon, not even for a moment, but finally, he looked, too.

Through the wide-open doorway, they saw something descending from the sky — a dark shape, like a giant black spearhead.

The fuck...

Earl squinted. It didn't look real, but he knew that it was, just as he knew *what* it was.

A goddamn spaceship!

This day was full of surprises.

The craft loomed large in the morning sky. It had to be at least a thousand feet long. Its dark skin shimmered and sparkled, illuminated by the dawn. It was headed directly for the abandoned runway, headed right for the old airplane hangar where they now stood, and it was coming in *fast!*

CHAPTER THIRTY

Carol Miyagi removed her helmet and stood in the Ark's domed control room, staring at the pilot's seat. There was something darkly magnetic in its disturbing, organic design, in its recessed folds and fleshy protuberances, that held her eyes helplessly captive. She had studied photographs of the Mayan sarcophagus for years, knew the carvings almost by heart, but seeing it here, fully realized in three dimensions, it possessed an odd sort of repugnant beauty.

Pacal's Rocket.

The biomechanical throne had sat empty for untold millions of years, waiting for someone to fill it; that someone was *her*.

Watashinounmei. *My destiny.*

She glanced over at Gagan and Alan. They were seated on the raised lip of the chamber, trying to secure themselves as best they could, lashing their bodies to bony railings with mountaineering gear.

The goat-man lifted his horned head and offered her a respectful nod.

Carol smiled and nodded back at him. But Alan...

Well, at least now he was behaving himself.

The man still wanted nothing to do with her. He refused to make any eye contact, acted as if she wasn't in the room, as if she weren't even alive. And at least in *his* mind, she supposed it was the truth; he had watched Carol Miyagi die out there on the slope, and there she remained.

To Alan Everson, Carol 2.0 was just a painful echo of the woman he loved. Nothing more.

For a moment, she allowed herself to think of the future, a time when this was all over, when they were safely back in Japan. What then? She couldn't just snap her fingers and cure Alan of his prejudices, make him sit down with her, have an intelligent conversation, finally accept her for who she was, no matter how badly she might wish it were possible. And she couldn't spend the rest of her life sleeping with one eye open, afraid of what Alan might do to her in his anger and his grief.

Would he just pack up his things and move out of her grand-mother's house, Carol wondered, would she be forced to make him leave? The thoughts bounced around in her skull like *Shuriken*, ninja throwing stars, shredding her brain. In many ways, she dreaded those conversations, those *arguments,* more than anything Hades' disciples had in store for her.

A tear welled in Carol's eye, but she took a deep breath and blinked it away.

Kari noticed just the same.

"What is it?" She reached over and cupped Carol's cheek. "Are you all right?"

"Fine," Carol lied, and she returned her focus to the pilot's seat.

Did she really want to go through with this? Did she have any choice? This was *her* plan, after all. So far, everything had worked better than expected, but in the end, everything hinged on *this*. After so many years in the ice and snow, was this wreck still capable of flight? Was she even qualified to pilot it?

Only one way to find out.

Carol moved away and climbed up into the control chair. Slowly, she reclined against its bony, textured surface, its sinews bulging and receding to embrace her unique shape. Her feet rested comfortably on a pair of contoured pedals and she stared at the nest of long tendrils that dangled over her head.

Probes wormed their way inside her body almost immediately, alerted to her presence by pressure, or heat, or perhaps some alien sense she knew nothing about. And this time around, it wasn't just her brain that they tapped. No, this time she felt the alien fingers wriggling into every orifice along her spine. They extended from behind her, slithering out from the back of the chair, each sliding into its own designated bio-port, plugging her in, making her one with the Ark.

As the umbilicals slid deeper, Carol tensed, and her hands reached out to grip the ribbed chair frame. *"Tawagoto!"*

Kari rushed to her side. "Carol, what is it?"

Carol looked up at her, at her sweat-stained tank top and her tousled red hair. And when she felt those tight rings of muscle close around every probe in her back, completing the many connections, Carol was finally able to relax. *"Daijōbudesu,"* she exhaled, then managed a grin. "It's nothing. I guess I am hardwired and ready to go. You'd better find a seat of your own now. This could be a very bumpy ride."

Kari nodded. She leaned down, placed her palms on the chair on either side of Carol's head. "I believe in you, you know," she told her, and Carol could see the truth of it there in her eyes. "All that bullshit you said you could do? You *can* do it. You can do anything you set your mind to, always have, always will."

Before Carol could say anything in reply, Kari kissed her.

That kiss...it was not a friendly little peck on the cheek for good luck. No, Kari's lips pressed against Carol's and stayed there.

Carol was surprised, but she did not fight it, nor did she shy away; in fact, she reached up, gripped Kari's shoulders, and pulled her closer. Kari's soft lips and smooth face moving over hers...the long-forgotten warmth of Kari's mouth, the gorgeous feel of her tongue as it caressed Carol's with such ravenous urgency, such intensity...

God, the taste *of her!*

It brought back so many memories — memories that, for *years,* Carol had not dared to recall. And yet it was far better than any of them, a kiss to end all kisses.

Then, Kari suddenly pulled back, her face deadly serious. "Carol, I—"

Carol made a shushing motion with her hand. Kari was going to tell her that she loved her, at least Carol hoped that was it. There had been so much genuine, pent-up emotion behind that kiss, on both sides, but if Kari said those words aloud, there would be no way Carol could let her leave it at that and just go on. There would need to be a *long* conversation, and now was not the time or place for it.

"Please," Carol begged, "tell me later."

Kari hovered over Carol for a moment, staring down at her with those beautiful eyes, not saying a word. Kari's bottom lip quivered slightly, almost imperceptibly, then she simply nodded and stepped aside.

Carol shut her eyes and tried to breathe, to refocus. Now, even without her helmet on, the darkness filled with a full tactical display. The Atlantean symbols and glyphs scrolled by, telling her that the Ark's systems were fully operational.

The ship is feeding me information, now, let's see if the connection goes both ways...

Carol thought for a beat or two, considering all the ways in which this interface might function. She pictured the Ark in her mind, imagined it free of Makalu's summit, saw it rising up into the night sky.

Hatsubai, her mind cried, *launch, lift off,* go!

The Ark evidently found something it liked and obeyed her command.

Somewhere behind and beneath her, Carol felt engines power up; her bones hummed with their vibrations. She heard a grinding bellow and the entire chamber began to shudder and shake. Her tactical display shifted, becoming a view of the stars and constellations over Makalu. After a moment, the pinpoints of light started to move closer.

No, the stars aren't moving. We are!

It was true. The Ark had slowly begun to lift. That rending noise she heard was the sound of the immense starship attempting to pull itself free of the melting ice and snow, to dislodge itself from mountain rock that had entombed it for untold centuries. The vessel trembled, growled and shrieked, as it rose from Makalu's jagged slope.

And then, it was done.

The Ark was loose.

Carol felt the shuddering stop, and that grating nails on a chalkboard noise also disappeared; all that remained was a soft, subsonic purr. Her tactical display suddenly flipped, became a sternward view, and she watched as Makalu, "the big black," caved in behind them. The peak collapsed into rubble, filling the vast chasm vacated by the rising Ark. Clouds of ice and snow billowed up into the atmosphere and cascaded down its steep face in every direction.

"We're out," Carol announced with a mix of satisfaction and relief. "We're *flying!*"

Gagan's joy was unmistakable, "You did it, Miyagi!"

"I knew you'd make it work," Kari said, and Carol could hear the smile in her voice as well, "I *knew it!*"

Next, it was time to pick a destination. Carol didn't know latitude or longitude. She didn't even have an address. Instead, she simply pictured North America, the other side of the globe. Memories of New York leapt to the forefront of her mind; she saw the city as it appeared from the air, recalled from numerous plane rides. Finally, she thought of Earl's message, of a place called Delancey Field.

The Ark must know where Earl's transmission originated, she realized. That's *where I want to go. The source of that message. Take me* there!

The ancient alien craft continued to ascend through the thin outer veils of atmosphere, picking up speed, its flight path shifting to obey Carol's will.

Alan finally spoke up from across the room, but unlike the others, his tone sounded far less cheery, "Not to rain on anyone's parade, but you all *do* realize that, now that we're not part of the mountain anymore, we're on everyone's radar. They'll probably mistake us for some Chinese or North Korean missile launch and try to blow us right out of the sky!"

"I've considered that," Carol assured him, "and *you* must realize that, to enter a planet's atmosphere without burning to a cinder, a ship this size would have to be fitted with some form of shielding."

As if on cue, she saw a familiar thread of Atlantean glyphs in the corner of her vision, *DEFENSE SCREEN.*

"And there it is," Carol told them, and then, under her breath, she whispered, "Here goes nothing."

She closed her eyes once more, focused in on the glyphs, and her wishes were made real. Through her internal display, she saw a veil of blue-white energy, the same power that coursed through the orb weapon, "the wrath of the gods;" now, it encircled the entire ship.

In addition to the friction of reentry, Carol hoped this new energy field would protect them from weaponry. Or perhaps it would act as some sort of cloaking device — make them invisible to earthly radar altogether? At any rate, Carol decided to keep the shields up until the last possible moment, until the Ark was on its final approach. Only then would she reveal the craft's location to American radar.

And when that happened, Carol hoped Earl Preston's boss, Special Director Patrick Tate, would get the message. She'd made a promise, after all, and Carol always kept her promises.

CHAPTER THIRTY-ONE

Patrick Tate, Special Director of Homeland Security, had made a promise, sworn an oath, in fact, that he would keep America safe from all her enemies, both foreign and domestic. The morning was still young, but already, he felt as if he'd failed her.

Around him, everyone looked as if they'd just had the living hell scared out of them and were waiting for the other shoe to drop. Tate could almost see their collective shudder. *"This can't be happening,"* their faces told him, *"maybe in Iraq, Afghanistan, London, or Paris, but not* here, *not in the greatest country on Earth!"* They were the same shocked, terrified faces he'd seen on 9/11, faces Tate never wanted to see again, and certainly not on his watch.

He rushed down a dim, prestigious-looking hallway lined with Greco-Roman columns; the sound of his dress shoes echoed as they clicked and clacked against marbled floor tile. His face was grim as he asked the obvious question, "Can someone please tell me how an object the size of the Empire State Building could just *appear* in the most heavily guarded airspace in the world?"

The director was followed closely by a mousy-looking aid, a man who kept trying to keep his glasses from sliding off the tip of his nose as he hustled. "Whatever this thing is," the man attempted to explain, his face red more from embarrassment than this sudden burst of physical activity, "it had to employ some sophisticated form of stealth technology. It didn't show up on radar at all until it was practically on top of us, and then it registered like a huge flock of birds, like a *living contact!*

"It's common for birds to flock in that area," the aid continued, "especially at dawn. If we scrambled F-16s every time a blip suddenly showed up on a screen somewhere, our pilots would never get to land! Because of that, most radar systems are programmed not to display living contacts at all, and when they do, the technicians have gotten in the habit of just ignoring them. They're more of a nuisance than anything else — what appears as a large, solid object on the screen one minute just breaks apart and disappears the next as the flock spreads out over the city. But this thing didn't do that.

"That's when the alarm finally sounded."

Tate nodded, still seething.

The aid pushed his glasses back up the bridge of his nose and went on, "By the time we knew the craft was there, we couldn't shoot it down without chunks of fiery debris raining all over the city! Whoever or whatever they are, they knew exactly what they were doing."

Tate's frown only deepened. "So, we're calling it a craft, now, are we?"

"Yes, sir. It made a controlled descent. There is definitely an intelligence at work here."

And that's what scared him; in his mind, Tate heard those hyena-children laughing again. "Where did you say this thing came down?" he demanded to know.

"Southeast of us, Delancey Field, just outside Brooklyn. It's an old airport, completely deserted."

Tate flashed him a dubious glance. His instincts were usually spot on. Right now, they told him that he would find those shape-shifting creatures massing at this airfield, preparing to carry out their plans, whatever they were. And if the monsters were there, then most likely, so was Earl L. Preston, Jr.

Link, your son's a chip off the old block, but there's no way he can tackle this one alone.

Tate continued down the hall, barking orders as he went, "I want black hawks in the air, and I want them *yesterday!*"

The aid pushed his glasses back up his nose again. "Yes, sir."

"I want boots on the ground, marines armed to the teeth, swarming every square inch of that old airport!"

"Yes, sir."

"Now, goddammit!"

———

The door of a helicopter was thrown open even before its runners had fully touched down. On the side of the chopper, the eagle and shield emblem of the Department of Homeland Security. As Tate lowered his head and he hustled across the rooftop helipad to meet it, a marine held out her hand and helped to pull him inside.

Whatever was happening at Delancey Field, there wasn't a moment to lose; in fact, Tate prayed they weren't already too late.

CHAPTER THIRTY-TWO

Vivian Song had prayed for this moment. She whipped her tail and looked out the hangar door; her vision was blurred at first, filled with white-hot sparks of pain, but she blinked her remaining eye and forced the world back into some sort of clarity. The sight that greeted her was a mammoth black arrowhead hovering high above a distant cityscape. Its descending shape loomed large in the morning sky, swooping like some prehistoric bird of prey. She heard no roar of rockets, no whine of jet engines, no sonic boom, just the hum of some unknown propulsion as it dove steadily toward the earth.

A chariot of the gods! It is *them! They're* here!

She stood in childlike wonder as a vessel the size of a large cruise ship lined up almost perfectly with the long-abandoned runway. This was the dream; this was *every* dream, the vision that had haunted Vivian's unconscious mind since birth, suddenly come to life. Now, it was for real.

The creators are back, for real and forever!

Her empty eye socket oozed tears of blood, her surviving eye simply wept.

The craft continued its dive, plunging ever lower until the point of its nose finally stabbed the ground. Loose dirt and chucks of asphalt were pried up into the air, thrown in every direction, as the triangular craft flattened itself against the tarmac. It deployed no landing gear, Vivian noted, no skids, no wheels; it simply raced toward the hangar, sliding on its belly.

As the vessel barreled toward them, many of the creatures retreated into the crowd, trying to get out of its way, but the craft was so massive, there was nowhere for them to go. Here and there, pockets of spectators collapsed to their knees in prayer, sobbing, just staring helplessly at the oncoming ship, their eyes wide with dread. Others remained on their clawed feet and stood their ground, their bodies stiffening, bracing themselves for the coming impact.

At the last possible moment, however, the alien ship swerved, turned sideways, and lost its momentum. It skidded to a stop in front of the wide-open hangar door, still silent except for that deep, rhythmic, internal hum.

A sound that reminded Vivian of a pulse.

She glanced up once more, looking to the watchful ball of flesh, another of the gods' living tools; the herald continued to hover, to observe, but it offered her no permission, no advice on how she should proceed. The dragon's scaly feet moved forward anyway, carrying her through the crowd and toward the downed spacecraft.

A large portion of the vessel's flank began to pry itself apart, spreading like huge plump lips — a door of some kind.

Vivian stopped in her tracks.

Curious mutterings arose from the diverse crowd around her, a multitude of languages. They stood there, Hades' disciples and Poseidon's children, gripping their guns and their spears, their clawed hands raised in either defense or praise, and they watched as an enormous creature skittered toward them from the starship's open hatch. Its multiple legs formed inhuman geometries; they were like those of a Dungeness Crab, but six feet tall and thick as tree trunks. The creature's head was equally huge; reptilian, threatening, its jaws filled with smooth fangs that were long and sharp as sabers. If Vivian didn't know any better, she would have sworn it was the head of a tyrannosaurus rex.

This T-rex-crab, for want of a better name, wore a harness, a *saddle,* and sitting on its back was another, much smaller creature. This rider wore a peculiar-looking suit and helmet, flayed muscle merged with corrugated tubing, and there were elements of coral, of seashells.

Just like our communications device, like the craft itself...

The rider's shape appeared roughly humanoid, and on its hand, a ball of energy glowed bright as the sun.

Something clicked in Vivian's mind.

An overseer!

But...it couldn't be, could it? Overseers were Zeus' warriors. This creature and its rider came down from the sky!

Whatever it was, the humanoid began to speak, to address the crowd, its resonant voice obviously deepened by the helmet it wore. Vivian recognized the language, the ancient tongue of the creators. She was shocked, however, to hear the creature mention *her* by name.

———

As Carol Miyagi sat in her saddle, Zeus' warrior perched high atop her caballus, both the last of their respective breeds, she raised her voice and addressed the throng of creatures before her. She spoke in

Atlantean. After all, the dead tongue was what Kari, Alan, and Gagan had first heard broadcast through the Ark's communicator. If Hades' disciples had been the source of that initial transmission, it stood to reason they would understand her now, no matter what their country of origin.

And Carol needed to be understood.

She needed to be *obeyed.*

When she finished speaking, her words were followed by an uncomfortable moment of silence. Then, she heard murmurs and whispers spread quickly through the crowd. Poseidon's children made it clear *they* knew what she'd been saying; the sea creatures laid down their bony spears and fell to their knees on the concrete, but Carol still saw a lot of confused faces out there.

She took a breath and repeated herself in English, "If you stand with Vivian Song, if you fight for Kronos' return, then by all means, you should remain standing.

"But," Carol warned, and she lifted the glowing orb high above her head, "if you want to *live,* I highly suggest that you all drop your weapons and *kneel.* Get down on the ground and stay there!"

———

Drop their weapons? Earl Preston could not believe what he was hearing. *Could this alien really be on our side?*

Every eye in the hangar suddenly went to Vivian Song, and Earl could tell that she felt them. The air grew suddenly quiet, tense. Earl let his empty TEC-9 fall to the concrete. He took another step back, bumped into a furry body, and found himself looking at Zuri.

She grasped him by the arm. "Are you all right?"

He nodded.

Chud was there, as well; he stumbled, dazed, clearly shaken by what just happened to Larry Neuhaus. The crocodile-man helped to pull Peggy onto her webbed feet, showing great tenderness. She looked hopelessly at the three of them, her face still knotted in grief, her lone remaining eye drowning in tears.

Earl felt for her, he truly did, but right now, if they didn't want to join Larry in the next world, they had to get a move on in this one; something was coming, something *bad,* and they all needed to take cover if they wanted to survive it. Earl waved frantically for the control panel, "Everyone, get down!"

They did as he said, ducked behind the bloodied stone slab for protection, and fell to their knees.

———

Carol waited, looking over the creatures' heads; a few more of them did as she commanded and went down on their knees, but not many. The bulk of Hades' disciples continued to stand tall on their hooves and their clawed feet. They were prepared to fight on, to fight to the death, if need be.

It was their funeral.

Behind the creatures, Carol could see the thirteen skulls glowing brightly. The portal was active, connecting this world with all the "sacred planets" of the universe, and God only knew what might now step through it.

Carol frowned inside her helmet. She glanced back at the Ark. "Now, Gagan," she called.

The satyr emerged from the belly of the craft, his ornately carved bow clutched in one hand and a quiver of arrows strapped to his back. He stepped out onto the ruined tarmac, his cloven hooves clacking against upturned rubble, his fur blowing in the breeze, and he yelled at the top of his lungs in Nepali, *"Dēvatāharūkō lāgi laḍnuhōs!"*

Countless Yeti suddenly charged from the Ark's open hatchway. The frenzied horde waved their jade axes, their swords, and their spears as they flashed past Carol and Gagan, totally ignoring them. They filled the air with their distinctive musk; with the deep, bone-shuddering sound of their snarls, their huge hairy feet pounding the ruined pavement as they thundered off into battle.

Maintaining a safe distance, Kari and Alan followed the berserkers out of the breach. They emerged blinking, each lifting a hand to shield their eyes from the bright morning sun. Kari still held Carol's katana; Alan clutched his pickaxe.

"So far, so good," Alan had to admit, sounding mildly surprised.

Carol gave him an appreciative nod.

They made brief eye contact, which Alan quickly broke.

Carol sighed, then bent down and held out her gloved hand to Kari, lifting the woman up onto the saddle behind her. "Ladies first," she said. "Stay close, boys."

"We are behind you, Miyagi," Gagan assured her, nocking an arrow and lifting his horizontal pupils to the slaughter that lay ahead.

"Lead the way," Alan agreed; he gripped the hilt of his pickaxe with both hands, holding it up like a Louisville Slugger.

Kari's arm moved around Carol's waist. "Girls always talk about 'a knight in shining armor,'" she leaned in, resting her chin on Carol's shoulder, "I get it now."

Carol smiled inside her helmet. She squeezed the caballus with her legs, signaling the creature to move forward. The chimera opened its massive jaws and bellowed up at the sky, then it responded to its rider's movement like a well-trained horse. It skittered ahead, its many legs scrambling over the rubble, carrying Carol and Kari into the hangar and into the fray.

Several disciples mounted an assault against them as they rode by. Carol flicked her wrist; the bone sword instantly extended, and she took off their heads with a single swipe. Another creature came face to face with the nightmare jaws of her caballus; it was lifted off the floor, bitten cleanly in two, and its furry legs were still kicking as they dropped back onto the concrete. Still another met Kari and the flashing blade of her katana; now, the thing stood gaping at a fount of blood spurting freely from its arm.

Behind them, Gagan let his arrow fly, then quickly nocked another.

A half ape half scorpion creature lashed out at Alan with the stiletto point of its tail; he batted the stinger away, then swung his pickaxe right through the beast's skull.

———

Earl heard the roar of countless beasts; it sounded like a fucking freight train plowing through a mountain tunnel, and with the noise came a lot of agonized screams. He dared to raise up, to glance across the control panel behind him, and he stared, mesmerized, as hundreds of hairy monsters swarmed through the open doorway in a savage attack. It looked like a damn avalanche, a white wall slamming into Hades' disciples at break-neck speed.

Snowmen, Earl thought, almost surprised that he should be shocked by the realization. *Abominable Snowmen...* Yeti!

These Yeti were not the simple white apes he had seen in countless drawings and questionable photographs. They carried Neolithic weapons made of carved wood and jade, and they stampeded over any creature who remained standing, the ones who had made their allegiance to Vivian Song crystal clear. Earl watched in awe as the enemy forces scattered, as they were mercilessly hunted down.

"What the hell is going on out there?" Zuri asked him, panting, still trying to remain low and out of sight.

He could only shake his head. "Girl, you wouldn't believe me if I told you."

Earl had never pitied Hades' disciples before, but as he watched a bunch of crazed Yeti hack and slash them to pieces right in front of him, he pitied them now. The poor bastards never knew what hit them!

Then, when he saw Vivian Song let loose with her fire, Earl felt sorry for the killer snowmen as well.

———

Vivian's phosphorus blast was like blazing magnesium, burning a wide gap into the heart of the advancing horde, turning them instantly into cinders. As she swung her horned head to and fro, the dragon looked down at the dead and dying creatures who littered the bloodstained floor, and she could not help but think once more of her slain lover. Benedict had given his life for the gods, and *this* was how his loyalty, how *her* loyalty, had been repaid?

These hairy white savages who were slaughtering her people, they were *Cerberus,* Hades' disciples; she could smell it on them. And yet, they had arrived in one of the creators' own vessels. Was this the retribution so many had tried to warn her about — a final purge, the gods washing their hands of this world and wiping the slate clean? Her advisors had all assumed such vengeance would be served through the open portal, not from some alien version of a Trojan Horse, but the results were proving to be just as deadly.

Now out of breath, she recalled the conflagration to her inner furnace, feeling completely abandoned and betrayed. The sphere of flesh still hovered there above her, a passive observer to all this bloodshed. She glared up into its ever-watchful eyes, her fury only intensifying.

"Is this *why you came?"* Vivian screamed at the thing, her tone turning rancorous. *"Was this all just for the gods' own amusement — some sick form of* entertainment?"

Of course, the living camera offered her no explanation, no confirmation or denial. Completely indifferent to her plight, it made no sound at all. But it *did* move; it began to float away from Vivian, abandoning her to a raging civil war.

As Earl watched the disintegrating battle, he saw that the floating, nasty-ass Madball had evidently seen enough. The sphere of eyes slowly retreated from Vivian Song and the carnage below, and he tracked its path back through the air toward the glowing gateway vortex. Were the aliens recalling their fleshy drone — cutting their losses and throwing in the towel? Or was Kronos planning to double down, to send even more bizarre and deadly living weapons across that interstellar bridge, tipping the scales yet again?

Earl did not want to wait around for the answers. He saw Graeme King kneeling on the concrete, halfway between him and the gateway arch. Staying low, Earl scurried over and grabbed the frightened physicist by the arms; he shook him, screamed into his face, *"How do we close the fucking portal?"*

Graeme blinked. "Remember what I told you and that para-medic back at Stanley?"

"Man, I've slept since then!"

"A massive amount of energy is fueling the wormhole, right —

holding it open? We just need to cut off its power supply. I thought, maybe, if we stopped the flow of blood, it—"

"We did that. It didn't do a goddamn thing. What else you got?"

The physicist licked his lips; he took a deep breath and said, "If we could remove one of the skulls, the circuit would be broken."

"Shit." Earl looked over at the brightly glowing crystals, at the blue-white electrical arcs and forks of actual goddamn lightning that shot from each of them. If he tried to touch one of those supercharged things now, he thought it would be like taking a piss on a spark plug. "There's gotta be another way!"

Graeme shrugged and regarded him grimly, his voice frightened but firm, "You asked, Agent Preston."

———

Preacher asked the gods for their divine forgiveness, for their infinite mercy. The old werewolf approached the portal slowly, the sounds of battle still loud in his long, pointed ears; clans killing clans. Life was brought into this world with screams, with *pain,* and was taken from it in the same way.

He had studied the gods his entire life, but he still did not understand their true power. Not the energy locked within the quartz, incredible as it might be. No. Theirs was the power of *creation.*

The power of blood.

Preacher held up his still-bleeding claw. The old werewolf lifted his dim, pale eyes to the brightly glowing skulls, to the doorway their combined energy had thrown open. He stared down that ghostly tunnel, a conduit constructed from nothing more than swirling blue-white light, desperate to see through to the other side. While he found nothing but darkness at the bottom of that deep well, he knew that the creators were there.

They were watching.

Judging.

Condemning.

Propitiation. Blood for blood. They had given so much of it over the centuries. So much blood. So much death. But it seemed the gods still demanded more.

If you need another life, my lords, please, take me!

Preacher stood poised at the gateway threshold. Every step he'd taken on his life's journey, missteps included, had led him to this moment. Now, only one more step remained.

One final leap of faith.

Something moved overhead. The messenger of the gods. Preacher watched as the fleshy sphere glided past him into the energy vortex; it became a streak of light spiraling off into darkness.

Preacher took a deep breath and moved to follow it.

Propitiation, my lords. My life for the lives of my people. My soul for theirs.

The old werewolf closed his eyes, stepped through the gateway, and disappeared.

———

Earl caught a glimpse of a silhouetted werewolf, watched as it vanished into the wormhole, then his eyes immediately snapped back to Zuri. Thankfully, he found that she was still crouched safely beside Peggy and Chud.

His elation was brief.

As he looked across the hangar, Earl saw Vivian Song soaring at him through the air. The dragon flapped her golden wings and lowered her legs, landing on the bloodied stone of the control console; she loomed over his lover and his surviving friends like the angel of death. "Preston," she hissed, spearing Earl with her lone remaining eye, "Stupid Zeus! You've turned the gods against us! You've damned us all!"

"Look around, Viv! Your disciples are gettin' slaughtered! Gods, aliens, whatever the fuck they are, at least they know the score. Game over, bitch!" He stood tall, his head cocked toward the portal. "All that's left now is to turn out the lights and go home!"

"You think you've *won?*"

The dragon leapt down off the stone. She took a step closer to him, bleeding from a dozen of more minor wounds that were all healing rapidly; her claws were outstretched, her once shiny scales now dim and grimy with gore.

"Time to *burn!*"

Earl felt the hot breeze, saw the sparks fly from Vivian's lips as she spoke, and he knew the flames were not far behind. He reached for the butt of his 9mm, pulled the pistol free of his waistband. He tried to sound strong, tough, but beneath it all, he was truly terrified, "Give it your best shot."

Vivian laughed at that.

"Those bullets would serve you much better if you used them on yourself, Preston." Her eye glanced down at the pistol in his hand, then met his stare; she smiled hideously. "Just stick that gun in your mouth and pull the trigger. It would be far less painful for you, quicker, than what I'm about to do!"

Earl stood his ground, his 9mm aimed squarely at the dragon's heart. "Then, do it, already!"

To his surprise, the dragon did not belch fire. Instead, she lashed out with her spiked tail. Earl ducked and tumbled, narrowly avoided being skewered.

Behind him, Graeme King was not so lucky.

Vivian's long tail spikes drilled him, tore through his chest, raking him up off the floor. Graeme thrashed in the air and coughed up blood. The clipboard slipped from his grasp, stained pages of mathematics and blueprints coming loose to carpet the concrete below.

The muscular tail lifted him higher, brought the physicist level with Vivian's snout. "Thank you again, Dr. King," she told him, "but it would seem your services are no longer required."

Vivian flung Graeme aside, hurled his perforated body off onto the left angle of the gateway. He slammed up against the blazing skulls and ignited like a fly in a bug zapper. For an instant, Graeme's wide eyes flared bluish white, jagged spears of lighting shot through him, making his entire skeleton shine bright as an X-ray, and then he was gone, disintegrated; atomized.

It was as if the physicist had never existed at all.

Earl rolled onto his hands and knees, stunned. To his right, Zuri, Chud, and Peggy stared on, all of them frozen in the moment.

Vivian turned toward them, slowly and deliberately, and her blazing eye narrowed down at Earl. "You killed Benedict!"

"No," Zuri blurted; the werewolf leapt up, her fangs bared and her claws glistening. "That was *me*. And you can now join him in *Hell!*"

Peggy suddenly sprang to her webbed feet as well, and Earl would have been hard-pressed to say which of the women looked more pissed off. "You took my heart," she growled, a mournful tear still streaming down her luminous face. "Now, I'm going to rip your chest open and *feed* on yours!"

Next, Chud stood up beside them; without a word, the crocodile-man leveled his M-16 and snarled.

Earl gave the trio a nod, then he too managed to climb to his feet; he flashed his friends a resigned, appreciative grin and aimed his 9mm squarely at the dragon's snout.

Vivian's lone eye swept over them. "How courageous," she said with contempt. "How *romantic!* Now, you can all die together!"

The dragon's horned head reared back, her mouth yawning, glowing like the open crater of a volcano about to erupt, and—

WHAM!

Earl reeled back as a huge, multi-legged form dove at Vivian's blind side, hurtled into her, tackling her to the floor — the T-rex crab and its armored alien rider. Vivian's snout pivoted as she fell, unleashing a geyser of fire at her attacker. Flames washed over the creature's spiny exoskeleton; it shrieked, but its rider quickly ducked to one side, dodging the brunt of the blast.

Vivian was on her jagged back now, bucking and writhing, staring up into the gnashing fangs of the huge dino-crab; her leathery wings flapped wildly as the alien creature's thick chitinous legs fought to hold her down.

"Preston!"

At the sound of his name, Earl forced his rapt attention away from the struggling titans. He saw a trio of newcomers run up to the opposite side of the control console and was surprised to find a familiar face among them. "Everson?"

Alan nodded. The marine archeologist was flanked by a redheaded woman Earl didn't recognize, and a furry satyr with an ornately carved bow and arrow.

Earl quickly noted that the creature's arrow was pointed at the floor, a non-threatening display, and his eyes shot back to Alan. "Where the Hell is Miyagi?"

"She's..." The archeologist was suddenly struck mute; he almost looked pained.

"She's right over there," the redhead finished for him, gesturing with the bloodied blade of a ninja sword. "That's Carol in the armor, the one fighting the damn dragon!"

———

As Carol Miyagi sat astride her mount, she signaled the caballus to halt its advance. The creature obeyed its rider; its skittering legs stopped moving and it lowered its body until it hovered just above the ground.

"What's wrong?" Kari asked, confused, the sudden change of motion causing her to tighten her arm around Carol's waist. "Are we getting off now?"

"*You* are."

"What? No! I'm staying with you."

"*Chikushō,*" Carol swore, "I'm wearing armor, Kari. You're not."

She could feel Kari's eyes on the back of her helmet. Carol's bond with the myrmidon had granted her many things, but the power of telepathy was not one of them. All the same, she could tell what Kari must have been thinking: *I'm not watching you go off and leave me behind again, Carol Miyagi!*

"I'm going up against a *dragon,* Kari, and I can't be worried about your safety while I do it. *Please,*" she begged, "for me."

Kari reluctantly withdrew her arm.

Carol turned her head; she watched as Kari awkwardly dismounted, joining Alan and Gagan there on the hangar floor, then she looked directly at Alan. "Keep her safe."

"I will," he promised, and she knew that he meant it.

Satisfied, Carol was off again; she squeezed the caballus with her legs and the creature surged forward, closing the gap. Together, animal and rider rammed into Vivian Song. They knocked the dragon off her clawed feet, skirting her flaming breath as they worked to pin her down and hold her there.

Carol took a swipe at Vivian; the jagged edge of her bony blade kissed the dragon's neck, but Vivian's claw shot up and caught her sword arm, halting the blow.

The ghost of a smile flickered across the dragon's snout; there and then gone.

With her free claw, Vivian reached up. Her golden talons slid beneath the caballus' snapping jaws, and she seized the beast by its throat. She then pushed the engineered creature back with all her might.

Her strength was incredible!

Somehow, Vivian managed to rise, to sit up beneath the caballus. Like a hydraulic lift, her chokehold raised the creature off the floor so that its spiny forelegs churned helplessly in the air.

The struggling caballus roared, thrashed its oversized head.

Vivian responded with a sudden furious twist. She overtook the beast; her body rolled on top of it, and she slammed it back against the concrete, nearly crushing Carol in the process.

Now that she had the upper hand, Vivian quickly shifted her grip. Her talons curled around the creature's teeth, her scaly muscles flexing as she worked to pry the jaws apart. Tender flesh at the corners of the beast's mouth cracked and tore, blood jetting from the widening splits. The dragon then opened her own mouth and exhaled down the beast's throat, filling its gullet with her white-hot fire, cooking it from within.

As Carol watched this shocking reversal of fortune, her vision tinted bright red. Flashing alarms on her internal tactical display informed her that Vivian's blaze had just spiked at over a million degrees Kelvin—

The temperature of an atomic blast!

—and her proximity to that unbelievable furnace instantly turned her armor into a sauna. The full weight of the caballus slumped against her right leg, and Carol found herself pinned to the floor.

Trapped!

Once again, she saw the glyphs for *DEFENSE SCREEN* appear on her heads-up display. She flicked her other wrist, waved both her arms, hoping her armor would respond and spontaneously morph into something useful.

Nothing happened.

I don't know what to do!

When the heat haze cleared, Carol could see Vivian Song glower down at her, curls of smoke painting spirals around her demonic head.

"Your ride is dead." Vivian released the burnt-out husk of her caballus, let the creature's still-flaming jaws drop to the concrete. "And so are you!"

––––––––

"Hey, you!" Kari hefted Carol's katana and sprang forward; she waved her arms, shouting, trying her best to draw the dragon's attention away from the woman she loved.

It worked.

Vivian growled and pivoted, catching Kari in her intense stare.

As she charged, Kari noticed movement to her right and was surprised to see Alan running up behind her. It didn't take long, however, for her to realize that he wasn't rallying to Carol's aid. He was coming after *her*.

Alan yelled out a warning and jumped at Kari, shoving her aside with one hand and lifting his pickaxe with the other. Vivian lashed out at him with her spiked tail; the impact sent Alan flying backward as Kari stumbled to the floor.

Kari gasped; the wind gone from her sails. When she looked up, she was greeted by the ominous, unbelievable sight of the dragon standing over her. She rolled onto her back and held out the katana, her hands trembling.

The dragon yawned, but before she could breathe fresh death, her sinuous neck bristled with a volley of arrows.

When Gagan saw that his friends were in danger, he showed no hesitation; the goat-man leapt up onto the ancient stone of the control console, drew back on his bowstring, and let his arrow fly.

I must protect Miyagi and Hannigan! I must draw the dragon away from them!

Gagan immediately nocked another arrow, and another, and another; the archer's motions were unnaturally quick, the accuracy of his aim precise.

The dragon flinched with each new impact. She roared in pain, in anger. Any one of those arrows should have had enough force to kill, but somehow, the beast remained standing.

Because this is no earthly creature. This is a primal force of nature, of the universe! *I would have more luck bringing down a typhoon!*

Gagan fired off a few more arrows, emptied his quiver, but it was a losing battle. To defeat this monster, he realized, it would take much more than swords and arrows.

It would take the power of a *god!*

The golden alien orb, the Wrath of the Gods, was still there on Carol's hand. As she struggled to free herself, desperate to slide her leg out from underneath the dead body of her caballus, to rush over to Kari and Alan, the weapon fed off her anxiety and fear, off her surging adrenaline. It glowed brighter, becoming a miniature super nova there above her wrist. Even with the heads-up display of her helmet, Carol had to squint against its powerful light. Energy surged through her, strumming her bones. She froze; stared fascinated, remembering her dream, her *epiphany*.

"*It's yours...It always has been...*"

She was *made for this*.

Carol nodded and looked over at Kari.

The dragon loomed over her, plucking Gagan's arrows from its neck and tossing them aside, preparing to unleash another blast of blazing fury, and there was nothing now to stand in its way.

With every ounce of energy she had left, Carol pushed against the dead weight of her caballus. She stabbed into the beast's flank with her bone sword, bent her elbow and flexed, her biomechanical armor bulging as she worked hard to prop the carcass up. At last, Carol had created enough space that she was able to shove her leg free.

She quickly stood and lunged at Vivian.

"Step back," Carol commanded with passion, with *authority;* she faced the dragon, moved between her and Kari, holding up the glowing orb like a talisman to ward off her attack. "Get away from her! Do it *now!*"

Vivian's lone eye went to the weapon on Carol's hand, reflecting its blue-white brilliance. "Zeus' warrior," she hissed.

It wasn't a question.

"I *am,*" Carol assured her.

They faced each other with stoic calm; two gunslingers at high noon, each wondering who would be fastest on the draw.

Vivian's scaly lip twitched, peeled back, and a gout of deadly flame shot from the widening gulf between her fangs.

At the same moment, Carol willed the alien orb to discharge, to project its full destructive power, and a beam of intense energy rushed up toward the dragon.

Both blazes collided; their combined destructive power ignited the very air between the two women, creating a small explosion, a fireball with a concussive wave that tossed Vivian backwards and sent Carol to the floor.

————

Earl lifted a hand to shield his eyes from the fireball, awed, trying to fathom what had just happened. *"Holy Christ!"*

When he lowered his hand again, he saw that Vivian and Carol had semi-recovered and were already attempting to get back onto their feet. Earl noticed something else as well: where the dragon had landed.

Vivian was on the gateway threshold, right at the glowing edge of the wormhole.

Break the circuit. That's what Graeme said, wasn't it — take out one or more of the skulls?

If Carol hit the metal scaffolding with another blast like that...

What the hell have we got to lose?

Earl stepped forward and yelled, curling his hands around his mouth like a megaphone, *"Miyagi!"*

————

Carol Miyagi rocked on her hands and knees. Her myrmidon had shielded her from the worst of the shockwave, but despite her protective armor and helmet, she felt as if she'd just had a bruising glance off a brick wall.

Someone called out her name.

Alan?

Still stunned, she looked back, but he wasn't there. She saw Gagan kneeling on top of the control panel, the bow and arrow still clutched in his clawed hands. Carol also saw the Poseidon woman, Peggy Neuhaus, and two other creatures, a walking crocodile and a werewolf. And there, beside them all, stood Earl Preston.

"Shoot the fuckin' gateway," the man yelled, *"blast it! Close it!"*

Carol struggled to stand, using her bone sword as a crutch to help her climb to her booted feet. Her gaze moved quickly toward the gateway, toward the thirteen crystal skulls, each alive and crawling with spectral energy. And as she stared up at them, she was reminded that her hand now glowed with the exact same power.

The heatshield that protected the Ark during re-entry...Same energy...

Carol turned to confront the dragon once more; the Atlantean glyphs for *DEFENSE SCREEN* still flashed insistently at the edge of her vision, and at last, she understood.

Kari was on her feet again now, standing at Carol's side.

Carol flicked her wrist, retracted her bone sword, and took Kari's hand in her own, pulling her close. "Get behind me," she murmured.

"What are you going to do?"

"You'll see."

Vivian scowled down at the women. She stood at the mouth of the gateway; her membranous wings, now backlit by the swirling vortex, seemed to glow from within. The dragon fisted her claws and parted her lips to disgorge more fire.

The killing blast came straight for Carol and Kari.

Carol raised the glowing orb, but this time, she did not propel the energy forward. Instead, she willed it to spread out, to create a bubble of blue-white radiance all around her, around Kari — a protective blister. Vivian's conflagration struck this newly formed defense screen and flowed harmlessly around it as if it were a boulder in the middle of a stream.

With Kari at her back, still safely within the confines of the energy bubble, Carol started forward.

Shocked, Vivian retreated. She stepped dangerously close to the wormhole, so close, in fact, that her golden skin was now painted in the shimmering waves of its light. Her long, catfish-like whiskers were seized by its gravity; they stretched back behind her horned head, reminding Carol of colorful streamers, the ones that once trailed from the handlebars of her childhood bike. The dragon ran out of breath, recalled her flames, and the look on her snout was as much wonder as confusion.

Now, it was Carol's turn. Vivian could not see the look of triumphant determination she wore within her helmet, but it was there.

"You want to see the gods so badly?" Carol shouted, lifting her arm even higher. "I'll send you to them!"

This time, Carol aimed above the dragon's head. The resulting burst of energy connected with a large section of gateway scaffolding, obliterating it. At first, Carol thought she had vaporized two of the skulls, but no, she saw that the crystals had simply landed on the floor atop a pile of metal shrapnel and debris. She briefly wondered if the alien artifacts could even *be* destroyed, and then she noticed that their glow had already begun to fade.

The circuit had been broken.

Metal grinding against metal drew Carol's attention back to the portal. Without a power supply to sustain it, the wormhole destabilized rapidly, and the massive gateway structure that surrounded it fell in upon itself. Carol saw the crippled steel bend and twist, watched rivets pull free and shoot like bullets into the depths of the spiraling gravity well.

Similar forces reached out and clutched at the dragon, yanking her back into the shrinking breach. Ruined and defeated, she continued to struggle, to *resist*, her wings flapping like an insect caught in a ghostly spiderweb. Finally, her claws blurred out and she grabbed hold of the warped metal framework on either side. The move kept her from being swallowed whole, but it only delayed the inevitable.

Vivian Song was dragged to Kronos in pieces.

Her wings went first, the molecules squeezed together and were ripped from her back in fiery streaks of light. Then, the entire length of her spiked tail was eaten away, dematerialized, the particles sliding and shifting as they swirled off into oblivion. Her arms and legs followed close behind, the limbs folding in upon themselves as the portal shrank around them. Huge gaps appeared in the dragon's torso; streams of atoms sucked into the collapse like water down a drain.

And through it all, Vivian shrieked; one chilling howl after another. It was as if the dragon could feel every cell as it was torn from her body and pulled halfway across the universe. The portal closed around Vivian's neck like a tightening noose. Super-heated energy sliced through scaly flesh, through jagged vertebrae, and at last, her screaming stopped.

Carol watched Vivian's severed head drop onto the cracked concrete floor. She heard it land with a loud sickening *SPLAT,* then slowly exhaled. "She's gone," Carol announced to no one in particular. "It's over."

Someone squeezed her gloved hand in reply. Kari. She stepped out from behind Carol, awed, and nestled up to her. "You did it."

Carol blinked, looked over at Kari, then back to the ruined gateway. The door to Kronos and the gods had been slammed shut. There was nothing between the misshapen steel pylons but empty air, and Carol could now look right through to the back of the old aircraft hangar. The crystal skulls had managed to survive the collapse; they were stuck in the superstructure, littering the floor, but all had gone dark, dormant.

She held up her hand, staring at the alien orb, watching as the spectral fire dimmed there a well.

Carol lowered her arm. She spun around and allowed her gaze to lock on Kari's smiling lips. In that sweet, victorious moment, Carol wanted nothing more than to strip off her helmet and kiss her, to hear her finish speaking the sentence she had begun in the Ark's control room, to say that—

Alan staggered toward them. There was blood on his clothes. Half a dozen red patches marked where the dragon's spiked tail had slapped him and pushed him away; they ran up and down the length of his torn shirt, growing larger with his every step.

He dropped his pickaxe and stumbled, about to fall to the floor.

"Alan!" Carol rushed over, caught him in her arms, and carefully lowered him onto the concrete. Then, she knelt beside him, inspecting his wounds, her helmet feeding her his vital signs; heart rate, oxygen levels, blood pressure, all of it diving rapidly into the red zone. "Hang on...I'll get you some help."

He shook his head. His hand reached up to touch one of the wounds, his voice clotted and hoarse, "Not this time."

Alan was right.

All his life functions were now critical. Given these readouts, even Carol could tell that he would be dead within minutes. She looked up, frantic, finding the downed spaceship sitting just outside the hangar doors. "We'll get you back into the Ark—"

"Don't you dare!" Alan's voice was weak, but still bright with anger and fear. He clasped Carol's hand in fierce grip, then his eyes shot behind her.

She turned her head and saw Kari standing there.

"Don't...you let her do it, Kari. Don't *you* do it. Don't make a...another *fucking* clone. Pr...promise me!"

Kari nodded helplessly.

"Promise," he cried, and the word was followed from his lips by a bloody cough.

"I promise," Kari said aloud, her eyes wet with tears.

Alan nodded, satisfied; he relaxed and closed his eyes in a slow, pained blink. "We...We did the right thing here. Carol would've..." He looked around, his pupils aimless at first, searching, then they seemed to find a point of focus. "Carol, is it really you?"

"Yes," she told him through tears of her own.

Finally, too late, he saw her for who she was; he had accepted her.

"I'm right here."

Alan shook his head lazily, dismissively, a slow-blooming smile on his bloody lips. *"Carol."*

She followed his gaze, saw nothing there but empty air. When she looked back down at Alan, however, she knew that he was smiling at *something.*

"Oh, I've missed you," he said to the nothingness, his voice no more than a whisper. "We...can be together again. I...I love you."

Carol swallowed thickly. She knew now that he wasn't really talking to *her,* but she answered him, anyway. "I love you, too."

Alan used all of his remaining strength to lift a hand, to reach out toward the emptiness. Then, his arm went suddenly limp; it hit the concrete with a slap, and he became still, lifeless in her arms.

"Watashi wa, anata o aishiteimasu," she said, then repeated it again in English, "I love you."

Carol blinked, sighed through gritted teeth as she laid his riddled body down.

"Sayōnara, watashi no ai. Goodbye."

Kari immediately knelt there beside her. She let go of the bloody katana she had been holding, reached out, and pulled Carol into her arms. "I'm so sorry, sweetie."

"Miyagi." Gagan was there as well; he walked up from behind, laid a furry claw on her shoulder, and said, "Mr. Alan fought bravely. He will be remembered."

Carol was grateful for them both, thankful that they had been able to remain safe through the battle. And when she spoke, her voice was thick with emotion, *"Arigatō,* my friends. Thank you."

The air grew thick with the chopping noise of approaching rotors. A fleet of helicopters, UH-60 Black Hawks by the sound of them, closing fast. Earl looked up to the rafters. Director Tate got his message after all.

Here comes the fuckin' calvary!

Earl shook his head bitterly. This was it, the moment he'd dreamed of, prayed for, fought for. They'd won, and yet, he found that he didn't feel at all like celebrating; he felt numb. His eyes moved from the twisted metal skeleton of the gateway to Alan's body, then from Carol to Peggy, feeling the weight of everything that had happened, everyone they had lost.

The price tag had been too damn high.

And now, with the arrival of those choppers, they had another potential problem yet to deal with.

Earl glanced back across the control console. Much of the hangar was still in chaos. Poseidon's children were all on their knees, but that army of killer Yeti continued to clash with Hades' remaining disciples. If Tate stormed into this place now with a bunch of heavily armed marines...

He slid his 9mm pistol back into the waistband of his torn and dirty slacks, then ran over to Carol. "Miyagi!"

She lifted her glowing eyes to him. Forget Lara Croft. In that armor and helmet, the archeologist was like a cross between Black Manta and the female alien from the movie *Species*.

"I'm sorry about Alan," he told her, "but if things don't change up in here, and I mean real fuckin' quick, Poseidon's children and all those pissed-off Wampas you brought, they're gonna get shot all to Hell!"

Carol whispered something under her breath, something in Japanese. Earl knew the language, but her voice was distorted by the helmet she wore, making the words unintelligible. She rose and stepped over to the wrecked gateway, over to Vivian Song's severed head. With a flick of her wrist, Carol extended a bony sword from her arm; she let out a primal scream, stabbed her blade down through the dragon's skull, and plucked it up off the floor.

Vivian Song's forked tongue hung limply from between her fangs. Her lone eye was wide and glassy, devoid of life.

"The fuck you gonna do with that?" Earl wanted to know, his face curdling.

Carol held the head up high above her helmet, triumphant. "I'm going to show these creatures that this murdering bitch is gone, and she's not coming back." Then, she locked eyes with Earl. "And I'm going to tell them that the fucking gods are never going to return."

The fact that Miyagi had just cursed in English for the first time since he'd met her was not lost on Earl. He nodded and offered her an appreciative grin. "Let the church say 'Amen!'"

———

Patrick Tate let the helicopter's runners touch down fully before sliding the door open and leaping out into the tall grass of Delancey Field. Several Black Hawks hovered protectively in the air above him. Others had already landed. Troops poured out, weapons leveled, advancing in a cordon toward the huge downed spacecraft and the equally large, supposedly abandoned aircraft hangar beyond.

As they hurried across the field, a lone voice cried out, nearly lost to the roar of the rotors, *"Don't shoot!"*

The director saw a single figure emerge. A man. African American. His clothing was ripped, covered in blood, and his hands were held high above his head; one of them was empty, fingers splayed, the other held up a badge and ID.

"Federal agent!" the man shouted.

Tate didn't need binoculars or scopes to know the man was Earl L. Preston, Jr.

Thank God! It's your boy, Link. He's safe.

"Stand down," the director yelled to his troops, rushing forward through their ranks toward Earl, *"That's an order, goddammit! Stand down!"*

They halted their advance, but Tate continued forward until he was no more than an arm's length from Earl. The two men paused there in the grass, staring at one another.

"A little late to the party, Director Tate," Earl told him, swaying on his feet, "but I ain't mad atcha."

"Son, you look like Hell."

"Well, sir, Hell is exactly where I've been."

"You can put your hands down now, Agent Preston."

"I don't know, sir." Earl's eyes skated over all the rifles that were still pointed right at him, all the fingers on triggers. "Black Americans, like myself, can't be too careful, even with a fancy badge. Growin' up, my mama always told me: 'Son, right or wrong, you get stopped, you watch your mouth, you use your 'yes sirs' and your 'no sirs,' like you was in *Roots*. You make eye contact, you keep your hands up, so they see you don't pose a threat, and then *maybe*, God willin', you don't get your black ass shot.' How am I doin' so far, sir?"

Tate frowned; his throat constricted. Earl's father had told him a very similar story back in the Gulf, and it pained the director to know that two men, growing up some twenty odd years apart, would need to hear such a thing in this country — a country they were both still willing to fight for and die to protect. "Well, I'm standing right here in front of you, son." He looked back at the troops, then returned his attention to Earl. "So if anybody shoots, they'll have to shoot through me."

Earl smiled at him and slowly lowered his hands.

Tate nodded at the hangar. "What's the situation, Agent Preston?"

"Party's over, sir. You're just in time to mop up."

"Are there any creatures, any werebeasts still alive in there?"

"Yes, sir," Earl informed him. "But you'll find that most of the ones who are still breathin' are playin' for the home team. I couldn't have saved the world without 'em, so I'd sure appreciate it if they didn't get shot, either."

The director thought of the woman who had been with Earl back in the hospital, the one who had changed into a wolf right before his eyes. "I understand," he said. "You have my word."

"Thank you, sir."

"Well done. You've probably earned yourself a medal today, Agent Preston. You've made me, your country, and I'm certain your father, immensely proud."

And, before he let himself get too emotional, Patrick Tate extended his hand.

Earl shook it, his eyes glistening in the early morning light. "Honestly, sir," he said. "I don't give a shit about the medal. I'm just really glad it's over."

PART THREE

The Legacy of the Gods

CHAPTER THIRTY-THREE

Peggy Neuhaus would be glad when this was all over. Another labor pain tore through her. She clenched her needle-like teeth together until her jaw ached. Her webbed talons clutched at her glowing, swollen abdomen; her lone eye stared into that translucent bubble, saw the shadowy life within her twist and flutter beneath ribbons of reticulated light and constricted muscle.

The pain ebbed away like the tide.

Peggy exhaled with a sigh. She allowed herself to relax for a moment. Just for a moment. But her midwife would not let her lie back against the rock.

"*Unum 'ukhraa,*" the Paralicht woman urged. These last six months since leaving New York, Peggy had studied the ancient language many of Poseidon's children used. While she still had her struggles *speaking* the words, she understood what her midwife had said.

One more.

"Unum 'ukhraa tulei!"

One more push.

Peggy took a deep breath, hoping it would help. Far from it. Her nostrils filled with a sulfur stench, the overpowering odor of the volcanic hot spring in which she now bathed.

Her birthing chamber.

Peggy wretched, then swallowed hard.

"Unum 'ukhraa tulei," the midwife begged again; she stroked the rigid fins that lined Peggy's legs; soothing, coaxing.

One more push. Sure. That's what you said after the last push, and the push before that.

The sharp pain of a contraction may have subsided, but the dull ache of her grief remained.

I want Larry. I want my husband. It isn't fair. He should be here right now. He didn't deserve to die. He deserved a chance to meet his child.

Even with the gateway closed, Peggy sometimes felt as if she were straddling two separate worlds. On the one hand, she found herself longing for Larry, wishing she could have just died in that aircraft hangar, could have joined her husband in the afterlife. But she also felt the overwhelming and conflicting need to live, *really live*, not simply to exist, to go through life as a shell of her former self; no, her baby deserved so much better than that. Boy or girl, this child had already lost one parent; Peggy would be damned if she let it become an orphan to misery and despair.

Whenever she felt depression closing in on her, a shadow circling her mind like a shark stalking its victim, Peggy told herself that she was far from helpless. She was no victim. She was *the shark*. Peggy could claw, and bite, and struggle on, and she did her best to do just that.

The fact that she was alive, that her child had been given the chance to continue to grow within her, to be born right now, was nothing short of a miracle.

Still, these past months, this miracle of life, feeling the baby stir and kick, had always been tempered by the ache of Larry's absence. She missed being able to discuss possible baby names with him. Being able to choose colors for a nursery. Being able to share all her joys and her every fear.

So many fears.

Peggy knew that every mother worried. But she had the added pressure of knowing this was her one and only chance to have Larry's baby, the pressure to make sure everything turned out okay. And she could not help but wonder what all that stress had been doing to their baby.

Her thoughts returned to that first ultrasound. Larry had been there by her side. He had taken her hand in his own, had given her fingers a gentle reassuring squeeze. It had been just what she'd needed.

"I'm right here," her husband had told her.

And somehow, Peggy believed it was still the truth.

I know, Rembrandt. I know. I just wish you were more than a ghost.

Larry's ghost.

That was one of the reasons why she did not return to their seaside home, afraid she would see him around every corner. His canvasses. His paints. His razor and his toothbrush by the sink...

One of the reasons, but not the only one.

Peggy remembered standing on that reef in Colonial Bay, Barbara DeParle extending a hand to her, inviting her to join Poseidon's children in the depths. That was years ago. Peggy had been in another place back then. She'd chosen instead to remain behind, to cling to the human world she'd always known. But after everything that had happened, all the fighting, all the *loss;* it was a world she no longer recognized. And when Christine DeParle's husband, Jason, offered to bring Peggy here, to New Poseidon, to welcome her as one of their own, this time, she had not refused.

It was what she needed, what her baby needed.

Peggy screamed; the sound echoed off the cavern walls. She reached for her knees, tightened her muscles, and strained.

The baby crowned. Peggy felt it. Not the rounded skull of a human child, but the pointed snout of a Charodon; its shark-like head stabbed into the water, thrashed between her legs like a second tail, its newborn gills pulsating. Once her child got its first taste of freedom, it grew impatient; its tail whipped back and forth, beating the walls of the birth canal as it worked to propel itself forward, *outward.*

And then, it *was* out.

Peggy's baby swam free of her and right into the waiting arms of her midwife.

"Is it okay?" Peggy asked, her voice full of worry and exhaustion, her cyclopean eye spilling tears down her iridescent cheek. "Is it...*Ua luderick ia?*"

If Peggy had pronounced it wrong, the Paralicht woman didn't let on. She lifted the baby up out of the water, smiled down at it, and nodded. *"Ita."*

'Ita'...Yes? Yes!

The child began to cry. It started as a gurgling snarl, morphed quickly into a high-pitched whine, and it was truly the most beautiful sound Peggy had ever heard in her life.

"You..." the midwife began, searching for the proper English, "have a son."

It's a boy, Rembrandt! We have a son.

A half-laugh, half-cry burst from Peggy's lips, full of joy, and sorrow, and relief, all in equal measure. She took the baby into her arms and held him to her glowing breast. He was indeed a Charodon, and the spitting image of his father. His cute little tail trailed down between her webbed fingers and slithered lazily across her belly. One of his tiny hands reached out for her thumb; his miniature claws wrapped around her much larger talon and squeezed.

His grip was *strong*.

Peggy gazed down at her son. These past months, she'd worried that her appearance might be too frightening for the child, that he might stare into his mother's burnt-out eye socket and never stop screaming. Just the opposite. As soon as her son looked up into her glowing face, he quit crying and began to coo.

"He's beautiful," Peggy said. "He's perfect."

All her fears, all her worries, every negative thought born out of dread...they all evaporated. In that first embrace, Peggy's heart melted, and she was filled with nothing but love.

———

Days later, the underwater city's ancient temple filled with all the clans of Poseidon; Charodon, Kraken, and Paralicht, hundreds of them, all lined up in neat rows. Peggy entered and walked leisurely through the center of the congregation; her newborn son cradled in her arms. Creatures on either side held their webbed hands out to her, blessing both mother and child.

Peggy looked at them all and smiled, moved by the gesture, by the entire ceremony. It had a regal feel to it, and she felt undeserving and unprepared.

At the foot of Varuna's statue stood the real royal: Christine DeParle. Jason sat in a carved seashell throne to her left with their tiger-striped daughter, Kohara, on his knee. The little shark-girl looked rather awestruck as Peggy approached and ascended the stone steps.

This was clearly a special event, one that did not happen every day.

As she turned her lone eye back to Christine, Peggy caught sight of the four crystal skulls that were now positioned around Varuna's carved feet. She remembered clawing at the base of the Colonial Bay statue, pulling out a stone cork to find the "Wrath of the Gods" hidden away within. Now, Poseidon's children had been entrusted to hide and protect another source of great power. A power that Peggy hoped would never again fall into the corrupt hands of monsters like Karl Tellstrom and Vivian Song.

"Today is a joyous day," Christine announced, her dark eyes sweeping the gathered crowd. "As a people, we have experienced much death, much pain and loss." She then gestured to the little shark-baby that squirmed in Peggy's arms. "But today, Poseidon's children welcome new life, a new member of the Charodon clan, into our ranks."

Her words were cheered by every member of the throng, but it was the Charodon who were the most vocal.

Christine lifted her talons to quiet them, her paddle-like tail swishing. Then, she returned her focus to Peggy. "What name do you give to your child?"

Peggy smiled down at her son, and her lips quivered with sudden emotion. "Rembrandt," she said at last. "His name is Rembrandt."

Christine nodded, intrigued. "A special name, indeed, composed of the Germanic elements for 'advice' and 'sword.' It was the name of a genuinely great artist."

"Yes," Peggy agreed, her single eye spilling a single tear. "It was."

CHAPTER THIRTY-FOUR

Wind whipped through the frozen mountain pass, spilling fresh snow. Gagan stood at the mouth of a large cave, a silent sentry, and he lifted his horned head to watch the flurries mound and drift. It was a beautiful sight; tranquil.

Peaceful.

Billions of snowflakes spreading out to cover the land, each one unique and distinct from all the others around it. And yet, after even the harshest of winters came the spring thaw. Then, all those untold billions would melt to form a single mountain stream, forging a path together, all going in the same direction, racing toward the same end.

The goat-man's thick lips curled up at the thought of it, and he ran his clawed fingers through his beard. His mind returned once more to Hannigan and Miyagi, the one-time strangers whom he now called his friends. He'd never really had friends before, and it had been difficult for him to leave them, especially after the death of

Mr. Alan. Gagan had not even been able to attend the man's burial. There had been no time.

After the battle, he had chosen to return with the Yeti, to act as their translator, to help bring them home, and he still believed it had been the right thing to do. There had been many soldiers flying along with them on the military cargo planes, acting as security for the massive airlift, trying to make sure the operation happened as quickly and quietly as possible. The humans had all been polite, yes, but Gagan had smelled the fear on them; he'd seen the mistrust, the *disgust*, in their eyes.

As openly and completely as his new friends had accepted him, Gagan knew the rest of the world was not yet ready.

Still looking out at the falling snow, Gagan recalled what he had said to Hannigan, during a quiet moment before they reached Makalu's summit, before they had stumbled upon the Yeti and the Ark. *"My whole life,"* he'd told her, *"I have lived a lie, afraid that people would find out the truth and reject me, beat me,* kill me. *But out here, in nature...there is no one to judge. I am free to be who I am."*

Here among the Yeti, Gagan did not have to hide behind a human façade. Here, he could be who he was born to be, and so could they.

And then, of course, there had been the matter of the crystal skulls. The Yeti had been entrusted with four of the powerful quartzes, had been tasked to hide and protect them here in these deep mountain caverns.

Gagan exhaled, the fog of his breath momentarily obscuring his view of the falling snow. The Yeti believed the Ark had sung to them from its prison on Makalu. Perhaps it had. Perhaps it had sung to him as well. All his life, Gagan had been drawn to these mountains, searching for his purpose in this world, his destiny. He had been tested in battle, and now, he had a sacred duty to perform.

The archer continued his watch. His bow was slung across his furry shoulder, a full quiver of arrows strapped to his back. They were there if he needed them, but he hoped and prayed no such need would arise.

Not tonight, or any other night.

No paths led to these caverns. No climbers ventured close. No planes flew overhead; there were not even any birds. This locale was truly remote, a frozen paradise where Gagan, the Yeti, and the skulls could remain hidden away. Forever, if need be.

In the months he had spent with them here, Gagan had learned much of the Yeti's history and culture through the songs they sang each night around their fires — important events, great men and women, all living on through words and music passed down from one generation to the next. And tonight, Gagan heard the tribe sing something new. Tonight, the Yeti sang about *him:* "*Gagan, Dēvatāharūkō Mēsanjara.*"

Gagan, the Messenger of the Gods.

Everything that had happened to him since leaving Kathmandu, since finding his new tribe, his new *family*, had now been immortalized in song. As long as there were Yeti in these mountains, Gagan's name would ring out. His life, however long it might be, will have had meaning. He blinked a single tear from his eye and it froze there in his fur.

"*Kē timīlā'ī bhōka lagēkō cha?*"

At the sound of that deep, familiar voice, Gagan turned to find the huge figure of Shekhar standing behind him in the mouth of the cavern. The Yeti chief clutched the shank of a Himalayan Tahr in his clawed hand, not a spear, not a sword, not an axe. The meat was fresh from the cooking fires, still steaming, and he held it out to the goat-man with a wide, yellowed smile.

Gagan smiled back at him and shook his horned head; he had eaten his fill earlier and was no longer hungry.

Shekhar shrugged. The yeti sat down upon a small boulder, bit off chunks of warm meat, then gnawed on the naked bone. Soon, no trace of his meal remained.

Nothing went to waste here.

Gagan hoped the same could be said for the second chance they had all been given; Hades, Poseidon, even Zeus. Outside, the wind subsided, and the air grew calm. How long it would remain that way, he could not say.

CHAPTER THIRTY-FIVE

Tom Savini, the make-up effects man behind the gore of *Friday the 13th*, could not know how right he had been. After years of simply finding new and slick ways to kill people on screen, he proclaimed that monsters, strange creatures, were going to be making a comeback. Savini's unusual creations had all been fake, of course, just foam and latex rubber molded over wires and servos; puppets and big-budget Halloween costumes, nothing more. But Dante "The Horror Show" Vianello was the real McCoy.

The once imposing killer, former hitman and would-be dragon-slayer, now sat slumped in an old, beat-up metal wheelchair, the best the Department of Corrections had to offer him. Scarred. Scruffy. His jet-black hair, no longer dyed, was now marred by that once-hidden skunk streak of grey. His hands lay folded neatly in his lap, and his deep-set eyes stared blankly off into space.

He was a pathetic sight, indeed.

Normally, the corrections officers would have had him handcuffed. It was standard practice, after all. The COs would have fastened a pair of leg irons around his ankles and forced him to drag a heavy length of chain between them as they shuffled him off to his brand-new digs. But of course, Horror Show didn't have any ankles, not anymore. No legs, either. All these pricks could do now was to push him along in that beat-up chair of his.

Sitting there like that, hands folded, vacant eyes staring, he appeared almost catatonic. He was no longer tall, but still brawny. Yet, despite his powerfully muscled arms, the staff no longer saw him as the threat he had once been. To them, Horror Show was nothing now but a helpless gimp. So, the COs kept their batons on their belts, and they pushed his ass around the prison like they were his own personal chauffeurs.

Horror Show almost smiled at the thought, but he fought to keep that blank expression firmly on his face, to show no emotion of any kind. Behind those vacant eyes was a gifted, savagely alert mind, a mind that had kept him at the top of his sordid profession for many years, a mind that now grew restless. He allowed his fingers to stir; they moved from his lap, slowly slid up his forearms. New flesh filled once pitted bite marks, and he felt the smooth ridges like a blind man reading Braille.

Let these bastards think I'm all weak and frail. Yeah. Preacher was good at that, wasn't he? Say what you want about the old man, but he knew the score. The COs never suspected what he was capable of, did they — the power he kept bottled up inside him?

He thought of the end of Hitchcock's *Psycho*, that little black insect crawling across the back of Norman Bates' pale hand.

Let these fucks think I wouldn't hurt a fly.

Horror Show nearly laughed out loud, but he managed to keep the sound bottled-up in his throat. Even if he had let it slip, the guards would have probably just thought he was crazy, and that would have been fine by him.

Crazy like a Goddamn fox. A fox in a fuckin' henhouse.

Preacher could have run D Block. Hell, he could have brought the whole prison to its knees. But he never took advantage of his...*unique* position.

Horror Show would not make the same mistake.

The COs stopped. Being in a wheelchair meant Horror Show was guaranteed a cell on the ground floor and the lower bunk in said cell. That was where his "special accommodations" ended. To the United States Attorney's Office, the Department of Corrections, the warden, and these here guards, he was just another inmate who was in here for life.

One of the COs opened the door to Horror Show's cell. The other pushed him inside. Then, he heard the loud *CLANG* as they both left him and locked the door behind them without saying so much as a word.

Looks like I'll have to handle the introductions myself. Good.

Deciding that he needed to wait a bit, he took a moment to reach the proper mindset, like an actor finding his character.

Over the years, the role of a killer had become a comfortable shoe Dante's mind could slip in and out of easily. Now, he knew that his body could do the same.

But he had to be cautious.

He had to be *smart*.

He'd learned a lot from his battles in Colonial Bay, from his confinement with Preacher, even from his pathetic loss to that dragon snatch, Vivian Song. Poseidon's children, Hades' disciples, and especially *Zeus*...none of them were invulnerable. Nobody was immortal. Bullets and blades could kill anyone, supernatural or not.

Yeah, but all these other fucks in the orange jumpsuits, these

Bagmen and Chesters, they don't need to know that shit. All they need to know is that I can ice them real quick if they don't do what I want, if they don't show me the proper respect.

What was it the devil supposedly said when he was cast out and banished to the underworld? Oh, yeah, *"It is better to rule in Hell, than to serve in Heaven."* Horror Show was ready to put that to the test. Yes, indeed. He was ready to be fitted for this prison's shitty little crown right now.

Horror Show's new cellmate hopped down from the upper bunk — a bearded spic with tattoos covering both arms, his neck, even his forehead. The convict took one look at the slumped form in the wheelchair and burst out laughing. *"Joder!* What have we got here? When did the rollers start delivering 'meals on wheels?'"

This punk was barely over five feet tall, but he was muscular, and he had the swagger, the *attitude*, of someone who did not make idle threats. Horror Show liked that about him already. Yes, he could tell that they were going to be good friends.

After all, every king needed a general.

The other inmate took a step forward.

One step.

That was when poor, pathetic little Horror Show sprang to sudden life. The stumps where his legs had been began to lengthen, forming slithering tendrils of flesh. Tentacles. New, sinuous muscles flexed; they lifted his shifting body up out of the wheelchair, made him now tower over his cellmate.

The Mexican instantly halted his advance; his eyes went wide, that cocky demeanor evaporating almost as quickly as Horror Show's body transformed. *"¡El demonio!"*

A hairy arm blurred out. Long talons wrapped around the man's neck; each point was as sharp as Horror Show's trusty pearl-handled straight razor had been, as deadly as Vivian Song's severed claw, but they were all a part of him, and now, they lifted his cellmate up off the concrete floor.

One side of Dante's head was bulbous and covered in a multitude of eyes: spider's eyes. The other half was scaly, horned, and reptilian. Before he'd slit their throats, his victims had often called him a monster. If only they could see him now! He had become a chimera unlike any the world had ever known, the blood of every clan on Earth now mingling and flowing together through his twisted veins.

Judging by his cellmate's face, *he* had clearly never encountered anything like it before; the Mexican struggled in the creature's grip and cried out, "What the hell are you, man?"

"Me?" Dante gave a throaty laugh; then he grinned, displayed gleaming white teeth. The rumor on the street had always been that he filed them down to points, like a shark. Now, it was more than just an urban legend, but there had been no file involved at all. The serrated daggers that stabbed from his gums were all natural, all *his*, and he was not afraid to use them. "I'm the gangster's boogeyman, the right hand of Death." He tightened his grip on his new cellmate's throat, careful not to pierce the meat. "I. Am. *'The Horror Show!'*"

The hulking chimera reached out with his other, more reptilian claw, his webbed talons smoothing the man's hair as if he were a faithful pet.

"And if you wanna live, my new friend, you better be fuckin' nice to me."

CHAPTER THIRTY-SIX

"Wow," Kari Hannigan tried to hide her shock, "you look...nice."

Carol Miyagi had gone and shaved off half of her luxuriously thick and shiny black hair. She'd kept it long up top and on the right, where her inky tresses still reached for the middle of her back, but the entire left side of her head, from her crown down to around her cute little ear, had been trimmed to a super short, military-style stubble.

"The girl at the salon called it a 'partial undercut," Carol told her, then she made a face, "and you hate it."

"No, sweetie—"

"*Usowotsuku na.*"

"—it's just..."

"I can tell that you do."

"It's a pretty dramatic change."

"*Anata ga tadashī.*" Carol ran the longer, uncut strands of black hair through her golden fingers then let them fall back in place. "That's exactly what I wanted, something truly *radical*."

Carol strolled across the carpeted floor of the New York apartment she and Kari now shared. It was pretty spartan, with few furnishings and even fewer personal touches. Carol had hung her grandfather's katana up on the wall, but everything else she owned was still back at her family's place in Japan. And Kari...Well, until now, Kari had never stayed in one place long enough to accumulate much of anything.

She tightened the belt on her fluffy pink robe. It was just about the girliest thing she possessed. Kari had been ready to step into the shower when Carol walked in, and now she stood there, staring, trying to hide her concern.

Evidently, she wasn't doing a very good job of it.

"Don't look at me like that," Carol told her.

"Like what?"

"Like you think I'm going through some midlife, or maybe *new life* crisis, some Britney Spears meltdown."

Kari shrugged. "Well, sweetie, I mean, I couldn't really blame you if you were. Lord knows, you've gone through more than your fair share of emotional trauma."

"This isn't a reaction to any *trauma*." Carol stood with her hands on her hips; even half-bald, she was as stunning as she was defiant. "It's more of a symbolic choice; out with the old, in with the new."

Carol's look might have been new to *her*, but it reminded Kari of something very old indeed, the "Half-and-Half." It was a true classic; a staple of burlesque shows everywhere. A solo performer, using a vertically divided costume and some clever choreography, created the illusion of a duet. Carol's right profile remained super fem, but her left side had gone through a bit of a "butch-up."

"That old hair had seen a lot," Carol went on to say. "Well, maybe not *that* hair, but...You know what I mean. Carol Miyagi dove to the bottom of the sea, climbed to the top of the world, even went into orbit, and she did it all with that same boring, very traditional hair. I am *far* from traditional, and I just felt it was time for a fresh start, time to finally let go of the past and look forward to the future."

Kari nodded. Carol had come back from the grave and into the world once more, and now, whenever she referred to life before that yeti spear, she spoke of herself in third person. It was as if she viewed her old body, her previous incarnation, as a different woman altogether. And just like Carol's frequent use of Japanese, it was a quirk Kari had simply grown to accept as they worked to blend their lives.

Carol paused her sexy, confident stride; she unslung her backpack and let it fall onto their new couch with a soft thud. As long as Kari had known the woman, she'd never seen her carry a purse, not even something as small as a clutch; it was always some big, bulky backpack. Carol was years removed from her Harvard classes, and she wasn't traipsing off through jungles or climbing mountains on some mysterious quest anymore, but the archeologist still carried her life around on her back as if she were a snail. She unzipped her leather jacket, revealing the government-issued ID card that hung from her neck on a lanyard. **DELANCEY FIELD** stood out in bold black lettering, right next to the eagle and shield of Homeland Security, and the smiling face it pictured was clearly Carol's, even if the hair no longer matched.

Kari thought of all the researchers and developers who now worked alongside them each day in the Ark, wondering how they might react when they saw Carol's new 'do in the morning. Many were young, just out of school. They'd probably think it was cool.

But there were enough who were older, stuffy, and in general, Western culture had this lingering taboo against women who shaved their heads.

Only half *shaved,* Kari's mind corrected, *and there are a lot of things that this supposedly "enlightened" society once thought of as taboo, things that are now completely accepted; long-haired men, short-haired women, tattoos, piercings, interracial marriage...*

Kari glanced down at Carol's naked fingers, thinking of the diamond ring she'd managed to buy in secret just over a month ago, the one that was still hidden away inside her nightstand drawer. She wondered what Dr. Walter Hannigan would think of his only daughter finally wanting to settle down, and wherever he was, she hoped he was proud of her, and of the work she now did on his behalf.

She had grown up with such hatred for the Ark, believing it had stolen her father away from her. Now, she understood its importance, its *possibilities.* Kari might never be able to give her father grandchildren, a descendancy, but she could ensure that his name lived on in another way, through the many fruits of his lifelong obsession.

Through the Ark.

Once the battle ended and the dust settled, Kari had fully expected the military to lock down the entire airfield, to cart them all off to some unknown black site and bar them from ever seeing the alien ship again. That was the way it always went down in the movies and on television, wasn't it? After a crash like that, some secret government agency swooped in, and soon any evidence of extraterrestrial spacecraft, of strange creatures and advanced technology, it all just mysteriously vanished; swept away, covered up.

Thankfully, that wasn't what happened at all.

Oh, Delancey Field was indeed locked down, placed under tight military guard; no one in or out without proper clearance and credentials, an unacknowledged black project; the new Area 51. Even the airspace above it was closed. Social media was all a buzz about it! One conspiracy theory after another floating around on the internet. Kari read some of them from time to time, whenever she was in need of a good laugh.

And Hades' surviving disciples, the ones who wanted to start a revolution, to enslave humanity — what happened to them?

Kari honestly didn't know. She had watched them all get carted off at gunpoint, whisked away in chains. But thanks to Carol's friend, Earl Preston, and their new boss, Director Tate, the other shapeshifters, the ones they called Poseidon's children, the Yeti, and most of all, Kari's friend Gagan; none of them had to share the same fate. That had been all Kari had cared about.

There had been a lengthy debriefing, and afterwards, the powers that be had put Carol in charge of the research team assigned to the spacecraft.

You didn't really give them a choice, did you, sweetie? I'd like to have seen them try and find another world-famous archeologist who not only reads but speaks *Atlantean, can effortlessly tap into alien tech, and has a giant alien mantis at her beck and call.*

There were times when Kari literally felt like Batwoman's girl-friend. After all, Carol could do just about anything she set her mind to, couldn't she? She even slept with an honest-to-God super suit, her "Myrmidon," hanging in the bedroom closet, ready to go if danger called.

"It's a little punk, don't you think?"

Kari blinked. "What?"

Carol ran her hand back and forth across the fresh stubble around her ear, then down the newly exposed side of her neck. "Makes me look like a rock star or something?"

"You're *something*, all right," Kari said, examining the top of Carol's head once more; it was bold, unique, just like her. "It suits you."

Carol smiled at that; her perfectly shaped, half-shaved head suddenly looking super sexy. "*Dōmo.*"

As she stood there, looking at the only woman she'd ever really loved, Kari smiled and thought to herself, *So* this *is what true happiness feels like?* Then, without even realizing it, she began to sing aloud, her voice so soft the words could barely be heard, "*Black is the color of my true love's hair...*"

Carol approached her with a look of fascination, her still thick, naturally shaped eyebrows raised. "What's that?"

"Oh..." Kari's face burned, the flush turning her normally pale skin the same hue as her own fiery hair; she felt suddenly ridiculous. "It's just something my father used to sing to me when I was a little girl. An old Scottish folk song."

"Please," Carol begged, "go on. I'd like to hear it."

Kari hesitated for a beat or two before giving in, her gaze locked with Carol's. *Those eyes...so intense, so beautiful. I can never say no to those eyes.* Kari was far from Adele, but she gave it her best shot, her voice cracking as she sang, "*Black is the color of my true love's hair.*" She brushed a few raven strands from Carol's forehead, then ran her fingers down her lover's golden cheek. "*Her face so soft and wondrous fair, The purest eyes, And the neatest hands, I love the ground on where she stands.*

"*And still I hope, That the time will come, When she and I will be as one.*"

"*Pinpōōn!*" Carol told her, smiling. "That was lovely."

"Thank you."

A lovely song for a lovely lady. The most remarkable woman I've ever known.

414 • MICHAEL WEST

Kari cleared her throat and said, "It's not like I wrote the song or anything. It's very old, and very Scottish."

"Like you," Carol paused and quickly added, "the Scottish part, I mean."

Kari laughed. "Yes, *very* Scottish."

"Descended from a long line of huggers, am I right?"

"And damn proud of it." She wrapped her arms around Carol's neck, gazed once more into those amazing eyes. "Not likely to change anytime soon, so if we're going to be friends, you're just going to have to get used to it."

"I think I can live with that." And from the look in Carol's eyes, Kari could tell that it was the absolute truth. "Now, kiss me."

Kari pulled her close and did just that, feeling the glorious warmth of her breath and the gentle sweep of her probing tongue against her own. Carol tasted of strong coffee; she smelled of lavender, and when she lifted a hand to cup Kari's breast, it sent ripples of heat flooding through her entire body.

Working alongside Carol in the Ark was wonderful, but it could also be a distraction. Carol usually wore a long white lab coat that hid her ass-hugging pants, but those eyes, those *lips*...Yes, this kiss was exactly what Kari had craved all day long, what she *needed*.

Carol suddenly broke contact and pulled back; her lips curled into a seductive little grin. "Now," she whispered, "*Omae no ochoko de yarashite kure yo na.*"

Kari cocked her head, her eyes playfully narrowed. "In English, Miss Miyagi?"

"Let me show you what it means."

As Carol took her by the hand and led her back toward the bedroom, Kari had a feeling that, whatever it meant, she was going to like it.

When they reached the foot of the bed, Carol Miyagi pulled Kari close to her for another ravenous kiss. How could she have ever denied her love for this woman — put her father's archaic sensibilities before her own happiness? Try as she might, Carol still had trouble wrapping her mind around it.

She undid the soft, fuzzy strap that held Kari's robe closed then took a moment to appreciate her lover's striking figure. Over the years, the archeologist had seen countless nudes immortalized in drawings, carvings, and sculptures from every culture, every era; these artifacts had somehow survived the ravages of time and the weathering of elements to become priceless. And yet, at least to Carol's eyes, none of them could compare to the beauty who now stood before her.

Kirei dayo, she thought, then said it aloud in English; a soft, sensual whisper, "You're so beautiful."

Carol's mind held the memories of what it was like to touch Kari, to *taste* her, but her flesh longed to experience those glorious sensations all over again. Still standing, she reached down between Kari's legs, her eager fingers parting those soft wet lips — stroking, teasing, circling the rim of Kari's opening with deliberate sloth.

"I need you inside me," Kari moaned.

And of course, Carol gave her what she wanted. First, she bathed one languid finger in Kari's warmth, then a second, probing deep, just as far as she could reach, searching for that most sensitive flesh.

Kari suddenly gripped Carol's shoulders. "Oh, *my God*, Carol."

Found it. Carol flashed a smug little grin. Her thumb pressed the swollen nub of Kari's clitoris as her fingers continued wriggling and thrusting.

Kari began to move, as well; she rocked her hips, grinding against Carol's hand.

Carol studied Kari's face, enjoying every moment of satisfaction she was giving to her. She continued gliding her thumb up and down, driving her fingers in and out. Deeper. Faster. She lost herself to the increasingly frantic rhythm of it all.

"Don't stop," Kari breathed as her eyes fluttered closed. "Don't fucking stop..." She tightened her grip on Carol's shoulders, arched her back, and then her lips parted in a stuttering sigh.

Carol felt Kari's soft, slick interior grow tight, constricting around her driving fingers, and she could not help but wonder if Kari experienced an orgasm in the same way she did. Did Kari feel that hot, tingling pulse surge through her entire body — the tension building, the fullness gathering deep within, begging for release?

When her lover's body finally stilled and relaxed again, Carol withdrew her hand. She licked her fingers, savoring the taste, then fondled Kari's breast, rolling the rock-hard nipple between her glistening thumb and forefinger. "So," Carol whispered, "was *that* what you needed?"

Kari nodded, her eyes half-lidded; she laced her fingers around the back of Carol's neck and pulled her toward her lips.

Even as they kissed, Carol felt hands working to undo the buttoned fly of her jeans, felt both her pants and her panties being drawn down her hips toward the floor. When they parted, Carol assisted by pulled her lanyard and shirt off over her head, allowing Kari to reach around her and unclasp her bra with relative ease.

Carol remembered the first time she'd ever stood naked in front of Kari, all those scary, nervous feelings of vulnerability, of *inadequacy*. Now, Kari's hands lingered there on Carol's bare back, fingers gently tracing the rims of those round access ports, the ones the Ark had installed along her spine. The orifices, and her obvious lack of a belly button, made it clear that Carol was *different*. This wasn't the same body Kari had loved years before, not even the same body that swam through the sunken passages of Atlantis, or dove into the temple of Colonial Bay, or climbed the slopes of Makalu.

Not the same Carol at all.

She frowned, grieving her former *normal* self, but the gloom was short-lived.

Carol felt one of those dorsal sphincters dilate beneath Kari's tender strokes, felt a finger slide into the opening and take a slow spin around its full diameter, igniting nerve endings previously unknown. She sighed and heard herself moan at this strange new intimate contact.

Ooh...Sore wa totemo yoi kanji...Totemo yoi...

For a moment, Carol wondered what it would feel like to have Kari tongue those ports, then Kari withdrew her finger and spun them both around.

Kari lowered her eyes to Carol's breasts and her hand slid between them; her palm pressed firmly against Carol's sternum. There was no hint of a wound there, of course, because *this* body was never injured. Kari gave her a gentle shove onto the waiting mattress, then she knelt down between Carol's spread legs. Carol felt Kari's tongue trace its way up her inner thighs to her sex, moving in leisurely strokes and dizzying spirals — warm, and soft, and wet.

Oh, my God...I'm so wet!

The sensation was incredible, and when Carol felt the tip of Kari's tongue work its way inside her, penetrating her with such delicious ecstasy, she could not help but cry out.

"Hai!"

Carol moved her hips, slowly at first, but as the sensations intensified, so too did her buck and her roll. Longing for release, she reached down, threaded her fingers through Kari's rosy hair, and pulled her lover into her, feeling the heat of the woman's breath, delighting in every swoop and turn of that expert tongue.

Finally, those incredible flutters gathered and shifted, becoming that *burn* Carol so craved, that hot, glorious pressure; it began to build, to *rise*, and finally...

"*Desō,*" Carol cried out again and again, her eyes rolling back as she climaxed, "*Desō!*"

She let Kari's hair slide through her splayed fingers as she fell back against the mattress, almost *melted* into it. In her whole life, Carol did not think that she had ever felt more relaxed.

Kari smiled. She climbed onto the bed, onto Carol, and when they kissed, Carol could taste herself on Kari's tongue. "I love you, Carol-kun," she said when their lips parted, her eyes dreamy. "Always have. Always will."

Carol felt another flutter, but this time, it was in the center of her chest. "Carol-kun?"

"Did I do that right?" Kari flashed an odd look that was a mix of both pride and embarrassment; even the tips of her ears blushed. "Google said that adding *kun* to the end of a name was a show of great affection in Japanese."

"Oh, it is." You *could* address a Japanese woman or a girl using *kun,* but it was a term of endearment usually reserved for a *man,* a boyfriend or a spouse. Still, the fact that Kari had bothered to look it up at all was a beautiful, romantic gesture. Carol smiled back at her, stroking Kari's lower lip with her thumb. "I love you, too, Kari-kun."

Kari kissed her thumb and said, "Enough to marry me?"

Carol froze. Had she heard that right? "You want—?"

"I really hadn't planned on doing this tonight, not this way."

Kari rolled off Carol and reached across the disheveled bedspread for her nightstand.

Carol sat up on the mattress in stunned silence, watching as Kari rummaged through the top drawer.

After a moment, Kari produced a small black velvet box; she held it to her breast as she turned to face Carol once more, sitting cross-legged on her side of the bed.

"I know, I know..." Kari tucked a few wayward strands of her fiery red hair behind her still-blushing ear. "This is probably, like, the worst proposal in human history. My dad got engaged to my mom in Vatican City. He got down on one knee in Saint Peter's Square. Did I ever tell you that story?"

Carol nodded absently. She didn't meet Kari's eyes at first. For a moment, all she could do was sit and stare at that little black box; it stood in stark contrast to Kari's pale, naked breast.

"See," Kari went on, "I've been holding off 'popping the question,' waiting for some equally perfect moment, and...dammit, we only have *so many* moments. In fact, it's nothing short of a miracle that we're able to be here together at all right now. And, after so many years apart, I don't want to waste any more of our time together."

Kari drew a deep breath, then she took Carol by the hand.

"Carol Miyagi, I feel truly blessed. Every minute I get to spend with you makes me the luckiest, happiest woman in the whole world, in the entire *universe*." Kari held out the little box and flipped it open. "Now, will you honor me by becoming my wife, by making me *your* wife; sweetie, will you marry me?"

Carol looked down at the ring and her breath caught in her throat. An *engagement ring,* white gold, crowned by a pair of Celtic love knots that framed a sparkling diamond solitaire; it was gorgeous, like something plucked from a fairy tale. Carol found herself reaching for the ring, running her index finger over the setting, a touch to confirm that it was indeed real, that it was *hers*.

Hai! *Yes!*

The words leapt joyfully to the front of her mind, as if they'd been there for some time, just waiting to be called upon, but they were followed closely by visions of Alan's final moments. Even now, Carol could see that joyous glow of recognition igniting there in his eyes, that blissful smile that brightened his entire face, just before he drew his last breath.

What was it, Alan — what did you see?

Still haunted, Carol slowly withdrew her wavering hand from the ring. She bowed her head, out of what — shame? Yes, but not the shame she feared from her father so many years ago. This was something else entirely. She felt...

Unworthy.

The uncut lengths of her hair hung like a black curtain in front of her face as she spoke, "I want to say 'yes' to you, believe me I do, but..."

"It's Alan, isn't it?"

"Well, yes, but—"

"I understand."

"I don't think that you do." How could she when Carol didn't really understand it herself?

"You're still mourning him."

"No." Carol shook her head. She had mourned Alan the moment he wished her dead. "I loved him, and I will always cherish the time we had together, but he..."

She let out a heavy sigh.

"He loved you, too, sweetie," Kari still held Carol by the hand; she gave her fingers a gentle, reassuring squeeze, "I know it."

"He loved Carol Miyagi."

Another squeeze, this one much firmer than the first. *"You're Carol Miyagi."*

"I used to be." She swallowed hard. "I don't know what I am now."

"You're the woman I love." Kari's voice was low, soft, but her every word held conviction.

Carol raised her head and brushed the hair from her face, her eyes locking with Kari's, her tone deathly serious, "When Alan was lying there, bleeding out onto the hangar floor, he *saw* something, something off in the distance."

"Like what?"

"Like the *real* Carol."

And there it was. The thing that had been eating away at her for months, finally out in the open.

Kari raised an eyebrow at that. "What do you mean 'the *real* Carol?'"

"*Tamashī.* Her spirit, her soul, essence, *ghost*, call it whatever you want. Alan was reaching out for her in death — Carol Miyagi, the love of his life, come to escort him off to the other side."

"Sweetie," Kari began, looking thoughtful, "he'd lost a lot of blood. He was *dying*. Whatever he saw, or *thought* he saw, he was probably hallucinating."

"But what if he *wasn't?*" Carol's throat felt thick; she choked back tears, hating how pathetic her voice sounded. "What if Alan was right about me all along? I'm just an imitation, an *imposter*; I have Carol Miyagi's face, all her memories, but *no soul.* I can't let you marry a lie."

"Would you like to know what *I* think?" Kari squeezed her hand yet again and flashed a slight grin.

"Onegaishimasu." Carol tried to smile back, but she wasn't

sure if she'd managed it or not; her bottom lip was trembling. "Please, tell me."

"You may not have a belly button, but you have a *beautiful* soul," Kari told her. "There is not a doubt in my mind about that. But...that doesn't necessarily mean you're wrong about what Alan saw."

"How can *both* be true?"

"There are those who believe that the soul, it's just like genetics, we get it from both our parents, along with our hearts and our minds, and I guess, whether or not we have the power to grow fangs, wings, and a tail."

They both chuckled at that.

Carol shook her head. *Oh, how far we have come!*

"And then," Kari went on; her smile widened, and she leaned in a bit closer, "there's this school of thought that believes God grants each new body its very own soul, a spirit different and distinct from any other that has ever walked the Earth. So, even if Carol Miyagi's soul left her body with that Yeti spear, that doesn't have to mean that Carol 2.0 was born completely soulless. In fact, the way I look at it, it means there's a very good chance that, one day — many, *many* years from now — Heaven might have not one, but *two* Carol Miyagis in it. And if that happens, my love, it will truly be a paradise."

Carol felt a warm tear slide down her cheek. She put her arm around Kari and buried her face in her shoulder. They stayed like that for some time, just holding one another, neither saying a word. Carol moved her hand leisurely up and down Kari's back, quietly thinking.

Of all the ancient mysteries she had dared to explore, none had proved more arcane, more complex, or more elusive than that of the human heart.

As a child, her father had watched his entire family perish in a Japanese internment camp. The horror of that experience, at so young an age, had petrified the man's heart, made it into an impenetrable stone. She had grown up craving his approval, his *love*, but he had never really wanted to get close to her, to *know her*.

And then, there was Alan. He'd been the exact opposite of Carol's father; her equal partner, giving her love, support, and so much genuine *passion*. But when he discovered she wasn't everything he thought she should be, he'd been just as quick to turn his back on her.

The only person in Carol's life who had truly known her, who had loved her unconditionally, who had never wavered, never denied her, was Kari.

But you denied your feelings for her, *didn't you? While she was crying her eyes out in that parking lot, telling you how much she loved you? You showed no emotion at all. Like father, like daughter, right?*

Wrong, her brain countered. *Not this time. Not this* Carol.

She lifted her head from Kari's shoulder, pressed her lips to her ear. And that word that had been leaping and dancing for joy at the forefront of her mind? Carol finally gave it voice, "Yes."

Kari pushed Carol to arm's length so that she could see her face and look into her eyes. "Yes?"

"Yes," Carol repeated. "I want to plan a future with you, to share in your dreams. If you'll have me, Kari, I want to be your *wife*."

And to prove it, she plucked the ring from its velvet cradle and slid it effortlessly onto her finger. It fit perfectly, like the myrmidon, like the golden orb, the "Wrath of the Gods", just as if it had been made specifically for her. And this time, there was no doubt in Carol's mind that it had been.

"It's yours..."

Carol shook her head. She had chosen to give up that golden orb, had begged Earl Preston to take it from her, in fact, to hide it away from everyone, like the skulls, somewhere beyond recall. The alien weapon would always crave another war, desire conflict, any chance to burn, to create more fiery ruins, and Carol was done with all of that. But *this*...this she would never take off.

Lamplight played across the surface of the diamond, making it sparkle like moonlight on waves, like the frozen skin of the Ark at night, and both women stared at it in mutual wonder.

"Kari Hannigan-Miyagi," Kari said at last, trying it on for size, grinning from ear to ear. "Has a nice ring to it, don't you think?"

Carol lifted her eyes to meet Kari's. "Does this mean I get to be Hannigan-Miyagi, too?"

"Whatever makes you happy, sweetie."

"*You* make me happy, Kari," Carol told her. "Always have. Always will." She reached up to caress her cheek. "*Anata o hontōni aishiteimasu.* I love you."

They kissed, then laid back against the bed, Kari curled around Carol in a tight embrace. Quiet and still, they stared up at the bedroom ceiling, simply content to be in each other's arms.

Hannigan-Miyagi. Yes, I do like the way that sounds.

Carol held up her left hand; she gazed at the ring on her finger and smiled, her strong new heart pounding beneath her breast. She was genuinely excited about what was to come for her and for Kari, all the *possibilities*. In fact, something told Carol that married life might just be her greatest adventure yet.

CHAPTER THIRTY-SEVEN

Standing at attention in front of Director Tate made Earl L. Preston, Jr. think of the day this adventure had truly begun, of lies spoken to another supervisor, of a motorcycle trip along the shore to Colonial Bay.

When he received this summons to the director's office, after months of bureaucratic bullshit, closed-door congressional hearings, seemingly endless debriefings, and mountains of paperwork; Earl assumed his days with the Department of Homeland Security were numbered. After all, it had been his idea to divide the crystal skulls between Poseidon, Hades, and Zeus.

Well, truth be told, I took that one straight outta J. R. R. Tolkien's Lord of the Rings, *but it was a damn good idea.*

As far as anyone could tell, those powerful lumps of quartz could not be shattered or destroyed, and it was much too dangerous to keep them all together in any one spot. The temptation for their enemies to try and steal them back again, to try and open another portal to Kronos, or God forbid, someplace worse, had simply been too great.

Uncle Sam kept the greater portion of the thirteen, of course; Earl knew he had to give "the powers that be" at least that much—

Mamma didn't raise no dummies.

—but better to let some of the crystals sit at the bottom of the ocean, or hidden away somewhere at the top of the world, where they'd remain a threat to no one.

And letting all those Yeti and Poseidon's children return to their far-off homes in the first place? That had been Earl's suggestion as well. Tate had fought tooth and nail to make it all happen, put all his clout and reputation on the line, but if the hammer came down, Earl knew it would fall squarely on him.

Now, Earl was left wondering just how much truth Tate had spouted during all those top-secret hearings, and how much of the man's testimony had been a *Beverly Hills Cop*-style crock.

"Senators, Earl L. Preston Jr. isn't just a federal agent. He's a God damn super-agent!"

Or perhaps the sight of that mousy, slight little detainee splitting out of his jumpsuit, transforming into a vicious bat-winged lion with the tail of a scorpion, right there on that hearing room floor, right in front of their bugged-out little eyes, had frightened those politicians so much, they just didn't give a shit what the director did so long as he was able to protect their asses from these monsters.

Yes, Earl thought, this whole thing smacked of the latter.

"I told you you'd be getting a medal, Agent Preston," Tate said, then he read from the open manilla folder he held in his hands, "and not just any medal: 'the Secretary's Award of Valor, the single greatest honor the department can bestow, given every year to recognize extraordinary acts of valor by an employee, occurring while on or off duty.'"

Is he dickin' me around?

Earl lowered his shocked eyes.

"So...you didn't call me onto the carpet to fire my ass?" he asked, then hastily added, "sir."

"Far from it." Tate smiled broadly; he rose from his chair to offer his hand. "Congratulations, son. Well deserved. I just wish your father were here to share in it with you."

"That makes two of us, sir."

And as he shook the director's hand, he could hear his father saying, *"You done good, Earl. I'm proud of you, Son. So very proud!"*

Even if it was only in his head, hearing Link Preston's voice speak those words...It was all Earl had ever wanted, and his eyes welled with joyous tears. He knew that his father was still with him. His father would always be with him. Earl cleared his throat, replying to both Tate and his father at the same time, "Thank you, sir. I'm honored. Truly, I am."

Tate motioned to one of the chairs in front of his huge wooden desk. "At ease, son. Neither one of us in the service anymore. Please, take a seat."

Earl relaxed and sat down, trying to act nonchalant as he wiped at his eyes with the heel of his hand.

Tate picked the folder back up off his desk. The director's office was the exact opposite of Earl's. It was spacious; everything was neat and clean and orderly. "And now," he said, "I get the added pleasure of offering you a brand-new assignment. I can think of no one in this country who's more qualified to head up the department's newly created Shifter Unit than you, Agent Preston."

"I appreciate that, sir, really I do..."

"But?"

"What the hell is a Shifter Unit?" Earl pushed forward in his seat, anxious for the answer. He pictured himself leading a platoon of were-creatures into battle for Uncle Sam, some nightmare version of Seal Team Six, a real-life *Suicide Squad*. Could that really be what Tate had in mind for him? Earl thought on this and smiled.

The director leaned back. His leather desk chair had a high back to it and appeared far more comfortable than Earl's. Tate removed his glasses, took a handkerchief from his pocket, and polished the lenses as he spoke, "Supernatural Hazard Intervention, Forces, Tactics, and Experimental Research. S.H.I.F.T.E.R. for short."

Earl could not stop himself from chuckling.

Tate looked hard at him for a moment, then cracked a genuine smile. "Come now, Agent Preston," he said. "It took a room full of very clever congressmen weeks to come up with that lovely little acronym. And let me tell you, they were *quite* proud of themselves."

"I'll bet they were."

Tate exchanged a look with him, then turned sullen.

"Son," the director began; he put his glasses back on and sat straighter in his chair, "based on the rather disturbing intel we've been able to gather from our...*unique* new detainees, Vivian Song managed to funnel *a lot* of military-grade hardware into unknown hands all across this country and around the world."

Earl nodded. He'd handled many of the interviews himself.

"We cut the head off a cobra, but its body lives on." Tate nodded to the office window and the New York skyline beyond. "It's still slithering around out there in the shadows, lying low, just biding its time until it can grow a brand-new set of fangs and strike us again. This country needs someone who understands the enemy, someone who can flush it out, someone who can stomp it into the ground once and for all."

The director made a fist and used it to pound his wooden desk, striking hard enough to rattle his coffee cup. Then, he pointed to Earl.

"That someone, Agent Preston, is *you*."

"Thank you, sir," Earl told him; he took a moment to think it over, then said, "I accept."

And though it wasn't even noon yet, he thought this was just about the finest day of his life.

———

"What did Director Tate want to speak to you about?" Andrews asked, turning to Earl as he came back down to their cramped little office space.

Crockett to my Tubbs, Earl thought with a grin, closing the door behind him.

Andrews had a degree in psychology. And as they spent their days interviewing shapeshifting monsters, Earl often wondered what went through that analytical mind of his. Andrews' right arm and leg were out of their casts and had both mended nicely. Sure, there was enough metal in those limbs to set off every detector down in the lobby, but when the man walked there was no longer any trace of a limp.

The dude's a regular poster child for the benefits of good physical therapy!

His bullet wounds and surgical incisions had all healed over, though some had left scars that would never go away.

Earl rubbed his own shoulder. Beneath his shirt, there was a raised ridge of flesh, smooth skin darker than the surrounding flesh; the spot where Benedict's foreleg had lanced clean through. It still bothered him whenever it rained.

Mama always says, "Wear your scars like a warrior, Son, they're a reminder you're alive."

To his partner, Earl said, "Boss man gave me some good news and some bad news, my friend."

Andrews ran a hand over his short, spiked hair. "And the bad news?"

"I'm getting a medal and a promotion. Looks like I'm *your* boss man now."

Andrews slumped in his chair. "Haven't I been through enough pain and suffering?"

Earl looked at him, shocked; he threw his head back and laughed, his hand on his belly. "Son of a bitch...Andrews...You finally got a sense of humor!"

Andrews flashed a smile, but otherwise, remained just as reserved as ever. "Congratulations, *sir.*"

"You can stop that shit right now." Earl held up his hand. "They're givin' me a title, but as far as I'm concerned, we're still partners."

"Well, then, what would the *good* news be?"

"We're movin' on up to some deluxe new office space," Earl sat down on the edge of his old desk, "not that we'll be spending much time there. Welcome to S.H.I.F.T.E.R."

Andrews eyed him warily. "S.H.I.F.T.E.R?"

"Yeah, don't ask." He held up his hand again and wagged his head. "Basically, we just do what we do."

"Who else is a part of this S.H.I.F.T.E.R?"

"Carol Miyagi's overseeing the 'Experimental Research' side of things," Earl told him. "Her team's still down there at the crash site, reverse engineering all that alien tech from the Ark. Can't wait to tell her I'm *her* boss. Hopefully, she's not wearin' that spring-loaded sword when I do it."

He rubbed his neck, still smiling.

"Anyone else I might know?" Andrews asked, even though it was obvious that he already knew the answer.

Earl nodded, his smile warming as it widened. "A couple of very close friends."

———

Uzuri Shujaa, "Zuri" to her friends, stood alone in front of a vacant West Side apartment building. She leaned back against the narrow trunk of one of the many trees that lined this New York street, enjoying the cool island of shade it provided. As heavy traffic drove by, and throngs of people filed past Zuri on the sidewalk. She was struck, yet again, by how far she had come from the remote African village of her birth, how much she had grown since that day when those soldiers came with their guns and snatched up that innocent, frightened young girl...

Joyous laughter rose above the drone of pedestrians.

She blinked and lowered her eyes.

A little black girl walking by; she held on tight to her mother's hand, her hair in beaded braids. The child's eyes lingered on Zuri. She smiled and waved her tiny, fisted hand happily in the air.

Zuri smiled back. She flared her nostrils, gave the air a subtle sniff. The girl was Zeus, human, and Zuri could not help but wonder what the child's reaction would have been if she had looked over and seen the wolf leaning against this tree instead.

One day, Zuri thought, *one day, we will all be free to show our true faces, and when that day comes, I hope to still see that joyous little smile.*

Hope.

Optimism.

Anticipation for the future.

Zuri was unaccustomed to such things, such *positivity*, but it felt good. In fact, she loved it. Just as she loved the familiar scent that now filled her nostrils.

Earl.

When she looked up, Zuri caught a glimpse of her beloved. He moved purposefully toward her through the milling crowd. She felt her heart flutter beneath her pawprint tattoos as he drew near; he was absolutely stunning.

"Damn, girl." Earl stood next to her in the shady spot. "You got one gorgeous smile."

Zuri nodded at the brick façade in front of them, staring at it with curious eyes. "Why are we meeting here?"

"For real? You gonna stand there and tell me you don't recognize this place?" He pointed to one of the abandoned apartment building's upper floors. "You pulled a knife on me, right up there somewhere."

"Yes, I know this, but why are we here again *now?*"

"Well, the feds confiscated this prime piece of New York real estate, along with every other holding Vivian Song's Operation Stargate had on the books, and today, good ol' Uncle Sam was nice enough to hand over the keys."

He pulled a jingling metal keyring from his pants pocket as proof.

Zuri felt her eyes grow wide. "You *own* this?"

"Don't trip. Like I said, it belongs to the United States government. I just get to work here now."

"And this is a good thing?"

"This is a *great* thing, Zuri."

She smiled, approvingly.

Earl flashed that cocky grin of his, jingling those keys. "Come inside and let me show you around."

Zuri nodded. She followed him across the sidewalk and up the steps to the entrance.

While the brick façade made clear the building's true age, the interior smelled like new — fresh paint on the walls and soft carpeting beneath her booted feet; the scent was so strong, in fact, that it would not have taken any supernatural senses to detect it. A security desk sat in the lobby, but it was currently unmanned. Zuri could detect no other heartbeats within these walls. She and Earl were alone here.

"They're still workin' on the upper floors," he informed her, "turnin' all those vacant old apartments into brand-new office space, re-wirin' this whole place for all the electronics and crap they plan to cram up in here. It will probably take 'em months to put it all together, but they were able to finish one thing."

"And what is that?"

Wordlessly, Earl pocketed that ring of keys and strolled over to a set of French doors. They were at the back of the lobby, to the right of the elevators. Two words had been stenciled in black across their frosted glass, *TRAINING ROOM*. He pushed one of the doors open and stepped aside, allowing her entrance.

Zuri's wide Afro brushed against the door frame. She immediately saw the punching bag in the center of the room; the bright red canvas hung down from the ceiling on a chain, just like the one in her underground chamber. The floor here was not brick or dirt, however. Instead, blue exercise pads gave softly beneath her feet.

"I insisted on all the padding," Earl called out from behind her. "You about broke my back the last time we sparred. And since I'm not gettin' any younger, and you're sure as hell not gettin' any weaker..."

"I do not understand." She turned slowly, taking it all in. Weights, jump rope, and other fitness equipment lined the walls. Finally, her appraising eyes swung back to Earl. "You had someone *make* this room? You had them make this room for *us?*"

"Well, not *just* for us," he admitted with a little shrug. "Other people will get some use out of it, too, staff, and Andrews has some exercises he does. Like I said, Uncle Sam owns the place. But I figured, you know, if we're gonna work together, you and me, stay in prime fighting shape, our Danger Room could use a little upgrade."

"Work together? Doing what?"

"Goin' after the bad guys. Homeland Security made me a Special Director. They want me to deal with all the supernatural bullshit out there, told me to pick my own team." Earl moved across the room to stand in front of her. "But I already got my team."

He reached out and placed his hand on her shoulder

"Come on, girl. I *need* you with me on this. You're my right-hand."

"Your right-hand," she repeated, her throat tight and her voice thick with emotion.

For so many years, Zuri had been afraid of being seen as a *left* hand, what the people of her home country referred to as the 'dirty hand,' something unclean, *unworthy*. But Earl knew her story, knew exactly what those soldiers and jailors had done to her, what she had done to *them* in return, and when he looked at her, she felt no sense of shame, no weakness or regret. She felt only acceptance, only love and respect. Despite her history, despite the Hades symbol tattooed on her wrist, despite *the wolf*, Earl saw only beauty. He saw only *strength*. And he wanted her by his side.

Someone who isn't afraid to fight for what she believes in, that *is what he sees. That is* all *he sees.*

In that moment, Zuri felt more love for Earl Preston than ever before.

"I will continue to fight alongside you, my beloved," she pledged, her voice husky and full of confidence, "as long as there is breath in my lungs and blood in my veins, and together, I know that we can defeat any enemy."

Earl kissed her, then abruptly pulled away. "Oops, I almost forgot."

He hurried over to one of the many weightlifting benches, picked up a white cardboard box that had been sitting there, then held it out to Zuri.

"Sorry, I didn't wrap it," he told her. "My mama will tell you; I can't wrap worth shit."

Zuri took the box from him; it felt light, but there was obviously something inside. "What is this?"

"Just a 'lil somethin' somethin'." He smiled knowingly. "Call it a thank you gift."

"'Thank you' for what?"

"For everything."

Zuri stared at him for a beat, studying his face. She listened to the beat of his heart, the sound of his pulse. He was excited about something, not for himself, but for *her*.

She returned her attention to the box in her hands and carefully pried off the lid. Inside, wrapped in tissue, she found black fabric, a T-shirt; she pulled it free and let the box fall to the floor. The image of a wolf's head had been printed across the front of the garment, surrounded by words; Zuri read them aloud, "*'If they stand behind you, give them protection. If they stand with you, give them respect. If they stand against you—'*"

"'*Show no mercy,*'" Earl finished for her, then added, "Ooh-rah. Told you I was gonna find you that shirt."

Zuri was overcome with emotion, and when she blinked, a tear streamed from her eye.

Earl reached out to rub her arm. "Hey," he said softly, "no need for all that now. It's just a T-shirt. It doesn't mean we're engaged or nothin'."

She shook her head, wiped at her eyes, and said, "Since I was a little girl, life has only taken from me. I guess I must now get used to being *given* things from time to time."

"Well, if you liked the shirt that much, you're gonna really lose your shit when you see *this*." He stooped down, picked the cardboard box up off the floor, and handed it back to her. "Look under the tissue paper."

Zuri draped the T-shirt over her shoulder then did as he asked, riffling through the wadded tissue. Beneath it, she found a large square slip of parchment paper — an official looking certificate, surrounded by an ornate boarder. At the top, *THE UNITED STATES OF AMERICA* stood out in all caps as if it were money. Centered at the bottom, in much smaller print, were the words *DEPARTMENT OF HOMELAND SECURITY*. And in the middle of it all, her own name, her full given name, had been printed in bold black lettering, right above the words *HONORARY U.S. CITIZENSHIP*.

"What is this?" she asked, her hands shaking and fresh tears welling in her eyes.

"What's it look like? You're in rare company, Zuri. In the whole history of this country, only eight other people have been given honorary citizenship, all of 'em white, and the only other two to get it while they were still breathin' were Churchill and Mother Teresa."

She stood there, slack jawed, reading the words again and again. Then, still clutching the certificate, Zuri wrapped her arms around Earl's neck and pulled him closer to her. "You did this for me?"

"Nah. You *earned it*."

"You make me very happy, Earl Preston, my King of the Badasses."

He gave her a little peck on the forehead, his voice low and sincere, "Every king needs his queen."

"*Queen* of the Badasses," Zuri ventured, and somehow, uttering the words made her feel stronger, stand taller. When she was born, her father had seen fit to name her "Beautiful Warrior." It had taken a lifetime, a fight to avert the apocalypse, but Zuri finally believed she was worthy of that moniker.

She was worthy of gifts and awards, worthy of a full and wonderful life, worthy of being loved and of giving love in return.

Zuri turned her face and her full lips up to Earl; they kissed. Then, she heard someone gently rapping on the French doors.

"Knock-knock," a low, gravelly voice announced from the lobby.

Chud.

Zuri took a step back and called out to him, "In here, brother."

The crocodile-man opened one of the French doors and stepped inside the Training Room, his thick scaly tail swinging behind him. He stopped just short of them on the blue exercise mats, his elliptical pupils taking in the newly renovated surroundings. "So…What's goin' on? Why'd ya have me meet you guys *here?*"

"Welcome to the party, Sleestak," Earl said; he stood with his arm around Zuri and quickly brought Chud up to speed.

As she watched them discuss Earl's new task force, and Chud's place in it, Zuri broke out in a happy buoyant smile. No matter what happened next, no matter what challenges or dangers might come their way, she knew that everything was going to be all right. They were all in this together.

They were a family.

Chud knew they were right.

Carol Miyagi had wanted no part of this thing! She'd seen what it could do in the right hands, but she'd also seen what it could do in the wrong hands. She'd given the weapon to Earl, and Earl, in turn, had handed it off to Chud, had told him to hide it away down here in this ancient forgotten labyrinth, somewhere where nobody would ever find it.

Never.

Ever.

The crocodile-man gazed down at the golden orb he now clutched in his claws, at the six sculpted talons that gripped it. His ancestors had called this thing "The Hand of the Gods," or "The Wrath of the Gods," but a fancy ray gun was all it really was, no different from the ones in the movies and on TV. Zeus had no claws, no fangs, no stingers or venom, but they had *this*.

This had made them strong.

This had made them *dangerous*.

A blue-white spectral glow enveloped the orb, lighting Chud's way as he marched down this tunnel, setting his scaly flesh all a tingle. Sculpted lips parted silently, revealing the orb's vacant interior, and the rhythmic pulse begged Chud to slide his own saurian fingers inside. It wanted to be used again; it wanted to *burn*.

Uh-uh.

Not happenin', pal.

That's the trouble with weapons, the crocodile-man told himself, shaking his snaggle-toothed snout. *Sticks and stones, swords and spears, guns, bombs, tanks, planes, drones, missiles, fucking* death rays...*sooner or later, that crap always winds up getting used.*

Chud jumped down off a rusted metal ladder and onto an

equally corroded catwalk. He had heard about far away fields in war-torn countries, grassy patches that were littered with unexploded mines — evil little seeds, buried in the soil, just waiting for a chance to sprout fresh death. And years, maybe even decades after conflicts had ended, there were still men, women, and children who were putting their feet down in all the wrong places.

Death.

Biding its time.

That's all the fucking gods left us, Chud thought, bitterly, as he stood there in the humid warmth beneath the city. *The skulls. These orbs. They're hidden around the world like a bunch of poison Easter eggs, just waiting for some asshole to decide to go and hunt for them — Poseidon, Hades, Zeus...*anybody!

It was only a matter of time.

Chud stepped up to the rusted railing. He stared out at a wall of white water before him, his eyes following it down into the churning manmade reservoir below. Over the years, he'd seen countless bits of garbage flushed into the depths of that roiling bilge; now, he had one more bit to add to it.

The crocodile-man held the orb out over the railing and let it drop. If there was a splash, the sound was lost to the deafening roar of the waterfall, but when Chud looked down, he could still see the glowing ball of light. It spiraled down through the effluent, growing smaller, dimmer, until it was gone from his sight.

How long would it take to hit bottom? Chud had no idea. But he pictured that all-powerful alien weapon sinking into a hundred years' worth of shit, and the thought brought a smile to his long scaly lips.

He rubbed his hands together until the tingling sensation went away.

Good riddance!

As Chud gave his back to that underground Niagara, he thought about the alien Ark. He knew it was still up there, stranded at Delancey Field. Just as he knew that, right now, Carol Miyagi and her team of government scientists were working to decipher all the gods' secrets, trying to grasp their understanding of genetics, the power of creation itself.

And then what?

Would the offspring of that knowledge do any better job with it, prove any wiser than their makers?

As Chud strolled on through the darkness of the catacombs, his smile faltered and slowly faded from his snout.

He honestly didn't know.

CHAPTER THIRTY-EIGHT

Preacher did not know if it was day or night. The old werewolf could not recall the month, nor the year. He was not even entirely certain of which way was down or up.

All he knew was pain.

Once, the newspapers had labeled him "The Holy Terror." Now, it was Preacher who was terrified. The walls closed in around him. They were not the cinderblock partitions of a prison cell, but living, *breathing* parapets of bone and sinew. Some of the alien surfaces were slick, slimed with a milky discharge, while others sat completely dry; columns like giant twisted spines, arches fashioned from gargantuan ribs, iridescent nodules, pulsating sacs that radiated faint bioluminescent light...It was as if, when Preacher stepped through the portal to Kronos, the gods had swallowed him whole.

The air was thick, overpowering his senses. It filled with a musky tang, like the scent of a dog in heat. He could also smell blood.

Preacher lay across a rippled plateau, a textured altar of hard ridges and tender swells that rose and fell against his back. His wrists and ankles were wrapped in slithering bonds that constricted as he struggled against them. Patches of his long grey fur had been shaved down to the bare skin. Long tubes were inserted, like hospital IV lines, tethering his limbs, the back of his head, and his genitals to reservoirs or mechanisms unseen; they trailed off into darkness, out into forever.

They...

Preacher's once keen eyesight was now blurred, warped. He was surrounded by shadows; strange figures, insect-like in form, their movements discontinuous and irregular. He blinked and tried to bring them into sharper focus, to impose order onto the chaos of their anatomy. Preacher had never seen the giant mantids that still roamed the Ark, but if he had, he might have concluded that these many-legged beings, these biological machines, were now a million generations removed from their predecessors, and as such, they were far more advanced.

He stared at the insectoid creatures with fascination and dismay, listening to the ticking of their mandibles and the crackling of their every move. Their forelegs ended in a series of highly specialized talons, like complete sets of surgical tools, shiny scalpels and jagged bone saws, forceps and clamps, even a spinning blade.

What they lacked was compassion, empathy, and of course, any form of anesthetic. Still, they took samples of his hair, of his skin, his tissue, and his bone; they performed biopsies, and one invasive surgical procedure after another.

Preacher felt like Prometheus, lashed to a rock; sentenced to eternal torment for his transgression. Each "morning," these twisted angels took away various parts of his anatomy, then he was stuffed into a gelatin-filled tube, put to sleep, given time for his flesh to heal, to grow back, only to have it plucked away again the next "day."

Preacher looked past his tormentors, gazed off into the gloom, searching for the immortal intellects that directed their cruel hands.

The gods were there.

In the distance, Preacher could see the darkness shift upon itself. The shadows coalesced into great behemoths with oddly contoured heads; with long, graceful limbs, and countless writhing tentacles or tails that whipped and stirred the humid air around them. He could feel the weight of their eyes upon him.

Preacher cried out to these horrors unseen. All his life, he had put his faith in them, worked to do their will on Earth. Now, the old werewolf pleaded with his gods in both English and Atlantean; he begged for their forgiveness, for their *mercy*. And then, he began to howl, a lone wolf baying at the moon.

His creators understood his cries, his pleas, but they offered him no reply. They looked down at him in the same way a disappointed scientist might look at a lab rat that had failed to navigate even the simplest of mazes, the way a frustrated inventor might scrutinize a malfunctioning piece of equipment that had given them no end of problems. Their only concern was finding out what went wrong with their rebellious creation and learning from it, *correcting it*, so that, when they seeded the next far-off world, their new garden would yield much better fruit, would flourish where the one on Earth had soured.

They only wished they had been able to retrieve more samples to dissect and study.

One of the insect creatures moved closer to Preacher; the circular saw blade on its hand came to sudden life and began to spin.

Preacher's frightened howls became screams of agony.

EPILOGUE

TWENTY-FIVE YEARS LATER...

P eggy Neuhaus heard screams and bolted out onto the weathered back porch. Through clumps of blowing sea grass, her lone eye spied a pair of familiar Charodon running across the rambling swath of dunes. Rembrandt trailed behind Kohara, and when the shark-man finally caught up to his new bride, Peggy watched him grab her around the waist; he lifted her up off the sand and spun her around in a circle.

Kohara's tiger-striped tail thrashed in the air and those high-pitched screams of hers morphed instantly into a fit of playful laughter.

Peggy exhaled and shook her head, relieved.

Newlyweds.

The couple had offered to accompany her here on the long swim from New Poseidon. Rembrandt could always smell how nervous his mother became in the weeks leading up to these annual writer's retreats. Every year, Peggy worried that a hurricane, or some other catastrophe, would have befallen the house in her absence, reduced it rubble and debris strewn along the sand. And every year, she came ashore to find that this place was more or less the way she'd left it the year before.

A cool breeze blew in from the sea, its invisible fingers combing through Peggy's hair. It was an odd, almost forgotten sensation. She shuddered, lifted a hand to smooth her re-grown mane, then stared curiously at the distant horizon. Peggy sniffed the air, but she could find no hint of rain or coming storms, nothing to spoil this beautiful spring morning.

The dawn of a brand-new day.

She turned away, moved back inside the home she and Larry once shared.

The house that monster porn built.

Peggy shook her head. That's what she used to call this place. They'd laughed about it, she and Larry, but it was the truth. The deed was in Peggy's name, the mortgage paid in full with money she'd earned from her published work; ongoing royalties from her various novels even took care of the property taxes. And Peggy had written *a lot* of books over the years.

Fantasies. Sci-fi. That's what the rest of the world think they are, anyway. All of them based in part on our lives, but none of them really real, none of them true. *None of them like the one I'm about to write now.*

She resumed her annual chore, grabbing fistfuls of fabric to uncover all the furniture hidden beneath. Dust clouds billowed into the air; Peggy coughed and waved her hand in front of her face, fanning the particulates away. After wadding the sheets up in her arms, she carried them down the hall toward the linen closet.

Peggy walked slowly, in no hurry, and every door stood shut along the way. She turned the knobs as she went, checking each room in turn, first the office, then the master bedroom, and finally, Larry's old art studio. It was just as her husband had left it decades before. After what happened, there had been no remains for Peggy to bury, not even a collection of ashes to fill an urn. This room...this was the closest thing she had to Larry's grave.

Larry's ghost.

Peggy stepped inside. The room was empty, but she felt her husband's presence all the same. Why had she avoided it for so long — this house, this *room?*

"Hello again, Rembrandt," she whispered aloud. "Did you miss me?"

A canvas still sat on the easel in front of her, a painted image only half realized. Larry last worked on it that fateful morning when they left to visit Dr. Brahm. The painting depicted a beautiful ringed planet, rising above the waves of some otherworldly sea. What more would her husband have created, Peggy wondered, what stories would his brushes and his paints have told if only he'd been granted more time?

"Our son got married." Tears scalded her surviving eye as she spoke the words; she blinked them onto her cheek, then lifted a hand to wipe them away. "He's very happy, our little artist. They recently added statues to the Hall of Heroes in New Poseidon, and *your son* carved them; he made one of Christine's father, the old innkeeper, Ed DeParle...and one of his own.

"You're a hero, Larry. To him. To me. To all of Poseidon's children. Future generations will know your name, what you did for us, for *everyone*. That's what this new book will be about, my love. I think I'm finally ready to write it all down."

She wiped away the last of her tears.

"At least, I hope and pray that I am."

Peggy swallowed hard, painfully, then left the room. She crossed the hall and grabbed a bathrobe off its hook. As she did so, she caught sight of her own reflection in the bathroom mirror. Gazing at her human face was like staring at the photo of some distant relative, someone with similar-looking features who was nothing more than a stranger. For the moment, her light blonde hair hid any signs of grey, but the lines on her face had grown deeper, had *multiplied* since she'd seen them last.

Old enough now for AARP, she chuckled to herself, *for senior discounts at the local diner, too.*

In many ways, old age was more surreal than being bitten by a wereshark. Peggy looked down at her hands, at the newly opaque crepe paper that covered her now blunted bones, and she was suddenly reminded of Barbara DeParle. Even after all these years, Peggy could still hear the woman's voice, soothing and sage, welcoming her into the clans, *"You're one of Poseidon's children...You and Larry aren't part of the same world now. You can be strong...you may not believe it now, but you can be. Remember what I told you, you're not alone."*

Of course, Barbara had no way to know how true her words would prove to be, or that, one day, their families would become so inextricably intertwined.

Peggy slipped on her robe and went to the office. Larry's paintings were in here, too, covering the walls. She moved to her desk, pulled open one of the drawers. Somehow, among all the clutter, she managed to find a blank steno pad and a working ink pen. Every year, on these return visits to "civilization," she became aware of new technological advances, a parade of ever-faster, more and more organic devices, but Peggy still preferred to write her books out longhand, at least when she was working on that first draft.

She made herself a cup of coffee, then stepped back out onto the porch. Watching Rembrandt and her daughter-in-law frolic in the shadow of this old house, walking along the beach, holding hands and smiling, Peggy could not help but smile herself.

I see so much of us in those kids, Larry, she thought. *We hope to leave behind a safe and healthy world for our children, a world so much better than the one we inherited. You've done that, my love. Thank you.*

Larry Neuhaus was not the first of Poseidon's children to give his life to protect his family, to give them a fighting chance for a *future*, but as Peggy looked out at her son and his new wife standing there on the sand, so young, so happy and full of so much promise, she hoped and prayed that he would be the last.

Peggy sat down. She wiped her eye, put pen to paper, and began to write their story.

THE END

ACKNOWLEDGMENTS

I want to thank my family, especially my wife, Stephanie, my sons, Kyle and Ryan, and my daughter-in-law, Grace, for their never-ending love, understanding, and support throughout this entire series, but especially during the lengthy creation of this final entry; Tony Acree, and the entire staff at Hydra Publications, for coming to my rescue when I needed it most; Enggar Adirasa for his incredible cover art and illustrations; my amazing pre-readers, Amanda DeBord, Sheri Morris Jarrell, Natalie Phillips, Stephanie Summers, and Judy West for putting up with all my emails, multiple delays, and as always, for giving me their honest opinions; your input and inspiration were invaluable to the completion of this fourth novel, and to the series as a whole; and, of course, my faithful readers everywhere, for sticking with me and supporting my work all these years. Thank you!

ABOUT THE AUTHOR

Michael West is the bestselling author of *Cinema of Shadows, Spook House, The Wide Game, Straitjacket Memories, Skull Full of Kisses,* and the critically acclaimed *Legacy of the Gods* series. He lives and works in the Indianapolis area with his wife, Stephanie, their two children, Kyle and Ryan, their daughter-in-law, Grace, and their dog, King Seesar.

West first began work on *The Legacy of the Gods* in 1989, when he was still a college student, working in a crowded computer lab, and printing out his manuscript with dot matrix printers because he did not own a PC. He now works from his home office, a room filled with movie posters and other science fiction and horror memorabilia, including the golden idol from *Raiders of the Lost Ark*, the Xenomorph from *ALIEN*, and a large werewolf statue that bears a striking resemblance to Zuri.

ALSO BY MICHAEL WEST

Harmony, Indiana

The Wide Game

Cinema of Shadows

Spook House

The Legacy of the Gods

Book One: Poseidon's Children

Book Two: Hades' Disciples

Book Three: Zeus' Warriors

Short Story Collections

Skull Full of Kisses

Straitjacket Memories

Made in the USA
Monee, IL
02 September 2022

12196925R00252